I0613794

WELCOME TO YOUR NEXT LIFE

The Arath Saga I

Xander Rose

Mythrunner Publishing

Paperback ISBN-13: 979-8-9989642-1-3
Ebook ISBN-13: 979-8-9989642-0-6

This book is dedicated to those who supported my wild ideas. To Heather for her review and edits. To my own real world Ella, you know who you are. And to all who read and enjoy the story that follows.

WELCOME TO YOUR NEXT LIFE
THE ARATH SAGA BOOK 1

by
Xander Rose

CHAPTER ONE

Life Sucks

Letting out a long-suffering sigh, Alex smacked the buttons on the clock for the third time, only this time, instead of hitting snooze he hit the off button. He stretched his length in the small bed and raked a hand through his dark hair. Sitting up he turned and placed his feet on the floor.

"One more and I won't be able to make it to work on time. I really don't want to go there again, but it pays the bills." He thought as he dragged himself from the bed and rubbed at his sleep-crusted eyes.

Mid-morning sunlight filtered through the slatted shades on his bedroom window, a further accusation of how late it had gotten. It dimly lit the small studio apartment allowing him to move about without tripping over the clutter of clothes and pizza boxes that made the floor a minefield as he dressed and went through the various tasks of getting out of the door and on his way to work.

Slipping his arms into his jacket he rushed out of the front door of the apartment building and turned his collar up to block the brisk spring morning breeze from going down his back. Turning he walked down the sidewalk dodging other pedestrians with practiced indifference as he moved through the city toward Dynamic Systems Inc., his daily grind of cooperate monotony.

"Wish it was more like in the books. Hells, I'd trade every coffee for a portal and a decent sword," he thought wistfully imagining pixelated health bars and epic loot tables. His mind drifting back to one of the most recent books he had been reading. LitRPG had almost overnight become his favorite genre when he was not playing video games or working, he was pouring over whatever new series he could find, more than just a little jealous of the different characters in them.

"Hey Alex, good morning! You want your usual today?" The cheerful voice of Samantha rang through the air and pulled him from his daydreams. As he returned to focus on the world around him, his eyes alighted on the cute brunette barista behind the window counter.

"Oh, hey Sam, yeah that would be great. Gonna need it to get through another day of work. I swear they invent new ways to bore us with code." He smiled at her as he placed a hand on the counter. She was a bright spot in his routine; he missed seeing her on days he didn't work. "Do you have any of those fresh croissants as well? I didn't get up early enough to eat today and my stomach is starting to tell me about it"

Laughing Sam set a small bag with the requested food on the counter and turned back to prep the coffee for him.

"I swear you never wake up early enough." She grinned at him. "Is this just an excuse to spend more time talking to me?"

"Well, not really, but talking with you definitely makes my mornings better," Alex said. He meant it too; their morning banter was often the best part of his day. He knew their flirting was never going to go beyond just the playful banter but hey a guy could wish couldn't he? "You sure you don't want to get lunch one of these days? I promise I won't go creepy on you... well no more than I already am," he joked as he waved his phone over the scanner to pay for the order.

Tapping a finger against her chin as if in serious thought Sam watched him a moment before finally speaking with a grin. "Nope, still don't think it's a good idea. I promised myself I would never mix work life with my personal life."

Same answer. Same banter. Another loop in a life on repeat. Same day. Same week. Same damn life. Alex sighed internally again at how nothing ever changed.

"All right, see you tomorrow then." He picked up his food and coffee then turned to continue his walk to work. A few more blocks and he would be able to get out of the crowded streets and ensconced himself in his desk.

Stepping off the sidewalk to cross the street he took a bite of the flaky pastry when a flash of color caught his eye. The brilliant vermillion hair distracted him for a moment as it disappeared around the corner of the building. A moment later the sound of a horn shocked him back to the present and he hurried across the road and into the office building of his work.

Making his way to his cubicle he quickly sat at his desk, powered his computer up, and then set his coffee cup next to the keyboard. His mind lingered on the hair he had noticed earlier as he pondered the likelihood of it matching one of the main characters in the book he started last night. "Must just be because the color was on my mind that I noticed it," he mused. "Just like when you buy a car and suddenly see the same car everywhere." Dismissing the thought, he turned his attention to the latest tasks in his queue and lost himself in the work.

Hours later he finally logged off the computer and rose. Throughout the morning his mind had kept returning to the brilliant hair color, something about it just stuck in his head and he could not shake it. Exiting the office, he hurried towards his usual burger place for lunch when once again the same woman caught his eye. That shade of hair was unmistakable, and he paused to see if he recognized her. While he looked closer at her she turned as if feeling her eyes on him and eyes the hue of evergreens in the deep forest locked with his.

Distantly he heard a horn again, along with squealing tires as the eyes holding his shifted from their mischievous mien to sadness. As his mind tried to process the sudden change his world erupted in overwhelming pain followed rapidly by darkness.

#

Alex winced as he sat up. His hands quickly ran over his body as the memory of the pain returned to him, but nothing felt out of place or broken. The air around him was still, almost too still. No distant city hum, no beep of the hospital monitors, not even the soft whir of a ceiling fan. Just ever present quiet. The scent hit him next. It was earthy, raw and slightly damp. He sniffed again trying to place the smell. Hay? Clay? One thing he was certain of is it was not disinfectant, asphalt, or rubber. He pressed his palms into the mattress and noticed his fingers brushing rough linen sheets over uneven wooden slats. It was definitely not his bed nor any hospital bed he had heard of. His gaze darted around the room. The light filtering in was not the artificial glow of florescent bulbs, it was warm, golden and... real. Like sunlight should be.

"Okay," he muttered, his voice cracking slightly, "this is not the ER." He tried to take stock of what happened and remembered seeing the strange woman right before the flare of pain. Realizing he had stopped in the middle of the road the last sounds returned to him. A horn and tires...

"Oh shit... where am I? Did I get hit?" He thought and once again he checked himself. Nothing was broken or even scuffed though. It was then he realized his clothes were different. Gone were the jeans and T-shirt he had put on that morning. They were replaced with what appeared to be simple woolen pants and a soft cotton shirt. As this realization settled in, he looked up and about the room. The silence was deafening, and it was not the bustle of an ER room or the back of an ambulance he would expect after a car accident. Instead, he found himself sitting on a small wooden bed in a simple mud and straw room. There were no decorations or other distinctive furniture besides the door in the far wall and the open window letting in light. Strangely he couldn't see anything besides that light through the window when he looked. Slipping from the bed he walked towards the door, pausing a moment he noticed he was barefoot and looked about for his shoes but there was no other clothing within the room.

As he placed a hand on the door it swung open to another room, this one had a table and two chairs though and one of those chairs was occupied. Alex stared slack jawed as the same woman who had caused his distraction when the car hit him turned to look his way and motioned to the empty chair across from her.

"I was wondering when you were going to wake Alexander David Eriksson." The light in the room didn't fall on her, it flowed towards her. The air around her shimmered faintly, not like the waves of heat, but more like the space itself bent slightly towards her presence. Every shift of her posture made the shadows lean away. And her hair, her vermilion hair caught the glow and danced with it, as if it had a life of its own. Most striking was her eyes, those deep, impossible emeralds, held more than color. They held ages. Her voice was silken and rich. The type of voice that one would expect to hear from trained singers or performers. The type of voice that one could listen to and lose themselves. "Please come join me, we have a lot to discuss before you make your choice."

That comment got him moving and he quickly closed his mouth and moved to the offered seat. Sitting in it he looked closer at the woman across from him. Her long hair flowed loose and wavy down past her shoulders and was the rich vermilion that had so enraptured him. A soft jade blouse draped her body demurely though it hinted at her form beneath. When she leaned forward placing her elbows on the table before resting her chin on her steepled fingers it drew his eyes up to her face. Full lips sat beneath a small slightly upturned nose creating a classically beautiful face. But even those features were subsumed by her eyes. Those orbs conveyed a world of emotions with just slight changes. The deep emerald drew him in and held him captive.

"Where am I?" He finally croaked after several long minutes of being pinned by her gaze. "Who are you? What happened? Am I dead? I was hit by a car! Wait, am I dreaming? And who are you?" His initial question broke the dam of his thoughts, and the others came out in a torrent. One question after another not permitting the woman a chance to speak or answer between them. Fear and worry started to build at the sudden changes to everything he knew.

The sadness he had noticed before the pain returned to her eyes and she nodded somberly. "You are in limbo, Alex. You have a choice to make. I didn't intend for your death to be so sudden, but it confirms you are who I was looking for." She sat back in her chair and watched as the emotions played over his features at her words. "My name is Danu, and I am here to ask you to help me."

"If I am dead, how am I supposed to help you? How does my dying help anyone? I mean sure I wasn't impacting anyone other than myself before but dying doesn't help anyone. And what is this choice you're speaking of? Kinda out of options being, I don't know, dead and all aren't I?"

His tongue loosened by the situation his tone became more heated the more he spoke. "Wait what do you mean you didn't intend for my sudden death? You were going to kill me eventually?" He pushed himself back from the table and moved to rise.

Danu reached across the table, her fingers brushing his. Warmth flowed through him, calm radiant, undeniable. Alex's entire being calmed suddenly and he stopped trying to stand only staring at her in a blend of awe and disbelief.

"Peace Alex. I did not intend to kill you. Your time was fated though it would seem my presence hastened it. Even the Ixyl," She paused a moment thinking, "I think you would know of them as the Fates, cannot see precisely how the weave of time and fate will form. Just hints and possibilities, since knowing changes it." She leaned back once again and studied Alex closely. "Your choice is a simple one. Help me or move on. When you were struck by the car and dealt a mortal wound, I was able to intercept your soul as it left your body and bring it here to have our discussion." Motioning behind Alex she pointed to two dark doorways. "You walk through that one," she pointed to the one on the left, "to help me. And the other," this time she pointed to the right doorway, "will allow you to pass on to the afterlife."

Alex turned towards the openings, eyes drawn not just to the doorways themselves, but to the carvings above the left one. Two faint sigils shimmered there, etched into the wood so delicately they seemed to hover in and out of sight, only fully visible in the shifting light. The first was hauntingly beautiful: a crescent moon delicately cradled a single, glowing silver thread. The symbol pulsed with quiet strength. The moon curved protectively around the thread, which shimmered with a faint inner light, like moonlight on still water. Though simple, it held a profound presence, as if it watched him back. He didn't know how, but he understood it represented her, Danu. The moon: her wisdom, her balance, her vision. The thread: fragile, yet unbroken. A line of fate stretching across lifetimes. Beside it, etched just as finely but radiating something altogether different, was the second mark, a fractured spiral surrounded by jagged lines. The pattern had clearly been broken once and reforged, its silver-blue glow flickering at the edges as though barely contained. There was a tension in it. A pull. Something ancient... and waiting.

Danu's voice was soft beside him. "The first is mine. A reminder that fate can be nurtured, woven, reshaped. The second..." she paused, "is the mark of the Kael'Sharyn. It recognizes you, even if you do not yet understand it."

The name stirred something deep inside him, recognition without understanding. A distant chord struck, vibrating in his soul.

"And the other door?" he asked, eyes shifting to the one on the right. It stood silent. Plain. Its frame was untouched by symbols or glow, as if the very wood refused to remember what lay beyond.

Danu followed his eyes. "That path holds no memory, no burden, no destiny. Only the stillness of what comes after." she said, her voice barely above a whisper. "Oblivion leaves no trace."

Alex looked to the doorways trying to see beyond their darkened frames at what might lay in store. Seeing nothing but shadows and darkness beyond them he turned back to the woman. "Wait, you caught my soul? Are you a god or something? I mean I didn't think they were real but... No, I must be in the hospital, and this is a coma-induced dream. This can't be real."

Once again, she reached out and placed her hand on his, the calm sensation suffused his body at her touch. "Yes, I am what you would consider a goddess. One of many, in fact, in the world I am offering you. If you decide to help me it won't be easy, but I won't force you to do anything. The world is dying, though it won't be for centuries, the path can be changed now if someone, if you, are willing to try."

"Why me?" The weight of her words settled on Alex even as her touch calmed his mind. Everything he had known in his life had been upturned in a moment, but she was offering him a new start it sounded like. "What would I have to do? Where would I go?"

Her smile brightened and her eyes sparkled seeming as if endless galaxies swirled in their jade depths. "What you do is up to you to figure out Alex. You would be given a new life on Arath aware that the world is tipping towards chaos and failure. You could drive it further towards that end and speed the eventual demise of the world forward, or you could become the balance and pull it back from the brink. I did say I wouldn't force you to do anything. The choice is yours here and there." A mischievous glint shimmered in her eyes again, "You have always dreamed of an isekai life, haven't you?"

Alex stared at Danu for a few minutes weighing her words and the possible choice. He wasn't ready to die and go to the afterlife, whatever it might be, yet. That left him accepting her choice. "Help a goddess or move on? That's the choice?" He thought to himself. Part of him wanted to laugh, another part screamed. He thought about his apartment, the rent he was still behind on, the overfull inbox he would never clear. His sister's birthday was next week, wasn't it? He had planned on calling her. Even as he had those thoughts, already, concerns of that life were slipping like water through his fingers. He couldn't even remember what he was supposed to get her as a gift. No, what he remembered clearly, almost achingly so, was the look in Danu's eyes. The sadness... and the hope.

"Guess no one else was lined up for the job," he muttered half to himself. Finally, he smirked slightly; did she actually just try to use the potential of an isekai experience to tempt him? Rising slowly, he turned towards the doorways. "Alright Danu, say I accept what happens when I walk through that door?"

Her smile remained warm on her lips as she rose and walked to his side. "Through that doorway, you start your new life. The world is different from Earth, it's more like the games and books you enjoy so it should have a special appeal to you."

He stood at the threshold of the left most door, the wooden floor groaned softly beneath his bare feet. Two paths were offered, one unknown and the other final. His hand brushed the frame, breath catching in anticipation. Some inside, his instincts screamed that the next step wouldn't just change his life, it would replace it.

"Here goes nothing," he whispered. He cast one last glance over his shoulder, but the room was empty. Danu was gone and only light remained in her place. Closing his eyes he stepped forward into oblivion. Her voice filled his ears as his foot broke the plane of the doorway and he vanished from the room. "Thank you, Alex," her voice whispered like wind between the worlds. "Good luck and welcome to your next life."

CHAPTER TWO

Becoming

Alex became aware of the vast emptiness surrounding him, weightless, formless, suspended in a silence that pulsed more like memory than air. A moment ago, he had been going somewhere, hadn't he? There was a destination... a beginning. But now, only stillness.

Then a voice stirred the void. "Welcome, Alex. Before you are released into your new life, you must decide how your thread will be woven."

The voice was feminine, calm, composed, echoing with a resonance that bent reality. As she spoke, the darkness rippled with light. A shape emerged from it: a figure bathed in glow, matching his body as he remembered it. Same face. Same hair. Same faint scar on the wrist. However, it was clothed only in coarse linen undergarments, like a canvas waiting for its first mark. Next to the figure floated a pane of light, translucent and gently pulsing, as if breathing:

Name: Unknown	**Level:** 1, 0%	**Age:** 32
Race: Unknown	**Alignment:** Neutral	**Languages:** Basic...
Reputation: 0 – Nobody knows nobody cares		

Stats		
Health: 100/100	**Stamina:** 100/100	**Mana:** 100/100
Attributes		
Strength: 8	**Agility:** 8	**Dexterity:** 8
Constitution: 8	**Endurance:** 8	**Charisma:** 8
Intelligence: 8	**Wisdom:** 8	**Luck:** 8
Resistances	**Skills**	**Marks**
None	None	None
Abilities		

Unbound Possibilities – Unlike native-born souls, you are not shackled by the limits of lineage or fate. You are blessed by Danu with potential unbound. The world's systems will attempt to guide you, but they will not constrain you.

Linguist – You can understand and speak all mortal languages, even those lost to time.

Alex stared. Why is my name unknown? He thought to himself. My name is Alex, isn't it? And race: unknown? That made even less sense, unless this wasn't just metaphor. Unless this was... somehow real.

"Uh... hello?" he asked aloud or thought aloud he supposed was a better description. "You said I had to decide how I start. What does that mean?"

The voice returned, steady and timeless. "You may call

me System. I am the weave through which your soul enters Arath. I serve as guide and framework, under the will of Danu, The head Goddess of the Veiled Pantheon."

The voice paused for a moment then continued. "Before you may begin, you must choose the body your soul will wear, your race, and the name by which the peoples of Arath shall know you. Be warned: in this world, names hold power. Your true name, the name of your essence, should be guarded as you would guard your very soul."

If he had knees, Alex might have dropped to them. This was no game, it felt so much more real, this was in fact an actual beginning in a new isekai world.

"Alright," he said slowly. "Let's start with race. What are my options?"

"As an Unbound Soul, you may select from the Core Races of Arath: Humans, Shě (Elves), Dorn'Vathrin (Dwarves), Fennari (Gnomes), Velethrin (Halflings), and Animari. Each race carries legacy, burden, and place within the world's living Pattern. Their traits and tensions are not only physical, but historical." Again, there was a short pause. "You may not access Advanced Lineages: Zar'kaan, Aetherborn, Draconic-blooded, or Celestial-Blessed, until those paths are earned."

"Alright," he said, voice steadying. "Tell me more. All of them, so I have an idea of what each consists of?" He finally asked.

System responded as though reading from a guidebook, her tone was bright but straight forward. "Humans – Versatile and short-lived, humans thrive in all corners of Arath. They are adaptable, driven, and not bound by ancestral memory or fate. They flourish in kingdoms, cities, and colonies, but they are also the architects of many conflicts. Among the dominant races, they possess the fewest natural gifts, but their ambition often tips the scales."

She paused for a moment and Alex could have sworn that if this wasn't non-corporeal, he would have heard her turning a page. "Shě (Elves) – Ancient, beautiful, and steeped in magic, the Shě see themselves as the stewards of order. Divided into lineages based on different heritages such as the Ge'shě or High Elves, Tu'shě or Wood Elves, Del'shě or Dark Elves to name a few. They rule the Elven Lands with iron elegance. As a race they revere law, tradition, and hierarchy. Station is identified upon birth, and it is highly unusual for one to change their position or place. Other races see them as aloof, elitist, and willing to enslave those deemed 'lesser'."

Again, she had the slight pause before continuing. "Dorn'Vathrin (Dwarves) – Masters of stone and steel, the dwarves are resilient and proud. They craft wonders beneath mountains and defend ancient strongholds with unyielding ferocity. Dwarves, while nearly as ancient a race as the elves, highly distrust the elves, remembering betrayals from past ages. Many now view outsiders with suspicion, believing strength is earned, not gifted."

A few moments passed before she continued again. "Fennari (Gnomes) – The smallest of the elder races, gnomes value invention, magic, and whimsy. Though often underestimated, they are cunning, perceptive, and difficult to deceive. Fennari communities are tight-knit but scatter easily due to their curious natures."

This went on again covering the last two races. "Velethrin (Halflings) – Cheerful and communal, halflings are rarely a threat and often a balm. Yet they are survivors,brilliant at disappearing or adapting. Many are content in obscurity, but others wander or spy for coin or cause. Some races dismiss them. Others suspect their happiness masks something deeper."

Pause. "Animari – Hybrid beings of beast and man, the Animari are bound to nature and spirit. Their subraces,

Duskhari (Pantherkin), Felvari (Catkin), Leporini (Rabbitkin), are some of the possibilities. They reflect a more primal ancestry. Once free and proud, many Animari are now enslaved, their blood deemed lesser by law in parts of Arath. Some serve as warriors, others as rebels. Most are feared or pitied, rarely trusted."

Alex let the knowledge settle. This wasn't a just a basic race selection option. This was politics. History. Identity. You didn't just pick what you looked like. You picked how you would be seen and reacted to.

"So... even race comes with enemies," he muttered. "Just like life."

"Indeed," System answered. "There is no neutral choice. Only choices with different consequences."

He paused, then said, "Then I'll go with what I know. Human."

The avatar pulsed. The figure solidified, becoming more vivid, muscle, sinew, skin, breath. The stat screen shimmered and adjusted.

> **Race set:** Human.
>
> **Physical age reset:** 18 years old (Young Adult)
>
> **Perk:** Adaptive Potential unlocked.

System waited, then asked, "What shall the world know you as?"

He thought again for a while, the idea of naming his character wasn't strange to him but the fact that this was going to be HIS name took a minute to consider. He was going to be stuck with whatever moniker he chose. Finally, a mental smile formed, and he spoke again. "Call me... Xavier." He spoke the name with the form he was more familiar with, and it came out sounding like ZAY-vee-ur. The fact that it was not too dissimilar from one of his nicknames from his youth, Xander, would also help him to respond to it when others spoke to him while he transitioned to the new world.

The name fell into the Pattern like a stone into deep water. It echoed back, affirmed. The figure brightened. The form was no longer hypothetical, it was.

> **Name set:** Xavier.
>
> **Primary Identity:** Locked.
>
> Unbound Path initialized.

A new voice boomed through the void, deeper, broader, carrying the weight of prophecy. "Xavier, the Pattern accepts your step into the weave." It thundered. "Will you rise as storm and tear through tyranny, or become fire that tempers a shattered world? Or will you crush your enemies, topple kingdoms and empires, and leave a path of destruction and pain? Know this: you are one, but not necessarily alone. Should you endure, your name may yet reshape the tapestry of Arath."

Light surged. Then darkness swallowed him whole.

CHAPTER THREE

A New Life

A whisper of wind stirred the canopy overhead. Leaves rustled in rhythm with birdsong, creating a melody both alien and familiar. Slowly, awareness crept back into Xavier's body. The first sensation to return was hearing that gentle chorus of the living forest surrounding him. Then his sense of smell was restored, it was greeted with the heady scent of rich earth mingled with the faint, sweet tang of crushed grass. He then realized that his cheek rested against something cool and soft, grass.

He then realized that beneath that soft grass was something far less forgiving. A sharp jab in his hip reminded him that while this place might seem peaceful, the ground was still ground. A stone, half-buried and jagged, dug into his side. Groaning, he pushed himself upward, feeling dirt clinging to his palms as he rolled to a seated position. His fingers trembled slightly, not from fear but from disorientation. Everything about this moment felt... surreal.

Sunlight filtered through the treetops in dappled gold, illuminating the glade he had awoken in. He took in the view slowly, as though his mind was trying to memorize it before questioning it. Wildflowers bloomed in chaotic bursts of color across the clearing. Dragonflies hovered in lazy circles above them, their translucent wings catching the sun.

Long grass swayed gently in the breeze, disturbed only by his movement. The hum of insects joined the birdsong, and somewhere nearby, the quiet trickle of water played its own soft tune.

"This isn't Earth," he murmured aloud, the words barely more than a whisper. It wasn't just the scene before him, it was the weight in the air. The land itself felt more awake, more alive.

His breathing quickened as the realization settled in. He was here. Wherever here was.

His memories rushed back all at once, the void, the voice of the System, the stat screen, his decision to begin as Xavier. There had been no grand arrival, no flash of magic or roar of thunder. Just... this. A slow, quiet rebirth in the heart of a foreign land. A sanctuary of wild natural life.

For all the peace and serenity the surroundings offered, his body screamed of needs. His throat was parched, his stomach a hollow ache. The instinctual needs of survival clawed their way to the forefront of his mind, pushing awe to the side.

He looked down and noted his condition. He was clothed, though barely. A rough-spun tunic clung to his body, coarse against his skin, and matching pants hung loosely from his waist, held in place by a crude rope belt. He had no shoes, no other gear to speak of, and no pack. Just the clothes on his back.

He stood carefully, legs stiff but cooperative. The muscles he hadn't used in what felt like days protested the movement, but didn't fail him. He turned slowly in a circle, surveying the clearing again. The sense of solitude was deep but not threatening, not yet at least.

A glint of sunlight reflecting off water caught his eye, and he moved toward it, the grass brushing against his ankles as he stepped forward. He emerged into a narrow break in the tree line where a spring-fed pool lay nestled against the edge of the glade. The water shimmered in the light, impossibly clear, and fed into a small brook that meandered back into the forest beyond.

He stared into the pool for a moment, and his reflection stared back. It was the same eyes and same face he had looked at every morning, but something had changed.

Smiling, he looked about the woods again. The land mirrored that truth. This world felt ancient, untamed, as though it had never been conquered like the majority of Earth, only respected.

He crouched by the pool, cupped his hands, and drank. The water was ice-cold and clean, shocking his senses back to full alertness. After several mouthfuls, he sat back on his heels and exhaled slowly. He was alive, and Arath, whatever it was, was real.

Now, he just had to survive it.

#

The cold water had revived more than just his body, it brought clarity. The haze of sleep and awe faded, and instinct took over. Xavier wiped his mouth with the back of his hand and looked around the spring-fed pool. The clearing felt safe enough, but safety was fleeting. Hunger gnawed at him now, a hollow pang that had shifted from nuisance to demand.

He glanced down at himself again. The rough tunic and pants were coarse but intact, stitched from undyed fiber. As he studied them, white-bordered prompts blinked into his vision.

You have discovered: Rough-Spun Tunic	Rarity: Common Armor Class: Light

	Durability: 10/10
You have discovered: Rough-Spun Pants	**Rarity:** Common **Armor Class:** Light **Durability:** 10/10

No stat bonuses. No enchantments. Just something to keep the wind off his skin.

"Well," he muttered dryly, "at least I'm not naked."

The sound of a splash drew his attention to the spring. Silvery flashes darted beneath the surface—fish. Fat and slow, their movements lazy in the crystalline water. He watched them for a few minutes, letting his mind trace their patterns. One of them looped in and out of a shallow divot at the edge of the pool.

Xavier shifted into position, crawling slowly until he lay prone just above the niche. He let his hand dangle in the water, careful not to move too suddenly. The minutes dragged. A dragonfly zipped past his ear, but he didn't flinch.

The fish returned and he struck.

Water sprayed as he scooped upward, flinging the slippery body onto the grassy bank. It flopped wildly. Xavier lunged, pinning it with both hands. The sensation was alien, wet, squirming muscle sliding against his fingers, but his grip held. Breathing hard, he forced his fingers into the gills and hoisted it into the air.

"Got you," he said to his freshly trapped prize. It wasn't graceful and it wasn't elegant. But food was food and he wasn't going to complain about the how's now.

He carried his catch a short distance from the pool and set it on a sun-warmed rock. He needed a fire. That much was obvious. A fire and tools, a knife, at the very least.

Moving to the trees, Xavier began collecting. Dry grasses

first, then bark, then sticks the length of his forearm. He gathered cautiously, never straying far from the clearing. The idea of getting lost in a forest he didn't know with no map, no compass, and no way to mark his way back was a risk he wasn't ready to take.

Twenty minutes later, he returned with an awkward bundle in his arms. He dug a shallow pit and arranged his kindling as best he could remember. Fire starting had been part of a youth survival course back in middle school. He'd mostly faked his way through it then. No one had cared much back then if he could actually start a fire or not, but this time, it mattered.

His first few attempts failed. The dry grass caught once, then sputtered out in a pathetic trail of smoke. He tried again, and again, bark scraped against stone as he struck one against another, stone against stone trying another way to improvise a spark. His hands blistered, his arms hurtm and his knees ached.

Then, as if a gift from Prometheus himself, flame. It was tiny and flickering, but real. He shielded it from the breeze, coaxing it gently to life with small twigs. When it stabilized, he fed in larger sticks and sat back, letting the heat warm his sore fingers.

Congratulations! You have learned a new skill: Survival (Level 1)

Many and varied are the things that need to be done to live off the land. You have taken your first step toward mastering them. This skill affects your ability to create impromptu shelters, campfires, and forage for edible foodstuffs.

Xavier let out a laugh that surprised even him. A skill, no, an actual skill prompt. He hadn't imagined it. He was now playing by the gamified rules of a world he barely understood, but the rules, and their inherent prompts, existed.

He picked up the fish again and frowned. Now came the part they never showed in games. Cleaning and gutting his catch. There were no icons. No instant meat filets. Just a rock, a fish, and fingers that had never done this before. After finding what he hoped was a sufficiently sharp rock, he winced as he cut into the belly, trying not to ruin the entire thing. It wasn't pretty, just a torn mess of entrails and bones but eventually, he had something vaguely edible. He rinsed the carcass in the spring, skewered it with a sharpened stick, and held it over the fire.

It was the smell that hit him first, the mouthwatering aroma of grilling fish flesh. Then the tantalizing sizzle of the meat as the flames worked their magic on the soft white flesh. His stomach growled loudly.

Congratulations! You have learned a new skill: Cooking (Level 1)

Hark and hear: by cooking your first meal, you have taken the first steps on a path oft overlooked. From humble fare to legendary feasts, cooking offers both flavor and power.

+2% flavor to prepared dishes+2% ingredient yield

You have discovered a new dish: Slow-Roasted Fish (Whole)	**Rarity:** Common **Quality:** Edible **Traits:** • Roasted over open flame. Lacking seasoning, but wholesome and filling. • Provides mild sustenance.

	• +1% future success with similar recipes

By the time he tore into the fish, it barely mattered what it tasted like. It was food, glorious food, and he ate every bite.

#

Smoke curled upward into the trees, a thin gray ribbon that dissipated quickly in the open air. Xavier leaned back from the fire pit, wiping sweat and ash from his brow. His earlier triumphs, catching a fish, making a fire, had dulled slightly under the weight of practical reality. He was alone. Utterly alone despite what the voice had told him before he woke in the forest.

And while he had warmth and food now, they were temporary victories. The forest was quiet, but it was not silent. Leaves rustled beyond the clearing. Something had moved earlier in the brush. Small? Harmless? He didn't know.

He glanced at the half-burned stick in his hand and stirred the embers again. The fish bones crackled slightly where he'd tossed them into the flames. It was amazing how fast those small successes had disappeared. Hunger and thirst were sated, but neither would stay gone for long.

Still, he allowed himself to breathe. The slow-roasted fish had not been a culinary masterpiece, but it had filled his stomach and left him with the mild warmth of accomplishment. He glanced at the prompts that remained floating faintly in the corner of his vision, the echoes of rewards earned then finally dismissed them completely. He had discovered while he was eating he could pull previously closed prompts back to view when and if needed.

He sat back, his legs crossed in the dirt beside the fire.

His tunic itched and he scratched where it chafed his skin. The rough-spun fibers were more like burlap than fabric. Still, better than nothing. He flexed his fingers slowly, still sore from stone and flame, and began scanning the treeline. There was no movement, no noticeable threats. Just the rustle of leaves and the creak of trees shifting gently in the wind.

"Okay," he murmured. "First fire done. First meal done. I can do this."

That thought came with weight. He hadn't panicked yet. He wasn't breaking down or crying or yelling at the sky. Somewhere inside, he'd always dreamed something like this to happen. Maybe not this, exactly, but some kind of escape from Earth. A fresh start on a new world with a different set of rules.

And he knew there were rules, he might not know them yet but they were there. The System, the stats, the skills. It felt like a game, but the pain in his fingers and the roughness of his breath reminded him it was not. There was no HUD, no minimap, and most importantly no floating inventory bag. He was alone, with the skills he earned and the tools he made. That thought sobered him.

He needed a plan. Fire was a start, but not enough. He needed shelter, tools, long-term food, information, civilization, allies and weapons. The list built in his head as he ran his fingers through the ash beside the cook pit.

Then he frowned. There was something faintly glowing beneath the coals. At first, he thought it was a spark, a coal flaring bright. But unlike coals that ebbed and surged with breeze, it pulsed, soft and steady.

He leaned closer and took a better look. Nestled beneath the blackened wood was a tiny, curved sliver of... metal. Copper? No. Brighter. It had patterns etched into its surface, runes maybe, or simple decorative filigree. He dug it free carefully with a stick and held it up. It was warm to the touch. Not hot, just warm. Like it remembered the fire that had birthed it.

You have found: Ember-Shard (Minor)	Rarity: Uncommon Type: Crafting Component Residual essence from a natural flame. Can be used in primitive crafting to enhance fire-based tools, items, or enchantments.

Xavier stared at the prompt, then at the shard. "So even campfires might drop loot?" he muttered. It was absurd. It was wonderful.

He tucked the shard into the rope belt at his waist and rose to his feet, brushing dirt from his knees. The stream still trickled nearby, its rhythm steady, patient. It led away from the glade and toward the unknown. He looked back at the fire pit. The flames were fading, but he knew now he could make more, and if this world rewarded effort, even small effort, then maybe, just maybe, he had a chance to shape it.

He doused the remaining embers with water and stirred the ash until no heat remained. The forest accepted the silence again. The last curl of smoke vanished into the canopy above. He turned toward the stream, adjusted the rope belt, and took his first step beyond the clearing. The path forward would not be easy, but it would be his.

#

The stream led him forward. It twisted through the underbrush like a silver thread, its banks lined with moss and pale-rooted trees. As he followed its path, Xavier felt the pulse of the world grow stronger around him. Each footfall sank slightly into leaf mold, the air rich with the scent of loam and dew. Birds still sang, but their voices were distant now, like a chorus watching him from afar.

He paused occasionally to scan the treeline. Every sound carried weigh, a branch shifting, a rustle in the underbrush. Most of it was probably harmless. He knew that was not true for all of the sounds. Arath, whatever it was, didn't strike him as a place without danger. Again, he lamented that there was no HUD to warn him of predators and do minimap to show where he was. Despite never having them on Earth, he never really felt like he needed them there. However, with the prompts and other system functions he found here he felt cheated by their lack. Instead, he just had instinct, and trust in his feet.

Time passed in that slow, wandering rhythm that only forests can teach. The sun crept higher, rays slicing through the trees in golden shafts. The stream grew wider, its murmurs turning to song, then to something louder. A rumble. He pushed through a curtain of low-hanging branches and stopped. Before him lay a cliff. Not a sheer drop, but a crag of stone that sloped steeply downward into a wide basin where the stream ended in a cascade of falling water. A waterfall, clear and clean, emptied into a deep lake whose far shores were lost in the shimmer of distance.

Mist rose in lazy tendrils from the basin below. Rainbow arcs danced in the light. The scene was perfect, so perfect, it almost didn't seem real.

And then came the sound of a glorious fanfare of trumpets. Faint at first but growing. Not from the trees, nor the sky, nor the lake instead it seemed to come from within himself. The sound resonated in his bones, like a distant fanfare struck across the strings of the world itself.

Above the waterfall, the sky shimmered. Words appeared as if they were written by a divine hand.

Welcome to Arath

They blazed in brilliant gold, not harsh, but warm. They felt ancient, like they belonged to a world that had been waiting for him.

He stared up at them, and a slow breath escaped his lips. "So, it really begins now."

The words lingered for several heartbeats, then faded. No prompt followed. No guidance. Just the wind, the water, and his own rising heartbeat. He stood there for a while, letting the moment settle into him. A quiet promise passed between earth and soul. This was his beginning, not just arrival, but an emergence.

His hand drifted down to the ember-shard tied into his rope belt. The warmth remained. A reminder of what he had already earned. Of what he could build, and he turned from the edge continuing down the path he had chosen.

CHAPTER FOUR

Predators and Prompts

As the golden letters faded from the sky overhead, the sounds of the forest rushed back in like a tide. The world was once again alive with chirping insects, rustling leaves, and birds overhead. It was as though the world had been holding its breath during that moment of divine revelation, and now, with the words gone, it exhaled. That exhale however brought a new noise.

A howl, low, guttural, and close enough that it prickled Xavier's skin. The kind of sound that bypassed conscious thought and went straight to the primitive brain. Something out there was hunting.

Another answered it, deeper in the forest. Then a third, higher-pitched and frantic. The calls overlapped in eerie harmony, forming a hunting chorus that seemed to fill the space between the trees.

The hairs on the back of his neck stood up. The forest, which only moments ago had seemed mystical and serene, now felt like a trap.

"No no no..." Xavier turned, eyes scanning wildly as panic took hold. Movement flickered between the trees, dark shapes slipping through the underbrush. Not just animals, their sleek forms and quick movements marked them as predators.

He ran to the cliff edge, scanning frantically for a way down. His breath caught when he spotted it: a narrow ledge jutted from the stone wall a few feet below. It wasn't wide, but it might be enough.

Behind him, something broke from the brush with a snarl. It was massive at least the size of what he imagined a dire wolf would be, but it was all wrong. Half of its body was covered in thick, bristling fur, the other in hardened, scale-like plates that shimmered with a wet sheen. Glowing red eyes locked onto him.

It raised its head and let loose another howl, louder this time. A challenge. A call.

He didn't wait for the answering howls. He swung his legs over the cliff and began lowering himself down, searching blindly for the ledge. His feet scraped rock, searching for purchase. The wind whistled in his ears. Then another figure appeared in the tree line. And another.

More of them, whatever they were. They fanned out like a practiced pack, as they moved in coordination, their howls falling silent as they crept closer. Predators in every sense. Their eyes never left him.

"Danu," Xavier whispered, barely daring to look back. "If you're watching... this is a hell of a place you dropped me in." Giving himself over to fate again, he let go.

His feet hit the ledge, and for a heartbeat he was safe. Then his balance shifted. The stone crumbled beneath his foot, and he fell, flailing, tumbling down the rock face. The world spun around him.

Branches tore past. Rocks slammed into his sides. Each impact ripped a ragged gasp from his throat. The fall felt endless. Finally, with a bone-jarring thud, he slammed into a thick tree trunk near the bottom of the ravine. He slid to the ground, gasping for breath.

Pain flared everywhere, his shoulder, ribs, back. A sharp ache pulsed in his thigh, but at least he was alive. As he shook the fuzziness from his head he noticed that three bars had appeared faintly in his vision, hovering in the top left corner like a heads-up display: Health, Stamina, and Mana.

The health bar had taken a hit, it was nearly halfway gone. His stamina was a little lower than full as well, he assumed that was from his frantic flailing as he tried to catch himself on the way down the hillside.

"Okay," he groaned. "So that's how that works. At least I didn't seem to break anything on the fall."

Above, the beasts gathered at the cliff's edge. Red eyes stared down. Then, one by one, they slipped back into the trees. Seconds later, the howls resumed, fainter but more ominous. They weren't done. They were hunting him now.

Xavier pushed himself up with a grunt, wobbling on legs that screamed in protest. "I get it," he muttered. "No safe zones." And with that, he turned and hobbled into the forest, the shadows swallowing him whole.

#

The forest closed around him like a curtain. Amongst the tree trunks he found branches that scraped his arms, thorns that tugged at his pants. Each step sent a fresh wave of pain through his bruised body, but he didn't stop. He couldn't stop, behind him he could hear as distant howls rose again, no longer frenzied, they were measured now, controlled.

They were tracking their prey, they were tracking him.

Xavier pushed deeper into the trees rushing as fast as he could push his battered form, following no path, and trusting only the flow of instinct and desperation. The canopy thickened above, turning day into dusky twilight. The moss beneath his feet was soft, but his soles ached from the effort, the bare skin slapping against stone and screaming with pain against broken branches. Leaves whispered around him like voices.

He noticed that the green bar in his vision was shrinking rapidly. His stamina was getting dangerously low, and he could feel it as his limbs moved more sluggishly and his muscles ached with each effort. Every gasping breath, every stumbling stride, drained it further. When he finally slowed to a limp, the bar hovered just above empty. He staggered to a halt beside a mossy log and leaned heavily against it, chest heaving. His stamina bar ticked upward. Slowly.

He peered through the trees, eyes flicking between shadows. He found no red eyes, no vicious feral shapes, but that didn't mean they were gone. The quiet was deceptive.

He crouched beside the log and listened, heart pounding in his ears. The forest remained still. Birds had stopped calling. Even the insects seemed hesitant. They were close. Or worse, he thought, they were clever. Xavier swallowed hard and tried to calm his breathing. His thoughts came in scattered bursts: I need a weapon. I need shelter. I need to hide.

He couldn't outrun them. Not like this, not in his condition, but... maybe he could outlast them, or out think them.

The moss beneath his hand was damp and cold, grounding him. He leaned back against the trunk and exhaled slowly. His lungs still burned. Sweat trickled down his neck, and every muscle in his legs screamed for rest.

A flicker of movement in the underbrush caught his eye, but it was only a squirrel darting through the ferns. He let out a shaky breath. "Game-like," he muttered. "That's what she said. Game-like."

He began scanning the forest floor, forcing his thoughts

into focus. He'd played enough survival games to know what came next. First fire. Then food. Then a weapon. At least he hadn't woken up on a shoreline only to be eaten by a damn spitting dinosaur like that one survival game.

Focus, He thought harshly to himself, One problem at a time.

The howls, now distant, echoed once more, they still present, still searching, but it would seem no longer closing in. He might have bought himself some time. He prayed it was enough to prepare.

Xavier's breathing had finally steadied. His body ached from the tumble and the desperate sprint, but his thoughts were clearer now. He knew what his next step was. He needed a weapon, any weapon really. That was the next step. He knew he couldn't keep running forever. In survival games one of the first weapons, besides a jagged rock, was always a wooden spear.

He scanned the forest floor again with a new purpose, eyes catching on a fallen branch that looked promising. It was long, relatively straight, and seemed dry. He walked over and tested its weight and grinned. It was light, but not too light. Solid enough to serve...maybe? It was one thing to do actions in a game on a computer. He was finding it quite a bit more involved to do them in real life, even if it was game-like.

Nearby, he spotted a rock. It was a little irregular, jagged, and sharp-edged. He crouched and picked it up, hefting it in one hand he found the rough texture bit at his skin. It would do he thought.

He moved to set his back against a tree, and he settled down at its base, placing the branch across his lap he began to scrape at the tip with the rock. It wasn't precise. It wasn't elegant either, but it was real.

Bit by bit, scraps of bark peeled away and wood fibers

frayed. He ground the point down, rotating the branch slowly, evening it with each stroke. Time passed in the rhythm of scraping and breathing.

The branch resisted in places, knots fighting against his shaping, but he worked through them with grit. At times, his hands slipped, and he scraped his knuckles, or the stone would slide across his palm like a cheese grater, or bark would end up slivered up under his fingernails Every time it would end up making him hiss in pain. Still, he pressed on.

As he worked, the weight of his situation slowly faded into the background. The world narrowed to the feel of wood against stone, the rasp of fiber, the tiny victories of shape taking form. It was oddly meditative. For the first time since arriving, he felt like he wasn't reacting, he was acting. He had chosen something, and now he was shaping it. There was something comforting about that. It was simple and tangible. A cause and effect in a world that had offered him precious little of either.

He paused only briefly to wipe his brow and flex aching fingers. Sweat ran down the inside of his arms and dripped from his elbows, darkening the bark beneath him. Forest sounds began to creep back into his awareness, distant birdcalls, the whisper of leaves, the sigh of wind through branches. It was almost peaceful once again and he nearly forgot about the wolf-like things that had been chasing him.

When the wood finally narrowed into something vaguely sharp, a faint chime echoed in his mind.

> **Congratulations! You have learned a new skill:**
> Woodworking (Level 1)
> Though done with the most basic of tools, you have crafted your first woodworked item. The intricacies of grain and fiber now open to you.
> **+2% to crafted item quality. +2% to wooden weapon damage.**

Another prompt appeared alongside it:

You have crafted: Rough Wooden Spear	**Item Class:** Common **Item Quality:** Poor **Weight:** 1 kg **Durability:** 10/10 **Damage:** 1–4 Piercing **Traits:** Pride of the footman, the noble spear has broken many a charge and pierced many a heart. This basic wooden spear was carved from a fallen branch and lacks true weapon capabilities but hey at least you have something. Crude, but functional.

Xavier stared at the floating text. A smile tugged at his lips. "Wait... was that prompt snarky?" He said aloud his focus on the prompt once again.

He gave the spear an experimental twirl. It was rough, uneven, and even splintered in places, but it felt solid in his hands. He jabbed the air a few times, testing the weight and balance. Yep there was no elegance, no grace, but it is mine. He thought to himself.

He grinned despite himself. There was something absurdly satisfying about it. The spear was terrible. He knew that. But it was his. Not something looted, not something gifted by the System, not something conjured from a prompt. He had made this.

He stood slowly, rolling his shoulders, shifting the spear from one hand to the other. His fingers wrapped tighter around the smoothed shaft of the wood. The pain in his legs and chest was still there, but now it felt distant, like background noise to the pulse of his own determination.

The spear was more than a weapon, it was a tangible reminder that he could shape this world. Even if only in splinters.

Around him the forest had grown quiet again. There were still no howls. No signs of pursuit. However, he swore he could still feel them out there. Waiting and watching, perhaps they were testing him, like the world itself was.

He adjusted his grip on the makeshift weapon and moved forward, deeper into the woods. One step at a time careful and cautious. Now, he wasn't just running to survive, he was preparing to fight.

#

Xavier walked carefully now. Each step he took was placed with intention. His hands gripped the rough spear, fingers tightening unconsciously with every creak of the branches overhead. The forest had grown hushed again, to Xavier, it was almost unnaturally so. Every sound was sharpened, every shifting shadow was suspected. He had the sensation that the trees were leaning in just slightly, listening.

Right when he thought his nerves couldn't take it anymore, there was movement. A rustle of underbrush just ahead. Xavier froze, crouching behind the trunk of a slender tree. He peered between the leaves.

Sitting in the undergrowth there was a rabbit. A plump, grey, oblivious rabbit.

It nosed at the base of a bush, nibbling at something unseen. Its ears flicked, but it hadn't spotted him. Xavier's stomach clenched at the sight, half in hunger, half in hesitation. He had eaten fish earlier, but somehow this was different. This was land game. A mammal. Blood, fur, warmth. A direct link to the predator-prey line he now found himself standing upon.

He lowered his stance, angling his shoulders like he had in gym class all those years ago. It was strange how old memories returned in moments like this. A throw in dodgeball, a lunge during PE relay races. Moments of aim and instinct. His primal brain called upon all those moments to guide him.

He steadied his breathing and let his heart settle. The spear's tip wavered slightly in his grip, and he forced his muscles to still. He exhaled slowly, then crept forward, careful not to snap a twig or displace a stone. He inched closer still, and crouching low, he drew back his arm the way he'd seen in videos on ViewTube and TakTik. A breath in. A heartbeat held. Then he threw.

The spear sliced through the air with surprising speed and struck.

The rabbit jerked, thumped the earth, then lay still.

Xavier didn't move at first. He blinked, surprised it had worked at all. His hands slowly dropped to his sides. A mix of shock, awe, and something darker stirred in his chest. He had done it.

Ding! **You have slain a Level 1 Rabbit.** **+10 Experience.**

His legs moved before he realized it. He jogged to the creature's side, heart pounding harder now than when he was running from wolves. Blood soaked the ground beneath it, bright and fresh. The rabbit had died quickly, but not instantly.

He knelt beside it and carefully reached out to touch its side. It was warm. That detail unsettled him more than the blood. The warmth was intimate. Immediate. A reminder that this had been a life, not an abstraction. It had not simply vanished. It had been snuffed.

He had killed before, in games. Monsters, bosses, nameless bandits. But this wasn't a pixelated trophy drop. This was a creature that had been breathing just moments ago. Now it lay still, lifeless because of his hand. It wasn't that he regretted his actions. Not exactly anyways.

But he felt the weight of them.

He sat there in silence, crouched next to the kill. In the distance, the wind rustled the trees. A bird called once and went quiet. The sound of the forest reasserted itself, pressing in around him.

He forced himself to swallow the lump in his throat. He needed this. It was needed food. It was needed materials. Maybe, even more importantly, it was needed progress.

He knew, however, more than that, he needed to prove to himself he could. That he wasn't going to freeze or fold. That when the time came to act, he wouldn't hesitate. That he could adapt.

He reached out and gently lifted the carcass. The body was heavier than it looked, solid with muscle and fur. The spear had gone deep, puncturing the chest cleanly. The shaft had splintered slightly at the base of the wound. A reminder that his tool wasn't made for this.

He pulled the broken shaft free with a wet sound that made him grimace, then wiped the tip against the grass, trying not to gag at the combination of blood and soil now smeared on the point.

The rabbit's head lolled to the side; it's little pink tongue partially exposed. Its eyes stared upward, glassy and unfocused. There was no twitch, no spasm. Just stillness.

He looked down at his hands. They were trembling. It wasn't the adrenaline of fear this time, not like with the wolf things. Instead, it was the adrenaline of excitement and achievement. He breathed through it and focused. He needed to focus on the next steps.

The fur would need to be removed. The meat prepared. He had no knife yet, no tools but what he could make or improvise. He had seen it done before, in videos and tutorials. A looped animation in his mind replayed the steps: find a blade, clean the kill, preserve what you can.

His gaze drifted to the brush beyond. What else hunted here? Would the scent of blood draw predators? Or more prey?

He turned back toward the last stream he had passed. Running water would help clean the body and maybe give him a safe spot to make camp. It would also, importantly, give him direction. The terrain there had been flatter, he remembered, open enough to spot anything coming.

As he walked, the weight of the kill settled into his arms, and his chest. He glanced down at it more than once, the image of the lifeless creature burned into his mind. This was his first true mark upon the land, not just a fire or a fish. This was a life taken in a deliberate act. It would not be his last.

He passed beneath low branches and over knotted roots, the forest once again folding around him. The sounds of nature resumed their rhythms. The wind hummed through gaps in the trees. A flicker of motion in the corner of his vision kept him sharp. His eyes swept the path ahead and behind, the hunter in him now wide awake.

He was different now. Not in some grand way, but in a quiet shift. A foundational moment. He had taken life to preserve his own. The logic was simple. It processed easily in the mind. The gamer knew the routine, but the soul, he suspected, would take longer to convince.

#

He welcomed the sound of the stream like an old companion. Its soft burbling filled the forest in gentle contrast to the eerie silence he had walked through. Xavier knelt beside the clear flow and rinsed his hands, watching blood ribbon away in pink trails downstream.

Before he had done that, however, he had laid the rabbit carcass gently on a rock nearby. When he returned to it, its fur was now drying into rough ridges where the blood had begun to congeal. It would not wait forever. He had to act.

The first challenge was obvious, he needed a blade.

Sighing yet again, at the lack of an inventory, and the fact he no crafted gear beyond his crude spear. He scowled. Game-like my ass, he thought to himself. But he had seen survivalists on videos break rocks into cutting tools. He scanned the riverbank, searching for something that resembled what they had called flint or shale, anything brittle enough to snap into an edge.

After several minutes of scouring, he found a likely candidate: a flat gray stone with streaks of black running through it. It felt heavier than it looked. He took it in one hand, then picked up a second, smaller rock and struck it against the edge of the larger one.

The first attempt produced a dull clack. The second, a glancing strike. On the third, the larger stone split with a satisfying crack, one edge flaking away in a jagged, serrated arc. It was primitive. It was dangerous. It was a start.

Congratulations! You have learned a new skill: Crafting (Level 1)

You have made your first tool through improvisation and intuition. You may now craft rudimentary implements and understand the nature of raw materials.

+2% to crafted items. +2% to tool effectiveness.

You have crafted: Crude Stone Blade	Item Class: Common Item Quality: Trash Weight: 0.25 kg Durability: 5/5 Damage: 1–2 Slashing Traits: Barely serviceable. You can cut meat, fur, or soft materials. May break under strain.

He rolled his eyes slightly at the quality assessment, then tested the blade against a strip of bark. It bit in, not cleanly, but enough. Satisfied, he turned to the rabbit.

The System, as if anticipating his need, painted a faint silvery line along the carcass's underside, guiding the incision point. Xavier gripped the crude blade and followed the line carefully, pressing just enough to pierce the skin.

The first slice was awkward. The second better. The third, smoother. As he worked, more guiding lines appeared. He surmised it had to do with his new survival skill. It seemed the system did have some guidance for skills. He wondered how they would change as skills improved.

You have discovered: Tattered Rabbit Hide	Item Quality: Trash Traits: Unevenly skinned and stained. With time and care, it could be cleaned or repurposed.

You have discovered: Skinned Rabbit Carcass	Item Quality: Raw Traits: Freshly cleaned meat, suitable for basic

cooking. No modifiers.

He set the hide aside on a flat stone, letting the sun begin to dry it. The meat he kept cradled in damp leaves. Now came the fire. He cleared a circle on the riverbank, gathering dry sticks and moss for tinder. There was no flint and steel. Just stones, friction, and the hope that his earlier fire wasn't a fluke.

Sadly, it took longer this time. His hands were blistered. His patience had waned, but eventually, a wisp of smoke curled skyward, followed by the faintest spark. He fed it gently, blowing until a flame caught the moss and spread to twigs. The relief he felt was physical.

He had fire. Again.

This time, he was more deliberate in his cooking preparations. He used the sharpened end of a new branch to skewer the meat and began to roast it over the flames. The scent of the cooking meat that rose was sharp, wild, and unseasoned. To him it was heaven, and it made his mouth water.

As the meat crackled and sizzled, Xavier sat back on his heels, watching the fire dance in the late afternoon light. His muscles ached. His stomach grumbled. Eventually he received a new prompt.

You have discovered a new dish: Slow-Roasted Rabbit (Whole)	Dish Quality: Edible Traits: Roughly prepared but nourishing. Grants minor satiety and warmth. Chance to improve future cooking: +1%.

There was pride in the exhaustion he felt. He had earned this meal with his hands, his sweat, and the bite of stone and spear. Gently he removed it from the fire and took his seat once again.

The first bite was stringy and uneven, but it was food. The second bite was better. Soon he was pulling meat from bone, devouring each mouthful with a mixture of reverence and hunger.

As he chewed, he studied the forest across the stream. Every shadow could be a beast. Every branch could conceal danger. But for now, next to the fire and enjoying his food, the space around him held.

No glowing eyes peered from the foliage. No snapping jaws lunged from the undergrowth. Just the fire, the food, and the quiet affirmation that he had survived.

When he finished eating, he buried the bones and doused the fire with water. Ash hissed and curled away in the breeze. The sun was dipping low. He would need to find shelter soon. But for now, he let himself rest for a moment longer, listening to the world breathe around him.

For the first time since waking in Arath, he did not feel hunted, or lost, or confused. He felt... capable.

#

The last light of the sun slanted through the trees, casting long golden beams across the stream and igniting the rising mist in a hazy glow. Xavier stretched his legs out beside the doused fire, the heat from the stones still radiating against his shins. His stomach, once knotted with hunger, now throbbed with the dull comfort of a full meal. He leaned back against the trunk of a broad, moss-covered tree and exhaled slowly.

His fingers brushed the dirt beside him until they closed around the haft of his spear. He did not want to sleep without it within reach. It was crude and likely not much use against a real predator, but it was still something. Proof of effort, of intent, of will to survive?

Above, the sky darkened into violet and charcoal. As the canopy thinned overhead, gaps between the branches revealed a night unlike anything he had ever seen. One by one, stars flickered into view, more than he remembered from Earth, clustered and layered like dust on glass. Constellations unfamiliar to him spread across the heavens.

What caught his attention most was when they came. Not one, but three moons. The first rose low on the horizon, a deep crimson orb etched with faint veining like garnet shot through with obsidian. The second followed soon after, it was smaller and blue, and luminous as a polished sapphire. The third was a pale-yellow crescent, it glimmered last and was tilted at an unfamiliar angle.

He sat in silence, watching their paths arc through the darkening sky. The air had grown colder, though not dangerous, especially with the still warm rocks of his fire nearby. Crickets sang nearby, and somewhere in the distance an owl hooted. Life went on around him, unconcerned by his presence.

The day was catching up with him. His body ached all over. His legs were scraped, his hands blistered, his shoulders sore from strain. But beneath the pain was something else, an ember of pride. He survived the first day. Hunted, bruised, alone, and unarmed, he had endured. He had found water, made fire, forged a blade, hunted food, and eaten beneath the open sky.

> **Milestone Reached: First Night in Arath.**
> You have survived your first full day on the surface without dying.
> This marks the beginning of your journey.
> **+25 Experience. Minor increase to Stamina recovery while resting in natural environments.**

Xavier smiled faintly. The text shimmered, then faded

like mist when he dismissed it. The System was watching, apparently, but not guiding. He was still very much on his own.

He shifted slightly and rolled the rabbit hide tighter, placing it beneath his head as a makeshift cushion. It was stiff and smelled faintly of smoke and blood, but it served. He lay on his side, the spear beside him, and listened.

Every sound of the forest now felt sharper. The crack of twigs in the distance. The whisper of wind through grass. The occasional flutter of wings. It was savage but none of it stirred fear, not anymore.

He closed his eyes and breathed in slowly. The scent of pine, ash, and the river filled his lungs. For the first time since he had arrived, he did not feel like a trespasser. He felt like someone who belonged. Not because he had been welcomed, but because he had earned the right to be here.

Sleep came slowly but surely. Fitful at first, with shifting dreams of teeth and shadows, but eventually settling into something deeper. He slept beneath three of the moons of Arath, wrapped in the memory of warmth and firelight, and did not wake until the stars began to fade.

He had survived his first day, and tomorrow, he would begin to live his next life.

CHAPTER FIVE

Rescue the Lost

Darkness stretched across the dreamscape like a canvas, painted with flashes of fire and shadow. Xavier drifted in the void of sleep, yet it did not hold peace. His mind burned with images, pulled from a tapestry not yet his own. He saw a brilliant meteor fall from the heavens and consume a golden city, flame pouring from the heavens as the ground split beneath a thousand screaming voices. He saw dwarves battling in the depths of unknown mountains, brothers cleaving at each other under banners of broken oaths. A desert bled shadows as a great skeletal hand emerged from beneath its sands, reaching for a shattered throne. Through it all, mortal champions rose, fell, rose again, each carrying blades etched in glowing runes, each making choices that scarred the world. Some bore a mark that glowed like fractured glass beneath their skin. Others screamed as it tore them apart.

A presence lingered in the periphery of each scene. Always there, always just beyond clarity. And when the light caught the presence just right, he caught the glimpse of a single, undeniable trait, hair the color of blood turned to flame. Brilliant copper at times, deep vermillion at others. It shimmered like a banner of fire through the shifting fragments of his dream, more real than anything else around him. It was not a voice, not a figure, but a sense. A watching. A pull. He knew it was Danu.

The goddess said nothing, yet her attention was undeniable. She did not guide the visions, but revealed them, like windows in a wall he had never noticed. Instinctively, he knew each glimpse offered a choice made, or yet to come. Roads that split and diverged, some bathed in light, others wreathed in blood. No path was safe, but all led forward.

Tentatively he reached toward one, just one, and it shattered like a mirror, scattering its shards into the abyss. As they fell, they began to glow. Red.

He gasped and sat upright.

Rain pelted his face, cold and sudden. The dream scattered like leaves in wind. He blinked against the droplets, disoriented. A soft hiss rose nearby where the rain struck last vestiges of last night's fire, quenching it completely. Smoke spiraled weakly from the wet coals.

The forest around him had changed. It was not a change in shape, but its mood. The hush of moisture gave every sound a closeness. The whisper of leaves, the pat of water against bark, the distant creak of shifting branches, all of it felt more intimate, more present.

He reached for the broken spear beside him without thinking. His fingers found it instinctively finding security in its feel. He scanned the glade. There was no movement, no threat. Just water.

Achievement Unlocked: Survive a night in the wilds Stepping stone for hunters, wanderers, and fools. You have joined their ranks. Look at you!

#

He snorted quietly. "Definitely snark."

Xavier pushed himself to his feet and stretched. His

muscles groaned in protest. His rough tunic clung wetly to his skin. The tattered rabbit hide he had used for a pillow was soaked through and managed to smell worse than it had the night before.

He walked to the stream's edge, cupped water in his hands, and drank deeply. The cold sent a shock through his chest. When he had finished, he washed his face and ran wet fingers through his hair. The rain had become steady, but not heavy. It was the kind of rainfall that soaked you slowly without realizing it.

He looked at his reflection in the water. Dark hair plastered to his forehead, eyes bloodshot and shadowed. He no longer looked like Alexander David Eriksson, the man who once worked an office job writing code and dreamed of something more. That name had belonged to a world that did not test him or make him feel as alive as this one had.

Yet he still carried the name, beneath the layers of this new place. A reminder of where he had come from. A tether. System had called it his true name and warned him to protect it so he would, locked away at the deepest part of his core.

He stood and packed what little he had, nothing more than the rabbit hide and his broken spear and stood at the edge of the clearing. Behind him lay the site of his first night, his first meal, and the site of his first kill.

Before him though, stretched the forest and a vast new world. He took a breath and walked forward.

#

The forest greeted him with stillness. Not silence, but something close. The rain filtered through the trees in a gentle whisper, pattering against broad leaves and the moss-covered ground. Xavier walked carefully, following no trail, letting instinct and the slope of the land guide him. He passed between ancient trunks, under branches heavy with moisture, feeling the cool drizzle soak deeper with each step.

He found he liked the quiet of the forest. It gave him time to think. Every moment of survival so far had been reaction, food, shelter, weapon, fight. Even last night was still a reaction of sort. This was the first time he felt like he was simply existing in the world, not scrambling to stay one step ahead of it.

He continued to walk along in quiet contemplation, then he smelled it. A distinctive scent of copper and iron. He slowed his pace but continued to move forward. The scent grew stronger with each step, until he crested a shallow rise and froze.

There on the path before him, even diluted by the rain, was a thick smear of red. Blood. Not old, not dried and rehydrated but fresh.

His breath caught in his throat. He crouched low, examining the ground. The blood had pooled and trailed through the mud, as though something had been dragged or stumbled through. Leaves nearby were streaked in the same crimson. Some crushed, others torn free entirely.

He touched a finger to a smear along a trunk. It was sheltered by the canopy overhead and still sticky. Definitely fresh, but not immediate.

He noticed that the forest had gone quiet around him. The distant birdsong had faded. Even the insects had dulled their chorus. Only the soft rhythm of the rain remained.

He rose slowly, his hand moving to the shaft of his broken spear. His eyes scanned the tree line. Still nothing moved and nothing called.

He could turn back. Find a different route. He would be lying if he said there was not a part of him that wanted to do just that, but a larger something in his gut rebelled at the thought. If something out here was wounded, there might be danger ahead... Or someone in need.

He set his jaw and followed the trail.

The path was erratic. Blood splashed against ferns, smeared across bark, dotted the roots of trees. Whatever it was, it was injured and trying to move fast. The drag patterns suggested a limp. Perhaps it had fallen.

He moved quietly, pausing often to listen. His own heartbeat seemed loud in his ears. He could feel the tension in his shoulders, in the tightness of his grip on the spear.

The trail ahead curved sharply between two old stones buried in the earth like the remains of something once greater. He followed it around the bend and came to a hollow where the trail stopped.

A deep pool of blood remained, and beside it, something small. A twisted, half-furred hand with long fingers and dull claws. He nudged it with the spear tip and swallowed hard. It was the size of a child's, but clearly not human.

It seemed almost rat-like.

He looked up. Beyond the pool, the trail resumed but now joined by deeper footprints. Larger, booted footprints.

It was then that another scent reached him, it was faint beneath the blood. The smell of smoke and wet ash. As he tried to identify the direction, the wind shifted, and for a moment, Xavier could almost feel the forest holding its breath, as if it, too, waited for what lay just ahead, beyond the bend and the blood trail.

#

Xavier stepped lightly over the thick puddle of blood and followed the new trail of prints. The booted steps were uneven, spaced irregularly, sometimes dragging as though the one who made them had stumbled or was bearing weight. They moved deeper into a stretch of the woods where the trees pressed closer together and moss blanketed even the lowest branches.

The rain eased to a mist, turning the air thick and cool. Every now and then he passed more blood, smaller spatters now, diluted by water. The smell of smoke was stronger here, clinging to the leaves.

Then he saw the first body.

Half-curled beneath the roots of a toppled tree lay a small, hunched figure. At first look he thought it was a deformed child, but as he knelt beside it, he saw the truth. It was covered in coarse fur that was matted with blood. A long snout, filled with sharp yellow teeth protruding from a cracked jaw marked its visage. It looked like an actual rat-man. The corpse had one glassy eye that stared skyward, while the other was gone, a splinter of wood embedded where it had once been.

A crude club lay in the dirt beside it. Xavier nudged it out of the way and searched the corpse. Filth, broken bones, rags of what had once been clothing. Nothing of value to be found, instead he moved on.

More bodies followed. Scattered among the trees and underbrush. Some slain by slashes, others by blunt force. Their wounds were brutal but efficient. Someone had killed them quickly and left them behind. Whatever had done this was either precise or in a hurry, and Xavier did not know which he feared more.

It was when he crouched beside the third corpse, noting the torn throat and crushed chest, that he found something of worth. This one had a jagged iron dagger gripped tight in its claws. A real weapon, not carved wood.

He took it.

You have acquired:	Item Class: Common

Rusted Iron Dagger	**Item Quality:** Trash **Weight:** 0.25 kg **Durability:** 2/5 **Damage:** 1–4 Piercing **Traits:** Rusted, low durability. Still better than nothing.

He wiped it clean on the wet grass and tucked it into the rope at his belt. The smoke he had noticed earlier had thickened here, no longer a distant trace but a lingering presence that clung to the trees. It was not the fading memory of a campfire but something more recent and raw, wet ash, scorched bark, and the faint sting of something unnatural carried on the breeze.

He slowed his pace given the bodies and pressed forward, more cautious now. The blood trail merged with another set of tracks, larger and deeper. Booted. Human or something like it. The spacing suggested urgency as if there was a chase.

The trail led toward a break in the forest. Stone jutted through the trees, covered in vines and lichen. Xavier pushed aside a curtain of hanging moss and stepped into a different world.

Ruins surrounded him juxtaposed against the vibrant forest he had emerged from. Crumbling walls stood like broken teeth around a central clearing. Archways tilted inward, threatening collapse. Statues too worn to identify leaned against fallen blocks. Roots tore through foundation stones, and thick undergrowth had claimed most of the floor. It had been a place of structure once. Now it was a tomb of memory.

He crouched beside the edge of a moss-covered path and studied the prints again. They moved directly through the ruin. Blood still dotted the stones. Bits of fur. A broken club.

Then he heard the voices. Guttural, wet, too low to be human. He pressed himself against the side of a crumbled pillar and crept forward. More rat-men, clustered in the ruins. He could not yet see them fully, but their snarls carried clearly.

Then a scream, raw and frightened, tore through the air. It was not an animal. It was human. A human female.

Xavier did not hesitate. He ran towards the sound.

#

He burst into the clearing with the rusty dagger in one hand and the broken spear in his other, his eyes immediately scanning for the source of the scream. It did not take long to find her.

Seven rat-men encircled a young woman who pressed back against a broken wall, her tunic torn and streaked with blood. She held a small knife, trembling, her feet braced against loose rubble. One of the creatures darted in and she slashed wildly, catching it across the snout. It hissed and recoiled.

Xavier moved without thinking. His legs surged beneath him as he sprinted into the fray, the mud beneath his feet spraying with each stride. He slammed into the first rat-man from behind, driving the dagger into its back with all his weight. The creature shrieked, flailed once, and collapsed. The others turned, the new surprise breaking their rhythm.

Another lunged towards him and Xavier barely had time to lift the broken shaft of his old spear, thrusting upward. The splintered point drove into the rat-man's jaw and burst out near its cheek. It twisted away, wailing and thrashing as its life force flowed out through the ragged wound.

You have slain a Level 1 Rat-Man.

+15 Experience.

The rest surged at him, their screeches rising in chorus as clubs swung from all sides. One clipped his shoulder hard, nearly knocking him off balance. Pain flared across his ribs. He tightened his grip on the dagger, pivoted, and plunged it into the gut of the closest attacker. Blood sprayed across his arm.

The rat-man gurgled and clutched at the wound. Xavier ripped the blade free and slashed across its throat, ending the struggle.

You have slain a Level 2 Rat-Man.

+30 Experience.

The blunt head of a club struck him full across the ribs. He doubled over, gasping for air, and another attacker tackled him and bore him to the ground. The cold mud rushed against his skin as teeth snapped inches from his face.

He reached out blindly and in desperation, his searching fingers found and closed around a loose stone. With a growl, he smashed it against the rat-man's temple. Once, twice, the third strike split bone. The creature sagged on top of him.

You have slain a Level 3 Rat-Man.
+45 Experience.

He rolled out from under the corpse and rose just in time to see one of the creatures raise its club toward the girl. Her weapon was gone, her hands braced against the wall. She was cornered.

Xavier shouted loud, hoarse and wordless. The sudden noise startled the creature, and the girl took the chance to duck low. Xavier scooped up his fallen dagger and sprinted forward driving the blade under the rat-man's arm, angling up between the ribs and into the attacker's vital organs. The creature wailed as blood burbled out of his mouth with each breath. He yanked the blade free and stabbed again, this time between the shoulder blades. The body dropped.

> You have slain a Level 2 Rat-Man.
> +30 Experience.

Only two remained.

The girl scrambled to her hands and knees, crawling toward her fallen blade. Xavier turned toward the last two.

One was bigger. Not just larger, but heavier, and more deliberate. Its matted fur was twisted into tight braids, woven with small bones. Its claws were dipped in pitch and glistened with oil. This was not a scavenger like the others. It was a killer.

The brute roared and swung a club of rusted metal, ringed with nails.

Xavier ducked the first blow by instinct. The wind of it ruffled the hair on his scalp. He stabbed upward, catching the brute in the ribs. The dagger scraped bone.

The brute howled and caught him by the arm, lifting him partially off the ground. Then it slammed him into the wall behind. The impact drove breath from his lungs. Stars exploded across his vision.

He stabbed again. The blade bit deep into the shoulder. The brute shrieked and dropped him. Xavier collapsed into the mud, coughing.

He scrabbled for anything, thankfully his hand closed around a broken plank. With a cry, he swung it like a club into the brute's leg. The creature staggered and Xavier lunged tackling it with every ounce of weight he had.

They fell. He landed on top and drove the dagger into its

neck. The brute thrashed, brutal claws raking along Xavier's side, but he held on.

He slammed the monsters head against the stone beneath them. Again and again. Bones finally cracked beneath his hands. The body spasmed, then went limp.

> You have slain a Level 5 Rat-Man Brute.
> +100 Experience.

He looked up, panting.

The girl had reclaimed her knife and she stood facing the last rat-man alone.

It lunged towards her. She screamed and twisted. Her blade flashed desperately once, twice, and caught the creature in the throat. It gurgled and collapsed atop her. She pushed it off, smeared in blood, her chest heaving with exertion.

> You have slain a Level 3 Rat-Man.
> +45 Experience.

His vision filled with new skill prompts and other information briefly obscuring his view of the stranger.

> **Congratulations! You have learned a new skill:** Tracking (Level 1)
> A footprint, smudged dirt, broken branch and disturbed leaves now paint a picture of passing to you. These are vital clues that enable you to follow your prey.
> **+2% to tracking prey.**

> **Congratulations! You have learned a new skill:** Spears (Level 1)
> Through blood and pain, you have discovered how to wield a spear. Woe to your foes because you now have reach with your weapon.

+2% to spear damage. +2% to attack while wielding a spear.

Congratulations! You have learned a new skill: Knives (Level 1)
Pride of thieves, assassins and just about anyone who sticks small pointy things into bodies, you have discovered the basics of wielding a knife. Go forth and continue to practice your stabby stabby skill.
+2% to knife damage. +2% to attack while wielding a knife.

Congratulations! You have learned a new skill: Clubs (Level 1)
Xavier smash! One of the most basic of weapons you now know how to swing a stick, be that a stick of wood, metal or stone.
+2% to club damage. +2% to attack while wielding a club.

Congratulations! For surviving the battle with the rat-man hunting party and aiding in the death of six of the creatures you have earned additional experience.
+250 Experience.

Hidden Quest Completed: Rescue the Lost I.
Your actions saved an unknown woman from death and danger. Who is she? Where is she from? More importantly can you trust her?
+500 Experience.

New Quest Offered: Rescue the Lost II.
Having saved the young woman from certain death or capture you now have the option of leaving her to the wilds or earning her trust. To continue this quest, try to get the woman to open up and learn more about her.
Potential rewards: A new traveling companion. +1000 Experience.
Do you accept?: Yes or No

Xavier collapsed to his knees, his chest shuddering with each breath. Blood ran freely down his side and mixed with grime and the reek of death. The dagger slipped from his hand and clattered beside him.

The ruins were quiet again. Rain pattered softly on stone. No more screams. No more snarls. Just the sounds of the two survivors labored breathing. Neither of them spoke.

#

Xavier crouched among the ruins, the pounding of blood in his ears finally giving way to the softer sounds of rain trickling over stone and through leaves. The battle was over, but the aftermath clung to him, on his skin, in his lungs, in the hollow beneath his ribs. Mud and blood caked his clothes. His arms trembled. The dagger, slick with gore, lay forgotten in the dirt beside him.

He wiped at his face, unsure whether the wetness was rain, sweat, or the slow bleed from a scalp wound. Probably all three.

He stared at the bodies. Seven of them. Some lay sprawled in grotesque heaps where he had struck them down. One still twitched faintly, nerves firing long after death. The largest, the brute, had a smear of Xavier's own blood on its nails.

He had fought. He had survived. He had killed. Not animals this time. Not abstract threats. These creatures had faces, voices, weapons, clothing, and even civilization, however crude.

People, he thought, or close enough to make him wonder.

He had ended them.

Then a crescendo of chimes sounded in his ears preceding the next prompt to fill his vision.

Hark and Hear! You have ascended in power. You are now level 2!

The touch of the divine lingers upon you, granting 6 attribute points to shape your destiny, an exceptional gift, elevated from the ordinary 4 points by the **Blessings of the Gods (Danu).** Choose wisely, for these points will define your path. You have 3 days to assign them, or they will fall to the whims of fate.

Rise, Seeker of Glory. The world awaits your will. Seek adventure, seek wisdom, seek love and let your legend be forged in your choices. LIVE!"

The chime in his head was almost comically cheerful. He sat back on his heels and laughed, it was sharp and bitter at first, then softer. Not hysterical, not quite. But it was a laugh all the same.

Then he looked at his hands. Blood soaked the creases in his palms. The drying red-brown flakes stood out against his skin like paint splattered on a canvas. His fingers curled slowly, reflexively. The image of the brute's face returned to him, the way it had looked just before he crushed its skull. Its eyes were not filled with rage or hatred. Instead, they had been filled with confusion.

He closed his eyes and exhaled. "No," he said aloud, his voice hoarse. "Not murder. Survival."

But the weight remained. It pressed against the back of his mind, quiet and cold. He did not know what these creatures had done before he arrived. Only what they had been doing when he did. That had to be enough.

A soft sound brought him back. A quiet breath. He turned his head towards where the other survivor lingered.

The girl still sat in the corner of the ruin, huddled with her knees drawn to her chest. She had cleaned some of the blood from her face with a rag torn from her tunic, but fresh welts marred her arms and collarbone. Her eyes followed him, watchful, unreadable.

He pushed himself to his feet with a groan. Every bruise, every scrape, flared with protest. His ribs ached sharply and even breathing hurt. His left arm felt half-dead from repeated blows.

Slowly he limped over to where her dagger had fallen and picked it up. Wordlessly, he held it out to her, hilt first.

She flinched at the movement. Her hands tightened around her knees. After a long moment, she reached forward and took the blade from him, fingers brushing his. Her touch was cautious, but not afraid.

He stepped back and knelt beside the brute's body. The stench made his stomach turn, but he forced himself to search it. Beneath the ragged tunic, he found a pouch knotted to a leather cord. Inside there were bits of bone, a loop of twine, and three small copper coins. Filthy but real.

He kept the coins and twine and tossed the rest aside. The pouch, after a quick wipe, was tied to his belt.

Next came the disposal of the corpses. One by one, he dragged them away from the ruined building. It was slow work. His body protested every effort. The girl said nothing, but she watched him drag each one beyond the brush line and drop them into the undergrowth.

On the last trip back, he noticed a shallow stone basin along the edge of the path. Rainwater pooled in its hollow. He bent and sniffed. No sulfur, no rot. He tasted it cautiously. It tasted clean and cool. With cupped hands, he washed his face, scrubbing the blood from his cheeks, neck, and chest. It helped, if only a little.

When he returned, the girl was sitting upright. She held the dagger in her lap now, both hands resting atop it. Her expression had changed subtly, it was still wary, but not hostile. Her eyes met his.

"My name is Xavier," he said quietly. "I... I don't know if you can understand me. But I want to help."

She said nothing.

"I don't know this world yet," he added. "I just arrived, not long ago. But I couldn't walk away."

He waited. No reply came.

He moved back to his gear, what little of it there was, and began to gather what he could. A few broken sticks, the remains of his splintered spear, his crude stone knife, and the dagger he had recovered. He looked at the girl again.

She still hadn't moved.

That was fine. He had done what he could.

He glanced upward. The rain had eased, turning into a fine mist that clung to the air like fog. Overhead, the clouds had thinned just enough to let filtered light touch the broken walls.

For now, there were no more enemies. No more screams. Just stone, silence, and the presence of someone who, like him, had survived. He would not walk away and leave her alone again... Not yet at least.

CHAPTER SIX

Joining Forces and Growing

Steadfastly refusing to dwell on what had just happened, the death, the blood, and the chaos. Xavier made his way back to where the girl still sat in the corner. She hadn't moved since the fight ended. Her knees were pulled to her chest, the dagger she'd used gripped tightly in both hands across her lap.

He kept his distance as he walked the perimeter of the ruined courtyard, gathering sticks, twigs, and several thicker branches. Every movement came with the slow ache of exhaustion. His legs felt heavy, and his arms bore the dull throb of bruises where clubs had struck. He welcomed the pain. It meant he was still alive.

In the center of the clearing, he began stacking the stones of a firepit. The work was slow, but deliberate. His fingers were numb, trembling slightly as he arranged the kindling. The flintstones he'd taken from the ruin's edge caught poorly at first, but finally, after long minutes of frustration, a spark leapt, then another, and then a flame. In just a few days he already was becoming much better at making fires.

The small blaze danced and cracked as it caught the tinder and began to grow, casting amber light over the broken stones and ivy-choked columns. It illuminated the wreckage of the fight: blood-stained earth, a discarded rat-man club, the still body of one he had yet to move. The fire's warmth slowly pushed back the cold mist hanging in the forest's breath.

He added a thicker branch, coaxing the flame larger. It felt primitive but comforting. A beacon against the dark. He sat back on his heels and glanced toward the girl.

She hadn't stirred, but her eyes, vivid and unsettling, never left him. The firelight danced in their depths. She sat with her back to the wall, her limbs tucked close, a posture born of both caution and fatigue. Her face, illuminated now by the flickering glow, was striking. Not just attractive there was something raw in her beauty. Something alive. Her heart-shaped features bore the wear of recent struggle, bruises shadowing her collarbone, dirt streaked across her cheek. Her dark hair, tangled and damp, fell in loose strands around her face, sun-touched highlights catching in the light.

It was not the look of a damsel in distress. She looked like someone who had survived. Someone who had been running a long time. Someone who had killed before and would do so again if needed.

The girl never moved. Her vivid jade eyes tracked every motion, though the dagger only lay across her lap it was clear she would try to wield it if needed. As the fire grew, dancing and casting its glow into the ruin, she finally spoke. Just one word. Soft. Threaded with something that could have been disbelief or anger or confusion. "Why?"

Even though it was quiet, almost a whisper, it cut through the night like a bell. Xavier looked up.

She had leaned forward slightly. The flickering firelight revealed her more clearly now. Despite bruises and dried blood, she was striking. Her eyes were an unnatural green, like young leaves lit from within. Her face, though smeared with dirt, had a graceful, heart-shaped symmetry: high cheekbones, delicate nose, full lips. Her skin was fair, tinged warm, and dusted with faint freckles. Her dark brown hair, tangled and damp, carried sun-kissed streaks of lighter tone where light had found it. It hung past her shoulders, though now loose strands framed her face wildly. She was beautiful in a way that felt alive, like the forest itself had chosen her.

It was more than her appearance; it was her presence that struck him. There was an old weight behind her gaze. Something that felt deep. Anchored. As if she carried stories in her silence.

He hesitated. Then he answered. "It seemed right. You were surrounded. You needed help."

She scoffed. "So, no expectations? You do not want me to fall into your arms with gratitude?"

The sarcasm stung, but he didn't flinch. "No," he said simply. "You're not a prize."

She watched him a moment longer, then hugged her knees. Her voice softened. "My name is Ella Bree."

"Xavier," he replied, offering a faint smile. He shifted to sit across the fire from her, careful not to intrude. "What were those things? And where are we?"

"Rat-men. Scavengers. They attack if they think they can win. They chased me through the woods." She glanced around. "This is the Silverwood. How do you not know that?"

"I'm new here. Woke up a few days ago. No idea how I got here. Just... lost."

He tossed another stick into the flames. "You have any food?"

She shook her head. He sighed. "Then we probably shouldn't stay long."

Ella stood, slipping the dagger into her belt. Now that he saw her upright, he took in her full form. She was lean but strong, built like a scout or a survivor. She stood perhaps a head shorter than him, just under average height. Her clothing was simple and worn, a pair of dark grey roughspun braes, loose green tunic, both faded and dirt-streaked. Her feet were bare, despite the forest's terrain.

Xavier stood as well. He found the straightest branch from the pile and began shaping it with his stone knife. He shaved it clean, but this time he hardened the point in the fire.

You have crafted: Rough Wooden Spear	Item Class: Common
	Item Quality: Poor
	Durability: 10/10
	Damage: 1–4 Piercing
	Traits: Basic, but reliable. A pointed stick that might give you a fighting chance.

Pausing a moment, he also retrieved the crude dagger taken from one of the slain rat-men and the small coin pouch from the brute.

You have acquired: Rusted Iron Dagger	Item Class: Common
	Item Quality: Trash
	Durability: 2/5
	Damage: 1–4 Piercing
	Traits: Rusted, low durability. Still better than nothing.

You have acquired: Tattered Coin Pouch	Contents: 3 Copper Coins, 1 Loop of Twine, Miscellaneous Bone Fragments
	Traits: Mostly worthless,

	but the pouch itself is serviceable for carrying small items.

She eyed him as he worked, tension still lingering. When the spear was finished, she took a step back.

"Are you taking me with you then?" she asked.

He shook his head. "Not unless you want to come. Safer together, that's all."

She considered that. Her gaze drifted to the ruins around them. "Back the way I ran. There might be something useful."

"Works for me." He replied.

He used a stick to scatter the fire's coals and smother the flame, careful not to burn his bare feet, then slung the crude spear over his shoulder. Together, they walked into the deeper shadows of the ancient stone.

#

They spent the better part of the day picking through the wreckage. Twilight was settling in when they finally stopped inside a mostly intact building near the center of the ruin. Though centrally located, this structure backed against a natural rock formation, and much of its rear wall was carved directly from the stone, lending it both strength and concealment. It was clear that while the ruin now seemed small, it had once been part of a much larger city. The scale of the worn streets and distant, half-buried foundations hinted at forgotten grandeur.

The windows and doors of their chosen shelter were no more than ragged gaps in the stonework, whatever wood or glass had once filled them long since rotted or shattered, but it felt safe enough. The layout meant there were only a few directions from which something could enter, which made them both feel more at ease.

While they searched, Xavier managed to spear several small rabbits. The customary prompt had appeared but was quickly dismissed. He had, to his relief, discovered a setting to minimize or ignore prompts for later review. The ability to filter what prompts and notifications he received was becoming more useful as the constant barrage of notifications had started to wear on him. During a quiet moment, he opted to allocate the attribute points from his recent level up and studied their effects, but before he made his choice, he looked into each attribute itself and read their description carefully:

Strength: This attribute is a character's ability to perform physical actions requiring physical power. It can affect a character's ability to carry objects, intimidate others, and increase damage when physically striking something. A character's weight carry capacity is factored by $100 + (Str*5)$ "When in doubt, punch it harder"

Agility: This attribute is a character's ability to move quickly and easily. It can affect a character's ability to evade attacks, land attacks, pickpockets, and pick locks. "Because sometimes running away is the smartest move"

Dexterity: This attribute is a character's ability to perform a difficult action quickly and skillfully with the hands or body. Dexterity controls a character's attack and movement speed and accuracy, as well as their ability to evade an opponent's attack. "The difference between a graceful disarm and accidentally throwing your sword"

Constitution: This attribute is a character's physical health. Constitution affects the ability to shrug off disease, poisons, and the individual's overall health. Hit points are factored by $100 + (Con*10)$ "Because taking a punch to the face is a valid strategy"

Endurance: This attribute is a character's ability to remain active and push past physical limits over periods of time. Stamina points are factored by 100 + (End*10) "When everyone else needs a nap, you are still standing. Barely"

Charisma: This attribute is a character's presence of personality. Charisma factors into persuasiveness, trade and bartering, leadership, and other factors when dealing with people. "Why fight when you can talk your way out of it… or into it"

Wisdom: This attribute is a character's self-awareness. Wisdom affects the ability to resist mental and magical effects. It also affects perception, restraint and insight. Mana is determined by 100 + (Wis*10). "For those who think twice before opening the cursed chest"

Intelligence: This attribute is a character's mental cognitive skills. It affects skill growth, knowledge, memory, reasoning and critical thinking. Intelligence factors into magical aptitude and mana regeneration. "Someone's gotta do the math around here"

Luck: This attribute factors into everything in some way or another. A pebble falling when trying to sneak, the mark happening to turn to talk to someone as the assassin take the shot, and a myriad of other esoteric factors. Who knows when the god of luck may curse or bless you traveler. "When all else fails, cross your fingers and hope the dice like you because, well, sometimes it's the only thing keeping you alive!"

After he had examined each attribute and been shown brief explanations. What stood out to him was that the baseline for most attributes seemed to be 8. Any benefit appeared to come from points added beyond that, which meant he had a solid foundation, but real impact would come from customization. The system even hinted that natural variation existed, but 8 was the common mortal norm.

Name: Xavier	Level: 2, 0.35%	Age: 18

	to Next Level	
Race: Human	**Alignment:** Neutral	**Languages:** Basic
Reputation: 0 – Nobody knows nobody cares		
Stats		
Health: 120/120	**Stamina:** 110/110	**Mana:** 100/100
Attributes		
Strength: 9	**Agility:** 8	**Dexterity:** 9
Constitution: 10	**Endurance:** 9	**Charisma:** 8
Intelligence: 8	**Wisdom:** 8	**Luck:** 9

He had split his character sheet to display only key pieces of knowledge. The way his skills had been growing, and the fact that it appeared he would not be limited in skills, he thought it would be best to look at those only when he wanted to. Overall, he was satisfied with the small changes that single level had given him.

Outside, night deepened.

Xavier let Ella Bree build the fire this time while he cleaned the rabbits he had caught earlier. Once both were prepared, he skewered the carcasses and hung them over the fire to cook. The scent of roasting meat soon mingled with the cool damp of stone and earth.

He leaned against the inner wall of the stone hut, the fire crackling beside them. Through a jagged hole where a window had once been, he watched the sky. The stars above glittered in unfamiliar patterns across a sky that no longer felt entirely foreign. Three moons hung overhead: not the same three he had seen that first night after fleeing the wolf-like creatures, when a crimson orb, a luminous blue sphere, and a pale-yellow crescent had risen into the sky like omens.

Tonight, it was different. One moon was silver and small like the one he had known on Earth, while the other two, one a deep violet, the other a radiant green streaked with golden veins, were equally alien, but somehow less jarring now. Familiar, if not comforting.

This wasn't Earth. It never had been. But with warmth, food, and another person beside him, it was starting to feel real. Maybe even like somewhere he could belong.

When he looked back at Ella Bree, she was tending to the fire with quiet focus. The flames painted her features in soft hues of gold and amber. For the first time, she looked less like a mystery and more like something tangible, present, alive, and for the moment, unafraid.

CHAPTER SEVEN

Cooking, Camping, and Learning

His stomach rumbled, a low ache that reminded him just how long it had been since he'd eaten anything real. He moved back to join Ella Bree by the fire, settling cross-legged on the opposite side. The rabbits rotated slowly on their skewers, crackling as juices hissed onto the coals. Xavier reached out, took over the turning, and let muscle memory guide him through the task.

The scent was rich now earthy, wild, tinged faintly with woodsmoke. The rabbits weren't seasoned, but hunger was its own spice.

You have discovered a new dish: Slow Roasted Rabbit (Whole) x 2	**Dish Rarity:** Common **Dish Quality:** Edible **Weight:** 2 kg **Traits:** This whole rabbit was slowly roasted over an open flame. The lack of seasonings gives it a gamey and stringy flavor, but overall, it is wholesome and filling.

A soft chime echoed in the air around him.

Congratulations! You have learned a new skill: Cooking

(Level 2)
By continuing to place ingredients to flame, you have taken another step down the path. From the simplest salad to the most robust entrée, cooking is the journey to gastronomic pleasure and status-enhancing buffs. Masters of this skill can craft delicacies that would make gods and kings weep with joy—and foods that empower armies.
+4% to flavor of prepared dishes. +4% yield from cooking ingredients.

He blinked, bemused. Just for roasting a couple rabbits? Still, the roasted meat did seem... larger. Fuller. Even the scent carried a richer depth than it had a few moments before.

He plucked both skewers from the fire and held one across the flame towards Ella.

She took it without a word, nodding her thanks. The flickering firelight caught in her green eyes again, and for a breath, her cautious expression softened.

They ate in silence. Not awkward. Not tense. Just two people sharing space. Watching each other, maybe, but without hostility. The forest noises outside had settled into a hush, distant chirps, wind against stone. The ruin felt still and safe, for now.

Xavier's gaze wandered around the chamber while he chewed. The room was broad, the walls curved and built partially into the stone behind them. The structure, though partially collapsed in places, had clearly once been important. Brackets along the remaining walls hinted that once, something had hung there, murals, banners, maybe torches. There were no carvings, no sigils, but the size and placement suggested some communal purpose.

"A meeting chamber, maybe," he murmured aloud, mostly

to himself. His eyes traced the layout, central location, elevated slightly above the rest of the ruined city, reinforced by natural stone. His gamer instincts flagged it instantly.

This was a central node, administrative hub... safe house?

It would've been defensible and commanding. Not a home, but something more. Ultimately he settled on it likely being a town hall of some sort.

He shifted, angling toward the back wall. The rock there was rough-hewn, not carved, but... something about the cracks caught his eye. There were lines etched into the surface that didn't look natural. At first glance they were just fractures, but now...

Xavier stood and stepped closer, careful not to draw Ella's suspicion. She was still eating, watching him out of the corner of her eye. His fingers brushed the stone.

It was cold, but his touch told him what his eyes were just beginning to suspect. These were not just weathering. These were runes. Faint. Worn. But deliberate.

He crouched, brushing away a layer of moss and grit. One symbol became clear, a spiral enclosed in an angular crescent. Another followed, two lines crossing through a hollow circle.

Familiar shapes, though he couldn't place them. They didn't match anything he recognized from Earth, but his mind stirred with something deeper. He didn't know how he knew, but these weren't just decorative. They meant something.

"Ella," he called quietly.

She came over, wiping her hands on her tunic. When she saw what he was crouched beside, she frowned.

"You know what this is?" he asked.

Her brow furrowed. She knelt beside him, studying the

lines. Her fingers didn't touch them, but she traced their shape in the air with a kind of reverence. "I've seen marks like this before," she said after a moment. "But only deep in the older ruins. Places people avoid."

"Why?" He queried.

"Because they were made by people who vanished. And the things that followed... weren't kind." Came her soft reply.

He looked at her sidelong. "You're not scared?"

"I did not say that."

They stared at the wall a moment longer. Then she stood and stepped back. "Whatever this place was... it might be older than the rest," she said. "We should be careful."

Xavier rose as well, brushing grit from his palms. "Yeah. Agreed."

Still, a part of him felt drawn to the markings. Not with dread, but curiosity. The same tug he'd felt in the forest. The same itch at the back of his thoughts since waking up in this world.

Something here was meant to be remembered, and he was beginning to think he was meant to find it. Shrugging slightly, Xavier turned back into the room. The weight of the day, exploration, battle, and the mental strain of this unfamiliar world, was beginning to settle into his bones. "We didn't see any other trace of the rat-men besides the ones that went after you. With their bodies dragged off into the forest, I doubt they'll attract scavengers tonight. I think we're safe enough here. We can figure out next steps in the morning."

Ella looked up from where she sat near the hearth, the orange light casting shadows across her face. She tilted her head slightly, as if listening to something beyond the walls, then gave a slow nod. "I had not seen any until they caught me. This may be a good place to rest, at least for a night. It has walls, a roof... and it feels sheltered. I think a storm is coming. The air has that weight to it."

Her words drew Xavier back to the dark window. He leaned on the stone frame, peering out at the deepening night. Sure enough, the moons he had seen earlier, those unfamiliar celestial companions, were now shrouded behind thick, rolling clouds. The air had grown heavier, dense with moisture and tension. Lightning flickered faintly in the distance.

Rain wouldn't just be inconvenient; it would be miserable without shelter. He stepped back from the window, nodding. "You're right. A storm's on its way."

He crouched near the fire and picked up a long, straight branch they had gathered earlier. One of the rabbit hides lay beside it. The failure of his last spear gnawed at him, he needed something better. Something that might hold if they ran into trouble again.

Settling near the fire, he started slicing the leather into strips. The crude stone knife dragged awkwardly through the hide, forcing him to saw more than slice. Ella watched, one hand half-covering her mouth. A soft giggle escaped despite her effort to hide it.

Xavier paused and gave her a side glance. "Glad you're in better spirits. What's so funny?"

She pointed to the stone blade in his hand, eyes bright with amusement. "Is... is that your knife? Do you not have any real tools?" Her expression was somewhere between amused and baffled. "Would you like to borrow mine before you cut off a finger?"

Still chuckling, she held out her dagger, hilt first.

He took it, grateful, if a bit stung. "I told you, I woke up in the forest with nothing. This knife and that spear were made from what I could find. I've been making do. Besides the dagger I took from the rat-men looks like its about to break already."

Ella's smirk softened, but she didn't argue. He resumed his work with her dagger, and the difference was immediate. The blade sliced cleanly, revealing sharp edges in the leather strip. He followed his instinct to notch the end of the shaft and affix the stone blade with the leather. It took only a few minutes to lash the head tightly in place. As he finished, a new prompt shimmered before his eyes.

You have crafted: Crude Stone Spear	**Item Class:** Spear **Item Rarity:** Common **Item Quality:** Poor **Weight:** 2kg **Durability:** 15/15 **Damage:** 3 – 8 Piercing **Traits:** Pride of the footman, the noble spear has broken many a charge and pierced many a heart. This crude stone spear was crafted from a carved tree branch and crude stone dagger. An improvement over the rough wooden variant. It is a step closer to being a true weapon.

Grinning with quiet satisfaction, Xavier turned to show Ella and offered her dagger back.

She raised one brow and waved her hand. "You keep it. You will get more use out of it than I will. Besides, I can always throw rocks."

To emphasize her point, she picked up a stone from the floor and flung it toward the far wall. It struck with enough force to chip stone and spark against the surface.

He whistled softly. "I'll try not to get in your way."

Inspecting the dagger, he was struck by its strange color. Not black, exactly, more like the sheen of oil on darkened steel. Its edge remained razor-sharp despite clear signs of frequent use. But what unsettled him most was the prompt. The color of the text shimmered and shifted as if it couldn't even define what the weapon was.

You have discovered:	Item Class: Dagger
Ella Bree's Unusual Knife	Item Rarity: Unknown
	Item Quality: Unknown
	Weight: 1kg
	Durability: Unknown
	Damage: 20 – 25 Piercing/ Slashing
	Traits: Ella Bree's knife is unusual in more than just looks. This blade is made of a metal unknown to you and defies your ability to understand anything more than the most basic of details about it. The edge retains a wicked edge despite obvious usage.

Back on Earth, he would have guessed this item was above legendary. Maybe even something mythic. But he couldn't be sure. "Where did you get this?" he asked, turning it over in his hands. "I can't make heads or tails of it."

Ella's smile dimmed. Her tone changed. "It was given to me at birth. I do not know who left it... only that it has always been mine. And... it always comes back to me."

There was something rehearsed about the words. Something old and worn and often repeated. He nodded slowly, filing it away for later.

They settled in, trading off shifts for watch. Xavier took first, letting her rest. He had placed the spear and her knife between them so they both would have access to them as they split the night's watch. As Ella curled to sleep, her fingers unconsciously reached out, resting lightly on the dagger beside them.

Xavier chuckled though his thoughts returned to her earlier guarded words about the blade. Whatever made her feel safe, he wouldn't question it. He leaned back, listening to the storm rage outside. Somewhere below, hidden beneath roots and stone, something sensing more than just animal life above stirred in response.

CHAPTER EIGHT

Heart of the Forge

Rain whispered across the ruins above, soft and steady. But deep below, in the stillness of the Warrens, something ancient awakened. From silence and sleeping stone, a pulse of light shimmered to life. She rose slowly from that breathless place, small, radiant, eternal.

Wings of living crystal spread behind her, shimmering like moonlit glass. Her hair drifted like mist, her limbs delicate and long, her presence shaped by something older than flesh. The air itself responded to her, walls humming with forgotten resonance as she drifted upward through the roots of the world.

Her eyes turned toward the surface, and her voice, barely a breath, named what she felt. "Otherborn."

Weaving through narrow passageways and sealed stone, she passed beneath aged supports and cobwebbed caverns until she found the fracture in the stone wall and slipped through.

Above, a fire burned low. Xavier sat beside it, stirring the coals, lost in thought. Ella Bree lay curled nearby, her back to the warmth, one hand on the hilt of her blade even in sleep.

The sprite hovered silently, watching. The girl... familiar. Known.

The boy however... Her gaze shimmered, and suddenly, she knew him. His skills. His traits. Even the one hidden gift, buried deep and marked by Danu herself. Unlisted. Unseen by others. But not by her.

A playful grin curved her lips and she drifted down beside him and whispered into his ear, "You have been offered a new quest: Heart of the Forge I."

A soft chime echoed in his mind.

Quest Offered: Heart of the Forge I

The ruins above once sheltered something vital. When the village fell, a piece of that legacy was taken. Return what was lost and awaken the path forward.

Objective: Retrieve the heart.
Reward: Unknown
Penalty for Refusal: None

Accept quest? [Yes] [No]

Xavier blinked, startled. He glanced at Ella, she was still asleep, then back to the screen before him. After a moment of hesitation, he selected Yes.

Another chime. A soft flutter of wings, and then... A laugh, bright as chimes, echoed beside him.

He turned, startled and nearly fell into the fire.

Ella sat up instantly, dagger in hand.

Then the sprite revealed herself. She hovered just above the floor, radiant and inconstant.

One... she flew. A pair of wings unlike anything Xavier had ever seen flickered at her back. They resembled dragonfly wings, yes, but they were more, larger than she was tall, translucent with the barest hint of iridescence, and seemingly immune to the laws of gravity. How they held her aloft, he could not begin to guess.

Two… she changed. Her appearance didn't remain static. Her skin shifted from the deep, warm hues of polished stone to the soft flicker of a living ember. Her hair turned from curling vines to threads of fire, rising like smoke from her head. Her wings pulsed with molten colors, glowing like flowing magma, then turned to delicate, lace-like patterns shot through with black veins. In one moment, she looked like a forest spirit. In the next, like something born of flame. And after that, a wraith of bone and light. Xavier counted at least eight distinct forms, shifting with no clear rhythm, only raw, graceful fluidity.

Ella, eyes narrowing then relaxing, slowly lowered her blade. "She's no threat."

"You've seen her before?" Xavier asked, still staring.

"Spoken with her once. She belongs to this place."

The sprite's grin deepened. "Aye," she said, her voice a clear, lilting thing touched by an accent that reminded Xavier of an Irish friend back home. "'Twas I who bestowed upon ye this quest. Now that ye have taken it upon yerself, I shall guide ye toward its end. Think of it as a trial, a proving of worth that I lay before ye. I must judge yer mettle afore I reveal aught more."

`As she spoke, her form continued to shift. The firelight caught the edge of her wings, casting fractured rainbows across the wall. Her voice echoed lightly with each change, first warm, then airy, then dark and echoing before becoming soft again.

"There's a path that winds from the ruins to the southwest," she continued, pointing behind and to the right of where Xavier sat. "It stretches for many miles, roundin' a small hillock. At the base of that hillock lies a cave. 'Tis there ye'll find what ye seek. The heart ye must return lies within, taken by dark creatures and fiercely guarded."

She hovered still for a moment, studying him, then added, "Fetch the heart and return to me. I'll be here when ye come back, and then we'll know yer true worth. And if ye be worthy of more."

Then she faded, folding back into the shadows as if she had never been.

Xavier sat slack-jawed.

Beside him, Ella let out a soft laugh and covered her mouth. "You should've seen your face," she said, the amusement in her voice barely restrained. "She really caught you off guard."

He glanced at her sidelong. "You think she's serious?"

"I do. And if she gave you a quest, then she sees something in you. We should follow it. But..." she pointed toward the half-shuttered stone window "...not until the storm clears. Traveling blind in the dark and rain is just asking to get lost."

Xavier nodded, the echo of the sprite's voice still lingering in his thoughts. He curled beside the fire, laying his head on his arm as Ella took the watch.

Sleep found him quickly. In his dreams, there were battles. They were against strange creatures, impossible odds, and nameless fears. There were shining women with burning eyes, voices that called from beyond the veil, and promises whispered from distant stars. But through them all, one presence endured:

A pair of fathomless emerald eyes, and a mane of wild, vermilion hair.

#

A soft nudge pressed against Xavier's boot. He stirred, groaning as he blinked blearily toward the source.

Ella stood over him, hands on her hips and a half-smile playing on her lips. The pale light of morning filtered through cracks in the ruined structure's stone, catching in her tousled hair and outlining her against the shifting sky.

"You snore," she said mildly, nudging him again with her toe. "Loud enough to wake half the Wildlands. You may want to fix that before some wandering beast decides to investigate."

Xavier sat up with a groan, brushing moss from his sleeve. "I thought I was being quiet."

"You were not."

He caught the faint humor in her tone, despite her deadpan expression. Beside her, she held the remains of their roasted rabbit, wrapped in a scrap of cloth. She handed him a portion and nodded toward the broken archway that marked the door.

"Come on. The rain passed during the night. The trail should be clearer now. If what the sprite said was true, we've a long walk ahead of us."

He stood and stretched, wincing slightly from the aches left by their previous battles. The cold meat was dry, but filling. He chewed as he followed her out into the ruined courtyard.

The storm had passed, but its mark lingered.

The forest around them shimmered with rain-slick bark and dripping leaves. Shafts of light broke through the canopy in broken beams, setting the underbrush aglow with soft, golden mist. Even after everything, the world felt impossibly alive.

Xavier took a slow breath. It smelled of wet earth, moss, and something faintly sweet—like blooming wildflowers hidden beneath the trees.

They walked in silence for a while, weaving through

collapsed buildings and fractured walls until they reached the outer edge of the ruin. There, mostly hidden behind a crumbling gatehouse, a narrow trail branched off through the trees.

It wasn't a road—just the faint passage of game or time-worn feet—but it matched the sprite's description.

Ella met his gaze and nodded once.

They followed it.

The path wound gently southwest, curling along the base of a ridge and skirting a shallow rise in the terrain. Trees pressed close on both sides, and the earth underfoot was soft with fallen leaves and still-damp from the night's storm.

They ate as they walked, tearing bits of rabbit from the bone in comfortable silence.

After a while, Xavier glanced sidelong at her. "So... when we met, you said your name was Ella Bree. Do you go by Ella, or the whole thing?"

"Ella," she answered simply. "I will tell you otherwise if the time comes."

She pulled a small leather bundle from her belt and held it out to him. "You forgot this."

He took it—her dagger, now wrapped in a plain sheath.

"I thought you said I could keep it?"

"You may borrow it." Her voice was dry. "But until I've something else sharp, I expect it back when I ask."

He gave a short laugh, tied the sheath to his belt, and slung the spear back across his back. "Fair enough."

They walked on.

After a while, Xavier tilted his head. "Any idea what we're going to find in this cave? I figure now's the time to plan."

"None," she replied. "That's what makes it dangerous.

Could be beasts. Could be something worse. We know only that it's guarded."

"Undead?"

"Possibly. Or Animari."

Xavier frowned. "What exactly are Animari?"

She gave him a sidelong look. "Beastkin. Folk who bear the traits of animals, some walk with claws, others with fangs, some with wings or scales. The Animari are many tribes and bloodlines. Some noble. Some savage. They follow instinct and ancestry both."

"Like the ones that attacked you?" he asked.

She shook her head. "No those were just rat-men. They are not the same. Rat-men are more like rats than people. Verminites are more like you and I. Rat-men will always have rat-men offspring. Verminites like other Animari can marry and breed with other races and produce half breeds." She paused again. "You truly do not know the difference, do you? You are very strange Xavier."

"So you have said." He muttered wryly. "Ok so rat-men are not Verminites which is a version of Animari. I think I understand so far. The Rat-men were easy enough hopefully it would just be more of them. I think we could handle them if that were the case."

She giggled at him again. "I would not be so quick to assume that. We fought a hunting party, not a den. If it is rat-men and they have a warren it would be a very difficult fight as there could be hundreds of them along with a warren king not just brutes." She spoke matter-of-factly about how difficult this quest might turn out to be. "We should just wait until we find the cave and see what we find before we make too many plans." Her suggestion made sense the more he thought about it and finally, he nodded in agreement.

After a while, she spoke again. "You speak strangely. You

ask odd things. And yet… you fight well enough. You are not from the southern lands. You are also not from the north. Not from the dwarves of the highlands. You bear no elvish grace. You also have no trace of any Animari I know." She looked at him curiously. "Where are you from, Xavier?"

He hesitated. This was the part he didn't know how to explain.

"If I tell you," he said, "don't laugh."

"I promise nothing," she replied. "But I will listen."

He sighed and nodded. "Alright. It started when I woke up for work…"

He told her everything, his death on earth, the darkness, Danu, the flight from the wolf-things, finding the ruins, the rat-men, and ultimately finding her.

When he finished, the forest had changed. The sun was higher now, and ahead, a hill rose through the mist.

Ella was quiet for several steps. Then, softly she spoke. "That is quite the tale. If it is true, and I think it might be, you would do well to keep it to yourself."

He glanced at her. "You believe me?"

"I believe you are sincere… And strange, but others would not. There are gods in this world, Xavier. Some do not tolerate rivals. If they thought, you were chosen by another… some might seek to silence you."

He gave a faint, humorless smile. "Noted."

She studied him for a moment longer, then nodded to herself. "If you will have me, I would travel with you. Not just for this task. I think your path will be longer than one cave."

A chime echoed in Xavier's mind.

> **The traveler Ella Bree has offered to become your companion.**

Do you accept? [Yes] [No]

The prompt surprised him. He'd assumed they already were companions. They had fought together, watched over one another's sleep, shared food and fire, but seeing it framed so clearly... officially... put something new in motion. He hadn't realized how much tension he still carried until now.

He focused on the word Yes.

The moment he did, the weight he hadn't noticed had settled in his chest lifted.

They were a party now. Not just two people surviving beside each other, but walking the same path.

He glanced at Ella. She was already looking ahead, her expression unreadable but calm. He gave her a faint smile, then turned his gaze forward.

A break in the treeline ahead revealed the hill the sprite had spoken of, rising gently through the mist. At their current pace, they'd reach its base within the hour.

And sure enough, just under half an hour later, they crouched low in the brush, hidden beneath the eaves of the trees. Below them, nestled at the base of the slope and half-swallowed by moss and stone, yawned a dark, narrow cave mouth.

You have found a place of interest: New Den

The message hovered in Xavier's vision.

He frowned. If the location's tag was accurate, and this world followed game logic like everything else had so far, it meant this den was recently established. No more than a year old. That didn't make sense. The village they'd camped in last night had been in ruins for far longer. Decades, maybe centuries.

Yet this... this was where the sprite had sent them.

He swallowed the unease crawling up his spine. Whatever waited in that cave, it hadn't been here long, and it hadn't come without purpose.

#

The forest around the hill fell into an uneasy stillness. The cave entrance yawned before them, low and uneven, choked with old root systems and half-swallowed by a fallen slab of stone. It was darker than it should have been. Not the shadowed quiet of a forest hollow, but the deeper dark that came with things unwelcome.

Xavier shifted beside Ella in the underbrush, spear gripped in one hand. She crouched low beside him, fingers sifting through the damp earth before plucking up a handful of smooth, hand-sized stones.

A flicker of movement at the cave mouth drew their attention.

A figure stood just within the threshold. It was gaunt, tall, and just a little too still. Its flesh had long since rotted away. Bone gleamed in the weak light that slipped through the trees. A skeleton, upright, animate, its skull twitching slightly as it scanned the treeline.

"Undead," Xavier murmured.

Ella nodded. "A sentry. Alone, but likely not unguarded beyond that entrance."

Xavier frowned. "My spear might not do much to bones."

"You used it like a staff before," she replied. "Do so again. Blunt force will break them."

She passed him a quick smile, then held up a stone. "I'll assist. You keep it focused on you."

He gave her a quick look, then rose from the brush.

The skeleton noticed him instantly. With a sharp rattle of

bone against stone, it stepped forward. Faster than expected.

Xavier barely raised the haft of his spear in time to deflect a clawed swipe aimed at his face. The strike rang against the wood, jarring his arms.

He pushed back, creating distance, then swept the blunt end of the spear toward the creature's legs.

It connected and bone cracked, but the leg held.

The skeleton hissed, a dry, rasping sound without breath.

Then a stone whistled through the air. It struck the creature's skull just below the jaw, snapping loose a portion of bone. The skull tilted at an awkward angle, but the body surged forward again, relentless.

It lashed out and one bony fist slammed into Xavier's stomach, knocking the air from his lungs. He staggered, but didn't fall.

With a snarl, he brought the butt of his spear around in a wide arc and slammed it against the creature's skull.

This time, the sound was sharper, and the skeleton reeled.

A second stone struck, this one embedding between the eye sockets. The skull shattered, and the bones collapsed in a pile at Xavier's feet.

> You have slain a Level 4 Skeleton.
> **+40 Experience**

Xavier bent over, hands on knees, breathing hard. "Well... that was unpleasant."

Ella emerged from the trees, dusting her hands. "You did well. Though next time, perhaps wait until I'm in position before drawing attention."

He managed a weak laugh, then leaned against his spear. "Noted."

She stepped closer, scanning the remains. "No armor. No

gear. Just bones. Which means whatever controls them is inside. Or worse, this place is steeped enough in death to animate corpses on its own."

Xavier frowned. "That's... comforting."

Ella stepped past him and then paused, her gaze falling to the side of the trail.

"Hold for a moment. See that?" she pointed.

Xavier followed her gesture. At the edge of a small rock, nearly hidden by moss, grew a fuzzy, low-slung plant with soft green leaves.

"That's forest sage," she said. "It's not much, but chewing it can help close wounds. Let's see if there's more."

She knelt beside it, tracing the stem with two fingers. As she finished the motion, the plant seemed to separate from the earth cleanly, lifting into her palm without cutting or tearing.

Xavier blinked. "How in the hell did you do that? I didn't see a blade. It just... let go."

"It's herbalism," she said. "A skill. You don't just grab it. You have to understand the plant first, feel it, know where it gives. The lower your skill, the more likely you'll ruin it."

She moved to another sprig and gestured him closer. "Touch it here, see where the stem meets the base? And here, where it bends."

He knelt beside her.

"You have to feel for the essence," she continued. "It's subtle. But once you sense it, the plant will guide you."

He placed his hands as she showed him and closed his eyes. At first, there was nothing just damp leaves and dirt, but then... a tingle. Faint, but definite, spreading from his fingertips up his arms. Something responded.

He felt the shape of the plant, not just physically, but its presence. Life, coiled and calm. His eyes snapped open. The stem gave a subtle twist in his palm, and rose free.

Congratulations! You have learned a new skill:
Herbalism (Level 1)
Herbalism is the art of gathering, identifying, and utilizing plants for their various properties, from healing wounds to crafting poisons. Those proficient in herbalism can locate and harvest rare herbs in the wilderness, identify the right plants even under tricky circumstances, and know exactly how to prepare them to get the desired effects. This skill also includes a deep understanding of plants' magical or medicinal properties and the knowledge to concoct everything from potent healing potions to deadly toxins. Some even say a skilled herbalist can hear the whispers of plants, guiding them to the rarest finds.
And yes, technically it means you can make tea, if you're into that sort of thing.
+2% herb effectiveness, +2% harvest yield

Xavier grinned and held up the sage. "That's... actually kind of amazing."

Ella gave a rare smile. "Now you can make tea."

They spent several more minutes combing the area for forest sage, careful not to strip it entirely.

When their pouches were half-filled, Ella stood and looked toward the cave entrance. "Lightmoss inside. See it glowing along the walls?"

He nodded.

"When we leave, harvest some if you can. It's used for alchemical light and night-vision tinctures. Much easier to carry than a torch."

She stepped toward the entrance. Xavier followed. The mouth of the den gaped before them, damp, dark, lined with that faint green luminescence. Deeper within beyond the mouth, something waited.

#

The cave walls narrowed quickly beyond the entrance. Faint strands of lightmoss clung to the stone, casting an eerie, greenish glow that flickered across their faces as they stepped inside.

It wasn't total darkness, but it wasn't far off either. The air grew colder with every step damp, still, and stale, like a place sealed too long from sky and sun.

Ella moved carefully along the left side of the passage, her hand trailing lightly against the stone. Xavier followed close behind, his spear angled low. Each footfall echoed a little too loudly for his liking.

After a bend in the tunnel, the floor began to slope downward. Ella paused at the edge, crouching low. Xavier peered over her shoulder. The descent wasn't long, perhaps twenty or thirty feet, but the incline was slick with moss and the runoff from the storm. Shadows pooled at the bottom, thick and still.

"Looks slick," she said quietly.

Xavier stepped forward without thinking. "I'll lead." The instant his foot hit the slope, he slipped. "Whoa…"

He landed hard on his backside and slid the rest of the way down in a clumsy blur of flailing limbs, scraping past rock and moss until he came to a graceless stop at the bottom.

"By the way, I did mention it's slick," Ella called dryly from above.

Xavier groaned from the floor. "Thanks. I got that part."

She began to descend slowly, one hand against the wall for

balance. She reached the bottom in moments, graceful and unbothered.

"You alright?" she asked.

"I think my spine's trying to leave my body."

She gave a small shrug. "You'll live."

The tunnel leveled out again, the floor solid stone now, worn smooth by time and water. The lightmoss continued deeper, painting the passage in green fire and the corridor ahead bent sharply to the right.

They crept forward, their weapons ready. As they rounded the bend, the passage opened into a chamber. Xavier froze.

Three figures stood in the center of the room. Two of them were skeletons, taller than the one they'd fought against above, and armed with cracked, uneven weapons. They didn't move. They didn't even breathe.

Between them sat a third being.

At first glance, the seated figure looked lifeless, slumped, hands resting on a heavy tome, something was wrong with what he was looking at. Its head sat cradled in its lap. Then it turned a page of the tome and he noticed that the heads eyes were moving as if reading the book before it.

Xavier recoiled instinctively. "What... is that?"

Ella was at his side in an instant. Her eyes widened as she took in the scene.

Her voice was a whisper. "Nekara's breath... that's a Gan Ceann."

Xavier turned to her. "Not undead?"

"No. A living race. Mystically sustained. The head detaches but it is still part of them."

The seated figure lifted its head with both hands, the void-like essence at its shoulders pulsing faintly in the dark.

It placed the head back upon its shoulders with a smooth, eerie grace. The eyes locked onto Xavier and narrowed slightly.

Ella continued, her voice low. "They are not to be underestimated. That one commands the dead, but it is not one of them."

Xavier clenched his jaw. "So how do we fight that?"

"Same way you fight anything else. It is still living and mortal just like you are."

The Gan Ceann stood now, motion smooth, almost regal. Its skeletal guardians shifted behind it, blades rising from stillness.

Ella handed him her dagger. "You take the Gan Ceann. I will hold the others."

He hesitated. "I've never fought something like that."

"You still won't unless you move."

He met her eyes, saw the certainty there and nodded.

Then, together, they stepped into the chamber.

#

The chamber beyond the narrow passage widened into a roughly hewn cavern. Lichen clung to the damp stone, glistening in the dim glow of residual essence pooled in crevices. At its far end, atop a low stone dais, stood the Gan Ceann, now fully risen. Its eyes open and fixed upon Xavier, as it watched him with quiet intensity.

Two skeletal warriors flanked the dais, their ancient weapons held low but ready. As Xavier and Ella entered the chamber, the skeletal guards stirred their shoulders creaking, eye sockets glowing with malevolent light.

Ella took the lead, hefting Xavier's spear with practiced

ease. Her eyes locked onto the skeletal guardians. "I will keep them off you," she said quickly. "You deal with the Gan Ceann."

Xavier nodded and gripped her dagger tight. The weight felt unfamiliar, but the resolve it stirred in him was firm.

The skeletons charged.

Ella moved like a storm, intercepting both with sweeping strikes. She slammed the spear across one's chest, knocking it into the wall, then spun and ducked under the other's swing, jabbing the butt of the spear into its ribcage to knock it off balance. Her movements were sharp, measured, deadly. Xavier hesitated for just a moment at the change in the woman from when he saw her with the rat-men.

Xavier darted left, circling the dais. The Gan Ceann extended one hand toward him, while its head began to chant in an eerie cadence. Shadows coiled around its arm, the air twisting with arcane energy.

Suddenly, violet light surged, and a bolt of ebon magic shot toward Xavier. He dropped to his knees, skidding across the stone floor just in time. The spell struck the wall behind him with a concussive thud, narrowly missing one of the skeletons that Ella battled. The chamber echoed with cracks and clashes as her spear met bone and steel.

Xavier surged forward and lashed upward with the dagger. The Gan Ceann moved to retreat, but not fast enough. The blade sliced across its outstretched hand, severing several fingers. A cry of pain burst from the head cradled in its arm. It staggered back, pulling the injured hand to its chest, then placed its head fully upon its shoulders with a glare of fury.

The chanting resumed, louder and faster. Both its hands extended, shadows gathering again in vibrant purple hues. Two lances of dark energy flew from its fingers. One struck

Xavier just below the knee; the other slammed into his right shoulder.

Pain exploded through his body. Nerve-searing, mind-shattering agony pulsed from the impact sites. He screamed but remained standing, legs trembling beneath him. Blood seeped into his clothes, but he refused to fall.

From behind came the sound of clashing blades and Ella's grunts of exertion. She fought fiercely, holding the skeletons at bay, giving him his chance.

Xavier switched the dagger to his left hand, his right now barely functional and pressed forward, determined. His slashes were weaker, but he kept the Gan Ceann on the defensive. It tried to cast again, raising its arms in preparation.

It had forgotten the book.

Its foot caught on the tome at its feet, and it stumbled. Xavier lunged. They fell together, and with the last of his strength, he drove the dagger deep into the Gan Ceann's chest.

Its eyes widened, then went still. The body twitched once and collapsed, lifeless.

> You have slain a level 6 Gan Caenn Dark Mage.
> **+120 Experience**.

Gasping in pain and exhaustion Xavier turned to try and help Ella only to see that the skeletons had also crumpled to piles of bones as well. The magic wielded by the dark mage that had been giving them unlife expired with his own death.

> You have slain a level 5 Skeleton Warrior * 2.
> **+100 Experience**

Ella dropped the spear and collapsed to the ground, her body once again covered in bruises and small cuts where the edges of the skeleton's fists and blades had broken the skin.

Her eyes were blackened, and her lower lip was bleeding where it had been split, but she smiled weakly at Xavier. They had won. More importantly, they had survived.

Xavier staggered over to her, his left leg throbbing with each step as he placed weight and strain on the wounded shin and muscle. Flopping to the ground next to her, he fished out some of the forest sage they had gathered earlier and began to chew it. Curious, he pulled up his status screen and just about spit the herb out. His hit points had dropped all the way from their 120-point maximum to a mere 11 points. He had nearly died from those two dark lances.

Quickly he resumed chewing on the herb, and he saw the bleeding debuff that he had not realized he had until that point, drop off his status and his hit points slowly start to climb. That prompted him to play with his status screen a little bit and soon three bars were hanging in the upper left corner of his vision. A bright red but mostly empty bar sat at the top, under it was a vibrant green bar that was already rapidly filling since he was sitting down and beneath that was a full deep blue bar, health, stamina, and mana respectively. He wouldn't be caught off guard at what his reserves were again.

Breathing a sigh of relief that he wasn't going to bleed out and die in this cave, he turned his attention to Ella and noticed she was chewing some of the sage as well.

As their pulses and breathing calmed and health returned to their forms, they started shifting more and each pushed themselves up to their feet once again. Now came the best part of the fight... The spoils to the victor. Each one took one of the piles of bones, but like the one outside there was nothing but bone.

Looking at each other, they crossed the room to where the final corpse lay. It was wearing dirty and almost ragged robes. It had been here a while, because as they were able to get a better look at it, it was barely more than a skeleton itself. Its cheeks were gaunt and looked as if he hadn't eaten in days. Yes, it was a male, they could tell that now they saw its features better. He had another dagger in his belt, but it was obvious his focus was more on magic since he hadn't bothered to draw the blade during the fight. Xavier moved to untie Ella's blade to give it back to her, but she simply shook her head and took the new dagger instead.

Another pouch tied to his belt held a handful of coins all looking to be copper in color. Besides the book resting on the floor, they could not find anything else of interest. Ella picked up the book and began leafing through its pages while Xavier rolled the corpse to the side to see if there was anything else to be found. That slight weight shift caused a loose stone in the floor to rise slightly on one side. The grating of stone against stone caught the young man's attention and he caught the edge of the stone as he gave the body a harder shove.

Levering the stone slab upwards, Xavier's breath caught. Nestled into the slight hollow beneath was a leather bag roughly the size of his fist. He lifted it from its resting place and let the stone fall back into place. He sat down roughly, and Ella came over to his side. She still held the book open, but her attention was now fully on the bag he held in his hands. Carefully he untied the knot and opened the pouch.

The room lit up with light shining from within the leather folds and he pulled out a delicately wrought sphere, the glow emanating from within its depths. As he held it up, a prompt filled his vision. Its border was a brilliant golden color.

You have discovered:	Item Rarity: Mythic
Heart of Creation	Item Quality: Unrivaled
	Weight: 5kg
	Traits: The heart of

creation is an object
from another age. This
marvelous item can be
used to elevate normal
buildings to near godlike
levels giving them traits
and capabilities beyond
anything that mortals
can build alone. What
will you do with such a
wonder?

#

CHAPTER NINE

The Syr'Vailen

Xavier sat quietly on the cold, damp stone floor of the cave, the faint luminescence from the Heart of Creation casting soft, shifting patterns on the cavern walls. His fingers trembled as he stared at them, stained crimson from the blood of the Gan Ceann. The chill from the stone beneath him crept through his clothing, but he barely noticed. The world had narrowed down to his bloodied hands and the dawning realization of what he had done.

He had killed someone.

His mind flashed unwillingly back to the moment of conflict: the Gan Ceann's eyes wide in surprise and pain, the dagger plunging into flesh, the sickening feeling of resistance giving way beneath his strike. Unlike the rat-men, whom his mind had easily classified as monstrous beasts, this had felt different. The Gan Ceann had possessed awareness, intelligence, intention. It had spoken, moved with purpose, commanded the undead. It had felt... human.

Bile rose in Xavier's throat, choking him. Was he a murderer now? He squeezed his eyes shut, breath quickening as his mind spiraled deeper into panic. Who was he becoming in this strange world? Was he still the same man who wrote code, spent his weekends gaming, who'd never even been in a serious fight before coming here? Or was he turning into something else, something dark, ruthless?

His breathing grew rapid, harsh, echoing sharply in the oppressive silence of the cavern.

A gentle touch on his hands startled him, causing him to jerk involuntarily. His eyes snapped open to find Ella kneeling beside him, her deep jade eyes filled with calm compassion.

"Xavier," she said softly, her voice steady and reassuring, "look at me."

He swallowed hard, struggling to control his breath, meeting her steady gaze. Her presence radiated calmness, anchoring him in the swirling storm of his emotions. Slowly, deliberately, Ella took his hands into her own, hiding the bloodstains from his sight.

"I know what you're feeling," she began quietly, her words carrying gentle authority. "It never becomes easy. It shouldn't. Taking a life is a burden, one you should feel deeply. But remember, this was no innocent victim. The Gan Ceann would have killed us both without hesitation. We fought for our lives, and we won."

Xavier exhaled shakily, the rationality of her words piercing the cloud of his despair. "It's different though," he managed, his voice tight with strain. "I didn't think it would feel so… personal."

"Because you're not a monster," Ella replied firmly. "You're not cold-hearted. If you were, this wouldn't bother you at all. Hold onto that pain, it's proof you're still yourself. It's proof of your humanity."

Her words settled over him like a soothing balm. Gradually, Xavier's frantic heartbeat slowed, and the tension gripping his chest began to ease. Ella's hands tightened around his gently, grounding him further.

Her words were soft but still filled the chamber they sat

in amongst the dead and bones. "Too many callously kill and maim without thought as to what that does to them or others. I think I am starting to see more of your nature the longer we are together. I want you to keep my blade for as long as I travel with you. As I said earlier you need a good weapon at least as a back-up." A glimmer of her grin returned as she eyed him a moment longer. "I think if we are going to keep exploring like this you need some actual armor as well. Cloth, unless it is enchanted, does not do much to turn a blade or a spell."

Xavier managed a weak smile at her practicality, a gentle relief washing over him. "I'll keep that in mind."

Ella nodded, reaching into a pouch at her side and retrieving some of the forest sage they had gathered earlier. She handed some to Xavier, who accepted it gratefully. Both began chewing the leaves, the bitter taste sharp but reassuring, the herb's medicinal properties slowly easing their aches and pains.

A soft chime broke the silence, drawing Xavier's attention away from his introspection. A glowing prompt filled his vision, its message bright against the dim cave.

You have completed a quest: Rescue the Lost 2
Your kind nature and willingness to help others has increased Ella Bree's trust in you, and she has gone from a mere traveling companion to an actual companion. As long as your goals and drives align, she will support you. Be wary, trust earned can be trust broken.
Rewards: A new companion. +300 Experience

#

You have earned 500 relationship points with Ella Bree.
Your loyalty from Ella Bree has increased from Cautious (-250 loyalty) to Eager (+250 loyalty). She will happily answer most general questions and provide general

---

> information that she knows.

He glanced back to Ella, whose eyes softened slightly as if aware of the prompt he'd just seen. The affirmation of their bond steadied him further, driving away the lingering shadows of self-doubt.

Ella finally released his hands, rising gracefully and retrieving the fallen Heart of Creation, placing it carefully back into its leather pouch. She handed it back to Xavier, who accepted it hesitantly, feeling the weight of responsibility it symbolized.

"We should return to the sprite," Ella advised gently. "Darkness will soon claim the woods, and the creatures that roam these lands at night are more dangerous than Gan Ceann."

Xavier took a deep, calming breath, and with a nod, pushed himself slowly to his feet. His body ached from the battle, muscles protesting each movement, but he felt steadier now, anchored by Ella's calm presence and the clarity she had helped him regain.

Ella smiled faintly as he stood, retrieving the spear she'd used during their fight. Xavier took a final look around the chamber, committing this moment to memory, a defining moment etched into his soul. Then, side by side, they turned towards the cave entrance and began their trek back through the winding tunnels.

Outside, the setting sun painted the forest in shades of amber and gold, but Xavier felt a deeper darkness looming. Yet alongside it, hope and determination stirred. He had survived. He had grown. And for the first time since waking up in this world, he felt a sliver of true purpose.

The journey back began in reflective silence, but Xavier felt stronger, ready to face whatever challenges lay ahead.

#

Xavier and Ella emerged from the cave into the twilight-lit forest, the soft hues of dusk casting long shadows across their path. A cool breeze stirred through the trees, rustling leaves and carrying with it the crisp, earthy scents of the forest after rain. Xavier inhaled deeply, finding comfort in the fresh, clean air after the oppressive atmosphere of the cave.

Their journey back to the ruins began quietly, both lost in their thoughts as they navigated the winding trail through the dense trees. Ella moved with a quiet assurance, her eyes continually scanning their surroundings, vigilant against any threats that might lurk unseen.

As they walked, Ella occasionally pointed out various plants growing along the path, identifying their properties with casual expertise. Xavier listened attentively, absorbing her knowledge, glad for the distraction from his lingering thoughts of the recent battle. Something about the small dungeon and the fact it held something so miraculous as the Heart of Creation didn't quite sit right with him, and he would have to figure out why that was. They paused briefly several times to collect more herbs, their actions methodical and careful, filling their pouches until satisfied.

Gradually, the ruins came into view ahead, their ancient stones bathed in the soft glow of dual moons, one emerald green and the other cerulean blue, that had risen since the sun had set below the horizon. The sprite, Aelriva, hovered gracefully in the center of the chamber where they had first met, her constantly shifting form shimmering with ethereal beauty. Her eyes brightened at their return, a playful smile tugging at the corners of her lips as she observed them.

"Ye've returned swiftly," she remarked approvingly, her lilting voice carrying a subtle melody. Her gaze drifted to the pouch at Xavier's side, where the Heart of Creation was secured. " Ye did find it, then. Curious, I thought that with as long as it's been lost, the task would be harder. Yet I be glad it's returned home at last... or mayhap it's not the true original. No matter, for now ye hold the means to restore the forge and perhaps the city itself to its former glory."

Xavier nodded, carefully retrieving the pouch and opening it to reveal the glowing sphere. Aelriva's expression softened, a faint wistfulness flickering in her eyes as she gazed upon the artifact. "Aye, that be it. Lost to time, but finally home again."

Her form shifted, the elements within her body briefly mirroring the patterns of the mosaic Xavier remembered from the nexus chamber. "Be cautious, though. Do not rush to rekindle the forge. Its power will attract unwanted attention, and ye're not yet ready to defend against those who might covet its strength." She paused, her expression turning serious. "Come, follow me. There's something ye must see."

Without waiting for a response, Aelriva turned and floated gracefully toward the back wall of the chamber. As she approached, the stones shifted silently aside, revealing a hidden passage descending into the earth. Xavier exchanged a brief, uncertain glance with Ella, who gave him a reassuring nod before they hurried after the sprite.

Xavier gawked at the well-wrought stonework lining the halls they walked through and mused that if this was the quality here then it was no wonder the ruins, as old as they seemed to be, were as intact as they were. Whoever built this place was amazing in their skill. He also pondered, for just a moment, if he could achieve that level of skill as well.

Descending the winding passage for about fifteen minutes, they eventually emerged into a spacious chamber deep below the ruins. The chamber stood about forty feet from side to side though it was circular instead of being squared off like the other chambers they had passed. Much of the floor was dedicated to an intricate mosaic. Eight distinct patterns touched in the center of the masterpiece and swirled out from it.

The mosaic was an s a breathtaking work of art. At the very center, where all eight different patterns touched, the tiles were arranged in a swirling, chaotic mix of colors that merged seamlessly into one another. Here, no single color or symbol dominated, creating a dazzling, hypnotic effect that symbolized the unity and interdependence of all the different sections. The nexus glowed softly, as if it possessed a life of its own, with faint magic pulsing beneath the tiles.

As they left this central point each pattern became more distinct, and Xavier could only assume they aligned with elements of magic or nature. One section was composed of shimmering white and gold tiles arranged in beams that fanned outward like rays of sunlight. Small pieces of crystal were embedded to catch the light, causing this part of the mosaic to glow naturally as light hit it. A sunburst was situated near the center and faded into golden rays extending toward the edge of the circle.

Directly to the right of that section was one filled with vibrant reds and oranges, evoking the image of roaring flames. Gold accents created the appearance of sparks and embers dancing within the fiery section. A phoenix sat boldly near the nexus, its wings reaching outward in a way that mimics flickering fire. The mosaic pieces in this section were arranged in jagged, chaotic lines to create a sense of movement and intensity.

That section was followed by a section depicted with greens and browns. The symbol, a tree with sprawling roots was prominently placed near the center and grew outward. The mosaic tiles in this section were arranged in solid, structured lines, suggesting the firm and unyielding nature of Earth. Hints of gold highlight the edges, representing the richness of soil and minerals.

Continuing around the circle came another section, this one somber and haunting, made of dark grays and blacks interspersed with pale blue highlights. Its symbol, a single raven's feather, is near the center, blending into mist-like patterns that dissipate toward the edges. The tiles were arranged in swirls, suggesting an eerie mist or smoke that faded into darkness, creating an unsettling beauty that contrasts sharply with the brighter elements. Xavier shuddered slightly as if someone had walked over his grave looking at that section and quickly moved to the next.

The next area was just as ominous though not as oppressive, it exuded mystery, and was crafted from midnight blues, purples, and blacks. A shadowed eye served as its symbol, placed near the center and ringed with faint stars or flecks of silver. The mosaic tiles were arranged in a way that created the illusion of depth as if one could fall into the darkness. Shadows seemed to seep from this section, blending into the adjacent elements in a subtle, graceful manner.

Thankfully the next section was fluid and soothing, rendered in shades of blue and green that created the illusion of moving water. The symbol, a wave, lies near the nexus, its lines flowing outward in graceful, undulating patterns. Tiles are arranged in waves and spirals, capturing the essence of water in motion. White tiles were used sparingly to create foam-like highlights along the edges, adding depth and vibrancy to this part of the mosaic.

The change continued onwards into the next section of the mosaic. It was light and ethereal, with pale blues and silvers arranged in sweeping arcs that mimicked gusts of wind. The symbol, a small swirling spiral, is placed close to the center, with faint lines that radiate outward as if caught in a gentle wind. The tiles were placed in a flowing, wispy pattern that gave this section a sense of motion as if the air itself were circulating above the mosaic.

Finally, the last section before it touched back to the starting point was vibrant and full of energy, with lush greens, yellows, and pinks that blended harmoniously. This section's symbol, a blooming flower, was placed near the center, radiating outward with delicate tendrils and vines. This section was arranged with intricate floral patterns, and tiny gemstone accents gave the impression of dew drops, capturing the vitality and beauty of life itself.

As Xavier studied the artwork, the color and light within each section seemed to beat along with his heart as it grew subtly in vibrancy and color. Each section seemed to glow with its own life and power.

"This," Aelriva announced reverently, "is the Syr'Vailen Nexus, the soul counterpart to the Heart of Creation ye retrieved. It holds the very essence of this place, the power that once made the city of Cael'Anthir thrive."

The sprite turned to face Xavier directly, her gaze intense. "By accepting the heart, ye've taken upon yerself the mantle of Ard'Maelor, the High Forgemaster. For that be the title of the one who leads this settlement, aye. 'Tis no mere name, it carries the weight o' duty, an' the hopes of all who dwell beneath yer banner."

Xavier felt a heavy sense of responsibility settle upon his shoulders, but also a resolute determination. "I understand," he said, voice steady. "I'll do what needs to be done."

Aelriva nodded approvingly. "Good. But remember, power always comes at a price. Take care ye do not lose yerself along the way."

As her words faded, Xavier's eyes were drawn once again to the glowing mosaic beneath his feet, the vibrant colors pulsing gently in rhythm with his heartbeat. The chamber seemed alive with quiet energy, and for the first time since waking in this world, Xavier felt a clear sense of direction and purpose guiding his path forward.

#

Xavier stood at the edge of the mosaic, absorbing the vivid, pulsing energy emanating from the Syr'Vailen. The swirling patterns seemed alive beneath his feet, colors flowing seamlessly from one element to the next. Each segment held its own aura of power, whispering ancient secrets to him as he gazed upon them.

Aelriva hovered gently above the mosaic's center, her ethereal form continuously shifting through the various elements depicted beneath her. Her voice resonated softly within the chamber, holding a solemn reverence. "The Syr'Vailen Nexus is the heart of everything Cael'Anthir once was. Each element here represents a fundamental aspect of life and creation itself. Mastery of these forces is key to rebuilding and safeguarding the city above."

Ella stepped closer, her eyes wide in wonder as she took in the mosaic's intricate beauty. "It's beautiful, Xavier. Powerful."

Xavier nodded slowly, his thoughts heavy with contemplation. "And dangerous," he added quietly. "Power like this would certainly attract those who seek to misuse it."

Aelriva's form solidified briefly into something resembling solemn acknowledgment. "Precisely, Ard'Maelor. Yer wisdom is encouraging. The Sylmyrians who built this place understood the need for balance and caution. That's why they concealed this nexus deep within the earth. It was both their strength and their greatest vulnerability."

Xavier moved cautiously toward the center of the mosaic, feeling the energies tug gently at his senses, inviting him closer. As he reached the nexus's core, a soft, golden light enveloped him, warmth spreading through his chest. It was comforting, reassuring, yet carried an immense weight of responsibility.

"You have chosen well," Aelriva continued softly. "But yer path will be fraught with peril. Those who walk it must remain vigilant and true. The elements demand harmony, not dominance."

Ella met Xavier's gaze, her expression serious yet supportive. "You're not alone," she said firmly. "We'll face whatever comes together."

Aelriva smiled approvingly. "Aye, unity will be yer greatest strength. Alone, ye might falter, but together, ye can restore Cael'Anthir to its rightful glory."

The glow gradually faded, leaving Xavier feeling subtly changed, as though the nexus had imparted a fragment of itself into his very being. He turned slowly, surveying the chamber once more. The enormity of his task settled fully upon him, daunting yet exhilarating.

"Then we start with caution," Xavier said, determination strengthening his voice. "We prepare, we build our strength, and we protect what we've found. Only then will we truly restore Cael'Anthir."

Ella and Aelriva exchanged approving nods, the bonds of their shared purpose growing stronger. The chamber seemed to echo softly in agreement, the elements resonating quietly beneath their feet, ready to be awakened once more.

Xavier lifted his arm, staring at it as a sudden, intense warmth surged through him. Golden light etched itself across his skin, forming an intricate mark, a hammer poised above an anvil, symbolizing his newfound status as Ard'Maelor. He felt a deep connection to the nexus solidify within him, an unspoken bond that affirmed his role as protector and leader.

The sound of rolling drums filled Xavier's ears, and a series of prompts filled his vision.

Know this! You have gained a mark: Ard'Maelor – The Grand Forgemaster.

You have claimed the title of Ard'Maelor. In centuries past the Ard'Maelor was the leader of the Sylmyrian peoples, a long-forgotten race. They were master crafters and built marvels unlike anything known in this world. Only time will tell if you have the drive and will power required

---

Congratulations! You have purified a lost village. As the Ard'Maelor of the Sylmyrian you have become the Lord of Cael'Anthir, The Shining Forge, this once marvel of an ancient civilization has fallen from its lofty perch to the ruins and remains you have discovered in the forest. Will you restore their city to its once former glory and revive the people anew or will you squander the potential you have been given.

Your village is level 1. As you increase the level of the village, more capabilities, powers and resources may be discovered. You are now bonded with the nexus Syr'Vailen: The Convergence of Essence. You have gain access to the magic and mana of the nexus location. Nexuses are places of power and mystery and to uncover their secrets requires intent and willpower. Discover and master them at your own peril! May the fates be with you!

Congratulation! You have been awarded +**600 Reputation** points.

Total Reputation: +600, your reputation has increased from 0 to +600.

This change in reputation has advanced your reputation level from "Nobody Knows, Nobody Cares – You're like a shadow in the corner of a tavern. If you disappeared into the mist tomorrow, the world would carry on without a single elf or dwarf noticing. Good luck finding a hero's welcome"
to

"Who Are You Again? – Your name might be whispered in the winds, but most can't recall it. If you were a knight, you'd be the one who gets left out of the battle plan. People might nod at you in the market, but they're mostly confused."

You have completed a hidden quest: Reforge the Past I

Your actions in returning an object to reinvigorate the Great Forge along with earning the trust of Aelriva and gaining the right to claim the nexus has not only increased your personal power and prestige it has granted you title and lands to go with them. You are now the Lord of Cael'Anthir and the Master of its lands. Arath may be forever changed due to this event.

Rewards: A settlement of your own. +2500 Experience

You have been offered a quest: Reforge the Past II.

Having gained mastery of Cael'Anthir it is up to you to restore it to its former glory and rebuild its people. Increase the settlement level to level 2.

Quest Objectives: See the Settlement Interface for details on increasing settlement to level 2

Penalties for Failure or Refusal: Stagnation of

settlement growth. As this is a settlement improvement quest for a settlement bound to you there is no capability to refuse.

Potential rewards: A level 2 settlement with increased powers and capabilities. +5000 Experience.

Ella watched silently, awe in her eyes, as the mark settled into his skin and slowly faded from sight. "You wear it well," she whispered, admiration clear in her tone.

Aelriva floated closer, her eyes reflecting approval. "Yer mark is more than just a symbol. It's a promise to yerself and to those who'll follow ye."

Xavier clenched his fist gently, feeling the lingering heat of the mark within. "Then it's a promise I intend to keep."

His voice echoed with quiet strength, filling the chamber with a sense of resolve. Ella stepped beside him, her presence steady and reassuring. Together, they stood united, ready to embrace whatever challenges awaited them in their quest to rebuild Cael'Anthir.

Turning their attention to a previously unnoticed archway at the far side of the chamber, Xavier approached cautiously, drawn by the subtle hum of power emanating from its intricate stone carvings. Ella and Aelriva followed closely, their curiosity piqued by Xavier's evident fascination.

The carvings shimmered faintly, ancient warding runes etched deeply into the stone, pulsating softly with protective energy. Xavier reached out, his fingers tracing the patterns reverently, the runes responding to his touch with a gentle glow.

"This leads deeper," Aelriva explained quietly. "To places beneath Cael'Anthir, rich with the raw materials the Sylmyrians once harvested. But now, darkness dwells below, kept at bay only by these powerful wards."

Ella glanced uneasily at the passage, then back to Xavier. "We're not ready for whatever lies beyond these runes."

Xavier nodded in agreement, withdrawing his hand slowly. "No, we're not. First, we secure what's above. Then we'll face what's below."

Aelriva smiled approvingly once more. "Wise decision. The depths hold their own trials and treasures, but they'll wait. For now, yer strength must grow, yer allies must multiply, and Cael'Anthir must rise again."

They turned from the archway, resolved and unified, ready to begin the task of restoration awaiting them above.

#

Xavier, Ella, and Aelriva ascended from the depths beneath Cael'Anthir, emerging once more into the fresh night air. The sky above was a tapestry of stars, glittering softly against the darkness, accompanied by the soft luminescence of the twin moons he had noticed earlier bathing the ruins in ethereal light.

Xavier turned sharply toward Aelriva, questions suddenly burning within him. "Wait, a forgotten race of people? What happened to them? Why are they no longer around? What are you not telling me? This place has been forgotten for how long?" His voice was edged with tension, suspicion flickering in his eyes as if sensing he had been guided onto this path without true choice.

Aelriva regarded him calmly, her form shifting gently through patterns that mirrored the mosaic from the nexus chamber. Her presence now felt humbler, less grand than when she had declared him worthy of Cael'Anthir. "Be at peace, mortal. What ye speak of lies in ages long past. Civilizations rise and fall upon this world, and those who vanish oft leave no trace behind. While I yet remain, with faint memories o' the Sylmyrian folk, there are others whose very names were swept away by time and fate. The Shattered Expanse is but one such place, when gods clash, nothin' is left in their wake. The peoples o' that land were erased from memory itself. Yet, as ye restore the city and its folk, the memories o' the Sylmyrian will return in time."

Xavier absorbed her words quietly, noticing now how intimately connected the sprite was to the elements and essence of this place.

The ruins appeared peaceful yet solemn, holding quiet reverence for the past they embodied. Xavier paused, allowing himself a moment to absorb the beauty and gravity of the place. He felt a profound sense of belonging, an unfamiliar but welcome sensation, as though the land itself acknowledged and embraced his presence.

Ella moved beside him, her gaze also lifted toward the heavens. "It's strange," she murmured softly, "how a place so broken can feel so alive."

"It's waiting," Xavier replied quietly, his voice thoughtful. "Waiting to be rebuilt, to flourish again. I can feel it."

Aelriva floated gently above them, her form shimmering faintly in the moonlight. "Yer instincts speak true, Ard'Maelor. Cael'Anthir yearns for renewal. It yearns for its people."

Xavier took a deep breath, the crisp air revitalizing him. "Then we'll start tomorrow. We'll gather resources, seek out allies, and begin restoring what we can."

Ella nodded, determination evident in her expression. "And we will grow stronger, together. We will protect what we have found and reclaim what was lost."

Aelriva offered a final, gentle smile before fading slowly into the night, her voice lingering softly in the air. "Rest now, champions. Tomorrow begins yer journey anew."

Left alone beneath the starlit sky, Xavier and Ella exchanged a quiet, resolute glance. With a shared sense of purpose, they moved toward the shelter they'd established earlier, the promise of restoration and renewal settling deeply within their hearts as they prepared to face the challenges ahead.

CHAPTER TEN

Or How to Build a Village

The fire burned low in the stone hearth, casting long, flickering shadows against the worn walls of what they were calling Hearthstead Hall. Xavier sat close beside it, cross-legged on the uneven floor, the gentle warmth at his back contrasting the cool dawn air that seeped through cracks in the old stone. The flicker of flamelight danced across his face, catching in his eyes, tired, alert, and distant.

He wasn't looking at the fire, not truly. His gaze was fixed on the shimmering interface only he could see, floating silently before him in the air. Names, numbers, symbols, all strange at first, now oddly comforting. His character screen felt less like a game mechanic and more like a reflection of who he was becoming.

Name: Xavier	Level: 3, 0.69% to Next Level	Age: 18
Race: Human	Alignment: Neutral	Languages: Basic
Reputation: 600 – Who Are You Again? - Your name might be whispered in the winds, but most can't recall it. If you were a knight, you'd be the one who gets left out of the battle plan. People might nod at you in the market, but they're mostly confused.		

Stats		
Health: 120/120	Stamina: 110/110	Mana: 100/100
Attributes		
Strength: 9	Agility: 8	Dexterity: 9
Constitution: 10	Endurance: 9	Charisma: 8
Intelligence: 8	Wisdom: 8	Luck: 9
Resistances	**Skills**	**Marks**
None	Survival: 1 Woodworking: 1 Tracking: 1 Herbalism: 1	Cooking: 2 Crafting: 1 Spears: 1 Clubs: 1 Knives: 1	Ard'Maelor - The Grand Forgemaster
Abilities		
Unbound Possibilities – While the inhabitants of Arath are constrained by rules limiting how they can grow and what they can learn you have been blessed by Danu to be unbound. These limits guide you but do not constrain you. **Linguist** – You have the capacity to know, understand, and speak any mortal language		

His breath left in a slow exhale. Not bad, he thought. Not great either, but better than where he started. And he had twelve discretionary points to allocate.

His eyes drifted to the broken spear resting beside him, then to the dagger Ella's gift, his first real weapon. Then the little pouch that held the Heart of Creation, pulsing faintly with dormant power. He hadn't yet dared to unpack what it meant to hold that. But this... this he could control.

With a slow breath and steady focus, he began assigning the points.

One into Strength, it only made sense, given how often he was carrying gear, scavenging, or fighting. Two went into Agility. Dodging those club swings back in the reliquary had nearly cost him his ribs. He winced slightly remembering all the club blows to his body and the pain of those injuries, granted he now had some herbs that helped but he was worried they would be lacking if the injuries were worse. One more went into Endurance, just to ensure he wouldn't tire as easily next time, stamina hadn't been a concern yet but the handful of fights and his running from the wolflike creatures had started to tax him and made him worry about how it would be if he had bottomed out.

That left eight. He hesitated. Combat stats were useful, sure, but he wasn't just a wanderer anymore. He was now, technically, a village leader. A founder. He needed to think ahead. He placed four points into Charisma, recalling every RPG he'd ever played. High charisma unlocked paths that didn't need to be walked through blood. Maybe it would help him talk his way through whatever Bramblegate threw at him. Two points into Wisdom, something told him intuition mattered here more than back on Earth. And the final two... into Luck.

He had no idea if that last choice made sense, but he'd been lucky so far, hadn't he?

A quiet chime sounded, and the stats confirmed their new values. Xavier let out a breath he hadn't realized he'd been holding and closed the screen with a blink. His eyes returned to the world around him, old stone, firelight, and Ella.

She was still sleeping, her back to the hearth, curled slightly beneath a worn hide they'd salvaged from their early hunts. Her breathing was steady, peaceful. He watched her for a moment longer, then turned his attention to something new.

Another tab had become available.

> **Settlement Interface** → *Statistics: Level 1 (Village)*
> Mana Cap: 1500 (Regenerates at 75/hour)
> Radius: 15 miles from the Nexus Core
> **Requirements to Reach Level 2:**
> ◆ Population: 100
> ◆ Individual Buildings: 15
> ◆ Settlement Quests Completed: 5
> *Description:* A quaint little gathering of huts, fields, and maybe a single ramshackle inn. The biggest excitement is when Old Man Barlow's goat escapes and terrorizes the local cabbages. Hardly a booming metropolis, but it's home... for now.

Xavier huffed a short laugh, his breath fogging slightly in the morning air. "Not exactly a glowing review," he muttered. But it was something. A framework and a goal. It also answered several questions about his settlement's limitations and requirements. He also noted that there were eight additional levels it could achieve, their details were all blurred out but again... a goal for the future.

He thumbed through the other tabs quickly, some blurred, locked beyond his level. Others hinted at capabilities he hadn't yet tapped. Skills, construction, resource management. One stood out though... Village abilities. Huh, he bookmarked that mentally.

Outside, faint birdsong began to stir in the trees, echoing through the still-sleeping ruins. The last few embers of night clung to the stonework, slowly giving way to pale light.

Xavier rose quietly and crossed to the doorway, stepping into the threshold and leaning against the worn frame. The air was brisk and clean, filled with the scent of dew-wet moss and pine. It didn't smell like danger. Not today.

He closed his eyes. "Thanks," he whispered, unsure if the words were for Danu or for the world itself. "For giving me another shot."

Behind him, the fire crackled. A moment passed. Then a soft hand touched his shoulder.

He turned to see Ella, eyes still sleep-heavy but alert, offering a faint smile. "My turn," she said, voice low so as not to disturb the morning's peace.

He nodded, stepping aside, and made for the bedroll near the hearth. He laid down, folding his hands behind his head as warmth from the fire touched his cheeks.

His mind still raced with stat points, Nexus powers, and the title now etched on his soul: Ard'Maelor. It was a lot to take in, but exhaustion crept in all the same. Tomorrow would begin the rebuilding. Tonight, he would rest.

#

The world pressed into his unconscious thoughts again with warmth and noise, birdsong flitting through the canopy, the gentle creak of wind through stone, and the faint scent of fire smoke lingering on his clothes.

Xavier stirred groggily, blinking against the sharp glare of sunlight slanting through the shattered arch above him. A single beam had found his face like a hunter's mark, cutting through the cool interior of Hearthstead Hall. He groaned and rolled onto his side, one arm flung across his face to shield his eyes.

A shadow passed across the light. Ella stood over him with an raised eyebrow.

She nudged his foot with the edge of her boot, amusement written plainly on her face. "Come on, sun-sleeper. The world isn't going to rebuild itself."

Xavier sat up with a yawn, stretching until his spine

popped in protest. His limbs ached from days of work and combat, but the ache was a welcome one as it was earned and familiar. He rubbed his face and grimaced. "My mouth tastes like old socks."

Ella laughed, the sound clear and easy. "Then I hope you didn't wear them yesterday."

Xavier smirked, then shook his head. "I'm going to need to figure out a new hygiene routine. I've been here what four or five days? No toothbrush, no showers, and the forest isn't exactly overflowing with toilet paper." He rubbed his eyes and stood, brushing bits of ash from his trousers. "Give me a minute. Nature calls."

He wandered out the broken archway, weaving between moss-choked ruins and shattered stone. The cool morning air wrapped around him like a blanket drawn from the earth itself, fresh, pine-scented, tinged with dampness. Birds chirped overhead, their calls unfamiliar but musical.

Behind a thick copse of scrub, he found a spot and took care of his business, grumbling under his breath about leaves and their shortcomings. While he moved to clean up, his gaze lifted to the trees, tall, thick-limbed, reaching like sentinels. The ruins felt smaller in the morning light, less oppressive than they had under the stars. The weight of history was still there, but now it seemed to breathe with him, not bear down on him.

When he returned, Ella was crouched in the grass beside the hearth, nibbling on a handful of dark red berries. She looked up and offered a satisfied smile. "Found these just past the third collapsed building down that trail. Sweet. Tart. Actually not terrible."

He raised a brow. "Any for me?"

She pointed with a berry-stained finger toward the trail. "Follow it down three ruins, veer left, look for the bramble cluster under the big flat stone. Watch for thorns."

Xavier grunted in mock irritation but followed her instructions. The path wound through the forest's edge where nature had crept into the cracks of the ancient settlement, reclaiming stone and mortar with moss and root. He found the bush easily, its bright berries glinting like rubies in the morning sun and picked a few carefully. The juice stained his fingers, sweet and tart on his tongue.

Returning, he found Ella sitting cross-legged beside the fire, contentedly eating and watching the breeze stir the trees. Aelriva had returned as well, her form suspended in midair, flickering between hues of green and pale blue like a prism struck by morning light. She hovered above the ground, arms folded, face contemplative.

"Yer tongues have been fed, then," Aelriva said, her voice like a whisper laced with wind chimes. "A good start. But ye'll need more than berries and banter if ye're to thrive here."

Xavier dropped into a seat across from her. "That's what I was about to ask. We've got food for a day, if that. Still no idea how to grow more, and unless we find more water than that puddle near the path…"

Ella motioned toward Aelriva. "She has a solution for that."

The sprite's smile tilted. "Aye. Follow me."

She darted off in a slow spiral of light, beckoning them like a will-o'-the-wisp. Xavier and Ella followed her through the ruins, across cracked stone paths lined with vines and collapsed beams. After several minutes, Aelriva stopped near a patch of crumbled wall. At first, Xavier saw only a moss-choked basin, until Aelriva raised her hand, and a shimmer pulsed in the air. A veil of illusion peeled back.

A wide stone well stood at the base of a gentle slope, tucked against the forest's edge. Water glimmered faintly at its surface, clear and fresh. A thin rivulet of it flowed from the rock face behind, feeding the pool with a steady trickle before vanishing underground through a narrow outlet.

"It's spring-fed," Aelriva said proudly, her form pulsing with soft green light. "Kept hidden to preserve its purity."

Xavier knelt beside it, cupping water into his hands and drinking deeply. The cold was sharp but clean, slicing through the fuzz of sleep with icy clarity. He splashed some over his face and sat back on his heels, blinking.

"That... is amazing." He almost cooed in pleasure at the taste and feel.

Ella followed suit, her expression more subdued but no less grateful. She let out a quiet sigh of relief.

"So we've got fresh water," Xavier said, standing slowly. "That's one thing off the list."

He looked at Aelriva. "I checked the settlement stats this morning. We need people. Buildings. Quests, apparently. But I've got no clue how to find people, or even where to start building."

Aelriva floated a lazy circle around his head. "Ye didn't read everything in the interface, did ye? There's a section ye missed... Village Skills and Abilities. Tucked away near the bottom."

Xavier blinked. "There's a what?"

"Typical," Ella said under her breath, smirking.

Aelriva tapped his forehead gently. "Look again, Ard'Maelor. Ye may find more tools at yer disposal than ye realize."

#

Xavier blinked twice and reopened his interface, flicking

mentally through the menus until he reached the bottom of the Settlement Tab. Nestled beneath statistics and quest tracking, a small, faintly pulsing label caught his eye: Village Skills and Abilities

He mentally tapped it and was rewarded with a brief flicker, then new options appeared—half a dozen abilities grayed out, but one glowing softly in green.

Summon Minor Forest Golem
Type: Summoning
Duration: 1 Full Cycle (20 Arathian Hours)
Cost: 150 Mana (Personal or Village Pool)
Description: Call forth a construct of bark, moss, root, and stone to perform basic labor tasks: gathering, carrying, clearing, and mining. Golems are simple-minded and require explicit, step-by-step commands.

He gawked at the screen. "How did I miss this?"

Beside him, Ella raised an eyebrow. "Didn't you say you were thorough?"

Xavier groaned. "I was… distracted."

Aelriva chuckled. "Ye're not the first to overlook what's in plain sight. But now ye ken the truth. These golems are the hands of the forest. Not smart, not fast, but tireless and loyal while bound to the Nexus. Perfect for yer needs."

Xavier stared at the ability for a moment, then focused. The mana cost shimmered in his mind, too much for his personal pool, but he could feel the quiet current of the village's mana, still untapped. With a breath, he reached out and touched it, it felt like dipping fingers into an unseen stream.

Power answered to his call and he activated the skill.

The ground trembled slightly, not violently, but enough to make the stones underfoot shift. Moss curled inward. Bits of bark and root lifted as if tugged by invisible threads. In the center of the ruined courtyard, debris and soil began to swirl in a slow spiral, as though stirred by a rising breath.

A minute passed as the mound grew and then the shape began to form.

First the legs, thick and knotted like tree trunks. Then a squat torso of bark-laced stone, hunched and broad. Arms followed, long and powerful, ending in thick club-like appendages. The head was last, a faceless orb of interwoven vines atop its broad shoulders, vaguely humanoid but devoid of expression.

It stood nearly four and a half feet tall, chest rising and falling with the creak of stretching wood.

Xavier took a cautious step back. "That… is awesome."

The golem stood still, silent, waiting.

He approached slowly, then pointed to a nearby pile of rubble that had once been a building wall. "Can you… tear that down? And maybe pile the stones over there by the forest edge?"

The golem did nothing.

Ella covered her mouth, trying not to laugh.

Aelriva sighed in mock patience. "Did I not warn ye? Ye must speak to them as if ye were explainin' to a very dim person. Vague directions will see them standin' there till the moons fall from the sky."

Xavier ran a hand through his hair and squared his shoulders. "Okay, fine. Follow me."

He led the golem to the edge of the ruin, motioning to a specific collapsed structure, half wall, sunken roof, debris strewn around. He picked up a stone, held it up for the golem to see, then walked over to the forest's edge and set it gently in an open space.

"I want you to do this," he said clearly. "Take apart all buildings that look like that one, and carry their stones over here. Stack them in this area. Like this."

He gestured for emphasis, careful and slow.

The golem tilted its head. A beat passed. Then it moved.

Its hands shifted club-ends extending into crude, root-fingered tools. It walked to the rubble pile and began lifting stones, one by one, and carrying them across the clearing. As it worked, its motions were slow but steady, like watching a glacier move with purpose.

Xavier exhaled, a grin blooming on his face. "Now that's more like it."

Ella joined him, watching the golem work. "That's going to save us weeks."

"Try years," Xavier muttered. He opened the interface again and summoned another, and then another, and another.

One by one, the ground gave rise to more forest constructs, ten in total by the time he was done, each drawing from the village's mana pool reducing it slowly until it had only a few points that had regenerated since he started. Each formed from the elements nearby, blending into the terrain even as they began their work, clearing rubble, stacking stone, and hauling fallen timber.

Soon, the clearing was alive with motion.

The golems were quiet workers, their steps muffled by moss and dirt. Occasionally, one would pause to reorient or mimic a motion Xavier had demonstrated earlier. But otherwise, they obeyed without complaint or hesitation. Their silence only added to the surreal beauty of the scene, living constructs of root and stone, reclaiming a dead city.

Aelriva hovered between them, arms folded as she

surveyed the work with a satisfied smile. "They'll keep at it for the full cycle. When the sun rises again, they'll fall apart into mulch and dust. But each day ye may summon more, so long as the mana flows."

"Can they build?" Xavier asked, watching one stack salvaged stones into neat rows.

"Not precisely," Aelriva answered. "They lack the finesse for masonry or carpentry. But they can gather, sort, dig, and clear, tasks that would've taken a dozen strong backs before. With yer hands free o' the grunt work, ye can focus on real craftin', planning, and seeking others to aid ye."

Xavier nodded slowly, watching as the first of the ruined buildings vanished beneath the methodical labor of the golems. "We might actually be able to do this..."

Ella bumped her shoulder gently against his. "We will."

For a moment, the early sun broke through the trees in golden bands, illuminating the ruins in soft light. Dust caught the beams like motes of memory, drifting lazily between the remnants of a forgotten city now breathing again under new hands.

#

The sound of stone grinding on stone drifted through the valley air, soft and rhythmic. The summoned golems moved steadily between ruined buildings and stacked stone along the tree-lined edge of the settlement. In the center clearing, freshly salvaged timber lay in sorted piles, casting long shadows in the slanted light of midmorning. A breeze stirred the scent of old earth and moss.

Xavier stood near the edge of what once must have been a plaza, his eyes sweeping across the growing signs of effort taking root. Hearthstead Hall stood firm at the center. An ancient forge, Mael'Anthir Aelriva had called it, loomed in silence near the north side. And beyond it all, he could just make out the glint of water catching light along the far eastern edge of the valley.

The Silverflow River, another name provided by the diminutive sprite, ran smooth and wide through the cleft in the land, its banks flanked by brush and thick-rooted trees. It was a lifeline. A natural border. And a reminder that beyond this place, the world still turned.

He turned to Aelriva, who floated at shoulder height, her form flickering gently in the elemental hues. "We've got fresh water. Food, more or less. The golems are handling the rubble. But all of that means nothing if it's just me and Ella here."

His tone wasn't frustrated, only matter-of-fact, practical he felt. The weight of reality was setting in now that the thrill of discovery had passed.

"We need people," he said. "Builders, foragers, crafters. Folks who don't mind living in the middle of a forest inside the ruins of a forgotten city."

Ella rose from where she'd been crouched, brushing dust off her knees. "And they'll need more than optimism to get them here. No roads means no wagon, and no idea what kind of life they'd be signing up for."

Aelriva tilted her head slightly, the air around her shimmering faintly. "Aye, and yet, there may be those willin'. There is one place I ken of still. Distant, but not unreachable."

She drifted a few paces ahead, then gestured for them to follow.

They walked with her past Hearthstead Hall and along an overgrown path once meant for more feet than theirs. The forest pressed close to the ruins here, roots creeping between broken flagstones, vines claiming the skeletons of old homes. As they reached the eastern edge of the valley's rise, the land sloped gently down toward the shimmering silver ribbon of the river.

Aelriva stopped before a moss-covered stone post. She placed her hand against it, and the runes carved into its face shimmered to life, glowing soft green and pale blue.

She turned and pointed northeast, beyond the curve of the Silverflow.

"Several days from here, if ye follow the river northeastward beyond the forest's edge, lies a place called Bramblegate. It stands where the treeline gives way to open hills and softer land. Trade once flowed through it, back when roads meant more than boundaries. Mayhap it still lingers."

Xavier followed her gesture with his eyes. He couldn't see the village, but the idea of it settled into his thoughts like a dropped stone. "So that's where we'll find people."

"If the village still stands," Ella said.

"If it does, then aye," Aelriva confirmed. "There, ye may find those with nothin' left to lose. Or those who dream of more. Some seek coin, others freedom. A few might simply want land to call their own."

Xavier rubbed at his jaw. "And if I walk in talking about being a forge-lord from a ruined valley, do you think they'll even take me seriously?"

"That depends on the shape of your words," Aelriva replied. "Truth told clear and steady carries weight. And those with eyes to see may look past your garb and see what you've already begun. Ye hold the Heart of Creation. Ye wear the mark of Ard'Maelor. Even if ye do nae share them, and ye should nae, it gives weight to ye words. That will mean something, to some."

Xavier looked to Ella. "What do you think?"

She didn't hesitate. "If it's a lead, we follow it. We need others. If Bramblegate can offer that, we go."

He nodded. "We'll need to prepare first. Food, supplies, better clothes. A pack, maybe some extra tools or weapons. I'm not heading into the unknown in what I'm wearing now."

Ella glanced down at his tunic, already patched in two places, and smirked. "Agreed."

Aelriva's form shifted, taking on the sheen of still water and weathered bark. "Wise to prepare. I'll remain here and continue summonin' golems each morning. They'll keep clearin' space while ye're gone. The forge will stay untouched unless ye say otherwise."

Xavier's gaze shifted toward the great dome of Mael'Anthir. "Make sure they leave the forge be. It is not its time, not yet. We've cleared the ruins, but we haven't earned the right to awaken it."

Aelriva's expression warmed. "Aye. Ye show wisdom already, Ard'Maelor. When the time comes, the forge will burn again. But not before the village lives."

Xavier stood quietly for a moment, the valley breeze playing through his hair, the hush of water whispering along the riverbanks below. Then he turned back toward the clearing.

"Let's finish what we can here. We gather, we hunt, we craft. And then we walk the river east."

Ella stepped beside him and gave a quiet nod. "Back into the wild."

He smiled faintly. "This time, we're walking toward something."

#

The sun crested the valley rim by the time Xavier and Ella resumed their sweep through Cael'Anthir's ruins. With the golems tirelessly clearing larger debris piles, the pair turned their focus to the structures that had weathered time with surprising resilience. Many of the buildings had long since collapsed under the pressure of root and weather, but a handful remained with walls still upright and door frames half-standing.

They moved carefully from structure to structure, stepping over tumbled beams and moss-covered stones. Each building told a different story, some with shattered furniture left where it had fallen, others long since emptied by weather or time. Still, a few had held fast against centuries of decay.

Ella paused beside one such structure, brushing aside a cluster of ferns near the foundation. "There's a door here," she murmured.

Xavier moved to help. The heavy wood was swollen with age and rot but still mostly intact. Together, they pried it loose, revealing a narrow stone stairway leading down into darkness. The air that rushed out was cool and damp, tinged with a rich scent of earth and something else faintly botanical.

He drew his knife, more from habit than fear, and led the way down.

The root cellar below was surprisingly spacious, the stonework still holding firm. Beams overhead groaned quietly, but nothing had collapsed. Shelves lined the far wall, crumbled under their own weight long ago. On the floor, a tangle of overgrowth covered nearly every surface.

At first, Xavier thought it was weeds. Then he noticed the orderly way the plants had grown, neat rows, rhythmic spacing, all pointing to a forgotten purpose. He knelt beside one of the clusters and tugged gently at a thick green stem. A squat, knobbly tuber came free, coated in soft, dark soil.

A small prompt shimmered across his vision.

You have discovered: Cave Tater	Ingredient Class: Common **Item Quality:** Raw **Weight:** 0.2 kg **Durability:** 5/5 **Traits:** A small, root tuber. "Boil 'em, mash 'em, stick 'em in a stew!"

He turned it in his hand, eyebrows raised. "We've got potatoes."

Ella moved to a second cluster nearby and unearthed another root, thinner and orange-brown in color. A new prompt appeared.

You have discovered: Cave Kraton	Ingredient Class: Common **Item Quality:** Raw **Weight:** 0.1 kg **Durability:** 5/5 **Traits:** A small, carrot-like root vegetable. Grows in low-light and subterranean conditions.

Xavier chuckled. "I think we just found our first crops."

Ella stood, brushing soil from her hands. "Makes sense they'd survive down here. No sunlight, but plenty of damp and old soil. Maybe some magical trace helped them endure."

They harvested a few of each, careful not to uproot everything. It was clear the plants had adapted to the cellar's environment, and removing too much might ruin a self-sustaining system. They bundled what they could carry in strips of salvaged cloth and moved back into the light.

Their next stop took them to a half-collapsed basement near the forge. The ground floor had crumbled inward, but the stone steps leading beneath were still accessible with some care. Xavier took point again, descending slowly into the dark.

Inside, the space had become a haven of mushrooms. Pale caps grew in uneven patches across the stone floor, clustered in corners and crevices. The damp, musty air was filled with the scent of growth and decay, a strange mix of rot and life.

Ella crouched near the largest patch and examined the mushrooms closely. "These are edible. Not just edible, some of these are actually pretty nutritious."

Xavier picked one and watched another prompt appear.

You have discovered: White Cave Shunt	**Ingredient Class:** Common **Item Quality:** Raw **Weight:** 0.02 kg **Durability:** 5/5 **Traits:** A hardy cave mushroom, filling and reliable. Grows in total darkness.

He found a second type growing along the wall, smaller and with a distinct shape—slightly curved, like an elongated ear.

You have discovered: Elf Ear Mushroom (Cave)	**Ingredient Class:** Common **Item Quality:** Raw **Weight:** 0.01 kg **Durability:** 5/5 **Traits:** A small, tan mushroom shaped like an elf's ear. Woody in texture, often dried for trail rations or stews.

"I think we've just doubled our food variety," he said. "Root vegetables, protein-rich fungus, and enough to keep us going for weeks if we ration it right."

Ella nodded. "We'll need to dry some of them. We can't store everything fresh, and the mushrooms will rot fast if we don't prepare them."

They gathered a small bundle of each variety, again leaving enough behind to regrow. As they climbed back into the daylight, the sun had shifted further west, casting the ruined village in warm amber tones.

Xavier looked at the plants in his arms and let out a quiet breath. "It's not glamorous. But it's a start."

Ella smiled beside him. "It's a harvest. One we didn't have yesterday."

They returned to Hearthstead Hall and added their findings to the growing cache. Potatoes and mushrooms were piled on a stone slab near the fire, joining the small reserve of smoked meat from the previous day's hunt.

The golems continued to work in the background. Their footsteps fell heavy and steady, muffled by soil. Though they never spoke, the rhythm of their movements had begun to feel almost like a heartbeat for the valley.

Xavier sat down beside the hearth and wiped the sweat from his brow. The aches in his back and shoulders were dull now, almost familiar. The day had been full, but not wasted. In fact, it felt like the first real day of building something.

He looked across the fire at Ella, who was sharpening one of their few remaining knives with a whetstone she'd scavenged earlier.

"You ever think you'd be farming mushrooms and root vegetables in the ruins of a forgotten city?" he asked.

She gave him a sideways glance. "No. But I've had stranger

weeks."

#

Evening settled softly over the valley, painting the Silverflow River in rippling streaks of gold and pale lavender. The last of the light filtered through the trees, casting long shadows across the mossy stones of Cael'Anthir. The golems continued their work with silent dedication, now stacking sorted timber into organized rows near the central clearing.

Xavier crouched beside a large flat stone they had cleared earlier in the day and laid out the materials he had gathered. A long, curved branch. A bundle of smaller, straighter sticks and a handful of feathers, mottled gray and white. Nearby, Ella returned from the small lean-to they had converted into a drying shelter, holding a strip of rabbit gut in one hand.

"Still smells," she commented, holding it out at arm's length.

"It's going to get worse before it gets better," Xavier said. He didn't look up. His attention remained fixed on the long branch, testing its give with steady pressure from both hands. It bent, not easily, but enough. The shape held promise.

"I'm going to try and make a bow," he said.

Ella tilted her head, crouching beside him. "You've done that before?"

"No," Xavier admitted. "But I've seen enough videos and survival guides to have a rough idea. Plus, the woodworking skill I got the other day might help guide things."

He could already feel it at the edge of his senses. As he laid each piece down, faint ghostly outlines traced across the materials. His mind filled in the gaps with images of how they could fit together. Not quite instructions, but suggestions. A whisper of potential.

"I'll work on the arrows afterwards," he said, nodding toward the shorter sticks. "The gut should be dry enough now to use for string. If this works, you'll have a ranged weapon that isn't just throwing stones or spears."

Ella watched him for a moment, then gave a short nod. "I'll handle the gut."

She moved with practiced efficiency, stretching the sinew between two upright branches they had hammered into the ground earlier. With careful hands, she began scraping the dried flesh from the strand, working it down into a thin, taut length that would serve as a bowstring. The motion was rhythmic, almost meditative.

Xavier turned his focus to the branch. With the flint knife at his belt, he began shaving it down, removing bumps and shaping the curve. The wood creaked as he worked, the sound sharp in the quiet air. Sweat gathered at his brow, but he didn't stop. He wrapped the middle with a strip of rabbit hide to form a basic grip. Retrieving the gut string from Ella, he attached it to both ends then tested the draw. The gut stretched and held, humming faintly with tension.

He smiled with pride at what he had accomplished.

Next came the arrows. He selected ten of the straightest sticks and began trimming them, using flakes of stone to form rough points. The feathers he tied in place with more sinew, not perfect, but serviceable. Each one took longer than the last, his fingers growing stiff with effort and concentration.

By the time the moons had risen, one silver, the other green, he held the finished bow in one hand and a fistful of crude arrows in the other. The bow wasn't elegant. It still bore splinters at both ends, and the grip felt uneven, but it was real. It was his.

You have crafted: Rough Short Bow	Item Class: Common Item Quality: Average Weight: 2 kg Durability: 15/15 Traits: A primitive shortbow crafted from wild wood, rabbit gut, and leather scrap. It lacks finesse but functions as intended. Accuracy and range are limited. Effective only at short distances.

You have crafted: Crude Stone Arrows (x10)	Item Class: Common Item Quality: Average Weight: 0.01 kg each Durability: 5/5 Traits: Hastily constructed arrows. Fletched with scavenged feathers and tipped with sharp stone. Not reliable beyond close range but better than throwing rocks.

#

Congratulations! You have gained: Woodworking (Level 2) Crafting (Level 2) +4% to crafted item quality +4% to crafted wooden weapon damage +4% to crafted tool effectiveness

Xavier let out a slow breath and looked up at Ella. She had

been watching him work for the last several minutes, her expression unreadable.

He handed the bow over. "Your turn."

She took it, tested the string, then selected one of the arrows. Without a word, she stepped to the edge of the clearing, sighted a nearby tree, and drew back.

The string creaked, then twanged. The arrow struck the trunk, not deeply, but enough to stick.

She smiled. "It'll do."

Xavier laughed and wiped his hands on his trousers. "Glad to hear it. I wasn't sure the string would hold."

Ella retrieved the arrow and returned, giving it a quick once-over. "Still usable. The tip chipped, but not enough to matter."

Then her brow lifted slightly. "You know... we'll need a quiver. Unless you expect me to carry these by hand."

Xavier winced. "Right. I didn't think that far ahead."

"No surprise," she replied, though her voice held amusement rather than criticism.

He glanced at the remaining scraps of hide they had. "I can try to make something simple. Might take a night or two."

"I can make do until then," she said, slinging the bow over one shoulder. "But I wouldn't wait too long. Carrying ten arrows in my arms while running sounds like a recipe for pierced ribs."

They sat together in the quiet that followed, watching the golems continue their work under the pale twin moons. Their breath misted in the air, and somewhere beyond the ridge, a nightbird called out with a lonely trill.

Xavier leaned back on his hands and stared at the bow

lying across her lap. It wasn't much, but it was something he had made. "We're getting there," he said quietly.

Ella nodded. "One step at a time."

#

By the third day, the golems had cleared much of the central ruins. Fallen beams, shattered walls, and moss-choked walkways had been gathered into tidy stacks of salvage. The bones of Cael'Anthir now breathed more openly beneath the sky, no longer buried beneath centuries of rot and silence, and yet, one place remained untouched.

Xavier stood before it now, the wind stirring his tunic and whispering through the cracks in its stonework. Mael'Anthir, the Great Forge of the Sylmyrian, rose ahead like a slumbering giant. The dome was massive, its curved roof lined with chimneys and fractured vents. Vines crawled across its surface, but even time had not fully claimed the building. A strange warmth clung to it, even in the shade.

They had avoided it for days, perhaps unconsciously. But now, with preparations underway and his curiosity too loud to ignore, Xavier stepped forward.

Ella followed without a word, her hand brushing the spear strapped across her back. Aelriva floated nearby, her form unusually still.

As Xavier reached for the heavy stone doors, the sprite spoke. "The Mael'Anthir remembers," she said quietly. "Even now, while cold and broken, its spirit lingers. Do ye feel it? That weight in the air? That breath beneath yer feet?"

Xavier paused, hand resting against the surface of the door. He did feel something. Not fear, not a threat, but a distinct presence. The same feeling he'd had in the nexus chamber. The sense that something ancient watched in silence, waiting.

"I do," he said.

Aelriva drifted closer. "Then heed me, Ard'Maelor. Do not awaken the forge. Not yet. When ye've gathered a people and built a village worthy of the name, then ye may give it back its heart. Until then, ye may enter. Ye may use its remnants. But the soul of this place must sleep a while longer."

Xavier nodded. He pushed gently, and the doors opened with a groan that echoed into shadow.

Inside, dust floated like pale spirits through shafts of fading light. The forge's chamber was massive, vaulted and circular, its central hearth long cold but unmistakably powerful. A cracked anvil stood at the heart of the room, etched with runes that pulsed faintly beneath the grime. Chimneys above opened to the sky, though many had collapsed inward, leaving jagged holes in the ceiling.

Scattered across the floor were the bones of creation. Broken tools, rusted blades, twisted pieces of armor. Some large enough for giants, others delicate and fine. Xavier stepped forward slowly, eyes wide.

He could feel the thrum of old magic in the walls.

"A forge built not just for fire," Aelriva said from behind him. "But for purpose. For soul. The Sylmyrians crafted here what others thought impossible. They forged weapons of balance, of truth, of will."

Ella approached the central anvil and knelt beside it. She ran her fingers over the runes carved into the stone. "They're like the ones from the mosaic room. Different, but… related."

"They are kin," Aelriva replied. "Wrought of the same thought. The same intention."

Xavier circled the chamber slowly. He passed workbenches that still bore shattered molds. Storage racks that once held rare metals now stood bare. Against one wall, a stone furnace sat dormant, its firebox dark but intact. He paused there and touched the rim of its opening.

"It feels like it's waiting," he murmured.

"It is," Aelriva said. "It knows ye're not ready, but it also knows ye will be."

Ella rose and moved to one of the outer alcoves, brushing aside old debris. Behind a partially collapsed support beam, she found a rack of unfinished tools, hammers, tongs, chisels, all too worn to use, but still bearing the marks of fine workmanship.

"This place could be incredible," she said. "If we had the right materials. The right knowledge."

Xavier walked to join her. He picked up a piece of broken metal, warped and pitted with rust, and turned it over in his hand. "We'll get there. One day."

He stacked the fragments they found beside the old smelter for future use. Some might be reforged. Others studied. For now, he just wanted to treat the forge with care.

As they stepped back outside, Aelriva lingered behind. She floated silently for a long moment, then drifted toward the anvil.

Her hand, small and luminous, pressed to the cracked surface. The forge pulsed once beneath her touch, barely visible, like a heartbeat in stone.

Ella saw the moment. She watched the sprite with quiet understanding and walked to her side. Without a word, she reached out and mirrored the gesture, placing her palm beside Aelriva's.

The glow grew stronger for just a second, then faded.

Xavier, still unaware of the exchange, stood outside blinking against the late afternoon sun. When the two rejoined him, neither spoke of what had passed.

But something had shifted, the forge had acknowledged them. and it would wait.

#

Time passed, not in great leaps, but in quiet rhythm. Each morning began with the low rumble of the golems stirring to life as Aelriva summoned them with practiced ease. They emerged from moss and loam, bark and stone, answering her wordless call with patient labor. Each day brought ten new hands to the valley, and slowly, Cael'Anthir began to breathe again.

The ruins changed shape under their guidance. Collapsed walls became neat stacks of stone. Broken timbers were sorted into piles for salvage or firewood. Pathways once buried in ivy and roots revealed old cobblestones beneath. The land was not yet tamed, but it no longer felt forgotten.

Xavier and Ella fell into their own rhythm.

In the mornings, they foraged. Ella's keen eye and steady hand made her well-suited to identifying herbs and game trails. Xavier followed close behind, learning to spot edible roots and signs of burrowing creatures. They tracked a few of the deer-like beasts they had glimpsed before. Though they were elusive, Ella managed to bring one down with a well-placed arrow near the riverbank. Its meat was lean and slightly gamey, but with the addition of mushrooms and root vegetables, it became a meal worth repeating.

The hides were stretched and cured beside the drying racks. Xavier, slow at first, began to take over the task of preparing leather. His hands fumbled often, and his knife slipped more than once, but each mistake became part of the process. The more he worked, the more intuitive the cuts and folds became.

At night, they cooked over a fire in front of Hearthstead Hall. Meals were simple: skewers of tubers and meat, occasionally a cluster of roasted mushrooms. It wasn't elegant, but it was warm and filling.

Congratulations! You have gained:
Crafting Level 5
+10% to crafted item quality
+10% to crafted tools

You have learned a new skill: Leatherworking (Level 2)
You've mastered the art of... not cutting yourself (as much) while working with leather. At this level, you can create basic pouches, straps, and other questionable-quality items that smell faintly of burnt flesh. But hey, everyone starts somewhere, right? Just don't get too ambitious and try making anything with "fancy" buckles.
+4% to crafted item quality, -4% to weight of crafted items.

Xavier's first successes were modest. A pair of crude water flasks. A small carry-bag tied with a looped cord. Then came a quiver for Ella, stitched from rabbit hide and padded with moss. It wasn't elegant, but it served. She took it without a word and wore it on her back the next time they hunted.

He also made a simple set of clothes for himself. Rough leather breeches and a sleeveless tunic. The seams were uneven, the shoulders too tight, and the collar stubbornly refused to lie flat, but it was better than the shredded tunic he had arrived in.

On the fifth evening, he stood at the edge of the cleared plaza, watching the golems as they carried the last of the rubble from a half-collapsed house to the salvage stacks. The stars above shimmered faintly, twin moons casting silver-green light across the stone paths. Hearthstead Hall loomed behind him, its old frame reinforced with salvaged supports and a patchwork roof that now kept out the rain.

Ella joined him, bow slung over one shoulder, a satchel resting against her hip. Her silhouette was steady and quiet beside him. She had taken to walking the village edge in the evenings, checking for disturbances, but tonight she lingered.

"We've done more in five days than I thought possible," Xavier said, arms crossed as he watched the valley. "It's still broken, but… it's taking shape."

Ella glanced at the forge dome in the distance. "It feels different here now. Like the ground remembers how to stand again."

Xavier chuckled. "Poetic."

She shrugged lightly. "Just true."

Aelriva approached from the edge of the plaza, her form flickering between soft forest hues and pale gold. "Ye've done well," she said. "The land feels it too. The golems move easier now. The ground resists less." She floated in a slow arc around them, then paused midair. "But it's time ye took the next step. The village is ready for its breath to reach beyond these stones."

Xavier nodded. "Tomorrow. We pack what we've made, what we've dried. Then we follow the river."

"To Bramblegate," Ella added.

"To whatever we find there," he agreed.

They lingered a little longer, watching the stars rise over the eastern cliffs. The Silverflow shimmered faintly in the dark beyond the trees, and the sound of water tumbling over distant rocks mingled with the quiet scraping of golem footsteps in the dark.

#

Morning rose slowly over the valley, casting golden light across the scattered ruins and catching in the mists that still clung to the banks of the Silverflow. Dew glittered on leaves and stone alike, and the first light of day painted the cracked dome of Mael'Anthir in soft hues of fire and copper.

Xavier stood outside Hearthstead Hall, spear resting across his lap as he leaned against the doorframe. The fire from their final breakfast still smoldered behind him, filling the air with the faint scent of smoked meat and roasted root vegetables.

His new clothes itched slightly, the leather still stiff in places. The tunic hung better than his first attempts, and the breeches were snug but serviceable. A pair of hide wraps encircled his forearms and boots. A new satchel hung at his side, packed with dried meat, foraged mushrooms, a few cave taters, and bundles of herbs wrapped in waxed leaves. They had filled both waterskins at the spring-fed well before dawn.

Across the clearing, Ella moved with quiet efficiency. Her bow was slung across her back, a fresh quiver of arrows resting at her hip. She had added leather bracers of her own and adjusted the strap of her satchel as she walked a final circuit of the plaza, checking their supplies and scouting the golem stacks one last time.

Aelriva floated near the entrance to the warrens of tunnels beneath the settlement, hands folded as she watched the preparations. Her form pulsed gently with morning color, shades of pale rose and amber layered through the elemental shimmer of her shape.

Xavier approached her once everything was packed. "We're heading out soon."

"Aye," she replied. "And well ye should. The land has given ye what it can. Now ye must reach beyond it."

Xavier nodded. "You'll continue the golem work?"

"I will. Each day, I'll summon them and direct their labor. The clearing will continue, and the materials ye've salvaged will be set aside for future construction. The forge will remain undisturbed."

Ella joined them, resting her hand lightly on the hilt of her spear. "Anything we should watch for along the river?"

Aelriva's gaze turned distant for a moment, as though peering beyond the valley walls. "Wild beasts roam the forest's edge, and the river draws many kinds. Some helpful, some not. The road will not be easy, but the river's flow will guide ye. And at its bend, ye will find Bramblegate."

Xavier glanced back at the village. It still wasn't much. Just cleared ruins, drying racks, stone stacks, and a patched-up hall standing where silence once reigned. But it was real now, tangible, and it was his.

He looked to Aelriva. "Will the village survive while we're gone?"

The sprite smiled faintly. "So long as ye return."

He nodded once, then turned to Ella. "Ready?"

She offered a small, steady smile. "Let's go see what the world has to say."

Together, they crossed the clearing, stepping onto the path that curved toward the valley's eastern edge. The Silverflow shimmered ahead, its current bright beneath the rising sun. The trees rustled with morning wind, and somewhere in the woods, a bird gave a long, trilling call.

As they passed beyond the last circle of standing stones, Xavier looked back once. Hearthstead Hall rose behind them, and beyond it, the silent forge. Aelriva hovered near the center, watching until they vanished into the trees.

He didn't speak as they walked. There would be time for words later. For now, there was only the trail ahead and the quiet promise of what lay beyond. They left Cael'Anthir behind, but only for now.

CHAPTER ELEVEN

Walk in the Woods

Xavier slept, his mind reeling with dreams again. Myriad possibilities spread before him, each begging him to select a path. Then it happened… a flicker among the infinite futures. He stood once more in that quiet wood cabin, the one with the single table and two chairs.

One chair was already occupied. A woman sat there, her vermillion curls unmistakable, her eyes replaced by bottomless voids filled with pinpoints of light. Though they should have disturbed him, he felt both comforted and captured in their depth.

He stepped forward, and in the blink of an eye, found himself seated across from her. Across from Danu.

"Well, you have surprised me in your choices so far, Alex… or should I call you Xavier now?" Her voice was smooth and warm, the kind that curled around his name like a memory. "Barely two weeks in the world, and already you've mastered a nexus and become a master of some ruins. And now, when you wake, you're going to go villager hunting as well. Very busy indeed."

Xavier blinked at her, struggling to focus through the flood of questions swirling in his head. "Yes, but I don't know how much of that has really been me," he said, voice low and honest. "How much of it was you nudging me in the right direction?"

She leaned forward, resting her chin in one hand, a half-smile curving her lips. "Oh, it's all been you. Yes, there are prophecies and foretelling's that speak of an individual such as yourself, but fate can be funny that way. Just because something is fated to happen doesn't mean it will happen at a certain time or by a specific individual. You are a convergence of possibilities yourself, Xavier. You could be the one who answers my hopes in stabilizing this world, or you could hide away in a little forest cave and never become more. If that happens, then it falls to another to make the attempt... and possibly fail. Come now, I know you read what the Norns and Fates were said to say about it. Where do you think the inspiration came from?"

Those last words gave him pause. He tilted his head slightly, studying her face. There was a stillness in her expression, not smugness, but certainty.

"You mean... you inspired legends in my world?" he asked, voice barely above a whisper. There was a quiver in it, a thread of awe. How long had she been involved in the affairs of Earth? Weren't gods just myths?

Her smile widened slightly, and she shook her head gently. "Now is not the time to discuss that, Xavier. Explore, grow, and learn more about the world you inhabit. It will answer some of your questions, though I imagine you will have more for me when next we meet."

He opened his mouth, trying to catch one of the countless questions now roaring through his head, but she simply reached out and touched his arm. Warmth spread from her fingertips, calming him, anchoring him in the moment.

"So, this isn't just a dream then?" he asked. "This is real? I'm really talking with you?"

She laughed softly. "Fate defined is fate changed. Chances are likely we will meet again, but to say one way or another alters the strands of your future. And who's to say this isn't your dream? How better to meet with a god, simply?"

His shoulders slumped. Her words only raised more questions, ones she clearly wasn't going to answer.

"I see," he murmured. "Still... thank you. For bringing me to Arath. I've felt more alive and happier here than I ever did on Earth. Even with the monsters and the fighting."

Danu's eyes softened. She reached across the table, her fingertips brushing his forearm once more. "I had a feeling you would feel that way. It's why I chose you."

Warmth and peace spread through him. His eyelids began to grow heavy.

"Our time is nearly over. You should wake for your travels rested, not worrying over what was said here."

Her final words rang gently in his mind as everything dimmed.

"I'm watching you, Xavier. Don't disappoint me."

Then the world went still.

#

Xavier slept deeply, and it wasn't until Ella nudged him with her foot, her now-customary method of waking him, that his eyes opened as he awoke with a sharp inhale, the final words of Danu echoing in the hollow between sleep and waking to the pale light of dawn. Morning light filtered through the canopy, dappling the mossy ground around him. A thin mist clung to the trees, silver threads drifting slowly above the forest floor.

He rose quickly anxious to continue their next step, the journey toward Bramblegate. Excitement stirred under the residual weight of dreams, and his mind still echoed with

Danu's final words.

Ella was already working. She had moved to stand at the riverbank, one foot braced on a stone, washing out a cloth darkened with last night's fire-smoke. The embers had long since gone cold. She didn't look back as she spoke.

"You twitched more than usual. Dream again?"

Xavier sat up, brushing dirt from his tunic. His limbs felt heavy, as if the dream had pressed down on him physically. "Yeah. Danu."

That earned a glance. "She speak in riddles, or warnings?"

"Both," he muttered, then shook his head. "She said it's still my choice. That I could be the one to change things, or... just fade. Said I'm a 'convergence' of possibilities."

Ella wrung out the cloth, the motion deliberate. "Sounds like she gave you her answer, and left you with the weight of it."

"Pretty much." He groused slightly.

They packed quickly, their routine efficient after so many mornings together. Xavier slung his spear across his back, double-checked his satchel for their dwindling stock of dried meat, and filled both waterskins from the Silverflow's edge. Ella stashed away a pouch of gathered roots and a few tart berries she'd harvested the day before.

They traveled in silence for a time, the sound of their boots muffled by pine needles and damp earth. The Silverflow ran nearby, wide and steady, its voice a soft constant. Birds flitted overhead between branches still bare in parts from the winter, their songs weaving through the canopy.

Spring had taken firm root in this part of the world. Wildflowers peeked from under brush, and the trees held the scent of growth. The path they followed was no road, just the natural gap beside the river's flow, carved over centuries by deer and other forest dwellers.

Xavier walked with one hand resting near the hilt of his dagger. Not out of paranoia, but readiness. The quiet was soothing, but it also held potential danger in its stillness.

"Do you think Bramblegate will take us seriously?" he asked finally.

Ella glanced over, adjusting her bow. "If they're desperate enough, yes. A village rising from ruins, a working forge, and space to call home? People gamble on less."

Xavier frowned. "I'm not exactly what most would call a leader."

"Leaders don't call themselves that," Ella replied. "They prove it... Or they die trying."

They walked on, her words sinking deep.

#

The evening campfire was burning low, and the forest had gone still.

Xavier sat on a mossy stone just beyond the campfire's edge, where the warmth could reach him, but not the light. The flames behind him crackled in soft rhythm, the kindling having burned low into a cradle of glowing coals. Smoke curled upward in lazy spirals, lost to the high canopy overhead. Somewhere behind him, Ella slept wrapped in her cloak, her breaths slow and steady. The Silverflow whispered nearby.

But the woods were silent, too silent. The quiet was wrong.

At first, he chalked it up to fatigue. Three days of peaceful travel, minor hunting, and foraging had lulled his instincts into something that almost resembled comfort. But now, now the hairs on his arms prickled with unease.

He leaned forward, elbows resting on his knees, fingers brushing the haft of his spear where it lay across his lap. The usual chorus of night was gone. No insects hummed. No frogs croaked. No owls hooted in distant trees. The air held the same stillness he'd once felt before a thunderstorm... pregnant with weight, as though the land itself held its breath.

Xavier's eyes narrowed as he scanned the dark. Something was off. His ears strained for anything... anything.

Then he heard it. A howl, long, low. Too deep for any normal wolf. Another followed it, then more still, dozens it felt like, rising in ragged unison, echoing through the trees westward, away from the river. The sound cut into him, scraping across memory.

He'd heard that cry before. It was the same sound that had chased him through the woods during his first days in Arath. Wolf-things, hulking beasts with too many teeth and hide like scaled leather. He hadn't seen them clearly back then, but he remembered their voices. The way they hunted. The way they ran. How close they had come to ending him.

His breath caught, and he stood at once, crossing swiftly to the bedroll where Ella slept. He crouched and shook her shoulder once, firm, not rough. Her eyes opened instantly. Sharp. Awake. Ready.

He held a finger to his lips and pointed westward.

She sat up without a word, listening.

The howls came again, closer now. Beneath them, snarls, barks and pitched yelps. The sounds of pursuit.

Ella's fingers closed around her bow. In a fluid motion she was upright, notching an arrow without needing to look. She cast a glance toward the fire. Then to the trees.

They exchanged no words. None were needed. They moved into the shadows.

The fire's glow fell behind them like a fading tether. Step by step, they slipped through brambles and pine brush, their boots careful not to break twig or stone. The deeper they went, the heavier the air became. Xavier's muscles tensed with every breath.

He could smell it now. Blood. Faint but rising.

Then came a terrible yowl. A snarl unlike the others. Louder and lower. Not one of the wolf creatures. Something massive. Then silence, followed by growls and rapid snarling. Something was fighting back and losing.

Xavier swallowed and slowed, crouching low beside a wide trunk. Ella eased into place beside him. They edged forward again, breath held, until the trees gave way to a broad clearing washed in starlight.

And there it was. A massive feline stood at the center of the glade, black as midnight, its fur slick with blood. The creature swayed as it moved, heavy-limbed and limping, but unbowed. Around it, four wolf-like corpses already lay in twisted heaps, their scaled hides torn and broken.

But three still remained. They circled the big cat in cruel formation, low to the ground, mouths open, eyes glowing faintly with animal fury. Barking, growling, feinting, and driving the creature back.

Xavier flinched at the sight. He had no name for the beasts, but he knew them. The same kind that had hunted him once before.

His hand tightened on the spear.

Ella touched his shoulder. Her fingers pressed, then pointed, low, between the cat's massive front limbs.

A cub. A small bundle of black fur shivered in the shadow

of the beast's paws. Its head lifted once, mewling, then pressed against the cat's chest.

Xavier felt his gut twist.

Ella scowled slightly pointing to the closest canine as she spoke, "Shardfangs."

As Xavier watched, waiting for the expected end and lamenting the death of such a young beast an arrow flashed into view sinking into the side of one of the shardfangs sinking into a gap between the scales as it moved and drew its attention.

"Ella!" Xavier hissed. "What are you doing?" He demanded hefting his spear in one hand and quickly drawing the dagger. "Even if we kill the wolves, shardfangs, whatever they are, the cat is still going to die."

She already had another arrow drawn.

"If we do nothing, the cub dies too," she said calmly. "It's old enough to survive I have never seen their like in these woods so it must be something rare or new to the area."

Xavier grimaced. He wasn't ready for this. He didn't feel like a fighter, or a hero. But the choice had been made, and so he stepped into the clearing, spear in hand.

#

As he stepped into the open with the spear leveled, he prayed the creatures hadn't noticed them yet.

It was too late, his prayers had gone unanswered.

The wounded wolf-thing, shardfang he corrected himself, its body covered in hardened scales that shimmered faintly in the starlight, had already turned, snarling with bloodied teeth. It charged without hesitation, padding low across the earth with terrifying speed.

Xavier braced, trying to still the panic in his chest. His muscles screamed to run. He didn't, instead he thrust the spear forward.

The beast twisted mid-lunge, slipping past the attack with unnatural grace. Its shoulder clipped Xavier's arm, spinning him sideways. His balance faltered, and he staggered.

A sharp whistle sounded through the clearing as another arrow sang past his cheek.

It struck the second wolf square in the haunch, burying deep between plates of armor-like hide. The beast shrieked, staggered, but didn't fall. It turned its head toward the trees, growling low.

"Keep moving!" Ella shouted. "Draw them! I'll shoot!"

Xavier gritted his teeth. "Easy for you to say!"

The third wolf was circling now, flanking left while the first pressed again. Xavier brought the spear up, but too slow. Teeth snapped at his side, barely missing the leather of his tunic. He stumbled back again, off balance.

Another arrow thudded into the wolf's rear leg, causing the beast to yelp.

Ella's bowstring creaked as she nocked another arrow. "You had better do something. I'm running out!"

Xavier backed toward the cat's body. The big feline still stood, barely, wheezing, blood running down its flank in dark ribbons. It lashed out at the third wolf with one paw, knocking it sideways, but the blow lacked strength. The creature was failing, but its body still blocked the cub, which crouched beneath it, frozen in place.

"I'm not going to let that thing die for nothing," Xavier muttered.

The first wolf lunged again.

Xavier turned the spear sideways this time, bracing it against his hip like a quarterstaff. The beast bit down hard, and the wooden shaft splintered between its jaws. Xavier grunted, forced back by the force of the impact. He slammed his foot into the creature's chest to drive it off.

Then he pulled the dagger from his belt. A strange warmth flickered through his arm the moment his fingers wrapped around the hilt.

The wolf lunged again.

Xavier twisted aside and slashed. He didn't expect it to connect. The thing was fast, too fast. But the blade, he could swear it shimmered, lengthened just for a moment, slicing across the beast's ribs. A deep gash opened along its flank.

Xavier froze, shocked. "What the hell...?"

No time. The second wolf was already on him.

He dropped low instinctively, the dagger coming up too late. The creature's teeth clamped onto his forearm. Pain exploded through his body. He screamed, shoving his arm deeper into the creature's maw to stop it from getting his neck.

With his free hand, he plunged the dagger down into the wolf's eye. The blade sank deep. The beast convulsed, its jaw locked tight. Xavier collapsed beneath its weight, pinned by the body. Blood poured over him in thick waves.

Ella loosed her final arrow.

It struck the third wolf in the shoulder. It didn't go down, but it turned, now bleeding from three wounds, panting, its tongue lolling. It hesitated. It looked at the dead. Then it howled, long and low, and turned, crashing into the brush and vanishing into the woods, three of Ella's arrows still protruding from its hide.

The clearing fell quiet. Then came the soft chime.

> You have slain a level 5 Shardfang wolf. ×2
> **+250 Experience.**

Ella rushed to Xavier's side, dropping to her knees. She grabbed the dead wolf's jaw and helped to pry it open, the tendons creaking as they forced the mouth apart. Together they rolled the corpse aside, and Xavier sat up with a groan, holding his forearm close to his chest.

He glanced at the wound, it was deep. Puncture marks rimmed in bruising, bleeding steadily.

Ella tore a strip from the lining of her cloak and began to wrap it. "How bad?"

He shook his head, grimacing. "Not... as bad as it could be."

He wasn't lying, though his arm throbbed, the bone hadn't snapped. He fumbled in his pouch for the crushed forest sage and packed the worst of the punctures, wincing.

Then silence filled the air once again. He turned toward the center of the clearing.

The large feline still lay curled protectively over the cub. Its head had sunk to the earth, and its sides barely rose with breath.

The cub let out a soft, plaintive mewl.

Ella rose and walked carefully forward, retrieving arrows as she went. When she neared the great cat, its head lifted slightly. Violet eyes, dim with pain but still sharp and unnervingly intelligent, watched her.

Xavier stood and moved to join her. Together, they looked down at the beast.

It was unlike anything either of them had seen before.

Its fur shimmered in the starlight, not just black, but a living void threaded with smoky trails and hints of silvery specks, like constellations trapped beneath its skin. Two long tails lay limp behind it, each ending in a wicked, curved barb. A low, weak growl rumbled in its chest.

The cub still huddled beneath it.

Xavier crouched slowly, whispering soft words under his breath as he held out his uninjured hand. The adult's ears twitched. Its lips curled slightly, but there was no strength behind the snarl. It leaned its head forward. Its breath was ragged.

It nosed the cub one last time, nuzzling its head gently. Then, it turned toward Xavier... and rested its heavy head against his hand. He felt the heat leaving its body. It exhaled, one last long breath and stilled.

#

Dawn crept slowly through the trees, soft and cold. The first light painted the clearing in faded gold, brushing over blood-slick earth, broken bodies, and the shadowed bulk of the fallen cat. Smoke no longer rose from the shattered campfire they had left behind, just the gentle warmth of a forest waking around death.

Xavier knelt beside the great feline's head, his fingers still resting lightly on its cooling fur. He didn't speak. He couldn't at that moment. The magnitude of the creature's final stand lingered in the still air like an echo. Every breath he took tasted of copper and ash.

The cub mewled softly and pressed its small body against the unmoving form of its parent. Its fur was the same shadow-black, but finer, more downy. When it opened its eyes, piercing violet and intelligent, just like the adult's, they glistened.

He watched it.

It climbed over the great paws, nuzzling under the chin,

pawing lightly at the jaw, confused. Xavier swallowed thickly and turned away.

Ella returned in silence, two arrows in hand. The others had broken or been too deeply buried to recover. She slid them away without a word and crouched nearby, giving Xavier space but not leaving him alone. After a while, she rose again and moved to one of the fallen shardfangs.

Her knife flashed as she began to cut, careful and practiced, working meat from the flank. She stripped narrow lengths of flesh, not much, but enough for the moment. She returned and cleaned the blade before silently offering the first strip to Xavier.

He accepted it with a nod, crouched low, and held the meat out toward the cub.

It didn't move at first. Then its nostrils twitched as the scent reached it. Cautiously, the little panther padded forward. It sniffed the offering, let out a tiny hiss of uncertainty, then bit down. The meat vanished quickly, the cub tearing into it with small, sharp teeth. As it ate, it made a low rumbling sound, half growl, half purr.

Xavier exhaled slowly.

He looked down at the blade sheathed at his hip. The blade Ella had given him. The one that had changed mid-strike in the heat of battle. Its presence now felt heavier. Not threatening, but aware.

Everything was changing too quickly.

"Another stray," he murmured. "Just what I needed."

The cub finished eating and sat, tail curling neatly around its paws. It tilted its head up to look at him.

Ella knelt beside him again. "It will not survive alone. Its mother gave everything to protect it."

Xavier nodded slowly. "I know."

They stayed like that for a while, just breathing. The forest slowly began to sing again, the sound of birds returned, and wind stirred leaves. The silence had passed, but it had left its mark.

By midmorning, they had stripped meat from the shardfangs, wrapped the cuts in scraped hides to preserve them, and cleaned their blades. Ella recovered what arrow shafts she could and fashioned makeshift fletching from feathers scattered in the underbrush.

Xavier worked in silence beside her, using his knife and a splintered branch to carve another spear. The memory of the fight burned behind his eyes, the impact, the blood, the overwhelming rush of helplessness turned survival.

The cub trailed them through the clearing, sometimes curling up near its mother's body, sometimes following them in wide circles, watching. When they were nearly ready to leave, the cub let out a low, questioning yowl. They turned. It stood at the body one last time, pressing its head to the cold cheek of the fallen cat. It let out a soft chuff and lingered, unmoving.

Then, it turned and padded back to Xavier. It rubbed against his leg. Xavier blinked, stunned. The cub looked up, ears slightly back, and mewled. Slowly, hesitantly, he knelt and extended his hand. The cub stepped forward, bumping its head into his palm and nuzzling. A faint vibration rolled through it, its purr, deeper now.

Ella smiled faintly. "It's chosen."

Xavier didn't smile back, at least not right away. His heart felt heavy, filled with something that wasn't just grief, it was the heavy weight of added responsibility. The weight of another life placed silently into his care.

He gently scooped the cub up. It was heavier than it looked. Dense. Muscled already, despite its youth, but it didn't resist, instead it curled into the crook of his arm, warm and quiet.

"Guess we're a pack now," he muttered.

Ella raised a brow. "You're naming it?"

He glanced down at the creature, its black fur shimmering faintly in the sunlight. Constellation-like spots shimmered under the surface as it shifted.

"Not yet," he said. "We'll see what fits."

They stood together and looked once more to the fallen mother. Ella stepped forward, placed one hand on the cat's head, and whispered something too soft for Xavier to hear. Then she stepped back.

He gave the beast a final nod, and as a new pack they turned and walked east, toward the river, and then on toward the trail to Bramblegate.

The cub nestled in his arms and did not look back.

#

The trail wound beside the Silverflow, narrow and sun-dappled. Birdsong had returned to the trees, timid but growing in confidence as morning wore on. The forest was still waking, Xavier, on the other hand, wasn't.

He walked in silence, the cub padding close to his boots. It had stopped needing to be carried, though it still occasionally bumped his leg as if reassuring itself he was real., or maybe it was the other way around. He wasn't sure anymore.

Ahead, Ella moved with ease. She hadn't said much since they'd left the clearing, not out of coldness, but respect. Letting the quiet speak. Letting them both think.

But Xavier couldn't think clearly. His thoughts were fraying at the edges, unraveling like loose threads pulled too tight. And at the center of it all, one persistent weight. The dagger at his side. It hadn't left his mind since the fight.

He'd struck with it once, maybe twice, but in that moment, just before the blade touched flesh, something had changed. He could feel it. The weapon hadn't been just steel and edge. It had reached, reacted, responded.

Finally, when the silence became too heavy, he spoke. "Ella."

She stopped, half-turning, one hand casually resting on the grip of her bow. "Yes?"

"That dagger. When I used it against the wolf-thing... it changed. Just for a second. It felt longer. Like it moved with me."

Ella didn't blink. She looked at him fully now, expression unreadable. "You're sure?"

"I'm not imagining it," he said firmly. "It wasn't just reach. It was like... like it wanted to hit."

Her gaze softened. "Then it's waking."

He stared at her. "Waking?"

She stepped closer, speaking low and even. "It's an ethyr'vael, Xavier. A soulblade. Forged with essence, spirit, memory. It's more than enchanted. It's alive in a way, and when you struck true with it, it responded to you."

He looked down at the sheath, brow furrowing. "I thought it was just a well-made dagger."

"It is," she replied. "But it's also a relic. One Aelriva claims is Sylmyrian in origin. I found it in the ruins before you arrived. It never responded to me, not like that. I held onto it because it felt... wrong to leave it behind."

Xavier's mouth went dry.

"So when you gave it to me...?"

"I didn't give it to you," Ella corrected gently. "I offered it, and it chose."

That hit harder than he expected.

He turned, walking a few steps off the trail until he found a low stone partially buried in moss. He sat, the weight of everything finally catching up to him.

The cub followed, hopping up and settling beside him, pressing its warm side against his hip. He barely noticed.

"By the gods," he thought, resting his elbows on his knees. "They are surely just toying with me now. There is no way this is all happenchance. Not the settlement, not Ella, not Aelriva, not this bloody knife, and now a strange cat cub following me around."

His eyes drifted upward, scanning the canopy but seeing nothing. Only memory and hearing only the echo of Danu's voice from the dream.

"I know she said I was a convergence... but this is too much." He raked a hand through his hair, jaw clenched.

"I came from Earth with nothing but the roughspun clothes on my back. Now I've got a city to rebuild, ancient magic blades choosing me, gods visiting my dreams, and a... what even is this cat? A shadow-panter-lion thing with two tails? I can't keep pretending I'm just some guy dropped into a fantasy land."

He exhaled shakily, leaned forward again, and whispered, "I need time."

Ella remained by the path, watching him. She didn't call out, didn't press.

Xavier's voice was barely audible. "I just need to think."

He wasn't sure how long he sat like that. It could have been minutes or even an hour, but the cub's small head eventually pressed into his arm, nudging insistently. Without thinking, he lifted a hand and scratched gently behind its ears.

The purring started again, deep, contented, and grounding.

Ella finally stepped forward. She crouched beside him, placing a hand lightly on his shoulder. "You're not imagining it. And no... it's not coincidence. Nothing has been, not since the moment you arrived."

He looked at her then, eyes hollowed by the weight of realization. "I didn't ask for any of this." He said quietly.

"No," she agreed. "But you're still here. You still chose. That matters."

He didn't speak, but he didn't pull away either.

Together, they sat in the quiet, and the forest moved around them, not waiting or judging. Just existing, as it always had.

#

The sun had climbed higher by the time Xavier stirred from his stupor.

He stretched slowly, his body stiff, his mind still fogged with too many questions. The cub let out a small yawn, stretching beside him before trotting a few paces ahead, tails flicking in idle curiosity. Ella had resumed her silent patrol during his pause, circling the edge of the trail in wide loops, keeping watch without making him feel watched.

The world had settled again. Birds flitted overhead, the trees swayed gently in the breeze, and the Silverflow chattered beside them as if nothing in the world had changed, but to Xavier everything had.

He adjusted the makeshift binding on his arm, the pain dulled to a low throb so he popped another bunch of forest sage into his mouth. Gods he was getting tired of the "furry" taste of the herb's leaves. Then he checked the dagger at his side, his soulblade, now. It felt heavier again, or maybe just real in a way it hadn't before.

He was still thinking of what Ella had said, of the blade's choice, of Danu's warning and everything that had pulled him deeper into Arath's impossible rhythms, when the breeze shifted.

It was warm, unnaturally so compared to previous days. It rolled down from the north, cutting through the cool scent of river and leaf with something sharper, acrid, dry, and bitter.

Xavier's nose twitched. Then his eyes widened. It smelled of smoke.

He stood abruptly, the sudden change startling the cub, which darted behind a root before peeking out again.

"Ella," he called, voice tight. "You smell that?"

She turned instantly. One deep inhale was all she needed. Her bow was in her hand before she answered. "Yes."

They broke into a jog, Xavier pausing only to scoop the cub into his arms. It let out a startled chirp but didn't resist, curling against his chest as they hurried through the thinning trees. The path angled upward slightly, rising toward a natural ridge. Branches slapped against them, underbrush snagging at their boots as they pushed forward.

Then, suddenly, they broke through the last line of pines and saw it.

A plume of black smoke rose high into the sky from far ahead, thick, roiling, and tinged with flickering orange near its base. The glow was unmistakable. Fire. The scent was stronger here, curling down into their lungs and clinging to their clothes.

Beyond the haze, just visible past the rolling hills and low forest line, rooftops danced with embers. It was Bramblegate, and it was burning.

Xavier stared, frozen for a breath. Then another. He swore he could hear the crackle already, though they were still a good distance out. "No. No, not now. Not when we were so close."

The cub squirmed in his arms, sensing his distress. Ella came to stand beside him, her jaw tight. She didn't need to say anything and neither did he.

They met each other's eyes... one moment, one shared look... and that was enough.

Xavier shifted the cub in his arms and started to run. Ella was beside him in an instant, her boots flying over rock and root. Their packs bounced against their backs, arrows clinking softly in their quivers. There was no time to question, no time to plan, just fire, and the unknown waiting beyond it.

CHAPTER TWELVE

Bramblegate

Xavier's legs burned with exhaustion, each step pounding against the forest floor like a war drum against his ribs. The rhythmic sway of Valkra's weight in his arms grew heavier with every passing minute, and when his stamina faltered, Ella would wordlessly take the cub, cradling her against her chest as they pressed on. Through sunlit canopy and into shadows of dusk, they ran. And when they could run no more, they walked... slow, dogged, resolute.

The smoke had drawn them, thick and ominous on the horizon long before they arrived. At first, Xavier had hoped it might be something benign, maybe a large fire for clearing land or burning refuse, but as the hours wore on and the wind shifted, his heart began to sink.

Now, the scent hit them full-force. It was acrid and sharp, like the bite of charred leather, and beneath it, the scent of something far worse. The air was heavy with the coppery tang of blood. This was not just a skirmish, it was a massacre.

By the time they crested a mossy ridge beside the Silverflow, dawn had surrendered to a smoky veil. Bramblegate lay below, if it could still be called that. Where once proud wooden walls ringed the village, only broken palisades and shattered stone remained. Fires smoldered like dying stars, casting a hellish amber light on what had become a charnel ground.

Xavier froze. His breath caught in his throat.

Embers drifted through the air like fireflies in a dream turned nightmare. The village square was a ruin of collapsed homes and half-burnt wagons. The docks that once stretched into the river were splintered and sagging, half-swallowed by dark waters. Rubble choked the thoroughfares. Blood painted the cobblestones, and amidst it all were the bodies.

It was not the bodies of warriors in neat lines of defense. These were civilians, struck down mid-flight or mid-plea. Men, women, children. Some held tools, not weapons, while others bore no arms at all. A few wore light armor, their corpses twisted among the rest, but they were the exception.

Xavier's jaw clenched. A tremor ran down his arms, a building fury chased away all thoughts of fear.

Ella crouched low beside him, emerald eyes scanning the devastation. The rain that began to fall did little to soften her expression. She looked like a statue carved from wrath and sorrow. "Too recent," she murmured. "Some of the smoke's fresh."

Xavier nodded. "They're still here."

Together, they slipped back beneath the cover of the treeline, circling to a vantage point. A narrow rise near the riverbank offered partial concealment and a wide view of the broken village. There, in the shifting shadows, the truth revealed itself.

Great iron-barred wagons, scorched and reeking, stood near the village center. Within them, prisoners. Dozens. Human, halfling, dwarf, Animari, all bound, crammed into too-small spaces, their limbs twisted in unnatural postures. Some bled openly, wounds bound with blood-soaked rags. Others simply stared blankly, eyes hollow.

Xavier's breath hitched as he took in the scene.

Screams broke the veil of rain. A woman, then another. The voice ragged and terrified.

Xavier didn't need to ask what was happening. He saw it in Ella's face before he heard it in the cries. Her jaw was clenched, one hand slowly reaching for the bow strapped across her back.

"We go in," Xavier said.

She turned to him, her gaze like flint. "We go in."

They laid Valkra in the shelter of a thick root hollow, wrapping her in Xavier's cloak. The cub whimpered softly, but did not stir. Xavier knelt beside her, resting a hand on her fur.

"Stay hidden. We'll come back." He comforted the small cub.

Then he rose, eyes locked on the burning skeleton of Bramblegate. Whatever remained inside, whatever beasts in human skin had done this, they would not leave alive.

Together, he and Ella stepped into the wreckage, and their hunt began.

#

The fires of Bramblegate whispered through the wreckage, hissing softly beneath the rain. Every step Xavier took was a negotiation with the chaos around him. Broken wood crunched beneath his boots, slick with blood and ash. Spilled entrails and twisted limbs marked the path forward. The acrid smoke clung to his throat and nostrils like a living thing. Ella moved beside him, bow in hand, her eyes scanning every shadow. Neither of them spoke, words felt too thin against the weight of what surrounded them.

They had entered through a fractured breach in the western wall, slipping through a gap where scorched timbers leaned outward like snapped ribs. The rain fell harder now, a cold veil that dimmed the world to muted greys. The streets beyond the fracture were a graveyard. Homes had collapsed inward on themselves, roofs bowed and cracked like broken spines. Doors hung askew, some blasted from their hinges entirely. Cloth banners and laundry lines danced in the wind, their edges singed and fluttering like flags of surrender.

The cries still came, distant, muffled, and ragged. Each one tore a deeper rent in Xavier's resolve to remain quiet and careful.

A sob, broken and rhythmic, cut through the rain to his right. He halted and Ella followed his gaze as he pointed toward a side alley choked with debris. He moved first, crouching low and picking his way carefully between the blackened skeletons of two homes. The sound grew louder with each step. There was no mistaking it, someone was in pain.

A flicker of movement just ahead made him stop short. He lowered himself behind a crumbling corner of stone, peering around it slowly. His stomach clenched at what he saw.

A young woman lay bent over a mound of cracked barrels. Her bare arms braced the wood, her knuckles white. Her dress was torn, bunched around her waist, mud and soot smeared across her back and thighs. Behind her stood one of the invaders, his armor cast aside and trousers bunched around his ankles. He moved with disgusting rhythm, one hand twisted in the woman's hair, the other gripping her hip. His grunts rose in volume with each thrust, uncaring of the world collapsing around him.

Ella hissed under her breath. Her eyes narrowed, and she raised her bow. The string creaked as she pulled it to her cheek, the arrow tip aimed squarely at the base of the man's skull.

Xavier reached out and touched her arm. She turned, fury blazing in her eyes. He didn't need to speak to his intentions, she saw the dagger in his hand, saw the way he pointed to himself. Her face tightened and for a moment, she looked as if she might argue, but then she nodded once and eased the bowstring down. She stepped back, blending into shadow behind the scorched remains of a doorway.

Xavier took a breath and moved. The rain masked his approach, a steady drumbeat of droplets against rubble and ruin. Each step he placed with care, the dagger tucked close along his forearm to keep its metal from catching the light. The woman's sobs came slower now, dull and hollow. Her head hung low. She didn't even notice him, but neither did her tormentor.

Xavier closed the final distance in silence. Then, in one fluid motion, he rose and locked his arm across the slaver's throat, wrenching him backward. The man let out a startled gasp, his arms flailing. Xavier's dagger bit deep into his neck, sawing through skin and muscle. Hot blood sprayed across the barrels and the woman beneath him. The man choked and gurgled as his legs gave way.

Xavier held him until the last twitch faded. Then, dropping the body and without pause, he delivered a brutal kick to the man's groin, a final act of rage before letting the corpse slump to the ground.

> You have killed a level 6 warrior.
> **+180 Exp.**

The woman screamed.

Xavier winced and raised a hand. "Quiet," he said gently. "Please. You're safe now."

She stumbled back, dress still disheveled, eyes wide and wild. Her gaze flicked from Xavier's bloodied hands to the corpse on the ground. He crouched slowly and pointed to the slaver's dropped sword, then gestured for her to take it.

She hesitated, trembling. Then she stepped forward and

picked it up with both hands. The blade dragged against the ground as she lifted it, but she held onto it with white-knuckled determination.

Xavier turned and led the way back through the ruined alley. Ella emerged from the shadows, her bow lowered. The woman saw her and collapsed into her arms. This time she cried not in terror, but in relief. Her sobs came in gasping bursts as she clung to Ella's tunic, seeking some anchor in the madness.

Xavier said nothing. He looked back the way they had come. Another scream echoed from deeper within the village. He adjusted the grip on his dagger. There were more cries, more victims. More monsters wearing men's faces, and he would not stop with just one. The fire of his anger had been stoked, and he was far from finished.

#

The alleys of Bramblegate blurred into a pattern of blood and ruin. Each turn led to another desecration, another echo of suffering. Xavier and Ella moved like specters, silent and watchful, shadows cast by the flames still licking at the bones of the village. Their footsteps were careful but unhesitating. Xavier had passed the point of fear. There was only purpose now.

A scream carried above the rain, high and piercing, not far away, they followed it. Around a collapsed cottage, Xavier slowed. He crouched low and signaled Ella to circle wide. She disappeared into the shadows as he crept forward and peered into the narrow alley beyond. What he saw twisted his gut.

A halfling boy, barely into his teens, was pinned to the ground by one man while another kicked something ahead of him with perverse glee. That something, Xavier realized, was not a ball. It was a severed head. A halfling woman's, her hair still braided neatly. Her body lay discarded by the alley wall, limbs askew.

Ella's arrow struck first. The man kicking the head dropped mid-step, an arrow protruding from the back of his neck. The other raider turned too slowly. Xavier was on him before the alarm could be raised. He drove the dagger upward into the man's armpit, angling for the heart. The man spasmed once and collapsed.

You have killed a level 5 warrior.
+150 Exp.

You have killed a level 6 warrior.
+180 Exp.

The boy scrambled to his feet and ran to the fallen body of the second raider. He ignored Xavier and dropped to his knees beside the woman's head. With shaking hands, he gathered it and placed it in her lap. Then he rose slowly, pulled the sword from the short sword out of the scabbard of the invader who had been abusing her. His face a rictus of anger he began to flail wildly at the man's body hacking it roughly to pieces in his outrage. Not for survival. Not for defense. For rage.

He cried as he swung, each blow a shriek of grief and fury. Xavier let him finish. When the boy's arms trembled too much to lift the sword again, he turned to Xavier with blood and tears streaking his face, daring him to speak.

Xavier met the boy's gaze, then nodded toward the sword still in his grip. "Come on."

The boy followed.

What followed was a grim procession. The cries led them, one after another, to the forgotten and brutalized. Each one a fresh wound in Xavier's heart. He and Ella killed in silence. Where one of the survivors could hold a weapon, they joined the cause.

Cynthia, the girl from before, stayed near Ella. The

halfling lad, Loram, never let go of his bloodied sword. They found others: Rilsa, a dwarven woman with a gashed arm but fire in her eyes; Hedra, a human girl who could barely walk but clutched a club like she meant to use it; Darra, an Animari female, wolf-blooded and half-mad with fury. The lone additional male was a young human by the name of Ferran.

Then came the Gan Ceann. Xavier didn't realize what she was until her head blinked at him from the dirt where it lay between her legs. It surprised Xavier at first having fought the one in the cave several days ago, he hadn't realized it was not a monster race but a people. She had been held down by two invaders, one with a foot on her back between her shoulders to pin her body, the other laughing as he assaulted her. Her head sat upright, bloodied but aware. She saw Xavier and gasped, eyes wide.

He raised a finger to his lips, and she nodded.

When the time came, it was swift. The human boy they had rescued earlier struck one from behind while Xavier slit the other's throat. The Gan Ceann woman retrieved her head, stood, and picked up a mace. She didn't look back.

By the time they neared the center of the village, there were eight survivors moving with them. They were grim. Bloodied. Clutching weapons with desperate purpose, and the tally of the dead grew.

> You have killed 15 additional enemies. Levels: 5–9.
> **Total Exp: +2600.**

Then came the notification Xavier hadn't expected as a crescendo of chimes rang in his ears.

> **Hark and Hear! You have ascended in power. You are now level 4!**
>
> The touch of the divine lingers upon you, granting **6**

attribute points to shape your destiny, an exceptional gift, elevated from the ordinary **4 points** by the **Blessings of the Gods (Danu).** Choose wisely, for these points will define your path. You have **3 days** to assign them, or they will fall to the whims of fate.

Rise, Seeker of Glory. The world awaits your will. Seek adventure, seek wisdom, seek love, and let your legend be forged in your choices. LIVE!"

Xavier dismissed the prompt. He would deal with it later. For now, the dead demanded attention.

The fires still crackled, but the screams had thinned. Few remained. Then he saw them. Six warriors in chain and leather, standing near two cage wagons. Another man stood out among them, clad in scale mail, shouting orders over the storm.

Xavier pulled the group back into cover. His eyes narrowed as he counted. Seven trained fighters against only eight of them, most of their number half-broken.

"We need a plan," Xavier said quietly. "We can't take them head-on." No one argued, not even Loram.

#

The rain deepened into a steady downpour as Xavier's grim band crouched in silence beneath the remnants of a ruined overhang. Water pooled in the ruts of the broken road and ran in rivulets down faces too exhausted for fear. Blood, sweat, and smoke clung to them despite the storm's cleansing.

Catching Loram's shoulder, Xavier pulled the group several streets back from the village square. "We need a plan," he said firmly. "We've had the advantage up until now, but we're outnumbered. We can't keep picking them off one at a time."

The rage that still smoldered behind the eyes of the villagers did not disappear, but it cooled just enough for their focus to return. Revenge still burned in them, but so did the understanding that throwing themselves into a hopeless charge would only ensure their deaths. They nodded, barely, but they nodded.

Xavier moved back through the rubble-choked streets alone, picking a path that kept him low and quiet. From the shadows behind a half-collapsed chimney, he watched. Seven figures lingered near the wagons. One stood apart from the others, a man in scale armor, taller, his presence clearly commanding. The rest milled about in chain and leather, idle, unconcerned.

Returning to the others, Xavier passed the body of one of the fallen raiders. The man's armor was mostly intact, soaked now but serviceable. A thought surfaced, one born from the games he used to play, where scavenged gear wasn't just valuable but essential. These men hadn't left yet. Likely they were waiting to strip their dead of armor and supplies.

A slow, wicked grin touched his lips. Returning to the others, he relayed the plan quickly. It was risky, but the rain and gloom would help. They stripped the dead, pulling on the grim remnants of their killers' armor. It didn't fit. It smelled. But it would do. In the dark and storm, it might be enough to fool the eye.

The rain worsened. Thunder grumbled overhead. The last fires sputtered into embers.

At the square, the leader of the raiders, Galdrik swore under his breath. He was missing men. They should have returned by now. He spat and frowned. They were likely still "celebrating" their victory. He would let them have their fun, but not much longer. The caravan had to move. They couldn't stay here much longer.

He turned to call for scouts but then paused as a small group emerged from the side street. They walked in loose formation, their faces mostly hidden by dripping hoods and slumped shoulders. Galdrik squinted. The right armor, weapons, and numbers. All resistance in this little shit hole had been crushed so he had no concern beyond that.

"About damn time," he muttered. He gave a sharp whistle, signaling the ox-handlers to begin preparations.

Xavier's heart thudded as they fell in line. There was no alarm and no questions. He drifted to Cynthia's side. "We don't have long. Get to the wagon. Let them know quietly. If they panic, this falls apart fast."

Cynthia moved, silent and calm. At the bars, she pulled back her hood just enough. The prisoners recoiled at first, but recognition flickered in their eyes. She beckoned a tall Gan Ceann man forward. He rested his severed head on the floorboards to listen. Her words were short and urgent. Then she turned and rejoined the others.

Xavier breathed deeply. His eyes scanned the nearest targets. The raiders walked apart, spaced to avoid clustering. Alone, relaxed, and inattentive.

He palmed the dagger, holding it along his forearm to keep the steel hidden. Each step forward was deliberate. The rain fell harder, and the world muffled.

The first raider never saw him coming. Xavier stepped in, wrapped an arm around the man's waist, and slit his throat in one clean drag. He held the body upright, muffling the gurgle until it stopped as the eyes on the captives locked on him. Cynthia's words were just now making the rounds of the huddled group, and they were shocked to see one of the invaders killing their own but kept to the silence requested.

> You have killed a level 8 Raider Thug.
> **+400 Exp.**

> **Congratulations! You have learned a new skill:**
> Subterfuge (Level 1.)
> Subterfuge is the fine art of deception, misdirection, and subtle manipulation. Masters of this skill can pick locks, forge documents, disarm traps, and tell lies so convincing they could sell ice to a frost giant. Whether slipping unnoticed into a noble's treasury or planting rumors to topple a kingdom, subterfuge is the go-to skill for anyone who prefers cunning over brute force. Of course, if subtlety isn't your thing, you could just call it "being shady" and move on.

Xavier's grin grew at the prompt, and he moved to slip around the back of the wagon seeking the back of his next target. He was able to mimic the procedure several more times. A second fell just as easily. Then a third.

> You have killed a level 8 Raider Thug.
> **+400 Exp.**

> You have killed a level 8 Raider Thug.
> **+400 Exp.**

One of the disguised villagers took the reins from the most recent victim. Still, no one noticed. Xavier moved again, circling around the wagon. Another throat opened beneath his blade.

> You have killed a level 8 Raider Thug.
> **+400 Exp.**

Then came the mistake. The fifth target shifted at the wrong moment, turning his head and sneezing violently. Xavier's blade missed its mark, slicing shallow across the bridge of the nose. The man bellowed and lashed out with an elbow, catching Xavier hard in the ribs.

"We've got traitors!" The injured man bellowed as he struck.

The armored leader turned at once, eyes wide. An arrow flew through the dark and ricocheted from his shoulder plate. Ella had joined the fray.

Xavier gasped and staggered upright. The rain swallowed all sound but the clash of weapons and cries of vengeance as the rest of the villagers surged forward.

The trap had been sprung, and the storm of blades had begun.

#

The clash of steel drowned beneath the storm, thunder rolling like a battle cry from the gods. Xavier barely had time to recover his footing before chaos erupted around him. Shouts rang through the muddy road, some from the disguised villagers who had dropped their act, others from raiders scrambling to make sense of the ambush.

The wounded raider who had raised the alarm stumbled back, clutching his bloodied face. He reached for the mace hanging at his belt, but before he could lift it, Xavier lunged. The two collided in the mud, sliding through pooling rainwater. The mace rose and came down with a thud, glancing off Xavier's lower back. Pain bloomed, but not quite enough to stop him. He twisted, driving one of his shoulders into the raider's gut.

They rolled. The raider tried to pin him, mud and blood mixing as they fought for control. The man was stronger, but Xavier fought with desperation, with fury, and most importantly with purpose. His hand slipped over the wet ground until it found the hilt of his dagger.

He wasn't fast enough though. The raider broke free and reared back to strike again... then stopped.

A sharp breath escaped his lips, then a gurgle.

Loram stood behind him, the boy's small frame shaking as he held the bloodied short sword embedded in the raider's back. He yanked it free and the man collapsed onto Xavier.

> You have killed a level 8 Raider Thug.
> **+400 Exp.**

A second notification followed.

> **Hark and Hear! You have ascended in power. You are now level 5!**
>
> The touch of the divine lingers upon you, granting **6 attribute points (12 attribute points remaining)** to shape your destiny, an exceptional gift, elevated from the ordinary **4 points** by the **Blessings of the Gods (Danu).** Choose wisely, for these points will define your path. You have **3 days** to assign them, or they will fall to the whims of fate.
>
> **Rise, Seeker of Glory. The world awaits your will. Seek adventure, seek wisdom, seek love, and let your legend be forged in your choices. LIVE!"**

Xavier rolled the body aside and rose, drenched and gasping. Around him, battle swirled. Ella's arrows whistled from the far edge of the square. Galdrik batted one aside with the flat of his axe, snarling. Rilsa, hammer raised, ducked beneath a wild swing and cracked her weapon across the leg of another raider. Ferran and Darra flanked a third, striking in awkward tandem but with fierce resolve.

Xavier grabbed his dagger and charged to reinforce them. The raider facing Ferran turned in time to parry Xavier's first strike, but the blow gave Ferran the opening he needed. The young man screamed and drove his borrowed blade into the man's ribs. Darra followed with a sweep of her spear, catching the raider across the knees.

The man dropped to the ground and Ferran finished it.

That left just the leader, Galdrik.

Blood and storm mingled in the air as the burly slaver surveyed the remains of his crew. His lips peeled back in a snarl, teeth flashing beneath a crooked nose. His armor was dented and streaked with soot, one side already darkened from an earlier wound. But there was still a dangerous energy in him, coiled, simmering, looking for a target.

Ferran stepped forward first, shaky hands tightening around the hilt of his chipped sword. His arms trembled, but the fire in his eyes held steady. Darra flanked him, crouched low, spear angled toward Galdrik's gut. Her wolfish ears flattened as a snarl curled from her throat. Behind them, Rilsa shifted into place, her blacksmith's hammer held like a war-banner. Her breathing was ragged, and blood was matting her sleeve from the slash she'd taken earlier.

Xavier approached from behind, silent as the rain, eyes locked on the man who had ordered the ruin of Bramblegate.

Galdrik roared and charged. The axe came in low, heavy, and fast. Ferran barely got his sword up in time. The impact sent the boy flying backward, the blade spinning from his grasp. He landed in a heap, dazed and gasping.

Darra lunged. Her spear darted out like a snake, but Galdrik anticipated the thrust. He twisted, steel bracer catching the point, and shoved it aside with brute force.

"Come now, pup," Galdrik jeered. "Is that all you have?"

He pivoted, axe sweeping in a brutal arc toward Darra's head. She barely ducked in time, the blade cleaving empty air.

He wasn't ready for Rilsa.

The young dwarf didn't shout a warning. She didn't hesitate. She simply moved, her hammer rising in a smooth arc. The head of the weapon struck Galdrik square in the ribs with a crunch that echoed louder than thunder.

The raider staggered, snarling. He lashed out blindly, the edge of his axe grazing Rilsa's shoulder and slicing through the chain shirt. Blood welled and she fell back, gasping.

He spun to finish her, and found Xavier.

The dagger gleamed in Xavier's hand, rain slicking the dagger's edge. Galdrik swung his axe in a downward diagonal, aiming to split Xavier from shoulder to hip, but Xavier didn't meet it head-on. He ducked low and swept his arm up, letting the dagger trace a wicked arc. The enchanted blade sheared through Galdrik's gauntlet and carved a deep line along his forearm.

The raider howled in pain and fury.

"Keep him busy!" Xavier barked, his voice cutting through the din.

Ella's answer came with a twang. Her arrow flew from behind a ruined wagon and embedded itself in Galdrik's thigh. The man staggered again, limping now, and his fury turned toward her.

"You'll regret that, wench!" he snarled and took a step.

Darra jabbed his wounded leg. He grunted, knee buckling. Rilsa didn't miss her cue. Her hammer crashed into Galdrik's elbow and bone shattered... his axe fell.

He dropped to his knees. Xavier stepped in front of him.

"This is for Bramblegate," he said softly, voice devoid of mercy.

Xavier's dagger rose and plunged upward, piercing beneath Galdrik's jaw. The blade slid through flesh and shattered bone, burying itself in the base of his skull.

The slaver convulsed once before he crumpled.

The fight was over, rain fell, silence returned.

#

The storm ebbed slowly, leaving behind only silence and the heavy patter of rain against ash-soaked earth. Xavier stood still amid the carnage, chest heaving as the adrenaline bled from his limbs. The bulk of Galdrik's corpse lay at his feet, its blood mingling with the mire.

Around him, the villagers began to emerge from the haze of battle. They were battered, bloodstained, and ragged, but alive. More than alive, they were free. Ella moved beside him, lowering her bow. She didn't speak, but her eyes found his, and there was something steady in them. A quiet pride.

Shouts filled the air from the captured villagers still locked within the carts. The cries shook Xavier from his momentary stupor. He dropped to a crouch beside Galdrik's corpse and began searching the slaver's pockets. It didn't take long before his fingers closed around a heavy iron ring... keys. He stood and tossed them to Ferran.

"Go," he said. "Get them out."

Ferran caught the keys and ran to the first cart. His hands fumbled at the lock, wet with rain and grime, but after a few seconds, one key slid home. The lock popped open with a metallic click. He darted to the next cart and repeated the motion. Within moments, both wagons were open.

The prisoners poured out. They stumbled into the mud... some sobbing, others silent, dazed, or shouting in confusion. A few fell to their knees and clutched the earth like it might vanish from beneath them. Xavier and Ella stood still as they were quickly surrounded. Villagers formed small clusters, comforting one another, sharing warmth beneath the cold rain. Faces streaked with ash and tears peered up at Xavier with cautious eyes.

Xavier counted silently. His final tally was forty-eight. Two Gan Ceann, sixteen Humans, eight Dwarves, ten

Halflings, six Gnomes, and six Animari of various bloodlines. They were bruised and gaunt, and none were armed, but they were alive.

Xavier's gaze drifted back down the path toward the smoking ruin of Bramblegate. That place, its hearths, it's homes, its families, was broken. He didn't know if any of these people would agree to follow him into the unknown, but he had to offer.

He looked again at the circle of huddled villagers. Their expressions were still shadowed by wariness. He had saved them, yes, but what did they truly know of him? Was he another lord seeking leverage? Another tyrant who traded chains for promises?

After several tense minutes, one of the Gan Ceann stepped forward. He was tall and broad-shouldered, holding his head in his hands. As he approached, he lifted it and set it upon his shoulders, securing it with care before meeting Xavier's gaze.

"Why?" the man asked simply. The question landed like a stone.

Xavier hesitated. Dozens of reasons swirled through his mind: Because it was right. Because he needed allies. Because he couldn't watch more innocents fall victim to cruelty. None felt honest enough. Eventually, he just shrugged and said, "I couldn't stand by and let what I saw happening continue. It wasn't right."

The Gan Ceann grunted. "Most of our coin and goods were taken. These were only the ones left to clean up after the raid. The others rode off north with the first batch of prisoners. Bramblegate..." He looked over his shoulder. "It may not survive this time."

Xavier stepped forward. "Then maybe it doesn't have to. I came to Bramblegate to ask for help founding something new. Deeper in the forest. Safer, perhaps, for its distance alone. I've reclaimed the ruins of an old city, far older than any I've seen. Game is plentiful. The land is rich. It needs people. Needs hands and hearts to build it into something lasting."

He met the man's eyes again. "I am Lord of those lands, and I will do everything I can to keep you safe, should you choose to come."

Murmurs rippled through the crowd. Xavier caught snippets, Cynthia's voice, Loram's, even Rilsa's, speaking of what they had seen, how he had fought for them, bled beside them. Trust, once fragile, began to take root.

The Gan Ceann rubbed his chin thoughtfully before he met eyes with Xavier again and gave the young lordling a nod.

"I am Braegor Voidiron," he said. "Blacksmith of Bramblegate, and its Ealdorman."

He straightened his shoulders. "I have no reason to distrust you, but also no reason to fully trust you either. Can you promise to protect them? Can you rescue the others?"

Xavier took a breath. "No. I can't promise that." He raised his hand before the murmurs could rise again. "But I swear I will try. If you stand with me, I will not rest until we have built something better. Something lasting. We'll find the others. We'll make sure this never happens again."

As he spoke, something stirred within him. A new strength, burning hot and bright.

You have gained a new trait: Unyielding Liberator Having witnessed the devastating aftermath of a tyrannical assault, your resolve is as unshakable	Effect: • **Strengthened Resolve:** Xavier gains a bonus to morale-based rolls and abilities when fighting against slavers, tyrants, or oppressors.

as your blade is sharp. The burning ruins of Bramblegate and the anguished cries of its people etched a singular purpose into your soul: to fight against oppression and to rescue the helpless from the clutches of cruelty. Your actions speak louder than words... when faced with the last raiders enslaving the people of Bramblegate, You and your companions delivered swift justice, leaving no room for mercy. For those who committed unspeakable acts of violence, revenge was precise, personal, and unrelenting.

- **Justice Over Mercy:** In situations involving the abuse or enslavement of others, Xavier will prioritize swift and decisive action, often at the expense of diplomatic solutions.
- **Fearsome Reputation:** Enemies who learn of his deeds are more likely to falter in battle, intimidated by his uncompromising sense of justice.
- **Unbreakable Loyalty:** Those he rescues see him as a savior, and his reputation among the oppressed makes him a natural leader and ally to rebel causes.

The general mood of the gathered people shifted. Where there had been exhaustion, now there was fire. Where there had been despair, now stood determination. The villagers stood straighter, their shoulders squaring, eyes kindling with a new light.

Ella stepped beside Xavier, rain beading on her lashes. "You'll need a name," she murmured. "One that honors what was lost and what will rise again."

Xavier looked to the dark sky, then to the blade in his hand. The word came without effort.

"Rynthavael," he said. "The Blade's Rebirth." He raised the dagger high. "For Rynthavael! For our people!"

Weapons and fists alike lifted. The word echoed as the call was taken up by the villagers. Xavier's new trait filled them with a resolve and loyalty that had been lacking moments before. "Rynthavael! Rynthavael! Rynthavael!" Three times the word echoed out and the universe answered.

> Your settlement has grown dramatically. Through your actions with the hostages of Bramblegate, you have increased your population by forty-eight souls. This sets you well on the path to one of the goals required to level your settlement. Take care young Lordling, such rapid changes can have consequences.

> Your trait **Unyielding Liberator** has improved the loyalty of all villagers rescued from Bramblegate. These villagers have gained a loyalty boost of +2000.
>
> Your overall settlement loyalty has changed from -1000: *Unreliable* to 1000: *Reliable*. +6% to settlement crafting, harvesting, and defense.

> Your trait **Unyielding Liberator** has improved the morale of all villagers rescued from Bramblegate. These villagers have gained a morale boost of +1500.
>
> Your average villager morale has changed from -1000: *Miserable* to 500: *Delighted*. +4% to settlement crafting, harvesting, and defense.

His new talent was a wonder! Just the effects of it alone shifted the loyalty and morale of the villagers he had rescued from pitiful negative effects to positive ones. Plus, it convinced them to join his settlement. He had grown his population by nearly half what he needed to increase the settlement to the next level. He knew he needed to focus on the other tasks for that as well, but he had his own people now. He smiled broadly and moved to sheath his dagger when he paused and studied it. Its prompt had changed since he last looked at it. The border now had a brilliant red tint to it.

You have discovered:	Item Class: Weapon
Vaeltheris "Eternal Song of the Blade" Unique Ethyr'Vael "Soul Forged Blade"	Item Rarity: Legendary Item Quality: Masterwork Weight: 1kg Durability: Unknown Damage: 30 – 45 Piercing/Slashing Traits: Though it appears sturdy, Vaeltheris is surprisingly light and perfectly balanced, almost as if it moves with the wielder's intentions rather than their strength. Its weight adjusts slightly to provide the ideal amount of heft for any strike, making it feel like an extension of the wielder's body. Material: Vaeltheris is forged from a silvery, semi-translucent metal that gleams faintly with an internal light as if housing the embers of a forge within its core. This magical alloy is unbreakable, resistant to the ravages of time, and

eternally sharp.

Form: The blade is slender yet slightly curved, designed for both grace and lethality. Faint, swirling patterns of runes and filigree adorn its surface, glowing softly when attuned to the wielder's emotions or magic. These designs are etched so finely they appear to shift and ripple like liquid under certain light.

Special Traits:

1. **Living Steel**: The blade repairs itself if damaged (though breaking it is almost impossible). If chipped, the missing piece regrows with a faint shimmer.

2. **Ethereal Edge**: The sword's edge can phase slightly into an incorporeal state, allowing it to bypass certain magical defenses.

3. **Additional traits may be discovered.**

Xavier's jaw fell open as he stared dumbstruck at the

blade. The thing was legendary! It was beyond anything he had ever expected of it. He looked at Ella in shock, she had a slight smirk on her lips as she shrugged at him and then turned back to watch the crowd. He sheathed the blade and looked as well. His people were ready to move, back to the Bramblegate, to salvage what they could and then on to their new home.

CHAPTER THIRTEEN

Home to Build

Xavier moved quietly to stand beside Ella, the weight of unanswered questions pressing heavily upon him. His gaze lingered briefly on her profile, noting the careful way she avoided his eyes. Finally, he broke the silence, voice measured but carrying the edge of tension he felt.

"You know more about Vaeltheris than you're letting on, don't you?"

Ella hesitated, shoulders slumping slightly as if the words themselves added a physical burden. When she spoke, her voice was sincere but cautious. "Yes, Xavier, there is much I haven't shared. It is complicated. Dangerous even." She lifted her eyes to meet his, vulnerability softening her usually guarded expression. "But you've proven trustworthy thus far. I promise I will tell you everything in time."

Xavier studied her carefully, the ache of withheld truths pulling at him. He knew trust had to be mutual, yet the distance her secrecy created gnawed at the edges of his resolve. Still, he chose faith over suspicion, stepping into the trust he hoped would bridge the gap between them.

"Alright," he said gently, placing a reassuring hand lightly on her shoulder, the warmth of his touch communicating more than words could. "But remember, we're in this together. Whatever burdens you carry, they aren't yours alone."

Ella relaxed subtly under his touch, a flicker of relief crossing her face. The silence between them grew comfortable, reaffirming their tentative partnership as they prepared to face the uncertain road ahead.

Xavier and Ella moved efficiently through the wreckage of Bramblegate, gathering the shaken and weary survivors who clustered anxiously around them. The air was thick with smoke and grief, the remnants of destruction evident in every scorched building and charred remnant of daily life.

"Listen, everyone," Xavier began, raising his voice enough to be heard clearly yet maintaining a reassuring tone. "My village, Rynthavael, lies southwest. Our resources are limited, but if we salvage what we can here, it should sustain us. I won't force anyone to join, but those who do, I ask for your commitment and cooperation."

Murmurs rippled through the gathered villagers, voices tinged with both uncertainty and reluctant hope. They gradually accepted the grim reality, understanding that their survival depended on unity. Slowly, the villagers began to search through the ruins, reclaiming whatever valuable possessions remained.

Finn and Theo, two halfling shepherd brothers, quickly took charge of the oxen, their natural affinity for animals calming the creatures as they prepared to lead the wagons. Xavier noticed how the brothers moved with quiet confidence, their soft-spoken words and gentle touches easily settling the frightened animals. He and Ella retrieved the shadowmane cub from its hiding spot beneath a bush, gently placing it among soft clothing in one of the carts. The little creature stretched sleepily, yawning to reveal sharp, tiny teeth before curling back into a peaceful slumber.

As the villagers continued their diligent search, gathering hidden caches of food, money, and practical tools, Xavier felt a growing sense of responsibility mingled with cautious optimism. He helped sift through the rubble, his heart lifting slightly as he discovered a collection of books tucked away in a half-collapsed building. Each volume was precious, a glimpse into the knowledge and culture of this unfamiliar world.

Amid the rubble, villagers methodically cataloged the supplies, calling out discoveries of cookware, tools, farming implements, and even a small stash of weapons. A young dwarf named Orrek Deepstone, soot-covered but resilient, led others to unearth mining equipment, noting their potential importance to Xavier. Meanwhile, Sylvie Tumblewick, the halfling tavernkeeper, efficiently organized recovered foodstuffs, rationing them into manageable bundles.

Despite the devastation, the collaborative effort bolstered Xavier's hope. Observing the villagers' diligence and mutual support reinforced his determination to ensure their safety and prosperity. Despite everything they had lost, they had enough resources and willpower to begin anew, building from the ashes towards a hopeful future.

#

Midday sunlight filtered weakly through the lingering haze of smoke, casting the ruined village in a ghostly, ethereal light. There was a single moment that broke the monotony of ash and silence... something that stirred even the grief-numbed hearts of those still standing. In the center of the town square, Willa, one of the young women who had been taken in the carts, sat with a small mandolin across her lap. She had found it where it had been kicked beneath a bed, the wood singed at the edges but the strings still intact. Her face was streaked with soot from the fires, with twin trails washed clean by tears.

She began to tune it quietly, her fingers trembling slightly, drawing uncertain glances from those nearby. Xavier paused in his task of dragging the invaders' bodies to a pile, watching her silently as the first hesitant notes spilled into the smoke-heavy air. The sound was so soft it barely reached him, a whisper against the weight of mourning. Yet it grew, tentative at first, like the breath of someone who had been afraid to speak, but slowly gaining confidence. The melody was haunting, sad, and resonant.

One by one, villagers paused in their labor. A man carrying a sack of tools stopped midstep. A young girl emerged from the ruins of her home, clutching a bundle of charred blankets. A pair of elders stood motionless, tears slipping down their cheeks without a word. They gathered instinctively, drawn like moths to a single fragile flame in the darkness.

Then Willa sang.

"Oh Bramblegate, oh home so dear,
Now lost to ash and bitter tear.
The fields we tilled, the hearths that glowed,
Are silent now, their warmth bestowed.

The laughter fades, the voices still,
As shadows claim the vale and hill.
Our mothers, fathers, friends we knew,
Now sleep beneath the morning dew.

Yet from the cinders hope may rise,
A flicker caught in tear-stained eyes.
For though the night has wrapped us tight,
A dawn will break, a newborn light.

So, sing with me, though hearts may ache,
For bonds we forge will never break.
Through grief, we find the strength to stand,

To build anew, a promised land."

Her voice faded slowly into the wind, the last note hanging like a prayer over the broken square. There was silence for a heartbeat, then another. No one spoke. No one moved.

Then a muffled sob broke the stillness. A woman in her middle years dropped to her knees, her hands clutching the hem of her soot-stained skirt as tears spilled freely. A child clung tightly to her side, face buried in her sleeve. An older man leaned heavily on his cane, eyes glistening, nodding slowly to himself. A few others knelt beside him, heads bowed, not in despair, but reverence.

The crowd had gathered without realizing it. Tools were set down, packs forgotten, and arms once burdened now hung loosely at their sides. The raw ache of loss trembled just beneath the surface of every face. But through it, something else began to emerge unity through shared pain and shared purpose.

Xavier stepped forward; his throat tight, moved by a feeling deeper than words. Willa's eyes met his, shining not with grief, but with unspoken challenge. He knelt beside her, taking a moment to steady himself, then rose again and addressed the villagers.

"Rynthavael will be everything Bramblegate was and more," he said. "I swear it to you, not as a stranger, not as a Lord, but as someone who believes in what we can build together. This isn't the end. It's the beginning."

The wind stirred the soot at their feet. Someone started clapping softly. Others joined, and soon the square echoed with the quiet rhythm of hands. Not joyful, not yet, but resolute. Hopeful. Willa smiled, a quiet thing full of sadness and strength, and lowered her mandolin into her lap as if it had finally done what it was meant to.

#

As dusk crept across the ruins of Bramblegate, the villagers gathered their dead. Each body was handled with quiet reverence, laid gently atop carefully constructed pyres. Friends and family members whispered parting words as they placed simple tokens, a ribbon here, a stone there, even a simple carved button, on their loved ones' chests. The scent of smoke mingled with the fading aroma of charred wood that already lingered in the air.

At a distance, a far less delicate heap of corpses marked the resting place of the invaders. The villagers had piled the slavers' bodies carelessly, dousing them in leftover oil and straw scavenged from the remnants of barns and carts. There would be no mourning for them, but they still would not be left to simply rot.

Torches were lit in silence. Flames touched the kindling, and the fire caught quickly, illuminating solemn faces and casting long shadows across the square. Willa played again, her mandolin's strings were soft and mournful, but she did not sing. The melody drifted upward like incense, wrapping around the rising smoke.

Xavier stood beside Ella, arms crossed tightly across his chest. The firelight flickered across his face, highlighting the weariness in his eyes. He leaned in slightly and spoke in a low voice.

"Is it normal to burn the dead here? I always thought people buried their dead. This feels... different."

Ella's expression flickered with a blend of surprise and solemn understanding. "Here? It depends. Some bury, yes. But magic runs deep in this land. Especially after something like this... a slaughter. A body left unguarded can be twisted, used, reanimated. Without someone of faith to consecrate the soil, fire is the only sure way to give peace."

Xavier glanced back toward the flames, the solemn pyres and the blazing heap beyond. "Magic's really that wild here?"

Ella gave a slow nod. "Wilder than most believe. It lives in the ground, in the air, in the things we leave behind. Especially when blood has been spilled."

That truth settled heavy in his thoughts. The ley lines beneath Rynthavael, the flickers of power he'd already felt, it all added up. Magic here wasn't something wielded from a distance. It was present. Intrinsic. And clearly, dangerous when ignored.

He stared into the fires, watching as the last shadows of Bramblegate gave way to ash. A sense of gravity filled his chest, one that told him this wasn't the last time he would see death turned to flame.

When the fires dimmed and the last note of Willa's playing faded into night, no one spoke. They simply stood together, silently remembering, silently mourning, and silently promising that something better would rise from the ruin.

#

As dusk crept across the ruins of Bramblegate, the villagers gathered their dead. Each body was handled with quiet reverence, laid gently atop carefully constructed pyres. Friends and family members whispered parting words as they placed simple tokens, a ribbon here, a stone there, even a simple carved button, on their loved ones' chests. The scent of smoke mingled with the fading aroma of charred wood that already lingered in the air.

At a distance, a far less delicate heap of corpses marked the resting place of the invaders. The villagers had piled the slavers' bodies carelessly, dousing them in leftover oil and straw scavenged from the remnants of barns and carts. There would be no mourning for them, but they still would not be left to simply rot.

Torches were lit in silence. Flames touched the kindling, and the fire caught quickly, illuminating solemn faces and casting long shadows across the square. Willa played again, her mandolin's strings were soft and mournful, but she did not sing. The melody drifted upward like incense, wrapping around the rising smoke.

Xavier stood beside Ella, arms crossed tightly across his chest. The firelight flickered across his face, highlighting the weariness in his eyes. He leaned in slightly and spoke in a low voice.

"Is it normal to burn the dead here? I always thought people buried their dead. This feels... different."

Ella's expression flickered with a blend of surprise and solemn understanding. "Here? It depends. Some bury, yes. But magic runs deep in this land. Especially after something like this... a slaughter. A body left unguarded can be twisted, used, reanimated. Without someone of faith to consecrate the soil, fire is the only sure way to give peace."

Xavier glanced back toward the flames, the solemn pyres and the blazing heap beyond. "Magic's really that wild here?"

Ella gave a slow nod. "Wilder than most believe. It lives in the ground, in the air, in the things we leave behind. Especially when blood has been spilled."

That truth settled heavy in his thoughts. The ley lines beneath Rynthavael, the flickers of power he'd already felt, it all added up. Magic here wasn't something wielded from a distance. It was present. Intrinsic. And clearly, dangerous when ignored.

He stared into the fires, watching as the last shadows of Bramblegate gave way to ash. A sense of gravity filled his chest, one that told him this wasn't the last time he would see death turned to flame.

When the fires dimmed and the last note of Willa's playing faded into night, no one spoke. They simply stood together, silently remembering, silently mourning, and silently promising that something better would rise from the ruin.

#

The work continued into the next day with a quiet urgency. With the dead honored and the village mourned, the survivors turned their attention to survival. The task was grim but necessary.

The villagers spread out through the ruins, moving with purpose now rather than despair. Hidden caches of food were unearthed, root cellars tucked beneath burnt homes, sealed jars of grains, bundles of herbs that had somehow survived. Coins, tools, and sundries were collected and sorted. Xavier noticed that despite the hardship, there was an efficiency to their efforts. They weren't strangers to labor or loss.

Sylvie, ever the organizer, took charge of cataloging the recovered goods, enlisting help from several others. Orrek Deepstone supervised the salvaging of heavier materials, stone, half-burnt timbers, usable iron nails. Even children were given tasks: gathering kindling, packing salvaged cloth, sorting pots and cutlery into crates.

Xavier helped wherever he could, his sleeves rolled up and face streaked with soot. He unearthed a half-collapsed home and discovered a stash of books, many slightly scorched but still legible. He gathered them reverently, brushing ash from the covers. Knowledge, he reminded himself, was a kind of power and here, it was rare.

One cart, in particular, drew his eye. It held what he privately considered the most valuable haul: not just tools and materials, but seeds, fishing line, soap, and even a few coils of fine thread. Essentials, yes, but also symbols of rebuilding. Additionally, nestled among the bundles was the shadowmane cub, it was again drowsing peacefully. Xavier smiled.

He reached in and gently scratched behind its ears. The cub stirred, blinked sleepy golden eyes, then let out a wide yawn that revealed tiny, sharp teeth before curling back into slumber.

A soft gasp drew his attention. Darra, a lean wolfkin hunter with amber eyes, approached slowly, captivated. "Is that... a shadowmane?" she murmured. "They're unheard of this far from the Kelari Mountains, especially a cub alone."

Xavier stepped aside to give her a better view. "We found it on the way here. Its mother was being attacked by shardfangs. We killed most of them, but... we were too late. Only this one survived. We couldn't leave it."

The cub shifted and gave a low, contented purr. Darra stepped closer beside the cart, gently running a hand down its back. "You're lucky. I've heard the Duskari train shadowmanes as companions, but it's not common. It takes time. Patience. And the Wild Bonding skill."

"I don't have it," Xavier admitted, watching the cub with fascination. "Not yet. But I want it."

Darra's eyes flicked to him, thoughtful. "It's rare. But if you learn animal empathy or survival instinct, that might awaken it. Or you could find a skill book, but they're not easy to come by."

"Could you teach me?" he asked, stepping closer, excitement rising in his voice. "Even just the basics. Anything that might help."

She shook her head. "I don't have it myself. But maybe one of the shepherds knows enough of the foundations to guide you."

Xavier nodded, his hand joining hers as they scratched the cub. The little feline leaned into the attention, rumbling loudly. "I'll figure it out," Xavier said with quiet conviction. "Whatever it takes."

Darra smiled. "Good. This little one already seems to like you. That's a start."

As the sun reached its peak, the villagers stepped back to assess their collective efforts. The carts were packed as full as they could be. There was not an abundance, but it was enough to begin. Enough to try at least and that, Xavier thought as he looked around at the tired but determined faces, was everything.

#

By late afternoon, the caravan was ready. The villagers stood in quiet clusters, holding torches or walking sticks, their belongings piled into the wagons. Some looked back at the blackened husk of Bramblegate, eyes shadowed by memory and loss. Others faced forward, lips pressed into firm lines, shoulders squared against the unknown. No one spoke of staying behind. Even those who had hesitated now fixed their gazes on the road ahead, driven by the weary, determined hope of people with nothing left to lose.

They moved as one. The wagons creaked and the feet of dozens shuffled along the ash-dusted trail. Xavier walked among them, stopping to speak with each person. Some he knew by name, others by role. There were hunters, tinkerers, miners, and shepherds. He made a point to ask what each had done before the attack, listening with care. Every skill mattered now.

He quickly began organizing them in his thoughts. A blacksmith and a smelter could handle tools and repairs. A miner would be critical for stone and ore beneath the village.

Hunters, a fisherman, and a farmer would help feed the settlement, alongside the two halfling shepherds. A gardener with knowledge of herbs might grow healing plants. A carpenter and a stonemason would be vital for rebuilding structures above. A few said little, uncertain or still shaken, but Xavier made mental note of them as well. Everyone had something to contribute, even if it was not yet known.

He smiled faintly as he moved through the crowd, placing each person into practical roles much like he had in countless strategy games back home. But this time, it was not a game. These were real people with real fears, real hopes. He did not want to control them. He wanted to lead them.

The forest was hushed around them, watching. The road ahead would normally take five days to travel at a steady pace, but their caravan moved slower still. Between the weight of wagons, the pace of children and elders, and frequent pauses to rest the oxen or scout for danger, it was clear this would not be a swift return. Dusk sank into night, and torches flared against the growing darkness. Somewhere in the distance, a lone wolf howled. The oxen continued their slow march, and the villagers moved in shifts, the hunters volunteering for the lead watch. They traveled through the night, stopping only when exhaustion made rest necessary. The farther they traveled from Bramblegate, the easier it seemed for them to breathe.

Ella remained close to Xavier, occasionally ranging ahead with some of the more agile scouts. She said little, but her steady presence grounded him. The shadowmane cub slumbered in one of the wagons, its rhythmic purring bringing comfort to anyone nearby. Children gathered around it now and then, whispering and pointing, giggling when it stretched or twitched.

It was well into the sixth day before the trail finally began to widen and the dense forest gave way to more open ground. Their pace had been slow, burdened by wagons and weariness, but they had endured Shafts of midmorning sunlight filtered down through thinning branches, casting golden light across packed earth and fresh-cut stone. The clearing below revealed the nestled heart of Rynthavael, tucked between low ridges and ringed with the steady rise of trees reclaiming the surrounding slopes. Xavier quickened his pace, a ripple of anticipation rising in his chest. The air smelled different here, clean, fresh, touched by something ancient and alive. And at last, there it was: Rynthavael.

The lead hunters came to a sudden stop, raising cautious hands. At the edge of the village, large stone golems moved purposefully about the ruined grounds. They shifted heavy stones, pulled stumps from the earth, and cleared brush. The markings tracing their limbs glowed with a soft emerald green light. A few villagers gasped, others reached for tools or weapons, instinctively bracing for danger.

"Easy," Xavier called out, stepping forward. "They're not hostile. They're here to help. They're part of the village now."

The words seemed to settle most nerves, though the tension did not disappear completely. Ella appeared beside him, watchful and quiet. Then a shimmer of light flickered in the air, and a moment later, Aelriva emerged from nothing, her form like a ripple across a pond.

"As ye can see, I've been hard at work," she said with a bright grin, her lilting cadence filling the clearing. "Drained the village mana each day to keep the constructs goin'. Thought ye'd prefer a bit more cleared ground on yer return."

Gasps rose behind Xavier as the villagers caught their first glimpse of her. Aelriva's shifting, radiant form shimmered with leyline resonance, part spirit and part something older. No one stepped back. If anything, they leaned in, drawn by the gentle pulse of her presence.

She scanned the group and nodded approvingly. "Ye've

done well, Ard'Maelor. Did not expect such a crowd. But where are ye plannin' to house them? We have no proper homes yet. The warrens will serve for now, but ye ought to finish explorin' them. I've felt little more than vermin below, but tunnels can twist, and deeper things hide in darker holes."

Xavier exhaled and gave a short nod. His list of responsibilities had only grown since leaving. But now, it felt like a burden worth carrying. He was no longer alone.

Turning to the villagers, he raised his voice. "Come on. We'll get you settled underground for now. It's dry, it's secure, and it's safe. Then we'll build something better together."

With heads held high, the caravan rolled forward. The last whispers of Bramblegate faded behind them. Ahead lay promise, possibility, and the first true steps toward a future worth claiming.

#

The procession wound through the valley floor, carts creaking under the weight of salvaged supplies, and villagers murmuring in low voices as they took in the strangeness of their new home. Above them, the ridges rose in uneven waves, their slopes dressed in thick green and silver moss, the valley a cradle of stone and silence. Birds called distantly overhead, the first real signs of life not touched by fire or grief.

The golems continued their steady labor, unfazed by the caravan's arrival. They moved with uncanny precision, hauling stones, lifting felled trunks, and clearing centuries of overgrowth. Their runes pulsed faintly with soft emerald light, illuminating trails of dust and the occasional shimmer of leyline essence drifting in the air.

Xavier led them past the skeletons of buildings long reclaimed by root and vine. The clearing had changed. Wide footpaths now wove between the reclaimed foundations, while mounds of stone and freshly cut timber stood ready for future construction. Where once there had been only ruin, there was now the beginning of intention.

They reached the central hall, that Xavier and Ella had sheltered in previously, an ancient structure carved of pale stone and marked by time. Vines crawled across its facade, but the steps were clean, freshly swept by golem hands. The arch above the entrance still bore faint symbols, half-erased by the ages, and yet warm to the eye. Xavier turned to the crowd gathered behind him.

"Inside is dry and defensible," he said, his voice steady despite the fatigue. "It will not be permanent, but it is shelter. We will use the rooms below until proper homes can be built."

Braegor stepped forward and gave a firm nod. There were murmurs of agreement behind him. No one resisted, their faces were drawn but willing. Comfort, even temporary, was enough.

One by one, they crossed the threshold. The carved corridors inside surprised them, smooth walls etched with flowing lines, long-dead sconces crackling softly back to life with crystal-lit glow. As Aelriva passed, the leyline energy stirred, causing dormant enchantments to flicker awake. A hushed awe settled over the villagers.

They spent the afternoon exploring the upper levels of the warrens. The chambers, though bare, had structure and strength. Rooms were selected quickly, most by families or small groups. Cloth was draped over old benches and stone shelves repurposed into sleeping ledges. Laughter returned, faint and halting, but real. Children darted through the halls, their echoing voices chasing one another around corners.

Several small rooms were found with deep-set stone shelves cut into the walls. These were quickly identified as storerooms and were soon stocked with tools, salvaged weapons, and whatever sundries had survived the journey. Darra and two others handled the cataloging, marking down quantities with charcoal on broken slates. The lists were then handed to Braegor, who took them seriously and promised to bring the essentials to Xavier's attention.

One wide chamber near the main stairwell was claimed by Frieda Deepstone. With practiced authority, she set up a rudimentary kitchen, directing the unpacking of pots, sacks of grain, and jars of pickled roots. Others followed her lead, chopping, peeling, and tending the fire she built against a shaped stone hearth. By early evening, the warm aroma of simmering stew filled the lower halls. Hunger pulled people together, and the tension of arrival began to ease.

Eventually, blankets and cloaks became bedding, with packs turned into pillows. Villagers lay side by side on the stone floor or repurposed shelves, surrounded by quiet murmurs and flickering light. The warrens, though cold and unadorned, felt secure. The stone beneath them was solid. The air was still. For the first time in days, there was no scent of smoke.

Xavier lingered at the edge of the main corridor, watching it all unfold. He saw Sylvie helping tuck children in beside their parents, Orrek mending a cracked tool handle, and Lorrin sketching a diagram into the dust with the tip of a spoon. These people, his people he corrected himself, were already beginning to rebuild.

Blankets rustled as bodies shifted, the final murmurs fading into soft breathing and scattered snores. The scent of stew lingered faintly, comforting in the stillness. Xavier moved quietly through the warrens, passing clusters of slumbering forms until he reached a side chamber where a quieter gathering had begun to form.

#

Blankets rustled as bodies shifted, the final murmurs fading into soft breathing and scattered snores. The scent of stew lingered faintly, comforting in the stillness. Xavier moved quietly through the warrens, passing clusters of slumbering forms until he reached a broader chamber not far from the ley mosaic of Syr'Vailen. Most of the villagers had avoided the nexus since arriving, whether from awe or unease Xavier was not sure, but this room rested just far enough away that it didn't disturb them. Private, quiet, and large enough for discussion, Xavier already envisioned it as the future council chamber.

The others filtered in slowly, each settling onto the stone floor with a fresh bowl of Frieda's stew in hand. Aelriva drifted into being along the wall, her luminous form echoing gently with leyline resonance. Braegor sat upright near the center, his ledger already open. Ella arrived shortly after, her quiet presence grounding as always. Rhett Calloway and Orrek Deepstone entered mid-conversation, the human carpenter and the dwarven stonemason having spent much of the day examining the ruins above.

Sylvie Tumblewick arrived next, her halfling warmth helping ease the edges of fatigue lingering in the room. Lorrin Thistlegear came with soot-streaked fingers and a restless energy, while Elric Stagstride stepped in last, his Animari calm balancing the group.

Xavier waited until everyone had settled before speaking. "As I am sure you have noticed, the village is rough. I imagine most don't want to stay in the warrens long, so we need to figure out what to build and when. Houses would be a good start, though maybe a communal structure first to get people above ground faster."

"I agree, Lord Xavier," Sylvie began, but he quickly raised a hand.

"Wait. Just call me Xavier. No need to bow and scrape."

"You are the Lord, however," Braegor said firmly, "If you are to lead, people—including you—need to accept that."

Xavier opened his mouth to protest again, but Ella placed a hand gently on his forearm. "Listen to him," she said. "These lands are yours now. They don't need to kneel, but they must recognize what you are."

Aelriva smiled. "The last Ard'Maelor was much like yerself, Xavier. Cared little for titles but knew his duty. Ye can lead as ye are, but if ye wish their loyalty, ye must let them honor the role. In here, we'll call ye Xavier. Out there? Ye'll have to be more."

He sighed, realizing this was not a fight he would win. "Alright. So housing, and then what?"

Rhett and Orrek raised their hands almost in unison. "Begging yer pardon," Rhett began, "Housing is important, aye, but people have beds for now. We think it's better to start with a construction shed. It'll let us set up properly for tier one structures, basic, sure, but solid."

Xavier tilted his head. "Why? Wouldn't that make more sense after homes are built?"

Orrek rumbled, "We can throw together housing hovels, aye, but they'd barely hold a good wind. What we need is somethin' proper. The hut lets us plan, draw, and design. Otherwise, we're just guessin', and guessin' leads tae walls that crack an' fall."

Xavier scrubbed at his face and gave a low chuckle. Of course, the dwarf had a brogue. Some part of him had hoped the stereotype wouldn't hold true, but here it was, gruff, earnest, and impossible to ignore. It almost made him feel like he was back in one of his games. Almost.

Then Xavier blinked as his mind caught up to what he was being told. "Wait, there are tiers to buildings?"

"Aye," Orrek said, "Tier one huts for now. Better ones once we get blueprints or skills."

Rhett added, "Even so, that construction shed will make all the difference. Average quality instead of poor. It means fewer repairs. Better long-term structures."

Xavier rubbed his face. "Alright, construction shed first. Then housing."

The group nodded and the decision was made.

Lorrin raised a hand next. "We're running out of space to store tools and supplies. I've cataloged what we have. Braegor has the lists. I'd like to start planning proper storage systems and facilities, lifts, ramps, even organizing flows."

Aelriva chimed in. "There's space near the river bend. I'll have the constructs start clearing there. The leyline's quiet in that stretch."

Xavier turned to Elric. "Thoughts?"

The druid's voice was steady. "They still believe in you. That belief will fade if we ask them only to endure. Give them work. Let them build. Towers to see from. Paths to walk with purpose."

That struck a chord. Xavier nodded. "Alright. Construction hut. Then housing. Then storage and defensive towers."

The council continued well into the night. Ideas were offered, some accepted, others marked for later. They agreed to expand toward the river. Aelriva and the golems would assist with lifting and hauling. Tasks would be distributed. Watch rotations would begin. They would have all the basics Bramblegate had and more.

Xavier stood and stretched. "This is what I wanted Rynthavael to be. Not a place I command. A home we shape together."

As the others filtered out, discussing next steps, Ella remained beside him. She walked with him back toward the chambers he had claimed. Her bedroll now lay beside his. Neither commented on it. Knowing the night watches had been assigned, the pair exchanged quiet goodnights and stretched out to rest. Morning would come fast, and with it, the first real day of rebuilding.

CHAPTER FOURTEEN

Growth

Xavier stirred beneath the rough blanket, a low groan escaping his lips as he stretched. His back ached from another night on stone, and he rubbed at the stiffness lingering in his shoulders. Sleep had come, but it had not come comfortably.

He sat up and looked around the dim chamber. He was alone once again. Ella must have risen early. He glanced at his bedroll, then the hard floor beneath it, and sighed.

"I really need to talk to someone about a proper bed. Wood, straw, whatever. Anything better than this."

He pulled on his boots and made his way through the winding tunnels of the warrens. The cool underground air clung to him, but light glimmered ahead. As he stepped out into the great hall and up toward the surface, warmth met him, and with it, the sound of life.

Sunlight poured through open archways and the fractured walls of the Sylmyrian ruins, illuminating the village square beyond. The air carried the scent of sawdust and fresh-turned earth. People were already hard at work.

At the edge of the woods, near the southern treeline, a small hut had begun to take shape. Rhett, the carpenter, and Orrek, the stonemason, stood at its base, giving instructions to several villagers who passed wood and stone between them. Tools rang against timber, and the structure slowly rose where none had stood before.

While he watched a soft voice pulled him from his thoughts.

"Here," came the quiet offering.

Xavier turned to find a young girl holding up a wooden plate stacked with steaming eggs and browned sausage. She looked up at him through a tangle of chestnut curls, her eyes uncertain but hopeful. It took him a moment to place her.

"Thank you, Emily. It smells wonderful. Please let Frieda know I appreciate it."

The girl beamed, pleased he had remembered. She was one of the youngest survivors of Bramblegate's fall, orphaned in the attack. Since then, the village had embraced her, and her bright spirit had become a symbol of hope. Her laughter often echoed through the camp, a sound that lifted more than one weary soul.

Emily gave a quick, enthusiastic nod, then darted off, likely heading back to the makeshift kitchen to help Frieda with the morning meal.

Xavier leaned against a stone pillar warmed by the sun, eating slowly as he watched the villagers work. They moved with purpose, carrying lumber, mixing mortar, planting new gardens. The shattered ruins of the past were beginning to look like a home.

`He brought up his interface, and the familiar hum flickered across his vision. A warning hovered near the top of his screen, reminding him that his unspent attribute points were on the verge of being automatically assigned. He had nearly forgotten about the new levels he had earned from rescuing the villagers. That would not do. He needed to have a better sense of his priorities now, both for survival and leadership.

He spread the points with deliberate care, aiming to balance his abilities while rounding out his weaker stats. Strength received three points, bringing it to a solid 12. Agility followed with two more, just enough to raise it to 10. Dexterity, already useful in both blade and bow, was boosted by three to match strength at 12. Constitution, which governed his resilience, also rose to 12 with a two-point increase. A single point went into endurance, just enough to round it to an even 10.

After interacting more with the villagers, he recognized the importance of presence and persuasion. Four points went into charisma, raising it to a respectable 12. Intelligence and wisdom, though not his focus, each received two points to lift them from their starting values to 10. And finally, he poured the remaining five into luck. It was the most intangible of the lot, but something told him it mattered more than it seemed. That put luck at 14, his highest score yet.

He reviewed the changes one last time, letting the numbers settle into place. The subtle sensation of attunement passed through him, like threads pulling tighter within the tapestry of his being. With a nod of satisfaction, he closed the interface and turned his full attention back to the village.

The village really was beginning to feel like something more than a stopgap. It was growing, taking root, and he, for all his uncertainty, was at the center of it. People waved as they passed. Smiles greeted him, not out of fear or obligation, but out of respect. Out of hope. Out of shared purpose.

He set his empty plate on a windowsill and pushed off the stone wall. There was still work to do. Xavier made his way toward the hut under construction and joined the others without ceremony. He took the offered timber, fell into rhythm, and lost himself in the labor of building something real.

#

The days passed in steady rhythm, each one beginning with the first light over the Silverwood and the soft bustle of a village slowly finding its footing.

Mornings in the budding village began early. The scent of hearthbread and simmering stew drifted up from the warrens, warm and welcoming, while the crisp air from the surface filtered down through the broken archways and weathered halls of the ruins. Villagers stirred with purpose, their movements already echoing across stone as they prepared for another day of building, clearing, and growing.

Xavier had begun to rise with them. He worked shoulder to shoulder with his people, joining wherever an extra pair of hands could help. Some days that meant lifting beams with Rhett, the carpenter, or mixing mortar under Orrek's watchful eye. Other times he helped Ferran's team near the riverbank, where their first planting beds had begun to take root in the dark, fertile soil. No task was beneath him, and slowly, that fact spread. They saw him not just as their lord, but as someone willing to earn that title through sweat and labor.

He made a point to speak to everyone each day. With so few settlers, it was easy to remember names and faces. Conversations grew longer with time. Smiles came more readily. The cautious respect they had offered at the beginning was giving way to something deeper, steadier.

Among them, the children were a constant presence. Laughing, shrieking, dashing between tasks or climbing where they shouldn't. They were the beating heart of the settlement's future.

Emily, smallest and youngest of the orphans, had

practically adopted the kitchen as her second home. She could be seen ferrying trays, dodging under arms, and sneaking tastes with a grin that made it difficult for anyone to scold her. Pip, the halfling boy, was her frequent partner in mischief, and wherever the two went, the gnome lad Perry followed, usually wide-eyed and always in trouble by association.

Nia, just four, rarely left her mother's side, though her curiosity was boundless. Jace, a six-year-old human orphan taken in by his cousin Tara, the weaver, had a knack for being wherever he wasn't supposed to be. He could often be found trying to scale the forge wall or dangling from support beams with no clear idea how he got there. Kedrik, the young dwarven boy, was the opposite. Quiet, methodical, and already helping his father with stonework. While the others ran wild, Kedrik built with focus and pride.

Xavier did what he could to be a steady presence. In the evenings, after the day's work was done, he often gathered the children near the central fire. There, surrounded by crackling flame and the scent of stew or roasted meat, he told them stories. Some were pulled from the books he had read as a child in his world. Others were pieced together from what Ella had told him of Arath, carefully reshaped to end with hope rather than tragedy.

Emily often curled into his lap while he spoke, her head tucked against his chest, eyes wide with wonder. The others clustered around on benches or furs, sometimes interrupting with questions, sometimes acting out scenes. Their laughter filled the ruins, echoing against the stone, and for a time, it felt like the past had never happened.

With Ella, the bond deepened more quietly. She remained nearby during the day, sometimes helping him move materials, sometimes vanishing into the woods to scout, but always returning with that faint smile he had grown to recognize. He would catch her watching him sometimes, eyes bright and unreadable, the curve of her lips betraying a private amusement.

He said nothing. She said nothing. The silence between them grew comfortable.

Still, a sense of unease had begun to take root in Xavier's thoughts. It stirred at odd moments, a prickling behind the eyes, a tightening in his gut. It was all going too smoothly.

Rynthavael had begun to thrive. The people were safe. The food stores were growing. The work never stopped, but neither did the progress. Yet Bramblegate lay just five days northeast, and its ashes had barely cooled. The same raiders, or worse, could come again. And the Shardfangs were not the only things lurking in the Silverwood. He could feel it in the earth beneath his boots, the way the wind sometimes turned cold without warning, or how shadows near the treeline lingered too long. The forest was watching.

At night, his sleep grew restless. Dreams curled at the edge of his mind like smoke. Half-seen corridors of stone. Halls lit by strange blue fire. A hum that pulsed in the dark like a heartbeat too deep to name. When he woke, he could never remember the words, only the feeling. Something old. Something waiting.

On the fifth morning, he found himself once more in the heart of the Syr'Vailen, beneath the mosaic where the ley lines converged. Aelriva hovered above it, her glow casting a gentle sheen across the worn stone.

"I know we've got the basics for the next level in motion," Xavier said, running a hand through his hair. "But we're going to need more people. More growth. I'm guessing that means quests. I just don't know where to find them, or how to trigger them."

The sprite's laughter was like chimes in the wind.

"I was wonderin' when ye'd finally start askin' the right questions," she said, spinning once in place before drifting lower. "The land's been whisperin' its needs since the day ye claimed it. There are nests in the woods, bringin' danger to yer borders. The ley lines lie dormant beneath yer feet, choked by silence. The Deeps stretch far below, forgotten and foul. And ye? Ye've barely scratched the surface." She pointed to the ground beneath them. "There's power here, Xavier. But it's sleepin'. And it's waitin' for its keeper to wake it."

As her words settled, three shimmering prompts appeared in his vision, their golden borders pulsing softly.

You have been offered a quest: Sleeping Lines I
The ley lines that make up the nexus beneath your settlement are dormant. Explore the Deeps beneath the mosaic and revitalize one of these lines to increase ambient mana and enhance settlement growth.
This is a settlement quest and has been automatically accepted.
Rewards: Increased ambient mana. Greater wildlife affinity. New quest opportunities. +500 Experience.

You have been offered a quest: Whose House I
While the lands surrounding your settlement fall under your authority, you are not their only master. Explore at least four unique locations and uncover their significance to assert dominion.
This is a settlement quest and has been automatically accepted.
Rewards: Reduced regional threat. Unknown benefits. +500 Experience.

You have been offered a quest: Drums in the Deeps I
The unknown Deeps lie beneath your settlement's mosaic. Creatures or forces may have claimed these

---

tunnels during centuries of neglect. Explore and reclaim the first level of the Deeps.
This is a settlement quest and has been automatically accepted.
Rewards: Increased resources. Hidden benefits. +500 Experience.

Xavier exhaled through his nose, wincing slightly at the mild rebuke in her tone. He had been focused inward, yes, but now the path was becoming clear. He already noted that two of the quests pointed to the same location. That would let him do more with less risk.

Xavier lingered in the Syr'Vailen chamber, eyes fixed on the mosaic beneath his feet. Aelriva's glow shimmered softly in the air above, her wings pulsing faintly in rhythm with the heartbeat of the land. The silence stretched as her earlier words settled in the corners of his mind.

"What do I need to know about the ley lines?" he asked finally. "Anything specific to revitalize them? Is there a right order?"

The sprite dipped lower, expression sharpening with the weight of what she was about to say.

"Each ley line holds its own unique requirements for bein' awoken and restored. Ye can choose the order in which ye approach 'em, but ye'll need to uncover what must be done for each. In the past, their awakening was tied to their very nature, so seek out what might be disruptin' their essence. As ye travel along a line, ye'll come across points of power. The more ye energize and set flowin', the stronger and more vital the line becomes. But mark me—each line has a core, and that core is the key to its awakening. Find it first, afore ye fret about increasin' its essence."

Xavier absorbed the words in silence, arms folded across his chest as he stared down at the faint lines etched into the ancient stone. So much was hidden beneath their feet. The Deeps were no longer just a curiosity; they were a crucible. If the ley lines were the lifeblood of this land, then the Deeps were its heart, buried and forgotten.

He would have to lead an expedition down there. Not immediately, not while the village was still finding its rhythm, but soon. Once homes were built and people felt secure. Then he could afford to face what waited below.

Part of him buzzed with anticipation—exploration, ancient mysteries, the possibility of restoring real power to the settlement. But another part hesitated. These people had already suffered so much. He could not allow his curiosity to outweigh their safety.

"All right, Aelriva," he said at last. "You've given me a lot to think about. I have an idea on how to move forward now. Any ideas where I might find some of those locations in my lands that you mentioned?"

Her wings beat once, slow and deliberate. Her tone sharpened.

"Did I not say I'm as bound to these lands as I am here?" she said, her voice edged with impatience. "There are five places within a short trek from the village. One lies north, toward the Ironpeak Mountains, about fourteen miles by foot. Another rests west by northwest, near the edge of yer domain, on the path one might take toward the elven capital of Eryndor, some fifteen miles travel. To the southeast, there are two: one eight miles from here, and another ten miles further, just past the boundary of yer land. And last, I sense somethin' due east, across the river. It lies two days away, not for distance but for the terrain. Any of these may be of interest to yer settlement."

Xavier gave a low whistle. "That's a lot of ground to cover."

"Aye. And none of it explored. Yer land's more than trees

and stones, Xavier. It's history, waiting to be claimed, or reclaimed, if ye've the strength."

He nodded and gave her a slight smile. "Then that's what we'll start with. The northern site first. It's within range, and it might tie into the ley lines."

She bobbed once in acknowledgment. "Choose wisely. And take care. I can travel with ye through the land so long as ye remain within yer domain. But the farther from the nexus I go, the dimmer my light becomes. Wake the lines, and my reach will grow. Build up the village, and I'll be able to do more still." Her form shimmered once more before vanishing like mist in morning sun.

#

Xavier exhaled and turned toward the exit. His path was clear, and the days of rest were ending. Climbing back through the winding tunnels that connected the nexus chamber to the surface, Xavier moved with quiet purpose. Sunlight filtered down as he reached the upper halls, and the familiar sounds of life greeted him. Hammers striking wood, voices calling out, the scent of damp earth and sawdust hanging in the air. Rynthavael was stirring, growing, and for the first time in days, he could see the outlines of something more than just survival.

He paused at the structure housing the warren entrance. Still too crude, too makeshift. More of a holding space than a proper gathering point. He would need to talk to Rhett and Orrek about expanding it into something worthy of a central hall. If they wanted a true village, it would need a proper heart.

Pulling up his interface, he flicked to the settlement ledger, letting the translucent display settle into place before his eyes. A tab marked Village Roles glowed with soft gold, prompting his attention.

The list populated quickly, most entries dimmed or obscured behind system warnings. He hovered over the blurred ones, and the familiar phrase returned again and again.

"You have not met the criteria for this role yet."

He frowned slightly and turned his focus to the few that had been unlocked. Titles arranged themselves in tidy rows:

- Steward / Mayor – Governance and day-to-day oversight.
- Healer / Herbalist – Responsible for tending wounds and preparing remedies.
- Carpenter / Woodwright – Overseeing woodworking, repairs, and structural reinforcements.
- Builder / Mason – Shaping stonework, reinforcing foundations, maintaining the ruins.
- Captain of the Guard – Organizing and commanding village defense.
- Blacksmith / Armorer – Listed but greyed out, with a note requiring a functional forge.

Simple roles, but essential ones. The foundation of a real settlement. Each one a piece of structure and order. And each one needed someone to fill it. He nodded to himself and closed the interface with a quiet breath. First things first, however, he needed Ella.

He found her easily enough near the northern edge of the clearing, standing in discussion with Coren and Kael, one of the Animari. Coren had taken to wearing his old soldier's leathers again, and though he still claimed to be retired, there was nothing idle in the way he stood. Kael, ever watchful, kept his arms crossed, his leonine features unreadable beneath his tawny mane.

All three turned at his approach, and in a motion that had already become habitual, raised their right fists to their chests in salute.

Xavier gave an exaggerated sigh and returned the gesture. "Still getting used to that."

The faint glimmer of amusement in their eyes told him they knew.

"I'm looking to improve my archery," he said, cutting to the point. "Planning to start exploring beyond the immediate area, and I'd rather be able to deal with something at range than wait until it's gnawing on my arm."

He tapped the hilt of Vaeltheris at his hip. The blade had once again adopted its dormant, unassuming form.

Coren raised an eyebrow. "Practical. You finally noticed your aim needs work."

Before Xavier could fire back a retort, Kael spoke in his usual low rumble. "Lorien and Amara were practicing near the riverbank. They had just finished patrol. If you hurry, they may still be there."

"Perfect," Xavier said, already turning. Then paused. "Actually... Coren, while I've got you. You've already taken on responsibility with the guard. Would you consider doing it officially?"

Coren tilted his head. "What are you offering, my lord?"

"I'd like to name you Captain of the Guard. I won't always be here, and the village needs someone reliable at its back. You're already leading. This just makes it formal." He hesitated before continuing. "There's no salary yet. Resources are thin. But once the economy stabilizes, we'll establish compensation."

Coren laughed, a low, genuine sound. "You're not the first commander to say that. I didn't come for coin. I came for a place to stand. I'll take the title, at least until someone better suited arrives."

Xavier stepped forward and clasped his forearm. "Thank you. I'll rest easier knowing someone experienced is watching the walls."

Coren's eyes gleamed with quiet mischief. "I'm going to start running drills. Just like the old days. You'll join us, of course. Wouldn't want the men thinking their lord is soft."

Xavier gave a pained smile. "After we return from our trip north. Ella and I leave tomorrow. Aelriva mentioned a location worth investigating."

Coren's expression darkened. "You're leaving the village already? With no escort?"

"I won't be alone," Xavier said, resting a hand lightly on Ella's shoulder. "And I'll be careful. We can't spare people from their duties yet. I'll recruit more soon, build up the numbers, then we'll move as teams."

Kael offered a solemn nod of agreement, but Coren still frowned. "Make recruitment a priority, my lord. Rynthavael is depending on you."

"I will," Xavier promised. "I'll speak with Braegor. He may know of nearby camps or wandering families. We've got homes going up. Now we just need people to live in them."

Coren offered no further argument, though his gaze lingered on Xavier a moment longer. Then he turned back to Kael, speaking softly.

As they walked away, Ella glanced at Xavier, her eyes gleaming with amusement. "You handled that well," she said.

"I felt like a teenager getting scolded by a strict uncle."

"And you still agreed to drills."

"I'm starting to think I regret that."

They both smiled, then set off toward the riverbank

together, the sound of hammer and laughter fading behind them.

#

The path to the riverbank curved gently through stands of young birch and weathered stone, the trees whispering softly above. Birds scattered from the underbrush at their approach, and the crisp air carried the scent of water and bark. Xavier moved easily beside Ella, his thoughts still turning over Aelriva's words and the quiet pressure of leadership.

Ahead, the muffled thud of arrows striking wood broke the natural stillness. As they stepped through the final veil of trees, the makeshift archery range came into view.

A dozen simple targets had been affixed to trunks and upright stakes at varying distances. Lorien stood poised at one of them, bow raised. Her feathered arms drew back the string with practiced grace. Behind her, Amara leaned in, offering quiet correction.

"Relax and slow your breathing, Lorien. Slow is steady. Steady is fast. Take your time, and your aim will follow."

Xavier stopped just at the edge of the range, watching.

Lorien's form was striking. Her Falconi heritage was unmistakable, plumage of deep brown and gold covered her limbs, and her keen golden eyes tracked the target with uncanny focus. Her bowstring twanged, and the arrow hissed through the air, striking just off-center.

Amara nodded in approval. The human ranger stood a few inches shorter than her student, her auburn braid trailing over one shoulder. Sunlight caught the freckles across her cheeks as she stepped back, arms crossed, letting Lorien loose another arrow.

Xavier studied the contrast between the two women. Amara, all grounded discipline and sharp practicality, stood beside Lorien's wild, avian elegance. Where the Falconi moved like a hunting hawk, light on taloned feet, Amara's stance was rooted, the product of years in the field.

"She's good," he murmured.

Ella smirked. "Better than you. Let's hope some of it rubs off."

He gave her a sideways look. "It was one time. One arrow."

"One near miss that almost tagged me in the ribs," she replied sweetly. "I still don't know whether the deer or I was the target."

Before he could respond, Lorien turned and spotted them. Her feathers ruffled slightly in surprise, and a soft pink hue flushed across her cheek-plumage. She lowered her bow, stepping back from the firing line.

Amara turned as well, her expression calm, though her eyes sparkled with amusement.

Xavier raised a hand in greeting. "You're both making this look easy."

"It isn't," Amara replied with a wry smile. "But it gets easier with practice."

He unslung his own bow as Ella did the same. "Mind if we join you for a bit? I could use a refresher."

Amara coughed slightly trying to hide her laughter at the emphatic nodding from Ella who was standing just far enough behind Xavier that he didn't notice. Lorien's golden eyes widened even more at the woman's actions but was already too embarrassed to laugh. Xavier glanced back at Ella who stopped just before she could be caught, an innocent smile on her lips. He narrowed his eyes slightly at her before turning back to the other women.

"As I was saying, I need to practice since Ella and I will be traveling soon." He stated.

Amara gestured toward the nearby targets. "Of course, Lord Xavier. Take a few shots and let's see where we're starting."

Xavier stepped into position and selected a shaft from the standing quiver. He nocked the arrow, drew it back with care, and exhaled.

The release was clean. The arrow thudded into the outer ring of the target. Not a miss, but far from impressive.

He fired again, then a third time. Each found its mark, but none with precision. His grouping was wide. His breathing inconsistent. His stance a little too stiff.

Behind him, Ella said nothing. Her smirk said everything.

He turned toward Amara. "Well?"

The ranger tilted her head slightly. "You understand the basics. But you're holding your bow like it's a staff. Too rigid. The wind shifts, the world shifts. You have to move with it."

"Relax the stance. Let your back do the work. Focus on the rhythm of breath, not just the moment of release."

Xavier nodded and adjusted. Over the next hour, he and Ella both trained under Amara's guidance. Lorien practiced alongside them, offering quiet encouragement when Xavier's shots improved or suppressing laughter when they didn't. The Falconi girl had a surprisingly gentle presence when not focused on her own target.

Amara moved between them with effortless precision, tailoring her advice to each student. Her corrections were subtle, but effective. By midday, Xavier was landing consistent hits near the center of the targets.

Then, the familiar shimmer of a system prompt slid across his vision.

Congratulations! You have learned a new skill: Archery

(Level 1)
Archery (Level 2)

You've begun to understand the art of ranged combat. Archery requires a balance of precision, control, and timing. Anyone can shoot. Few can hit.

+4% accuracy with bows and crossbows
+4% arrow damage
+4% chance to recover arrows

He blinked at the message, then made a face.

Ella raised an eyebrow. "Something wrong?"

He tilted the prompt toward her so she could read it, then deadpanned, "Even the world seems to think I'm bad at this."

She laughed aloud, a clear, musical sound that turned a few heads. "Don't worry," she said. "You're only mostly hopeless."

They spent a few more minutes gathering arrows and packing the training materials. Amara gave Lorien one final pointer before waving them off.

As they made their way back to the village, the scent of roasted meat and fresh bread met them on the wind. The midday meal had begun. Villagers clustered around long tables near the fire pits, laughter rising in the warm air.

Xavier took a place among them, greeted with nods and easy conversation. He felt the bond forming, threads of shared effort, shared hope, shared belonging.

He watched the children chase each other near the fire. Saw the builders speaking over timber plans. Smelled the stew that someone had added aromatic herbs to for the first time. Rynthavael was growing, not just in size, but in soul.

He rose after the meal and stepped onto one of the flat stones near the central courtyard. As the voices quieted and eyes turned toward him, he raised his hand.

"My people. We've only been together a short time, but already you've shown what kind of village this will become. Look around you. Homes are rising. The fields are beginning to turn. The forge will soon burn again."

He paused, letting the moment breathe. When he spoke again the words seemed to come from something beyond his own thoughts and feelings. Words formed that felt heavy with portent. "We have our roots in the past, our strength in the present, and our hope for the future."

The villagers echoed the words instinctively, voices rising as one. "Roots in the past. Strength in the present. Hope for the future!"

> **Congratulations! You have set the motto of Rynthavael.** These words reflect the village's ties to the ancient Sylmyrian ruins, their determination to rebuild and thrive in the present, and their collective aspirations for a brighter future.
> **Morale +200**
> **Loyalty +200**

Xavier smiled as the cheer rolled across the courtyard. Across the crowd, Ella raised her cup to him, eyes bright, her grin wide and proud.

CHAPTER FIFTEEN

Echoes of Innocence

The last golden threads of daylight stretched across the clearing as Xavier returned from his final supply check. The preparations for their upcoming descent were complete. Packs sat loaded with dried rations, flint, spare cloaks, tools, and coils of rope. Ella had double-checked the contents, her practiced hands moving with quiet efficiency. Between them, they had tried to account for every unknown. Still, Xavier's instincts pulled him toward something less predictable.

He left the supply shelter behind and made his way westward across the clearing. The evening air carried the scent of roasted root vegetables and smoked fish from the communal fire pits. A soft breeze rustled through the canopy, tugging gently at his shirt as he neared the hunters' area.

There, stretched atop a flat rock warmed by the day's fading sun, lounged a familiar shape. The shadowmane cub was curled with her paws tucked beneath her body, her fur catching the light with an almost silken sheen. Her belly, noticeably round, gave away that she had eaten well—and likely not by hunting.

Xavier chuckled under his breath and approached. "You really are spoiled," he murmured, kneeling beside the rock.

The cub cracked one eye open. Recognition glimmered in

the slitted amber gaze, though she made no effort to move. Instead, she began to purr, a low, steady rumble that vibrated through the stone beneath her.

He reached out and ran his fingers through her ebon fur, marveling again at how soft and thick it had become. She had grown. Not just in size, though her frame was heavier than he remembered, but in presence. There was a quiet confidence to her now, a sense of self that extended beyond instinct.

"Enjoying the easy life, are you?" he teased, rubbing behind her ears. Her purr deepened, and she pushed into his hand with the full weight of her head.

He sat there for a while, letting the calm of the evening wrap around them. A few hunters passed nearby, nodding in acknowledgment. One of them, Darra the Lupari, smiled warmly at the sight.

"She's got you wrapped around her paw, you know," she said, tossing a cut of meat over to the cub.

The panther snatched it out of the air without opening her eyes.

"Seems mutual," Xavier replied, watching as she gnawed contentedly. "You've made a friend for life."

Eventually, the sun dipped below the treetops, and shadows lengthened across the clearing. Xavier scooped the cub into his arms, grunting at the weight. She gave a soft huff of protest, but her claws remained retracted as she allowed herself to be carried.

"You're getting heavy," he muttered. "Might have to make you earn your meat soon."

She licked his chin once and then tucked her head against his chest.

He carried her back through the village and down into the

cool embrace of the Warrens, their path lit by the occasional wall sconce. The cub dozed in his arms the entire way, utterly unbothered by the movement. When he reached his quarters, he set her on the bedding with care before stripping off his outer layers and settling beside her. Sleep came quickly.

A soft rumble pulled him back to the waking world. His mind surfaced slowly from dreams of firelight and shadowed halls, unsure of what had woken him. Then he felt it, warmth curled against his side, and the unmistakable vibration of a deep feline purr.

He opened his eyes to find the shadowmane sprawled across the edge of the bed, half on the blankets, half on his leg. Her breathing was slow and steady, but her gaze met his as soon as he stirred.

"You really need a name," he said groggily, reaching down to scratch beneath her chin. "Calling you 'cat' or 'little one' just isn't going to cut it anymore."

Her eyes narrowed. One paw lifted and slowly pressed a single claw into the blanket atop his thigh. Not hard enough to draw blood, but just enough to send a clear message.

Xavier yelped and flinched. "Alright, alright. You understood that, didn't you?"

The claw retracted. She yawned widely, flashing rows of tiny fangs, then gave him a look that could only be described as unimpressed.

He laughed and scratched behind her ears, earning another pleased rumble. "You've got attitude. That's good. You'll need it." He paused, then added, "What do you think of Valkra?"

The name hung in the air between them. "It's from a myth," he continued, his voice softer. "Valkyries. Guardians of warriors, fierce and wise. Seems fitting for you."

The cub blinked once. Then, slowly, she leaned into his hand again. Her purring grew stronger. She kneaded the blanket with her forepaws in quiet approval.

"Valkra it is," he whispered, smiling. "You ready to go hunting with me and Ella tomorrow? Might even find you something bigger than scraps."

V alkra stood, stretched, and hopped down from the bed with a feline grace that made no sound. She glanced back over her shoulder, ears twitching, as if to say, Well, what are you waiting for?

Shaking his head with a quiet chuckle, Xavier rose and dressed. He tightened the straps of his leathers, checked his satchel, and drew Vaeltheris a finger's breadth from its sheath to ensure its balance felt right. Satisfied, he adjusted the blade at his side and followed Valkra up toward the surface, the soft pad of her paws leading the way like a silent herald.

#

They climbed together toward the upper chambers. His mind was on the journey to come, the unknown below the village, and the feeling, steady now, that something waited in the dark. But he wasn't prepared for what awaited above.

As he stepped out of the Warrens and into the main hall, the atmosphere hit him like a wall.

Sylvie stood to one side, clutching her son Pip tightly, her knuckles white. Her eyes brimmed with tears she refused to shed. Tara was already past that point. She wept openly as she spoke to Ella in hiccuped sobs.

"She's gone," Tara cried. "Emily's gone, Ella. I woke up and she wasn't in her bed. She's never up before me, not once. I checked the whole house, then outside, everywhere. I don't know where she could have gone!"

Ella's voice was steady, but her expression carried the same weight of worry. She placed a calming hand on Tara's arm. "We'll find her. I promise. She can't have gotten far. Coren is already organizing the hunters."

Xavier felt the blood drain from his face. He stepped closer, trying to gather the situation, when a glowing prompt appeared before his eyes.

You have been offered a quest: Echoes of Innocence. The orphan child Emily has vanished. The village is in panic, and Tara and Sylvie are desperate to find her. Track her down and return her home safely.
Rewards: Increased morale and happiness within the settlement. +1000 Experience
Penalty for refusal or failure: Decreased morale, possible resentment from Tara and Sylvie.

Do you accept?: Yes / No

His answer came without hesitation. Mentally, he focused on Yes. The quest locked into place.

He moved toward Ella but paused. Valkra was sniffing the floor, her nose low, her tail twitching with curiosity. She snuffled at the path leading back into the Warrens. Her movement was focused, deliberate.

"Notice something, girl?" he asked, crouching beside her.

The shadowmane looked up, met his eyes, then turned and padded silently back down into the tunnels.

Xavier followed. Ella's voice called after him.

"Where are you going?"

"Back down," he called. "Valkra's onto something. I think she's tracking Emily."

There was a pause, then Ella's boots echoed behind him. "You really are starting to sound like a ranger."

"She's acting like a bloodhound," he said, glancing back at the cub. "Wouldn't surprise me if she starts talking next."

Valkra led them down through the echoing tunnels. Her paws made no sound, her body low to the ground as she moved with purpose. The path curved until the mosaic room came into view, the glowing relief of the Syr'Vailen sprawling across the floor, but Valkra didn't stop. She padded across the nexus tiles and halted at the far archway. Something lay at the threshold.

A small stuffed bear, slightly worn, propped gently against the wall like it had been placed there on purpose. Xavier's breath caught and Ella gasped.

"That's hers," she whispered. "Emily never goes anywhere without it."

A strangled sob behind them announced Tara's arrival. She had followed at a distance, desperate for answers. The sight of the bear stole her breath. She staggered, collapsed to her knees, and began to cry.

Xavier crossed the chamber swiftly and wrapped his arms around her. "We'll find her. I promise you. We will bring her back."

He turned as Braegor entered, silent and imposing. Xavier nodded to him. "Take her home," he said. "Keep her from following. We'll search the Deeps."

Braegor's head dipped. "What should I tell the others?"

"Tell them we're following a lead. Ella and I will find Emily. No matter what's down there."

As Braegor lifted the grieving weaver into his arms, Xavier bent and picked up the small bear. He tucked it into his satchel with quiet reverence. When he straightened, Ella was already adjusting her pack.

He grabbed a torch from the wall, lit it, and stepped into

the archway that led into the darkness below. The archway swallowed the light behind them. As Xavier stepped through first, torch raised... the world changed.

#

It was not just a descent into deeper stone. The moment he crossed beneath the keystone of the arch, a sensation rolled over him like a silent tide. The pressure was immediate and strange, as though he had stepped through a curtain of heavy water. There was no resistance, no sound, but everything beyond felt different.

A shimmer passed across his skin, not visible to the eye but undeniable in sensation. For the briefest moment, something tugged at the edge of his awareness, a quiet recognition that the world had shifted. Then he was through.

The warmth of the Warrens vanished. In its place came a sudden, raw cold that sank into his clothes and wrapped around his chest like damp cloth. The air grew dense, filled with the scent of wet stone and lichen. Every breath carried a hint of decay, a metallic note beneath the damp, like old iron and forgotten blood.

Behind him, Ella stepped through in silence. Her breath hitched, and she turned slightly, glancing back toward the arch. A faint shimmer still clung to its edges, but even that faded as they moved forward.

"It felt like the air changed," she whispered.

Xavier nodded without looking back. "It did. We're not in the same place anymore."

The boundary behind them felt absolute. Though the arch was no more than a few feet wide, it had cleaved the world in two. On one side stood the village, warm and alive. On this side was something older, sealed away for good reason. That boundary had not been made for convenience. It was a ward. A veil, a magical barrier crafted to keep the Deeps and whatever lived within them from ever reaching the world above.

He shifted the torch higher, its flame flickering as if reacting to the change. A cold draft wound upward from the unseen stair below, carrying the scent of earth and rot. It brushed past his face like the breath of something long asleep. They descended.

The stairwell spiraled downward, hewn stone steps worn smooth by time and moisture. Moss filled the cracks. Water ran in thin trails along the edges, trickling toward some unseen depth. The walls sweated with condensation. Every surface glistened in the torchlight, dull and glimmering like the hide of some buried beast.

Ella walked a few steps behind him, her hand trailing along the left wall for balance. Valkra padded ahead in silence, her form sleek and low to the ground, never straying too far ahead. Her paws made no sound against the slick stone.

The deeper they went, the heavier the silence became. There was no echo of their steps. No sound from the village. No birds, no insects. Only the slow drip of water and the soft hiss of the flame as it danced against the moist air.

When the torch burned low, Xavier paused on a landing. He glanced back, breath steady but alert. Ella drew a fresh torch from her pack and lit it against the dying one. The new flame sparked to life, flaring bright before settling into a steady glow that pushed back the dark.

Xavier reached to his side and drew Vaeltheris.

The dagger pulsed faintly in his hand, its surface catching the light and answering with a subtle, inner gleam. Not firelight, but something older and colder. The runes etched into the blade shimmered faintly, reflecting neither gold nor silver, but something else, something more elemental.

It felt heavier here. Not the weapon itself, but its presence. Like it remembered this place. They descended further, lighting a third torch before the stair finally ended. The narrow passage opened into a vast chamber. Xavier stepped into the space, torch lifted high, and froze.

Stone columns loomed like petrified trees, stretching beyond the reach of their light. The vaulted ceiling was lost in shadow, but the faint echo of dripping water suggested an enormous height. The air tasted ancient, mineral-heavy and still. The floor underfoot bore the marks of purpose: worn tiles arranged in careful symmetry, though many had cracked and shifted with time.

It was not natural. This place had been carved, crafted, meant for something. The hall spoke of Sylmyrian hands.

Xavier could feel it in the patterns, in the curve of the walls, in the precision of the stonework that refused to crumble. This was no cave. It was a memory of civilization, half-swallowed by time but not yet lost.

Several dark passageways branched out from the far side of the chamber. Between them were benches of carved stone, long since worn smooth by water and time. Moss clung to them like burial cloths.

He dropped to a crouch and ran his fingers along the floor, inspecting the stone. Nothing. No footprints. No disturbed dust. No signs of movement. It was as if Emily had stepped off the stair and vanished.

Throwing caution to the wind Xavier started to call out. "Emily! Are you here? Yell if you can hear me, help us find where you are." He walked about the chamber as he called out.

Valkra sniffed at the ground, turning tight circles, her ears twitching with frustration. She gave a low whuff, then lifted her head and stared at the far wall.

Xavier followed her gaze. Something faintly reflected the torchlight. A shimmer. A shape. He crossed the chamber without a word, Vaeltheris casting its pale glow forward in tandem with the flame. As he neared the wall, the torchlight caught an enormous carved relief. His breath caught.

The serpent was the first thing he saw, coiled in an endless loop, its mouth consuming its tail. A perfect circle. The Ouroboros, a symbol of cycles, of death and rebirth. He had seen it before. But not like this. Despite the obvious weathering of the stone in the rest of the chamber, this was in perfect condition, as if it had been carved just hours ago.

The upper loop of the serpent was alive, covered in gleaming carved scales, each one patterned with delicate vinework. Tiny runes gleamed faintly between the leaves. Jera, Uruz, symbols he recognized of harvest, strength, life.

The lower loop changed... Here the body turned skeletal. The scales gave way to exposed bone. Ribs arched outward, and the vines curled inward in decay. New runes filled the spaces, Kaunaz and Thurisaz, again old Norse runes, but these were for suffering and transformation, symbols of fire, pain, and endings.

Between the two loops, rising from the intersection of death and life, grew a tree. One he could not help but recognize, Yggdrasil.

Its roots burrowed into the lower ring, dark and gnarled. Its branches climbed into the upper ring, blooming with leaves that shimmered faintly, as if resisting the stone they had been carved from. It was both beautiful and unnerving.

At the tree's center, where it aligned with the loop of the serpent, lay a rune Xavier did not recognize , it seemed as though Jera and Thurisaz, life and death blended to create a starburst pattern of intersecting lines, symmetrical yet alien. It felt wrong and right at the same time. It pulled his gaze like gravity.

The blade in his hand grew warmer. Vaeltheris shimmered, and the strange rune answered, beginning to pulse softly with alternating light. Golden brilliance faded into deep black, then returned again, as if breathing.

He raised the dagger toward it. The light deepened. Something in the wall responded to him. Instinctively he reached forward.

"Xavier!" Ella's voice sliced through the silence.

He turned, startled. She stood near one of the side tunnels, eyes alert.

"I heard something," she said, voice low. "Down there. A girl's voice. Singing."

Xavier's heart lurched. He crossed to her side without hesitation. "That means she's alive. Let's move."

They slipped into the darkened tunnel with Valkra leading the way, the serpent and the tree fading behind them into the breathless silence of the stone.

#

The tunnel closed around them, as Xavier and Ella stepped into the passage, the worked stone of the Sylmyrian ruins continued for only a short distance. The floor beneath their feet was still even, still laid with purpose, but already the edges had begun to crack. Vines crept along the seams. The precision of the architecture softened with every step forward.

They moved quickly at first, propelled by the faint sound of singing echoing ahead. It was Emily's voice, delicate and haunting, drifting through the corridor like a melody wrapped in mist. The tune was unfamiliar, but its quiet sadness clung to the walls.

Xavier's grip on Vaeltheris tightened. "We have to find

her. Now."

They broke into a jog, torchlight bouncing along the corridor as they ran.

The change came gradually. The even stone floor began to buckle. Cracks split the tiles. Moss overtook the edges. The Sylmyrian elegance they had grown accustomed to was giving way to nature's slow reclamation. Roots pierced through seams in the ceiling above. Carvings faded into crumbling reliefs beneath veils of lichen. Then the worked stone disappeared entirely.

Raw earth surrounded them now, and the path turned soft underfoot. The corridor widened into a narrow cavern. The air changed with it, damp, thick, and fragrant with loam. Bioluminescent moss clung to the walls in glowing patches, casting dim green and blue light. Fungi bloomed at intervals along the ground, their gills pulsing with faint inner luminescence.

They slowed their pace, realizing the ground was growing too treacherous for haste as the floor dipped unexpectedly. Stones jutted like uneven teeth. Any misstep could turn an ankle or worse.

Valkra continued forward, low and silent, the torchlight catching in her eyes like amber fire.

Mushrooms sprouted in spiraling clusters. Lichen spread in leafy sheets across the walls. The deeper they moved, the more the natural tunnel shimmered with quiet, alien life. It was beautiful, in a strange and breathless way.

Until the smell changed. t first, it was only a faint bitterness beneath the loam. Something just slightly off. Then it thickened, becoming acrid and wrong. The sharp edge of rot tainted the air, sour and clinging.

Ella raised her sleeve to cover her mouth. "Something's rotting."

Xavier scanned the walls and floor. His eyes narrowed as he noticed the shift. Moss blackened at the edges. Vines curled inward, their tips dark and cracked. Spores wept from sagging mushrooms and hissed where they landed on the stone.

"Not just rot," he murmured. "This place is turning. Something down here is poisoning it."

They continued more cautiously. Vines thickened around the walls and ceiling. Fungal growths crowded the path in irregular patches. The light of their torch began to blend with the ambient glow of the plants, until it was no longer needed. The torchlight dimmed, and Xavier lowered it. Bioluminescence guided them now.

Ahead, a hazy fog of golden-green spores floated across the corridor. the cloud shimmered like sunlight on water, dancing slowly in the air. Xavier wrapped a cloth over his nose and mouth, motioning for Ella to do the same. They pressed forward into the cloud. The spores stung immediately. Eyes burned. Breath grew tight. The world narrowed to blinking shapes and muffled footfalls. After a slow half-minute, they emerged coughing into a broader tunnel where the air, while damp, was clearer.

After hours of careful navigation through the developing underground swamp of rot and decay they came to a change in the tunnel. Before them stood a carved stone arch. It was Sylmyrian. That much was clear. Tree motifs curled up both sides of the archway. Among the roots and branches were creatures, wolves, birds, serpents, deer, woven into the stone as guardians of a long-forgotten gate. The arch was overgrown with roots, but the runes etched at its base still glimmered faintly. Vaeltheris responded to the glow and the runes pulsed once with light as if in recognition. A breath held and released by the stone itself.

Beyond the arch, the tunnel ended, and the world opened

up. Xavier and Ella stepped onto a natural ledge overlooking a vast underground grove. The sight stole the breath from his lungs.

The cavern stretched wide and deep. Bioluminescent trees stood like silent sentinels, their bark lit from within by veins of soft green and pale blue. Vines draped across the upper canopy. Sprawling plants spilled glowing petals across the ground. Pools of dark, still water mirrored glowing fungi that bloomed in ringed clusters.

However, not all was peaceful. Decay had taken root.

Some trees sagged, their limbs twisted and blackened. Fungi lay slumped in puddles of rot. Vines curled like dying snakes, their ends frayed and brittle. Mold crept up from the floor in wide, dark veins. And beneath it all, a slow pulse ran through the earth, an unnatural rhythm, not unlike a fevered heartbeat.

At the center of the grove stood a raised platform of stone, half-consumed by roots. At its heart rose a single pillar. Emerald veins pulsed within its surface, steady and calm, like breath. Clinging to its side was a small form... Emily.

She sat curled at its base, arms wrapped around her knees, her forehead resting against the glowing stone. Her lips moved, forming words almost too soft to carry. A lullaby drifted up, just audible, fragile and filled with longing.

Xavier took a step toward the spiraling ramp that wound along the outer wall.

Ella caught his arm abruptly stopping his decent.

He turned to her, confused, until he saw where she was looking. Below, the grove was not still. Among the trees moved shapes.

Golems. Not like Aelriva's, however, these were twisted things made of rot and vine, bark crusted in fungus, eyes glowing faintly through the decay. They walked slowly between the roots and pools, half-patient, half-predatory. Guardians, perhaps. Or remnants of something that had once protected this place before falling to whatever corruption now crept through its soil.

Xavier crouched beside Ella and moved closer to the ledge, scanning for a path below. As he settled into place, his hand brushed against a loose stone.

It fell and clattered as it struck stone below the ledge. The sound rang through the grove like a struck bell. Everything below stilled. Emily's head lifted.

She turned slowly, and her eyes found his. They widened, filled with fear, then something else. Recognition. Hope. Her small fingers clung tighter to the pillar, and Xavier's heart cracked.

She looked so small. Dirt streaked her face. Her eyes were glassy, her arms thin, wrapped around herself like she could hold in the fear by sheer force of will. The light of the pillar touched her skin, and it was the only thing that seemed to be keeping her anchored.

His breath caught in his throat. Seeing her like that, alone in this place, clinging to something ancient and failing, filled him with a helpless fury he had no place to put. It was not right. She should have been chasing butterflies or sneaking extra sweets, not curled up in a grove of death and ruin.

He stood slowly, not to threaten, and not to act. Only to let her see him. To make sure she knew she was not alone. He raised his hand, palm forward.

Wait. We're here. We see you.

Emily did not speak. She only nodded once, almost imperceptibly, and then pressed herself tighter to the stone. A faint tether of light shimmered from her chest to the pillar. Whatever held her here was not just physical, and whatever else this place was, it had not let her go.

#

The air remained unnaturally still.

Xavier and Ella exchanged a glance, then began to creep slowly down the winding ramp that spiraled along the cavern wall. Their steps were light and measured, careful not to disturb the heavy silence pressing down on the grove.

As they descended, more of the corrupted garden revealed itself. Crumbled arches lay buried beneath moss and rot. Statues slouched among overgrown roots, their faces long worn smooth. Shattered pathways peeked from beneath the carpet of lichen. Stone benches lay sunken and broken beneath creeping vines. A black, sluggish stream wound through the grove's center, branching around the roots of giant fungal trees and the cracked remains of fountains.

The grove had once been a sanctuary. Now it felt abandoned by time, overtaken by sorrow and decay.

When Xavier's foot touched the floor of the grove proper, a pulse of awareness swept over him. A prompt filled his vision.

You have discovered a quest: The Seed of Renewal
You have found one of the dormant cores of the Ley Lines tied to the Syr'Vailen. This place, once sacred to life and healing, has fallen into corruption. Additionally, it seems as if the missing child Emily has found her way to the core and seems to have an unknown role to play in what transpires here. Restore the core of the Life Ley Line and cleanse the surrounding area of the rot and corruption.
Possible Rewards: Purification of the Life Ley Line.
Restoration of access to Life magic.
Rescue of the child Emily. +1000 Experience

Penalties for failure: Further corruption of the Ley Line.
Spread of decay to the lands surrounding Rynthavael.

Death of Emily. Quest *Echoes of Innocence* will fail.

This quest has been automatically accepted.

A second prompt followed as soon as Xavier dismissed the first.

You have discovered a quest: Balance Restored
A corruption has taken root deep within the Life Ley Line's sacred grove. The origin must be found and addressed before the core can be stabilized. Explore the surrounding deeps to find where this corruption is coming from. Only by restoring balance can the life of Emily be saved. Beware your actions could tip the scales in one direction or the other instead of creating balance.
Possible Rewards: Renewal of the Life Ley Line. Additional unknown reward.
Access to Life magic. Rescue of Emily. +1000 Experience

Penalties for failure: Permanent loss of Life Ley Line access. Increased corruption in the region. Death of Emily. Catastrophic imbalance in the Syr'Vailen. Quest *Echoes of Innocence* will fail.

This quest has been automatically accepted.

Xavier exhaled slowly, lowering his hand from the prompt's fading glow.

"Shit, fuck, shit, dammit." He swore as he stepped back on the ramp and stopped Ella from moving further. "Fuck more quests and these ones have some serious penalties if we fail." He told her.

Ella moved beside him. "No easy answers here."

The sentient plant life seemed blissfully unaware of the small group on the ramp as they paused. Emily, who had stopped singing when they reached the bottom of the ramp, started to softly sing again. Her voice seemed to have a calming effect on the twitching and shifting life. They approached the girl carefully. She still clung to the pillar, her head resting against the stone. The tether between her and the crystal at the top glowed gently. The golems had not moved. The vines had not twitched. Everything watched.

Xavier crouched a short distance away. "Emily," he said softly.

She stirred, then looked up. Her eyes were rimmed in red but alert.

"We're here to help you," he said. "We want to bring you home."

Her arms tightened. "I can't. If I go too far, it hurts."

Ella knelt beside him. "The tether is real," she murmured. "The core has latched onto her essence."

Xavier's voice lowered. "Did someone tell you to stay?"

Emily nodded faintly. "The roots. They whisper. I don't understand them, but they're afraid. Sad."

Ella looked around. "The corruption is alive. It remembers what this place used to be."

Xavier reached slowly into his satchel and pulled free a worn bundle of cloth and loose stitching. "Someone was waiting for you," he said. "He wouldn't let us pass without him."

Emily's eyes widened. "Mr. Bear?"

He tossed the toy forward with care. It landed beside her. She lunged forward, grabbed the bear, and hugged it tightly to her chest. The tether pulsed brighter. The light steadied, and around them, the grove seemed to settle. The vines stilled while the fungal trees quieted.Even the twisted golems stood inert.

Then she began to sing once more. It was the same

melody they had heard echoing through the halls. A lullaby, soft and wavering, but it resonated with something deeper than words. The grove listened. The corrupted growths pulsed slower. The hostile tension in the air eased.

Ella's eyes widened slightly. "She's holding it back. The song... it soothes the core."

Xavier looked around. "She's part of it now. A living anchor."

The melody wavered as she looked up at them. "Please don't go," she whispered.

Xavier's heart twisted. "We will come back," he promised. "But we have to find what broke this place. It's the only way to bring you home."

Tears welled at the corners of her eyes. She nodded, but the movement was small. Reluctant. Her expression held both silent plea and weary understanding. She knew they had to go. She just didn't want them to.

Xavier crouched closer, voice soft and steady. "We'll be back, Emily. I promise you will be home where you belong."

She said nothing, instead her arms tightened around the bear. The lullaby continued, a fragile thread of sound echoing faintly in the gloom.

A light tap touched his shoulder. He turned to find Ella beside him, one hand raised, motioning silently back toward the ramp, the only entrance they had seen.

His shoulders sagged for a breath, the weight of failure pressing in before resolve returned to his features. He gave one last look to the girl below.

She had returned to the base of the pillar, seated once more in the moss, clutching her bear. The light that linked her to the core still pulsed with each quiet note of her song. Tears slipped down her cheeks, but her gaze remained fixed on them, watching, waiting. The lullaby did not stop.

Xavier stared a moment longer, burning the image into his mind, then he turned, jaw set, and followed Ella up the winding ramp. They passed through the arch without a word, and left behind the quiet song of a child too strong to let go.

CHAPTER SIXTEEN

Echoes of Eternity

The return through the tunnel was quieter than before, the silence broken only by the soft pad of boots and the occasional whisper of fabric brushing against stone. The air had changed since their first passage. Where it once felt stifling, choked with overgrown roots and vines, it now carried a subtle dampness, cool against the skin. Faint traces of floral musk lingered where the strange flora had bloomed, now wilted and drained of their unnatural vibrancy. They passed tangled clusters of brittle vine husks and torn stalks, the remnants of their earlier struggle, now inert and broken. A few leaves still clung to the walls, their edges curled and brown as though the life had been stolen rather than faded.

Valkra moved with her head low and ears flat, tail twitching at each soft sound that echoed back from the stone ahead. Xavier kept his hand near Vaeltheris, but no threat came. It was not danger that lingered in the corridor now, but a hollow ache, as if the tunnel itself mourned the child left behind.

Eventually, the tunnel began to widen, and the clinging plant life fell away completely. Rough natural stone gave way once more to the clean angles of worked masonry. The transition was slow at first, marked by a few squared blocks nestled between patches of worn rock, then all at once the rough passage gave way to smooth stone flooring. Ornate carvings emerged along the lower edges of the walls, nearly hidden by dust and the passing of time, but present all the same. Each step forward felt like crossing a boundary between the wild and the forgotten.

They emerged at last into the wide chamber at the base of the great staircase. Its vast stillness greeted them like a held breath.

Though the pressure to act quickly remained, the absence of an obvious path forward forced them to pause. Without Emily's distant song guiding them, they turned their attention fully to the space around them for the first time.

The chamber was not simply a room, but a junction. A total of seven archways branched out from the central space, including the one behind them that led back to the surface. Three arched passages lined the left wall, three mirrored them on the right, and the final wall held the towering relief of the coiled dragon, opposite the staircase. The whole chamber had a design of deliberate symmetry. The air carried a faint thrum of dormant power, like the heartbeat of something that had once been alive.

The passage they had taken to reach the corrupted Life Ley Line, the place where Emily now waited, was the second archway on the right. That path remained open and unobstructed, a faint trace of green light still flickering faintly near its mouth. The others, upon closer inspection, were far less promising.

The first passage on the right had collapsed completely, filled with jagged slabs of rock and earth that looked ancient and undisturbed. The third right-side arch curved slightly around a bend before ending in a blank stone wall, as if the passage had never been completed or had been deliberately sealed. On the left side, two archways were choked by cave-ins, their depths hidden by rubble and dust. The final left-hand arch led forward for about twenty feet, then turned sharply, only to end abruptly in a sheer wall of smooth, seamless stone. No seams. No markings. Just stone.

Xavier and Ella stood together near the center of the room, surveying the chamber. The mosaic of the dragon stared out from the far wall, its expression unreadable. There was a sense of waiting here, an unfinished task set in stone. A crossroads, not just of stone paths, but of purpose.

#

They stood in the center of the crossroads chamber, surrounded by archways that led nowhere, or worse, to ruin. The air held a weight that pressed down with more than just silence. It felt like a question waiting to be answered.

Ella stepped forward; her gaze fixed on the massive relief at the far end of the chamber. The carved image of the coiled dragon dominated the wall, its body split between two halves. One half bloomed with depictions of flourishing life, leaves, roots, and streams spiraling through intricate scales. The other withered into the likeness of death, barren branches, curling smoke, and the stillness of final breath.

"There," she said, pointing toward the dragon's living side. "Those runes. I have seen them before."

Without waiting for a response, she darted back toward the tunnel they had emerged from. Her voice echoed across the chamber. "Look. They are part of the archway here. Faded, but they're here."

Xavier moved quickly to her side. He narrowed his eyes and began to trace his fingers across the weathered stone. The carvings were faint, almost consumed by time, but now that he knew what to look for, he could see them. A handful of life runes, matching the ones carved into the dragon mural, lay hidden in the remnants of decorative stonework.

Their presence confirmed what he had begun to suspect.

He stepped back and turned toward the relief once more, thoughts spinning in his mind. The quests had spoken of renewal and balance. One, The Seed of Renewal, was clearly tied to the corrupted garden and Emily's imprisonment. The other, Balance Restored, hinted at something greater, something incomplete. There had to be more.

"Balance," he muttered as he approached the wall again.

He stood before the dragon, studying the two mirrored halves. The symbolism was obvious now... life and death held equal weight here. It reminded him of the infinity symbol, or the old myths of the ouroboros, devouring its own tail in a cycle without end. Life flowed into death, and death returned to life. The meaning felt more than philosophical. It felt like instruction.

His eyes drifted to the passage directly across from the one that had led to Emily. It was one of the collapsed tunnels, utterly impassable. If that path mirrored the life ley line's location, it likely led to the death ley line core, or had, once. But if that were true, and the physical path was destroyed, then where was the balance supposed to be restored?

His gaze shifted to the next archway over. This one had ended in a smooth, blank stone wall. No debris, no carvings, just silence and stone. He narrowed his eyes.

The mural loomed behind him. Carefully he crossed the chamber and approached the blank wall, letting his hand rest against its surface. The stone was too smooth, too perfect. It had no tool marks, no texture. It was unnaturally clean, as if someone had gone out of their way to erase whatever had once been there.

He ran his fingertips slowly across the face of the stone, eyes narrowed in concentration. The second time he passed over the keystone above the arch, he felt it, small indentations, barely noticeable, too faint to see.

"Ella," he called, "come here. I think I've found something."

She abandoned the mural and crossed quickly to his side. Together, they traced the faint marks, a series of shallow depressions invisible to the eye but clear beneath their fingers. They formed a line across the keystone, like the ghosts of runes worn flat by time.

"This was important," she said softly. "But too much has been lost."

Xavier's eyes lit up with sudden inspiration. He reached over his shoulder and drew Vaeltheris. The blade shimmered faintly in the dim chamber, pulsing with an inner light. As the blade neared the stone, the runes responded. A soft shimmer passed across the surface of the wall, and then, faint at first, a series of symbols emerged where the indentations had been.

They were not in any language Xavier knew, yet the meaning pressed against the edge of his mind like a memory half-remembered. Then the familiar chime of a system message sounded, and a prompt flashed before his eyes.

Congratulations. You have learned a new language: Ancient Sylmyrian.

The symbols shifted and reformed in his vision, resolving into clarity. He could read them now. He spoke the words aloud, each syllable heavy with meaning. "Vytha'rin si'alenth, solah na'vylah, durna ven'valith, yn thar'nok vael ren'talah."

Then, with care, he translated them. "Life begins as the seed, rises to flourish, falls to decay, and from dust is born again."

Ella inhaled sharply and turned to look at him. Her expression had changed and now suspicion flickered in her eyes. "How did you know what that meant?"

He met her gaze with a small shrug. "When I saw them clearly, I got a prompt that said I learned Ancient Sylmyrian. After that, I just understood them. Can you read it?"

She did not answer at first. The suspicion faded, replaced by something more guarded, more distant. She studied him for a moment longer, then looked away. "What do you think it means?" she asked. "We do not have any seeds. And we cannot wait for one to grow and die."

Xavier turned back to the relief. "It's not just about plants. It's a cycle. A full pattern. Life and death. I think there's another ley line nearby. Death, to counterbalance the life one. Maybe the reason everything is rotting is because they are not fully awake and are unbalanced." He hesitated. The memory of Emily's quiet humming echoed in his mind. "She's tethered to the life pillar. That might be part of the problem. I don't want to believe that, but if it's true, we have to understand the whole cycle before we can free her."

He raised Vaeltheris again, letting its light play across the wall. As he moved closer to the mural, his hand brushed a ledge that ran the circumference of the chamber, waist-high and coated in dust. As his weight shifted, he felt something shift beneath his palm.

He jerked back instinctively, bracing himself for a trap. Nothing happened.

He stepped in again, brushing the dust away. A small wheel of stone had rotated slightly under his touch, half-embedded in the ledge. As more dust fell away, more wheels appeared, eight in total, each carved with a series of different images.

One showed a seed. Another a sapling. A third depicted a full-grown tree. The next bore a pattern of four crossing lines, forming a star. Others showed a withered tree, a skeletal one stripped bare, a small mound of ash or dust, and finally, a sprouting seed. Only the one he had touched was misaligned. The rest all showed the sprouting seed face up.

Ella moved beside him, peering closely at the carvings. "Well," she said dryly, "I think we've found what the inscription refers to. Now we just need to make sure they're in the right order."

#

Xavier studied the stone wheels, brow furrowed as he reached up to scratch at his chin. The stubble there was rougher than he liked, another reminder of how long they had been down below. He sighed and turned his focus back to the puzzle laid before them.

"Life begins as the seed," he murmured, repeating the line from the wall. "That would mean this one." He pointed to the wheel showing a simple, smooth seed, then carefully rotated it so the seed faced upright once more. "Then sprouting seed, sapling, and full-grown tree. That's the flourish."

Ella nodded. Without a word, she reached for the next two wheels and adjusted them. Sapling, then tree. Her movements were precise, but cautious, as though she expected the stones to bite back.

"That covers the rising phase," she said. "Then comes the fall. Withered tree... then skeletal tree."

Xavier followed the rhythm of her thoughts, his fingers tracing the next two wheels. He adjusted the one with a leafless, slumped tree, then the skeletal trunk stripped of even bark. "And that leaves these," he said, gesturing toward the final two. "From dust is born again. So the pile of dust here... and then the star? Spirit returning?"

Ella hesitated, lips pursed. "It would make sense. Essence reborn. The riddle fits."

Xavier turned the dust wheel into place, then rotated the last so the four-pointed star faced up. He and Ella stepped back.

For a moment, nothing happened. They glanced at each other, puzzled.

Then the faintest click echoed from beneath the stone, and all eight wheels snapped back to their original position with a grinding sound. A dark hiss followed. A thick cloud of shadow burst from the dragon's nostrils, engulfing them in a freezing shroud.

Xavier coughed and dropped to his knees, eyes watering as searing cold flooded his lungs. Beside him, Ella collapsed to her hands, gasping for air. The cloud pulsed with a sickly green light, and in the edge of his vision, Xavier saw his stamina bar plunging like a falling blade.

The pain vanished as suddenly as it had come, leaving only a heavy weariness behind. His limbs trembled with the effort of staying upright. Ella hunched beside him, her breath ragged and her hair damp with sweat.

Gritting his teeth, Xavier opened his status interface and pulled up the combat log. A pair of new entries scrolled at the top:

You have been struck by necrotic cloud (Death Magic).
You will lose 20 points of stamina per second for the next 10 seconds.

You have been struck by necrotic cloud (Death Magic).
You will temporarily lose 1 point of Constitution for the next 24 hours.

He checked his attributes. His Constitution had dropped from twelve to eleven, marked with an asterisk. His maximum stamina bar had visibly shrunk.

"We cannot make that mistake too many times," Ella

stated. "It nearly knocked me unconscious, and I have a feeling that is the last thing we want down here."

Xavier groaned as he pushed to his feet and offered her a hand. She took it without comment. They returned to the ledge, this time keeping their hands to themselves as they studied the wheels once more.

"We must have had something in the wrong order," Xavier said. "But which part?"

Ella squinted at the symbols. "The riddle felt correct. It matched the imagery."

Xavier crouched and began sketching the line of runes from the inscription in the dust beside the ledge. "Vytha'rin si'alenth," he recited softly. "Life begins as the seed. Or maybe… essence of life as seed of beginning."

He drew a small circle. "That's the seed, no question."

"Solah na'vylah," he continued. "Rises to flourish. That's still the growth stage. Sapling, tree."

He marked those beside the seed. "Then durna ven'valith. Falls to decay. Withered, skeletal." The next two were added. He paused, then glanced over his shoulder at Ella.

"The last line. Yn thar'nok vael ren'talah. It's more complex than just 'from dust is born again.' 'Yn' is and. 'Thar'nok' is from the dust. But 'vael'… I think that means spirit, or maybe essence, and 'ren'talah' is reborn."

He stood slowly, drawing Vaeltheris from its sheath once more. The blade pulsed faintly in his grip, he thought about the name of the blade new insight given with his understanding of Ancient Sylmyrian. "Vaeltheris," he said under his breath. "Essence of harmony. Or soul of balance."

He looked over at Ella. "Is that what your blade's name means?"

For a moment, she said nothing. Then she gave the

smallest nod. "Something like that. I never really looked into it. I was more focused on surviving."

Her voice had changed. It was now softer, distant. It was the first time she had let her guard slip. Xavier filed the moment away. Whatever she was hiding, it was something she wasn't ready to talk about yet. But when they got out of these tunnels... if they got out... they would need to talk. No more secrets. Not if they were going to rely on each other.

Turning back to the ledge, he rested a hand on the wheels again. "So if 'vael' means spirit, and that line talks about spirit being born again... then maybe the order is wrong at the end. Maybe the star is spirit, and it comes after the dust."

He pointed to the final wheels. "Then it should be dust, then star. But then the cycle would demand something after that. Rebirth. That could be the sprouting seed."

Ella leaned forward. "That would mean the first seed represents the beginning and the sprouting seed is the return."

"Then that means we had it wrong before," he said. "We started with the sprouting seed. That belongs at the end."

He reached forward, wiping dust from the symbols and began adjusting the wheels once more, his fingers steady despite the ache in his muscles.

"Seed," he whispered. "Then sapling. Then tree. Then withered tree. Then skeletal. Then ash. Then star. Then... sprouting seed."

He stepped back, motioning Ella to do the same. For a moment, silence held the chamber still. Then came the click.

This time, the wheels sank slightly into the stone and locked in place. A deep hum rose from the floor, vibrating through their boots. The dragon on the wall stirred with light, runes flaring to life along its form. They moved in sequence, beginning at the head and trailing across the body until they met the tail, then circled back again.

The light grew brighter with each pass, the speed of the runes increasing until they raced across the dragon's shape like lightning through storm clouds. It gave the illusion that the dragon was shifting, rising from the wall in a rhythmic pulse of energy.

Xavier shielded his eyes, breath caught in his chest. "Now what?"

Ella gave a shrug, her tone dry. "Touch it?"

He turned to look at her with a withering glare. "That is terrible advice."

She gave an innocent shrug again.

Sighing, he stepped forward and raised his hand. The runes on the dragon's head flared as his palm hovered above them. As they lit once more, he pressed his hand firmly against the stone.

The response was immediate. The runes froze in place, illuminating the entire form of the dragon. A hiss of air escaped from the blank stone wall within the archway. Its surface shimmered, wavered, and vanished, revealing a dark stairwell descending into shadow. A gust of air rushed up from below, dry and ancient. It smelled of dust and stone, but beneath that lingered the faint metallic sweetness of decay.

A voice, deep and disembodied, drifted forth with the wind. "The balance restored. Enter, seekers of eternity."

#

You have updated a quest: Balance Restored
A corruption has violated the essence of the life ley line and its surrounding gardens. You have found a hidden passage. Signs indicate it is the way to the death ley line. Only by restoring balance can the life of Emily be saved.

Beware your actions could tip the scales in one direction or the other instead of creating balance.

Possible Rewards: Possible renewal of the Life Ley Line and the Death Ley Line.

Possible access to Life magic and Death magic. Rescue of Emily. +1000 Experience

Penalties for failure: Permanent loss of Life Ley Line access and/or Death Ley Line Access. Increased corruption in the region. Death of Emily. Catastrophic imbalance in the Syr'Vailen. Quest *Echoes of Innocence* will fail.

This quest has been automatically accepted.

The voice faded into silence, but its echo lingered in the bones of the chamber. The archway stood open now, no longer sealed by stone but by dread. The stairway beyond was shrouded in blackness, and the air that flowed from it chilled more than just the skin. It carried a weight that whispered of endings.

Ella took a tentative step toward the opening, but Valkra held back. The panther cub let out a low, uncertain whine and pressed herself against Xavier's leg, tail curling tight beneath her body.

Xavier crouched and gently scooped her into his arms, brushing her fur back from her ears. "Afraid to go deeper, little one?" he murmured.

He reached into one of his belt pouches and pulled out a strip of dried meat. Valkra snatched it from his fingers, devouring it in two bites. When she looked up at him again, her golden eyes shimmered with something more than animal instinct. There was understanding in her gaze, trust, and resolve.

He lowered her to the stone floor and watched as she padded forward, hesitating only briefly at the edge of the threshold before stepping inside. She glanced back once to be sure he was following.

"All right," he said quietly. "Let's see where this leads."

Ella lit a torch and handed it to him. Its flame flickered as if nervous, casting jagged shadows across the stone.

The stairwell was narrower than the one leading back to the surface, but far more refined. Each step had been precisely carved, fitted with craftsmanship that spoke of care, reverence, and ancient purpose. The walls bore no cracks or wear. The air here was undisturbed, untouched by the collapse and overgrowth that had claimed other parts of the ruins.

As they descended, the light danced along the stone, revealing detailed carvings etched deep into the walls. At first glance they appeared abstract, but closer inspection revealed a flowing progression of symbols and shapes. Blossoming vines interlaced with skeletal hands. Flowers opened in full bloom before curling into decay. Human figures wept beneath withered trees while spirits rose above them on arcs of curling flame and dust.

The further they went, the heavier the air became. It was not just in weight, but in silence. Sound itself seemed to falter. The torch crackled weakly. Their footsteps landed without echo. Even breath seemed muted, as if the very stone absorbed every sound out of respect.

At the base of the stairs, an archway framed their destination.

It opened into a vast crypt, its ceiling arched high and supported by rows of graceful pillars. Every surface gleamed with untouched polish. Marble floors reflected the flickering torchlight like still water, and ornate alcoves lined the walls, each housing a statue of a Sylmyrian guardian.

Each statue bore unique armor, yet shared the same aesthetic, stylized plates etched with flowing symbols, half worn in battle-readiness, half in ceremonial repose. In one hand, each guardian held a blooming flower carved of white stone. In the other, a withered branch blackened with age. The balance was unmistakable.

The silence deepened within the chamber. Xavier could feel it pressing into his ears, not loud but absolute. Then, at the edge of hearing, something shifted. A whisper. A faint breath that did not belong to either of them. Then another. Words, fragmented and unclear, flitted through the gloom like dying embers in wind.

Ella took a step closer to him. "Do you feel that?"

"I do," he said, voice low.

Then the thrum began. It was soft at first, almost indistinguishable from a pulse, a sensation more than a sound. But with each moment it grew stronger, resonating through the stone, then through their bodies. The frequency was familiar. They had heard something like it before, near the Life Ley Line. But this was deeper. Colder. It pulsed with the cadence of endings.

With each beat, the chamber changed.

For an instant, the pristine marble cracked. Veins of blackened stone tore through the floor. The walls buckled with invisible pressure, and the statues shattered into piles of broken limbs and sundered weapons. Alcoves crumbled, spilling dry bones across ruined tiles. The torchlight flickered wildly, then steadied.

The room returned to its perfect state. Then the thrum came again, and again the crypt distorted.

This rhythm continued, as if two realities overlapped, the tomb as it once was, and the hollow ruin it had become.

Xavier stood in stillness, caught between the two images, one full of peace, the other of corruption.

Ella shuddered, folding her arms tightly as if to keep something cold from seeping into her ribs. "This place... it's broken."

Xavier took a cautious step forward. The world pulsed once more and a new prompt slid into view before his eyes.

You have discovered a quest: The Echoes of Eternity
You have found one of the cores of the ley lines that make up the Syr'Vailen. This majestic crypt housed generations of Sylmyrian nobility. Their spirits were held in gentle repose by the power of the Death Ley Line. The sudden awakening of its opposing force, the Life Ley Line, has disrupted the balance and caused corruption to fester.
Possible Rewards: Renewal of the Death Ley Line. Access to Death magic. +1000 Experience

Penalties for failure: Permanent loss of Death Ley Line access. Increased corruption in the region. Death of Emily. Catastrophic imbalance in the Syr'Vailen. Quest *Echoes of Innocence* will fail.

This quest has been automatically accepted.

Xavier exhaled slowly. So that was it. The dual quests now made sense. The other chamber, the garden one where Emily had been tethered, was tied to the Life Ley Line. This, below, was its counterpart. One could not be cleansed without the other. To heal one while ignoring the second would only widen the imbalance.

He looked toward the center of the crypt where the air shimmered faintly, a nexus of deathly stillness and flickering motion. Whatever lay ahead, it was no longer dormant, and the scales of balance were tipping with every breath.

"We need to be careful," he said softly. "If we fail here… we lose everything."

Ella nodded once. Her fingers tightened around the hilt of her blade, and together, they took another step into the shifting dark. The air thickened with every step Xavier took, as though the chamber itself pressed back against his presence. The torches barely held their flame, flickering as if caught between two realms, neither welcome in the world of the living nor the dead.

Behind him, Ella moved with silent focus, her face taut. Valkra stalked at their heels, her small body low and tense, fur bristling faintly along her spine. Even the panther cub, so bold when chasing after phantom scents or strange vines, now moved with solemn awareness. None of them spoke.

They stopped just beyond the first row of guardian statues, their dual symbols of life and death seeming to watch from unmoving eyes. At the center of the room, a platform rose from the floor, ringed by low steps and inlaid with symbols that shimmered with residual energy. A faint light pulsed beneath the platform, deep and sluggish like a heartbeat slowed nearly to stillness.

Xavier turned his gaze upward to the arched ceiling. The carvings continued above them, spirals, skeletal wings, trees woven with curling bones. Everything here had been crafted with reverence, not fear. Death was not depicted as horror or shadow, but as transition both necessary and sacred.

He found himself whispering, almost without thinking. "This place wasn't built to frighten. It was meant to honor."

Ella glanced at him, her expression softening for a moment. "The Sylmyrians did not see death as an ending. Only as part of the return."

He nodded slowly. The weight of realization settled deeper now. Everything they had seen, Emily's imprisonment, the corruption in the garden, the crypt's shuddering illusions, all of it stemmed from imbalance. They had touched the Life Ley Line, even if only briefly. Its energy had surged, and now, with nothing to temper it, it overflowed. The rot, the vines, the dreams, they were not signs of renewal, but of life gone wild without death to counter it.

The corrupted garden was not dying. It was refusing to die. And in doing so, it threatened to consume everything.

Xavier's fingers tightened around the grip of Vaeltheris. "They're connected," he said quietly. "The two ley lines. If we restore one without the other, it'll spiral out of control. The energy will flood through the land and twist it into something worse. Too much life becomes something unnatural. Too much death becomes desolation. We have to do both. Purify both."

Ella tilted her head slightly, watching him. "If we restore life first, without restoring death, the balance tips too far. That much we've seen."

"And if we restore death first," Xavier added, "we risk extinguishing what remains of life. The garden. Emily. Maybe even Rynthavael itself."

She lowered her eyes to the glowing platform. "Then we must restore them together."

He nodded. "Or at least one after the other, quickly. Before the imbalance catches up."

For a moment, neither spoke.

Then Xavier looked around the chamber once more. The statues stood quiet, but he sensed the presence here was no longer passive. It waited, watched, and judged.

"This is bigger than her," he said. "But she's still the heart of it. If we fail… Emily dies. And the corruption spreads." His words hung heavy in the air.

Ella gave a small nod, her voice low. "Then we will not fail."

Valkra gave a quiet growl, the sound more like a vow than a warning.

Xavier took another step forward and felt the platform tremble beneath his boots. The room pulsed in answer. The challenge was set. The balance awaited its reckoning.

CHAPTER SEVENTEEN

The Crypt and the Garden

Xavier stepped forward into the breathless dark, the weight of their vow still hanging in the cold air. The crypt stirred around them, neither living nor dead, as if holding its breath in return. Behind him, Ella followed in silence, her expression carved with quiet resolve. Valkra padded between them, fur bristling along her spine, twin tails twitching in wary arcs.

A second step carried him into the open space beyond the central platform. The silence broke.

Light surged along the walls as sconces erupted to life, their blue flames flickering against stone worn smooth by time. The glow crawled across the chamber, pushing back shadow but not banishing it, illuminating the edges of a place suspended between two states. Pristine lines of ancient artistry clashed with creeping veins of decay, and the walls flickered between the two like a dying dream struggling to remember what it once was.

Xavier crouched low, Vaeltheris held at the ready. The pulse of the place was familiar now, an echo of the garden, but colder, slower, more solemn. Here, life was not overgrown, it was absent. A void of presence.

Ella came to his side, scanning the walls. "It's like the garden," she said softly, "but... reversed. This isn't wild. It's waiting."

"If it didn't keep shifting," Xavier murmured, "it might even feel peaceful."

Valkra nosed cautiously at the floor, then pressed in close to Ella's leg with a quiet whine.

Xavier moved toward one of the statues lining the chamber's outer ring. The figure stood tall and broad-shouldered, though its stance held no aggression, only a quiet, regal strength. Stone fur rippled down the sides of its arms and shoulders, carved in layered tufts that hinted at a thick, shaggy coat built for frigid winds. Horns swept back from its brow, curved and ridged like polished antlers. Its face bore a mix of cervine grace and lupine solemnity, with elongated features and deep-set eyes that watched the chamber with mournful calm.

This was no Duskhari, no Lupari or Aelori. It was decidedly not feline, not lupine or avian. Though close it was not one of the Cervari either, not entirely. He stepped closer and studied the details: hooved feet, muscular hind legs bent slightly in a posture both ready and rooted. The markings etched into the base of the statue's robe-like armor were floral and spiraling, reminiscent of old growth forests and frost-touched leaves.

"Not one of the lines seen in the village," he murmured. "But definitely Animari."

The resemblance aligned most closely with the Thalrani, the Elkkin. A reclusive subrace, seldom seen beyond the cold highlands or ancient boreal woods of the north. Known in scattered lore as lorekeepers and soulbinders, the Thalrani were rumored to speak to trees and spirits with equal fluency. He had only ever read of them, never seen one.

His gaze drifted to the other statues. Each was distinct. A dwarven elder with a smith's hammer. An elven, Shě he corrected himself, priestess mid-chant. A robed human with open palms. A child with large foxlike ears and a scroll cradled in their arms. Every statue here was different in race and bearing. There was no single lineage preserved.

"They weren't just honoring the dead," Xavier said quietly. "They were honoring everyone. All people. This wasn't a tomb for a single bloodline. It was built for a people bound by belief. Odd," he said, stepping between them. "I had thought the Sylmyrians were a race. But this... this looks more like a people. A kingdom. Something broader."

Ella ran her fingers along the base of one of the statues and responded almost offhandedly. "They were. The Sylmyrian Dominion was one of the great empires, several epochs back. There were others, Arathorian Empire, Thanik Empire, the Phoenix Empire, Darnathian League, Ilvani Theocracy." She ticked them off absently on her fingers. Then she hesitated, glancing at him. "At least, that's what I've read. Nothing remains of them now. Just ruins."

Xavier frowned. "But the history book we found in Bramblegate didn't even mention the Sylmyrians. The others, yes. But not them. The only place I've seen anything of them is here. And in the ruins we're building Rynthavael on."

Ella didn't answer his statement directly, instead her voice dropped to a murmur. "Gods, I do not like this place."

"That makes two of us," Xavier said. A soft whine rose at their feet. "Make that three," he added, reaching down to gently run his hand along Valkra's back.

Now that the light filled the room, the true structure became clear. Several archways led outward, but in this phase, only one remained clear of debris. The others were choked with fallen stone, blocked by time and collapse.

Xavier motioned to the open path. "Do we try that way? Climb the rubble into one of the others? Or wait for the next shift and see if something changes?"

Ella eyed the passage, then shook her head. "Too easy. As if it's guiding us. Like bait in a trap." She hesitated. "Maybe we should go back. Help Emily. If we purify the Life Ley Line, maybe it will stabilize this one."

He considered that for a long moment, but a sinking realization settled in his gut. "I don't think that's how it works. Everything here points to balance. Symmetry. I think if we purify one without the other, we're just making things worse."

She winced. "You're probably right. Too much of either, and the system collapses." She turned to him, eyes uncertain. "So... who goes back, and who stays?"

Her reluctance was clear. She hated this crypt. Xavier didn't blame her.

The low thrum sounded again, vibrating through the floor. The chamber shimmered, shifting back into its pristine form. Walls straightened. Arches cleared. The lingering weight of decay lifted slightly, though the stillness remained. A soft blue light replaced the sickly hue, tranquil and almost reverent.

Xavier reached down and lifted Valkra into his arms, then passed the cub to Ella with quiet care. "Take her. Go to the garden. See if you can reach the heart of it. Save Emily."

Ella didn't argue. She only leaned forward and pressed a kiss to his cheek, a brief warmth amid the cold. Then she turned, cradling Valkra close as she climbed the steps and vanished into the corridor beyond.

Xavier's hand lingered at the place her lips had touched.

He drew in a breath, then turned toward the archway now clear before him.

#

Xavier stepped forward into the breathless dark, the weight of their vow still hanging in the cold air. The crypt stirred around them, neither living nor dead, as if holding its breath in return. Behind him, Ella followed in silence, her expression carved with quiet resolve. Valkra padded between them, fur bristling along her spine, twin tails twitching in wary arcs.

A second step carried him into the open space beyond the central platform. The silence broke.

Light surged along the walls as sconces erupted to life, their blue flames flickering against stone worn smooth by time. The glow crawled across the chamber, pushing back shadow but not banishing it, illuminating the edges of a place suspended between two states. Pristine lines of ancient artistry clashed with creeping veins of decay, and the walls flickered between the two like a dying dream struggling to remember what it once was.

Xavier crouched low, Vaeltheris held at the ready. The pulse of the place was familiar now, an echo of the garden, but colder, slower, more solemn. Here, life was not overgrown, it was absent. A void of presence.

Ella came to his side, scanning the walls. "It's like the garden," she said softly, "but... reversed. This isn't wild. It's waiting."

"If it didn't keep shifting," Xavier murmured, "it might even feel peaceful."

Valkra nosed cautiously at the floor, then pressed in close to Ella's leg with a quiet whine.

Xavier moved toward one of the statues lining the chamber's outer ring. The figure stood tall and broad-shouldered, though its stance held no aggression, only a quiet, regal strength. Stone fur rippled down the sides of its arms and shoulders, carved in layered tufts that hinted at a thick, shaggy coat built for frigid winds. Horns swept back from its brow, curved and ridged like polished antlers. Its face bore a mix of cervine grace and lupine solemnity, with elongated features and deep-set eyes that watched the chamber with mournful calm.

This was no Duskhari, no Lupari or Aelori. It was decidedly not feline, not lupine or avian. Though close it was not one of the Cervari either, not entirely. He stepped closer and studied the details: hooved feet, muscular hind legs bent slightly in a posture both ready and rooted. The markings etched into the base of the statue's robe-like armor were floral and spiraling, reminiscent of old growth forests and frost-touched leaves.

"Not one of the lines seen in the village," he murmured. "But definitely Animari."

The resemblance aligned most closely with the Thalrani, the Elkkin. A reclusive subrace, seldom seen beyond the cold highlands or ancient boreal woods of the north. Known in scattered lore as lorekeepers and soulbinders, the Thalrani were rumored to speak to trees and spirits with equal fluency. He had only ever read of them, never seen one.

His gaze drifted to the other statues. Each was distinct. A dwarven elder with a smith's hammer. An elven, Shě he corrected himself, priestess mid-chant. A robed human with open palms. A child with large foxlike ears and a scroll cradled in their arms. Every statue here was different in race and bearing. There was no single lineage preserved.

"They weren't just honoring the dead," Xavier said quietly. "They were honoring everyone. All people. This wasn't a tomb for a single bloodline. It was built for a people bound by belief. Odd," he said, stepping between them. "I had thought the Sylmyrians were a race. But this… this looks more like a people. A kingdom. Something broader."

Ella ran her fingers along the base of one of the statues and responded almost offhandedly. "They were. The Sylmyrian Dominion was one of the great empires, several epochs back. There were others, Arathorian Empire, Thanik Empire, the Phoenix Empire, Darnathian League, Ilvani Theocracy." She ticked them off absently on her fingers. Then she hesitated, glancing at him. "At least, that's what I've read. Nothing remains of them now. Just ruins."

Xavier frowned. "But the history book we found in Bramblegate didn't even mention the Sylmyrians. The others, yes. But not them. The only place I've seen anything of them is here. And in the ruins we're building Rynthavael on."

Ella didn't answer his statement directly, instead her voice dropped to a murmur. "Gods, I do not like this place."

"That makes two of us," Xavier said. A soft whine rose at their feet. "Make that three," he added, reaching down to gently run his hand along Valkra's back.

Now that the light filled the room, the true structure became clear. Several archways led outward, but in this phase, only one remained clear of debris. The others were choked with fallen stone, blocked by time and collapse.

Xavier motioned to the open path. "Do we try that way? Climb the rubble into one of the others? Or wait for the next shift and see if something changes?"

Ella eyed the passage, then shook her head. "Too easy. As if it's guiding us. Like bait in a trap." She hesitated. "Maybe we should go back. Help Emily. If we purify the Life Ley Line, maybe it will stabilize this one."

He considered that for a long moment, but a sinking realization settled in his gut. "I don't think that's how it works. Everything here points to balance. Symmetry. I think if we purify one without the other, we're just making things worse."

She winced. "You're probably right. Too much of either, and the system collapses." She turned to him, eyes uncertain. "So... who goes back, and who stays?"

Her reluctance was clear. She hated this crypt. Xavier didn't blame her.

The low thrum sounded again, vibrating through the floor. The chamber shimmered, shifting back into its pristine form. Walls straightened. Arches cleared. The lingering weight of decay lifted slightly, though the stillness remained. A soft blue light replaced the sickly hue, tranquil and almost reverent.

Xavier reached down and lifted Valkra into his arms, then passed the cub to Ella with quiet care. "Take her. Go to the garden. See if you can reach the heart of it. Save Emily."

Ella didn't argue. She only leaned forward and pressed a kiss to his cheek, a brief warmth amid the cold. Then she turned, cradling Valkra close as she climbed the steps and vanished into the corridor beyond.

Xavier's hand lingered at the place her lips had touched. He drew in a breath, then turned toward the archway now clear before him.

The hallway beyond the arch yawned like a throat into darkness.

Xavier stepped through, and behind him, the sconces guttered out one by one. The chamber he'd left was plunged once more into that gray liminality, its stillness sealing behind him like a held breath. Ahead, the spectral torches along the corridor flickered to life in sequence, casting pale light down a corridor of stone and shadow.

The weight of it was immediate. The passage ahead was long and narrow, with evenly spaced alcoves carved into both walls. Each alcove held a small platform, empty, for now. Xavier's boots rang faintly against the smooth marble as he approached the first one, the air changed.

Without sound or warning, a form coalesced atop the platform: a tall, ghostly human male. The specter stood still and noble, one hand resting atop a forge hammer. His eyes glowed faintly with inner calm as he looked down at Xavier, not judging, merely observing. His mouth moved, and though the words were in Ancient Sylmyrian, the gift of from Danu rendered them clear.

"Sul'mir yn durn'vyr, vael yn kal'dormis."

Death gives rest. Life brings motion. Balance binds them. The meaning settled over Xavier like a shroud.

The unsettling pulse sounded through the hall. The same deep thrum that marked the cycle, pristine to ruin, and back again.

The change was swift. Hairline fractures raced across the walls. The soft white stone cracked, weeping lines of violet light like veins in dead flesh. The platform beneath the ghost crumbled into aged rubble. And the figure itself...

Gone was the serene forge master. In his place stood a rotting horror, the corpse of a man held together by sinew and will. Skin sloughed from his face, one eye drooping, the other black and glowing. He leaned forward, skeletal hand stretching toward Xavier with slow, inevitable hunger.

Xavier staggered back and slashed on instinct. Vaeltheris surged to life, the blade hissing with radiance as it met the outstretched hand. The specter burst apart in a flash of light and shadow, vanishing into smoke.

Xavier caught his breath, his heart pounding, and looked

down the hallway. There were more alcoves. Many more. The thrum passed through the environment again, once more sending it back to pristine. He pressed forward.

Each new alcove awakened as he passed, each offering a vision of the past. A tall dwarven woman in ceremonial robes. A massive bear-like Animari in radiant plate, likely an Ursari. A delicate, waifish girl with silver hair and sharp, intelligent eyes.

Each vision offered a phrase in Ancient Sylmyrian:

"Draen'vir os val'sul, thyrris os yn nol'myrin."

Strength lies in unity, the balance of flame and water.

"Nol'ys varrith, sul'nar eyl'ar'mirael."

At twilight's breath, stone and air find peace.

"Nor'thar sul'nol, vel'ys mir'nar."

In the cycle of dusk and dawn, harmony prevails.

The symbolism of balance, again and again. Every phrase was a variation on the same truth. No single force could stand alone.

Then the thrum came again. The hall twisted, and every vision turned.

The armored bear-knight's chest was torn open, fur matted with gore, armor rusted and black. The robed dwarf's eyes had been hollowed out, her hands now skeletal claws. The child, dear gods, the child, smiled with jagged rows of needle teeth. Her eyes glowed with purple flame, and a long, black tongue flickered out between her lips like a serpent's.

Xavier's stomach turned as they stepped from their platforms.

One after the other, dragging broken limbs and weapons that weren't there. The husks of memory, twisted into mockery. The hall filled with rasping whispers.

"Essence... broken... death claims... silence reigns..."

"Cycle... lost... shadow overcomes..."

"Balance... fractured... all fades..."

Xavier backed away, blade raised, breath catching.

Then the bearkin lunged. He met it head-on, driving Vaeltheris into the creature's chest. The light pulsed, and the spirit shrieked, vanishing in a wave of heatless flame. But not before its massive claws raked across Xavier's side, leaving deep tears in leather and skin.

He spun to face the child next. She was faster than expected. She leapt onto him, needle claws digging into his arm as her teeth sank into the flesh of his hand. The cold that followed was worse than pain, it was hollow, numbing, as if his soul were being siphoned through the bite.

His health plummeted. Lines of corruption traced out from the wounds, black and green.

Gritting his teeth, he flung her off and plunged his blade into her back. She shrieked and vanished, leaving nothing behind but a smear of necrotic rot across the stone.

The dwarf came last. She advanced slowly, robes in tatters, bones creaking with every step. Her fingers clutched at him again and again, and he was forced to hack them away one by one, until at last he drove Vaeltheris into the hollow of her skull.

The hall went still. Xavier staggered, bloodied and breathing hard. His arm throbbed violently, and the corruption had already begun to fester. Pus oozed from the wound, and the lines crawling up his veins pulsed with a sickly hue.

"No... no no no"

He sheathed his blade and fumbled for his belt pouch. Fingers trembling, he found the forest sage, bit down, and chewed. The bitterness bit back at his tongue, but he forced it down, praying it would be enough to hold off the worst of the infection.

The next thrum came. The hall shimmered once more, pristine again. He didn't wait. Gritting his teeth against the pain, Xavier ran.

#

Ella ran and Valkra darted at her side, nimble and swift as a shadow, paws silent against stone. Together they raced down the tunnel that led back to the garden chamber. The twisting corridor, once dim and overgrown, now felt tighter, more tangled. The further they went, the thicker the vines grew, clinging to the walls like veins beneath translucent skin.

But there was no mistaking it now, the taint they had seen before had deepened. The wildness was spreading.

The first time they had entered this space, the overgrowth had seemed defensive, aggressive, but passive, an echo of imbalance. Now it pulsed with purpose. The air was damp and choked with the musk of bloom and rot. A low, constant hum echoed through the roots underfoot, like a heartbeat out of sync.

They reached the overlook, and Ella froze. Where once she had been able to see the pedestal at the chamber's center, she now saw only chaos. Massive trees rose where there had been none. Their branches reached nearly to the cavern ceiling, woven together in thick snarls. Vines hung like drapes, choking the space between trunks. Fungal blooms, bright, luminous, and pulsing, fought with twisted bushes for control of every patch of ground. Pools of water glistened in the distance, their surface a sickly green, bubbling faintly.

The garden had devoured itself.

Ella dropped into a crouch, dragging Valkra with her behind a thicket of roots. Something moved below.

What she had mistaken for a patch of dark shrubs stirred, then padded forward on four legs. The shape was feline, but wrong. Its hide was bark, its eyes like amber set in moss. As it moved, lichen curled from its shoulders, and its tail twitched like a creeping vine.

The garden shifted. A low thrum vibrated the ground beneath her, and in answer, the flora surged. Branches thickened. Vines snapped taut across gaps. Flowers burst open in violent bloom, spraying pollen into the air in hazy clouds. The growth was not natural. It was manic, fevered.

Ella swore under her breath. "No waiting."

She stood and vaulted down the ramp, spear gripped tightly in her hand, as she plunged into the madness below. Every few steps, she was forced to cut her way forward. The vines clawed at her boots. Roots shifted underfoot, trying to trip her. Creatures that had once been passive now lunged and attacked, plant-animals, bark-skinned predators with thorny limbs and leafy hides. Mushrooms burst apart in clouds of choking spores, forcing her to double back, hacking and coughing as her throat closed with irritation.

Valkra stayed close. Once, the cub pounced a creeping vine before it could entangle Ella's leg. Another time, she drove her twin tails into the eye sockets of a lurching plant-beast that had once mimicked a badger.

They fought through the growth together, two lone figures in a living nightmare.

Panting, Ella dragged her spear free from the chest of another enemy, a quadruped twisted from tree roots and moss. It shuddered, collapsed, and finally stilled.

She looked around. No spores hung in the air this time. No scent of acid or decay. Just the heavy silence of temporary reprieve.

Valkra padded over and butted her head into Ella's hand. The woman gave her a tired smile, brushing bark and blood from the cub's fur.

"I take back everything I said about the undead," Ella muttered. "Ghouls would be a welcome change."

Valkra gave a low chuff of agreement.

Ella's spear was growing heavier in her hand. Her arms burned from strain. Her body bore a dozen shallow cuts and one deeper gash down her thigh. The forest sage in her pouch wouldn't last long, and it was already slowing in effectiveness. She pressed on.

They ducked around a sulfurous pool that hissed at the touch of overhanging vines, hugging the trunks of massive trees that formed walls more than pathways. The natural layout of the garden had been replaced with something maze-like, maddening.

Finally, they broke into a clearing. In the center stood the pillar, the heart of the garden and the Life Ley Line core, but Emily was gone.

Ella's heart lurched. She surged forward with a cry of alarm, only to freeze when she heard movement near one of the gnarled trees to the right.

A small shape stirred in the roots. Ella approached slowly. Emily lifted her head from where she sat nestled against the base of the tree. Her eyes glowed softly, their emerald light pulsing in tandem with the ley line beneath the earth. She looked exhausted. Her skin was pale, her limbs trembling.

"You came back for me," Emily said, her voice richer than it should have been, deeper than her size suggested. "I knew you would."

She opened her arms out towards Ella. Ella knelt and

pulled her close.

The tether was still there. Thicker now. The thread of ley energy that had once connected her to the pillar had grown into a vine, roots digging into the earth around the child like a nest.

"I cannot leave," Emily whispered against Ella's shoulder. "If I do, it dies. And so will I."

Her eyes brightened. Her voice deepened. "We need the child. Her life sustains us. The balance is amiss, and it will destroy us."

Ella drew back sharply, still holding Emily, but now at arm's length. "Who are you? What are you doing to her?"

"We are the Life Ley Line. Without us, the land withers. The forest fades. Death takes hold. We do not wish harm... but we must live."

Tears welled in Ella's eyes.

Emily, sweet, young Emily, had become the fuel for something ancient. A sacrifice to a system she never agreed to, but Ella couldn't accept that. She wouldn't accept that.

"There has to be another way," she said, voice trembling. "Tell me what to do. Please."

Silence followed. Then came the thrum.

The growth surged once more, and Emily shuddered in her arms. Light flared through her body, and for a moment, she didn't look like a child at all.

"There is... one way," she whispered. "Balance must be restored. Death was once sustained by sacrifice. So must life be. But there is still a seed. A dying tree holds it. Deep in the maze. Find it. Plant it here. It will restore the ley line and release me."

Her voice faded again. The light within her dimmed.

"I'm so sleepy." The little girl murmured.

"I'll be back soon," Ella whispered. She cupped Emily's cheek and gently set her down near the roots of the tree. The child curled up like a fading blossom, breath soft and slow.

Valkra lay down beside her, protective, silent. Ella rose, turned, and vanished once more into the heart of the wild.

#

Xavier – The Reflecting Pool and the Obelisk Chamber

Xavier burst through the archway, breath catching as the haunting cries from the corridor behind faded into silence. The hallway of horrors was behind him, but the weight of it clung like shadowed residue.

The new chamber opened into a wide circle, its perimeter marked by carved stone pillars and aged sconces. One by one, those sconces ignited with pale blue flame, casting a soft, cold glow across the walls. The illumination danced across worn carvings and moss-fringed stone.

At the far end, across a shallow, perfectly still pool of water, stood two more archways. Neither was sealed. Neither blocked. For the first time in what felt like hours, Xavier exhaled.

He crouched at the edge of the water. The surface rippled faintly in response to his proximity, yet his reflection failed to form. Only the chamber's ceiling shimmered faintly across the mirrored surface. The water was clean but void, still and unnatural.

He pulled back his sleeve and examined his arm. The wounds from the spiritual assault had not closed. The bite, swollen and discolored, now oozed with slow, pulsing lines of black-green corruption. His fingertips trembled faintly. The lines had stopped spreading quickly, but they had not stopped entirely. The corruption clung to his flesh like a second, rotting skin.

He flexed his fingers and hissed through his teeth. There wasn't time to delay. He would need to finish the trials, claim whatever lay at their end, and return to the surface. Hopefully the healers in Rynthavael could cleanse the taint before it claimed the entire arm, or worse.

He gazed into the water, seeking calm. But as he watched, the surface shimmered, then changed. His own reflection stared back, yet it was no longer his. The face in the pool was emaciated, rotted. The jaw hung askew, attached by a single joint. Hollow eyes, clouded with death, locked with his own.

He recoiled, scrambling back from the edge. His heart pounded as his hands flew to his face and arms, frantically checking for signs of decay. His skin was warm. His flesh intact. But his mind struggled to reconcile the truth his body confirmed against the vision he had seen.

"Fuck, I hate this place," he growled, voice breaking from the strain.

The light shifted again to that eerie purple glow. Shadows danced along the walls, morphing into ghastly shapes with every flicker. Each movement made him flinch.

Rising to his feet, Xavier skirted around the pool, deliberately avoiding another glance at the water. He reached the archway at the far end and ducked through, glad to leave the cursed chamber behind.

The hallway gave way to another chamber, larger and colder. The sconces here burned with violet light, illuminating a central obelisk composed of bone. The walls were covered with intricate geometric arrangements of skeletal remains, woven together like a macabre mosaic. Runes etched into the bones glowed faintly, casting long, splintered shadows. On the far side of the room, a pair of sealed stone doors waited beneath another arch.

Xavier moved cautiously along the wall, giving the obelisk a wide berth. His eyes scanned for traps or wards, but no threats leapt out. When he reached the doors, he pressed against them. They didn't budge. Bracing himself, he pushed harder. Still, they refused to open. He sighed and turned back to the obelisk.

It stood at the center of a series of concentric rings. Each ring held a series of rune tiles, jagged or smooth, clearly representing different domains.

The outer ring was marked with harsh, angular runes: Thar'nok, Ven'vaalith, Syr'noloth, Durnan, Erlath, Vorin, Sul'varis, Ilyn'coris... Void, Decay, Shadow, Wither, Rest, Corruption, Dust, and Drain.

The inner ring displayed smooth, flowing glyphs: Si'alenth, Solah, Illuvah, Vythalir, Na'vylah, Arin'var, Ren'talah, Nalu'varis... Seed, Growth, Light, Vitality, Flourish, Spark, Renewal, and Purity.

He crouched between the rings and tested them. The tiles shifted easily under his hands, each rune sliding from its ring into the blank middle section between them. It became clear he could match pairs, concepts from life and death.

At the base of the obelisk, an inscription read: "Vytha yn thar'nok, vael yn ren'talah, solah yn valithar."

Xavier translated softly. "Life to dust, spirit to renewal, growth to decay." A slow smile touched his lips.

He moved swiftly, slipping runes from each ring into paired notches between them... Seed and Void, Growth and Decay, Light and Shadow. When the central ring was complete, he stepped back, proud. Nothing happened. He scowled, turned to the doors, and tested them again. Still sealed.

Over the next several minutes, he tried new

combinations. Adjusting, swapping, reordering. None brought results. Then the chamber thrummed.

Everything shifted. The rings cracked. The obelisk aged before his eyes. The bone murals on the walls, once faded and brittle, now reformed. Flowers bloomed and decayed in one mural. A river teemed with life then dried to dust in another. Light touched a meadow that fell into shadow. The puzzle was frozen.

He tried to move the tiles again, but they no longer budged. Time, rot, and age had locked them into place. Defeated for now, Xavier stepped back, running a hand through his hair. The doors remained closed. With a final glance at the ruined murals, he turned and made his way back to the reflecting pool, intent on exploring the remaining passage.

Ella – The Maze Deepens

Ella's path through the overgrown maze had grown no easier. The forest pulsed with each thrum, and the vines grew thicker. What had begun as small plant creatures the size of Valkra were now the size of tigers, their claws like daggers, their speed terrifying.

Blood dripped from cuts along her arms and legs, and though the forest sage numbed the pain, it could not keep up with the damage.

She circled a massive beast, its body dense with bark and moss. Its eyes glowed green with twisted vitality. Her spear had barely dented it. It rose onto its hind legs. She charged.

The spear drove into its gaping maw, the one place unarmored. The creature froze, then collapsed. Ella fell with it, gasping, sweat soaking her tunic.

Her arms trembled as she retrieved the spear. She thought of Xavier.

She prayed she would reach the seed in time. She had

faced danger before, nearly died more times than she could count, but this was more than a fight. It was a race against the end.

Gritting her teeth, she stood and pressed on. She rounded a corner and screamed. The ground vanished beneath her.

She slid down a hidden slope, bouncing off roots and stones. Her world spun until she tumbled into a crumpled heap at the bottom.

Pain exploded through her body. Her shoulder dangled at an odd angle.

She moaned, dragging herself upright. Her spear lay nearby, intact, somehow. Her fingers closed around it as she pulled herself toward a small sapling.

Closing her eyes a moment at what she knew needed to be done she braced her dislocated shoulder in the crook of the Y-shaped trunk, she took a breath, then jerked.

A blinding flare of agony dropped her to the ground. Her body went still as darkness claimed her.

#

Xavier skirted the pool again, unwilling to face the image of his rotting reflection for a second time. His mind still recoiled from what the water had shown him. Ducking through the final archway, he hastened down its short tunnel, determined to uncover what other horrors this crypt held.

The tunnel opened into another circular chamber, just as the thrum pulsed again. The ruins shimmered back into pristine condition before his eyes. This room, however, was different. At its center stood a short pillar, and atop it hovered an orb of pure, shifting energy. Xavier stared, transfixed, as black, green, gold, and purple hues twisted and writhed across its surface. Within the orb, something small floated, an object that pulsed evenly with all four colors. It was suspended, unreachable.

Tearing his gaze away from the orb, he examined the chamber more closely. In each of the four corners stood smaller pillars. Above each one, a shaft of light descended from the ceiling, but the beams flickered and faded, their energy unstable.

He stepped into the room. Behind him, the archway slammed shut with a sudden crash, a stone shutter dropping from the ceiling to seal the passage. The floor rumbled. Stone grated. From the ground, more columns rose, eight of them in total, each topped with angled, polished reflective surfaces.

Xavier's stomach sank. The setup reminded him of light puzzles from the MMOs he used to play. He had to redirect the beams, figure out which light belonged to which pillar and at what intensity. But there were no markings, no glyphs, no helpful clues.

Approaching one of the new reflective columns, he touched it lightly, half-expecting a trap. It moved under his fingers, rotating in a fixed arc and adjusting its angle to redirect light.

He turned it toward the golden beam and aimed it at one of the pillars. A flash of blinding light erupted.

Heat blasted across the chamber. Xavier dropped to his knees, covering his face. His skin prickled and blistered. Gritting his teeth, he shoved the column away, knocking it from alignment. The light died instantly.

Panting, he pulled back his sleeves and winced. His arms were burned. He had only a bit of forest sage left and didn't dare use it yet.

He eyed the remaining colors warily. A mistake with any of them could be worse. He looked again to the orb at the center. Reaching for it directly would be idiotic.

As he studied the chamber, the thrum returned. The beams flickered out. The reflective columns crumbled into dust. The corner pillars cracked and fractured, spilling heavy chunks of stone to the floor. Only the orb remained untouched, floating in its eerie stillness.

Xavier shook his head. "Of course it wouldn't be that easy. Damn magic and traps. Why is everything so hard?" After hearing his words aloud, he reassured himself that it was only slightly whiney.

He moved to inspect the broken pillars. The first was a smooth column of black stone, split near the top. He tapped it with the tip of Vaeltheris, wary of triggering a harmful reaction. Nothing happened. He touched it with his hand. Just cold, inert stone.

The second pillar was also black, but delicate golden veins ran through its core. He grinned. Rushing to the third, he found strands of deep purple. The fourth shimmered with faint green threads like emerald fibers.

That was the key. Each light must correspond to a pillar with matching coloration. He waited for the next thrum.

When the room restored again, Xavier sprang into action. He moved the reflective posts into place, redirecting each colored light toward its matching pillar. As each beam struck home, the orb grew brighter.

But then, the light within the orb surged. A wave of cold pulsed outward. The reflective columns were thrown askew. Xavier dropped to his knees as exhaustion washed over him. His stamina bottomed out, leaving him gasping.

At least his constitution held. After a short rest, the familiar green bar in his vision began to refill.

"Ok," he muttered, "got part of it right. Now I have to factor in the orb's fluctuations."

He searched for something he had missed. He returned to one of the original corner pillars and touched it carefully. This one felt different, rougher now. It turned under his hand, becoming porous like volcanic rock. Holes of varying size dotted its surface.

He twisted it experimentally, finding that he could widen or narrow the holes. He crouched, eyes narrowed, studying the orb again. The dark energy seemed dominant, but only the third most frequent overall. He watched the colors twist and braid around each other, noting their strength and order. Then the thrum came again. The room reset.

The pillar beside him cracked once more. He remained focused on the orb, and saw it change. The dark energy now surged as the most dominant, overtaking the others. His carefully calculated plan collapsed.

"Of course," he growled.

Frustrated, he kicked the nearest broken column. Pain shot through his toes and he cursed, hopping on one foot before plopping down hard. He sighed. This would take time, but he was not giving up. Not that he could go anywhere with the archway closed. Ella still needed to reach the other side, Emily still waited for salvation, and the balance between life and death demanded to be restored.

#

Ella slowly stirred, consciousness returning in waves of throbbing pain. Her shoulder screamed with lingering agony, though it had lessened from the blinding torment of dislocation. Gritting her teeth, she carefully eased herself free from the twisted limbs of the tree that had caught her fall. Every subtle motion reignited fiery bursts of discomfort, but at least her shoulder was back in place... functional, if barely.

She stood gingerly, testing her arm's movement. The

shoulder protested sharply yet held firm. Retrieving her spear from where it had fallen, she cast cautious eyes over the surrounding brush. The heavy silence reassured her that nothing had found her unconscious and vulnerable, but the thought was little comfort against the trials ahead.

Her gaze drifted upwards, tracing the steep, treacherous slope she had tumbled down earlier. The incline was daunting, a future concern she quickly pushed aside. For now, her path lay forward, deeper into the thickening maze.

Taking a steadying breath, she pressed into the dense wall of vegetation. Each thrust of her spear through tangled branches and clawing vines drew fresh sparks of pain, but determination propelled her onward. Sweat soon soaked her brow, her breathing labored from the strain and agony alike.

Gradually, the vegetation thinned. With a final, defiant shove, she stumbled into a clearing dominated by a massive, corrupted tree. Ella halted abruptly, breath catching sharply in her chest. The sight was harrowing, an image of decay personified. Once golden bark now lay cracked, charred, and blackened, marred by deep wounds leaking thick, viscous sap. The foul substance oozed slowly from the gashes, glistening ominously in the dim, sickly light.

The air was oppressive, thick with the pungent scent of rot and festering vegetation, mingling nauseatingly with the acrid stench of the sap. The grove itself was littered with the desiccated husks of fallen branches, brittle leaves crunching underfoot, whispering forgotten memories of vibrancy lost. Twisted roots clawed desperately at the barren earth, resembling skeletal fingers grasping at fading life.

As she stepped forward cautiously, Ella sensed a faint pulse emanating from the heart of the corrupted tree, a rhythmic heartbeat, a fragile echo of ancient magic buried beneath layers of corruption. The pulse called to her, drawing her attention to a deep fissure in the tree's trunk. Nestled within its dark depths was a softly glowing seed, delicate veins of radiant gold and emerald pulsing faintly along its surface.

Ella took another tentative step closer, drawn toward the seed by an instinctive pull. The moment her foot touched the ground, a subtle yet profound fragrance wafted toward her. It was a curious blend of spring blossoms, fresh summer rain, and fertile earth. It contrasted sharply with the oppressive rot, heightening the surreal duality of life and decay within the grove.

Another step closer, and the tree suddenly shuddered awake. Limbs groaned and cracked violently, ancient wood splintering loudly as massive branches swung with brutal speed toward her. Reacting on pure instinct, Ella leapt backward, barely avoiding being crushed as the heavy limb slammed into the earth, scattering splinters and debris.

She quickly understood the horrific truth, the tree, corrupted by the ley energies, had gained a primitive yet vicious sentience. It knew the seed both sustained and doomed it, and it would defend its precious heart to the death.

Ella ducked and rolled, narrowly dodging another devastating strike. Her spear proved futile against such strength, and she abandoned it without hesitation. Agilely weaving through the barrage of swinging limbs and erupting roots, she sought an opening, her mind racing for a strategy amidst chaos.

A smaller branch whipped downward, embedding deeply into the ground beside her. Without pause, Ella seized it and hauled herself upward. The limb immediately thrashed violently, attempting to shake her free. Bark tore her hands raw, branches and twigs clawed at her face and shoulders, reopening wounds and sending fresh torrents of agony through her body. Her dislocated shoulder screamed mercilessly, pain threatening to wrench her consciousness away once more. Yet, through sheer, stubborn determination, she clung tightly and ascended.

Near the trunk, the air grew thick with the choking scent of corruption, and the sap oozed dangerously. Hesitating only briefly, Ella thrust her hand deep into the fissure. The corrosive sap immediately engulfed her skin, burning fiercely and clinging stubbornly. Tears blurred her vision as she forced her hand deeper still, fingertips desperately probing through layers of foul, molten darkness.

Finally, her fingers brushed against something warm, pulsing with life, pure amidst corruption. Clenching her teeth, she closed her grip around the seed and yanked it free with a fierce cry of triumph and agony.

The reaction was immediate and violent. The tree let out a terrible, mournful scream, shuddering and convulsing as if its very soul had been torn away. Limbs cracked and splintered, thrashing wildly before collapsing limp and lifeless. The great trunk itself fractured with a deafening groan, splitting apart as the essence sustaining its corrupted form was stripped away.

Ella, still clutching the softly glowing seed, slid down the ruined trunk, landing roughly among the debris below. Her entire body trembled with exertion, pain, and overwhelming relief. For a moment, she lay there, panting, the seed's gentle pulse reassuring against her chest.

With supreme effort, she gathered herself, reclaimed her spear, and rose shakily. Limping heavily, battered and bloodied yet fiercely resolute, she turned her back to the fallen guardian of decay and hurried toward where Emily waited, though weakening with every passing moment.

In her hands, the seed continued to pulse softly, a beacon of hope amidst ruin, promising renewal if she could reach Emily in time.

#

In the crypt, Xavier stood, almost patiently, waiting for the next thrum of sound to bring change to the room he occupied once again. When it finally came, he moved with urgency, aware of how much time had already passed—even if he had no real way of tracking it.

The orb still hovered at the chamber's center, spinning slowly, its glow pulsing with rhythmic intent. The four colors, gold, green, purple, and black, flowed in a complex dance across the surface, casting strange shadows across the floor. He studied it for several long moments until he spotted the pattern of coverage.

Dashing between the columns, he twisted each in turn to adjust their openings. The golden one he left widest, to match the majority of the sphere's coverage. That was followed by the dark purple column, then the emerald, and finally the plain black stone. Once satisfied with the alignment, he turned to the risen reflective columns.

The beams of light had reappeared, more stable now but still needing precise control. Xavier moved deftly, twisting the mirrors to direct each radiant shaft toward its respective pillar. The room began to brighten with each alignment, the glowing energy cascading in brilliant arcs across the floor and walls. As the last beam struck the open golden column, the chamber bloomed with light.

However, it was no longer the scorching blaze that had punished his earlier mistakes. This time the light was warm, comforting, like sunlight through high clouds. He shut his eyes, not in pain, but in awe.

Moments later, the grinding of stone echoed around him. The sealing slab at the far end of the room began to retreat, revealing the passage back to the reflecting pool. Further mechanical sounds echoed in the distance.

He opened his eyes and looked toward the central pillar. The swirling orb of energy was gone. In its place stood a small pedestal, atop which rested an ornate miniature version of the ouroboros symbol he had first seen at the crypt's entrance.

Reverently, Xavier stepped forward and lifted the item from its stand.

You have discovered: Sigil of Balance	**Item Class:** Epic **Item Quality:** Mastercraft **Weight:** 0.25 kg **Durability:** 500/500 **Traits:** This wrought sigil depicts the ancient understanding of the balance between life and death, darkness and light, and the rest of the elements.

The sigil felt alive in his hand. Its surface twisted and shimmered subtly, never releasing its own tail, locked eternally in its infinite loop. It pulsed faintly, as if acknowledging its new bearer.

With no other path forward, Xavier slipped it into his belt pouch and exited the trial chamber, emerging once more into the reflecting pool room. As he passed the water's edge, he noticed his reflection was whole again, unmarked, unscarred.

A small light now shone from the hallway he had left earlier, the one with the strange mechanism he had previously abandoned. Curiosity rising, he followed it.

The room beyond had changed. Though the twin doors remained closed, the runes etched into the floor now glowed softly, like embers beneath glass. The obelisk mechanism had returned to its original configuration. The noise he had heard earlier had been the room resetting.

He moved with purpose now, stepping to the obelisk and adjusting the rotating rings. He aligned the runes carefully, sliding each pair into place until they clicked home and locked.

Only one pairing remained. Ren'talah and Sul'varis... Renewal and Rest.

He hesitated, then closed his eyes and whispered a quiet prayer to Danu. He slid the final runes into the center ring. A breathless pause.

Then a voice, soft and clear, filled the chamber. "Yn valithar si'vytha. Yn ren'talah si'vael."

Xavier exhaled slowly, translating the words in his mind: In harmony, life flows. In renewal, spirit rises.

Stone ground against stone, and the great twin doors parted slowly inward. A deep violet light spilled from the chamber beyond, and he stepped forward into the heart of the crypt.

The chamber was massive, dwarfing all others he had entered. At its center stood a monolithic black pillar laced with veins of glowing purple, all converging at a brilliant gem set at its apex.

Xavier knew instantly, this was the Death ley line core but reaching it would not be easy.

Swaths of the floor were bathed in the same necrotic light that had nearly drained him before. He could see no safe path between the patches. Even stepping near them caused the hairs on his arms to rise. Frustration built in his chest. So close. So damn close.

He scanned the edges for a route, then looked again at the pillar. Faint etchings of the ouroboros caught his eye. He drew the sigil from his pouch.

"Worth a try," he muttered.

Stretching his arm forward, he extended the sigil into the nearest field of draining light. It shimmered, then vanished, as light receded.

Xavier gave a startled laugh and strode forward, using the sigil to clear a path directly to the core. As he reached the pillar, the chamber flared with full illumination. That was when he saw it, a stone throne at the far end of the room.

Seated upon it, perfectly preserved, was the corpse of a robed elder. Xavier passed the core and approached, reverent. The figure's hands rested on the arms of the throne, head bowed slightly, as if asleep. This was no ordinary corpse. This crypt had been built for him.

Xavier knelt in respect. Then he turned, moved back to the pillar and placed his hand on the ley core. The world vanished.

He stood in a chamber similar to the crypt housing the ley line core as before, but changed. The throne beyond was occupied not by a corpse, but by a living man, eyes glowing with violet light.

"By what right do you defile the sanctity of this crypt?" the figure thundered.

"I... I come to awaken this ley line and restore its power to the Syr'Vailen," Xavier replied, struggling to speak.

The being rose from its throne slowly and paced toward the entrapped man. Xavier found he could not lift his hand from the gem and panic began to rise within him. The being walked slowly around Xavier studying him with those glowing eyes before stopping in front of where Xavier stood trapped. "You bear the aura of Aelriva and the mark of the Ard'Maelor. I am Kintral Amerit, the first Ard'Maelor of the Sylmyrian Dominion."

Xavier's breath caught.

"It has been millennia since I last beheld that mark on a new individual. Do you have the power to awaken the core young lord? It has faded to near extinction, and I can feel its corruption even through this tenuous bond with you." The corpse not corpse continued

Xavier hesitated.

Xavier didn't respond immediately. The question felt stilted to him as if his answer would set things into motion that could twist the outcome beyond his ability to control if even survive. He thought back to everything he had seen and been through in the crypt, every lesson pointing to balance. Lifting his eyes to the radiant purple orbs of Kintral he spoke softly. "I do not. But there must be a balance struck to stabilize it. Can you guide me towards what must be done?"

Kintral smiled genuinely at Xavier's words and nodded. "Death requires death to energize it just as life requires life. The two cores must be balanced when they are revitalized, or one will overwhelm the other. I sense another returning to the life core, carrying the essence of life though weak to try and restore it. What would you sacrifice to this core in balance?"

Kintral's gaze was all Xavier could see. He couldn't turn away from the being now and felt trapped like a fly in amber. His mind raced as he struggled to find anything, think of anything that could be offered. Then he knew, but before he could speak Kintral did.

"Are you sure young lord? Your predecessors in the past would come here to speak with the dead and learn from their wisdom. The dead know many things, see many things, and hear many things. You could learn much and grow rapidly if you followed their path."

Xavier swallowed hard, he could feel the power and

knowledge radiating from the being before him and oh how he wanted to tap into that font, but he nodded slowly. "I am sure, it is the only safe way to restore the core."

Kintral bowed his head approvingly to the young lord as Xavier's hand came free of the gem. The vision ended.

Xavier stood once more in the crypt. The core blazed bright with purple light. A beam surged from it to the throne, engulfing the corpse of Kintral in radiance. Moments later, it crumbled to dust.

The light dimmed to a steady glow. The rest of the crypt lit up as all the sconces flared back into life at once filling the halls with the gentle blue glow. Xavier knew, however, what was lost.

Xavier placed the sigil into a notch atop the pillar. It locked in place, the shape of the ouroboros aglow with soft purple light.

Balance had begun.

He turned and walked toward the exit. The halls were silent now. The dead were gone.

You have completed a quest: Echoes of Eternity

Weakened and corrupted the core of the Ley Line of Death required sacrifice to restore its vitality. You were given a choice though unknowing of the consequences you sacrificed knowledge and power, the wisdom of the dead who had long advised your predecessors to the needs of the core choosing to forge ahead unguided as opposed to risking your own final death. Kintral seemed to approve of this choice before he vanished, a final guidance to a new lord. What will this choice do for your fledgling settlement, what was lost in this sacrifice? Only time will tell young lord.

Rewards: Purification of the Death Ley Line. Access to

Death Magic. +1000 Experience. A final piece of wisdom
from the past.
Choices have consequences… even those whose weight
you may never know.

#

#

At the same time Xavier worked through cryptic trials,
Ella ran with fierce determination through the winding
paths of the maze. The seed pulsed faintly in her grasp, its
light dim but steady. Her other hand still burned, the acidic
sap of the corrupted tree clinging to her skin like poison.

She did not stop to bandage it. Every second mattered.

A thick vine dangled over the slope she had fallen down.
She slung her spear and bow into place, then wrapped her
uninjured hand around the vine and began to climb. The
earth was soft beneath her feet, the slope slick with rot
and moss. She moved carefully, pausing to wedge her boot
between jutting stones or brace herself against the trunk of a
dead tree. Each pull burned her muscles. Each shift of weight
strained her limbs.

When she finally rolled over the top of the slope, she
collapsed onto her back, gasping. Her heart thundered in her
ears. She remained there only long enough to breathe. Then
she stood and she ran.

The way back through the maze was not easy, but she had
marked it well in her memory. No wrong turns. No wasted
steps. She avoided the pitfalls and dead ends that had cost her
time before, navigating the twisted grove with a grace born
of necessity.

When she reached the clearing where the Life Ley Line
core pulsed faintly, she slowed.

Valkra lifted her head immediately, bounding forward

to greet Ella with a soft chuff. Emily stirred, her emerald-glowing eyes opening as Ella approached.

Kneeling, Ella opened her damaged hand to reveal the seed. Its glow had strengthened.

Emily smiled, but the resonance returned to her voice. "The seed must be planted and nurtured for it to feed us. We did not know how weak it had become. The corruption was far greater than we suspected." The voice softened. "The child will not survive the transition. The seed will need her vitality to renew the core of life."

"No." Ella's breath hitched. "No, there is another way. I am certain of it."

She cupped Emily's cheek, leaning her forehead against the girl's. "We promised we would bring you home. Xavier and I both did. I will not let that promise be broken."

Rising, she walked to the pillar that cradled the Ley Line core. She knelt beside it, digging into the soft soil with her fingers. Her hands were shaking. She ignored the pain.

The hole was small but deep enough. She placed the seed inside, covering it gently.

A screen appeared before her. She barely read it before she looked back to Emily and smiled.

Then she made her choice as she accepted the prompt before her. The screen vanished from her view and Ella collapsed across the turned earth, unmoving.

On the other side of the first level of the deeps, unseen in its sheath as Xavier was lost to his vision with Kintral, Vaeltheris surged in radiance briefly then faded, diminished from what it once was.

> **You have completed a quest:** The Seed of Renewal
>
> Weakened and corrupted the core of the Ley Line of Life

required sacrifice to restore its vitality. As you were given a choice so was your companion, Ella Bree. Her choice freed the child Emily from her fate but at what cost? Return to the Life Ley Line core to retrieve Emily and Ella Bree so you may complete Echoes of Innocence and Balance Restored

Rewards: Purification of the Life Ley Line. Rescue of Emily. Access to Life Magic. +1000 Experience. Insight into the unknown.

Xavier reviewed the new prompt that had appeared while he was otherwise engaged. He scowled deeper and quickened his pace. Balance begins to return. But at what cost?

#

CHAPTER EIGHTEEN

The Syr'Vailen Awakens and History Lessons

As Xavier moved through the restored halls of the crypt, he noticed a shift—an absence more than a presence. The low, ever-present hum he had grown accustomed to had softened, its rhythm evening into something serene. The dissonant thrum that once warped the air and seemed to gnaw at the edges of his awareness was gone. He furrowed his brow, instinct already stirring before his thoughts fully caught up.

Then, his interface flickered. A new icon appeared in the upper left corner of his vision, just beneath the familiar trio of health, stamina, and mana bars. It was a miniature portrait of Ella, her image grayed and streaked through with a stark white X. Worse still, her health bar showed only a sliver of red. He felt his stomach twist.

She had never been so hurt before. The system had likely hidden her data until now, but something in her condition had changed that. The interface wasn't subtle when it came to warning of danger.

Xavier sprinted forward, his boots thudding against the smooth stone with increasing urgency. The crypt's pristine condition allowed him to move unhindered, a stark contrast to the treacherous terrain it had once been. Two steps at a time, he took the staircase to the central chamber, lungs burning but resolve ironclad.

He would not lose her. Not now. Not after everything they had survived together. The time since his arrival was hard to track, blurred between days and weeks, but the thought was gone in a heartbeat. There was no room for distraction now. Ella needed him.

Vaeltheris burned in his hand with anxious heat as he surged through the passage toward the garden. He barely registered the change in flora. The wild overgrowth that once clawed at everything had receded, replaced by a tranquil display of nature shaped with intention. Faintly glowing moss and flowering vines adorned the walls like quiet sentinels.

Bursting onto the overlook, Xavier came to an abrupt halt. The cavern had transformed.

Gone was the chaotic jungle of thorns and decay. In its place stood a radiant expanse of manicured paths, cultivated hedges, and carved stone pavilions. Walkways traced elegant patterns through blooming flowerbeds and arching willows. The ley line pillar still rose at the center, its gem now glowing with a deep emerald radiance.

At the base of a vast tree near the core, nestled among its massive roots, he saw them. A child curled protectively over a motionless woman's body. A shadowmane cub paced beside them, head low and movements wary. Xavier's breath caught in his throat.

There were no threats in sight, no twisted vines or corrupted creatures. Without hesitation, he sprinted down the slope, boots flying across the immaculate paths.

Valkra whirled, her hackles raised, a low growl vibrating in her chest. Her golden eyes locked onto him, and for a heartbeat she crouched, ready to pounce. Then recognition sparked. With a low chuff and flick of her tails, she turned and bounded back toward Ella and Emily.

Xavier dropped to his knees beside them, pain flaring as stones beneath the grass tore at his skin. He ignored it. His eyes swept over the trio.

Emily was conscious. Tear-streaked and trembling, but unhurt. His attention immediately shifted to Ella.

Her body was limp, her skin pale as marble. Faint cuts and bruises marred her arms and face, but nothing severe enough to explain her condition. Her health bar told the truth. She was barely clinging to life.

Emily looked up, her eyes shimmering with an eerie green glow, faint but unmistakable. "She saved me," she whispered through her tears. "The ley line needed life. It spoke of a seed. She gave it what it asked for, and when she did, it let me go." The girl's voice broke. She collapsed across Ella's body, sobbing harder.

Xavier gently wrapped his arms around the child and lifted her aside with care. He laid her next to Valkra, who pressed her side comfortingly against the girl's shoulder. With the way cleared, he leaned over Ella, studying her more closely.

Her breath came in the barest flickers, like mist fading on morning glass. He lowered his cheek to her lips, waiting. There, a whisper of warmth, a thread of breath.

Relief struck him like a hammer. She was alive. Barely, but alive.

Almost laughing in relief, he gently lifted the woman into a princess carry and rose to his feet. No one noticed as her arm fell between his arm and body allowing her hand to briefly touch the hilt of Vaeltheris, nor the brief pulse of light from the blade when it happened.

Ella stirred. A quiet moan escaped her lips. Her eyelids fluttered, and her gaze, dazed and unfocused, drifted upward until it found his face. "X... Xavier?" she murmured, voice raw and brittle.

"I'm here," he said, tightening his grip to steady her. "Let's get you back up top. Someone up there might be able to help." His voice softened. "You're the closest friend I've got in this world. I'm not about to lose you now. We have too much ahead, and I still need you."

Her lips curved into a faint smile before she leaned her head against his chest, eyes drifting closed once more. "It worked... didn't it? The seed... the core said it needed more life. It would have taken Emily."

"Hush," he said gently, brushing hair from her brow. "She's safe. Both of you are. Just rest."

Emily's tears quieted at the sound of Ella's voice. She reached out with one small hand, curling her fingers around Ella's. Ella cracked her eyes open again, her smile tinged with weariness but no less real. She seemed relieved to see the glow in Emily's eyes had dimmed, though a faint trace still lingered.

Xavier got the group moving as he carried Ella back towards the incline, moving slowly to avoid jostling her. With careful steps, he began the walk back toward the incline.

The garden passed around him like a dream. No longer wild and dangerous, it radiated calm and harmony. Paths lined with flowering trees crisscrossed between sculpted lawns and shallow brooks. Bridges arched over streams that glittered with faint ley energy. The ley core shimmered behind him, pulsing in time with the breath of the chamber.

A strange serenity settled over him as he walked. Though exhaustion tugged at his limbs and fear still gnawed at his thoughts, something deeper took root... hope. They had saved Emily. The core had accepted Ella's sacrifice. Whatever power rested in this place had begun to awaken.

He knew they would return. There was more to uncover in the Deeps. This was only the beginning.

#

The climb out of the Deeps took time. Xavier moved slowly and deliberately, cradling Ella's unconscious form in his arms with the care one might offer a wounded bird. Her breathing had stabilized, but the sliver of red in her health bar remained, a grim reminder of how close she still hovered to death.

Emily walked quietly beside him, one small hand resting on Valkra's shoulder for balance. The shadowmane cub matched her pace with gentle grace, her golden eyes ever flicking between the girl and the path ahead. The eerie stillness of the garden had followed them, its serenity clinging to them like the scent of blooming jasmine that still lingered faintly in the air.

When they stepped through the archway into the mosaic chamber, the shift in atmosphere was immediate. The stone walls here were warmer than below, but felt almost expectant, as though the chamber itself had been waiting for their return.

Sylvie was the first to spot them. The halfling woman froze as her eyes found Emily. For a heartbeat, nothing moved.

Then Sylvie let out a cry of joy, the sound raw and unfiltered. She dashed across the floor and scooped the girl into her arms, clinging to her as though afraid she might vanish again.

"Thank you, Lord Vael," she sobbed. "You brought her back. She's like a daughter to me. I do not know how to repay this."

Before Xavier could answer, his interface flared with new prompts.

You have completed a quest: Echoes of Innocence. Ella Bree's sacrifice enabled the rescue of Emily from her connection to the Life Ley Line. Though not intentionally harming the child, her life essence was empowering the failing line. Ella Bree provided another source of energy. Speak with her to learn more about what happened.

Rewards:
- Purification and revitalization of the Life Ley Line
- Rescue of the missing child Emily
- Access to Life Magic
- +1000 Experience
- Insight into the unknown

You have completed a quest: Balance Restored. The opposing elements of life and death have had their ley lines restored. This balance ensures that one no longer threatens to subsume the other. Rejoice, harbinger of balance—your influence has already shown its effects on the world.

Rewards:
- New access to challenges in the Deeps
- Passive Effect: Ley Line Resonance
- +1000 Experience

Xavier blinked away the messages and muttered under his breath. "I really need to change those to appear only when I call for them." The idea of prompts appearing in the middle of a battle or diplomatic standoff made him shudder.

He looked back to Sylvie and the other villagers gathering in the hall. "I would do the same for any of you," he said simply, his voice calm but firm. "I gave my word. If you chose to stand with me, I would do everything I could to restore what was taken from you. We haven't yet found a way to retrieve those stolen by the slavers... but I would not leave Emily to that place below."

He continued forward, still cradling Ella's limp form in his arms. As his boots touched the central mosaic, the very ground beneath him quivered. The ancient stones stirred.

A tremor, subtle yet unmistakable, rippled through the floor. It wasn't seismic, it was something else, something more intimate. The chamber responded to his presence as though recognizing him, as if the very stones themselves remembered what had been lost and now awakened to welcome the one who had helped restore it.

The moment both of his feet came fully to rest on the mosaic, the air thickened. The weight of unseen potential pressed in from every direction, not heavy with dread, but charged with long-dormant purpose.

Then the Life section exploded into color.

Brilliance surged from the tiles beneath his boots. Lush greens, vibrant pinks, and golden yellows burst to life, momentarily blinding him. Patterns that had once seemed faded and forgotten now glowed with a vigor that pulsed like a heartbeat. The petals of blooming flowers unfurled across the stone in slow, graceful spirals, as if freed from a binding silence. Vines etched into the mosaic twisted upward in real time, animated by ancient will, their tendrils reaching toward Xavier like the arms of an old friend embracing him after an age apart.

At the center of the section, the symbol of Life, a radiant blooming flower, flared with light. Energy pulsed outward from it in gentle, steady waves. The air shifted. A warm breeze stirred, brushing across every face in the chamber like the caress of early summer sun. The scent of blooming lilies, new grass, and citrus blossoms filled the space.

From unseen corners of the room came soft sounds... the rustling of unseen leaves, the quiet murmur of growth and breath. Every inhalation brought a feeling of renewal, of being made whole, a sensation that whispered: Life has returned, but with it came the echo of its twin.

The Death section stirred as Life danced. Shadows deepened, and the once-muted hues of gray and dusky blue sharpened into chilling clarity. The raven feather, its sigil, blazed with ghostly light. A curl of blue streaks wound upward from it like smoke rising from unseen coals. Then came the mist.

It billowed up from the stones in curling tendrils, pale and cold, ghostly white tinged with sapphire. It gathered around Xavier's legs, brushing his skin with a tingling chill that stole his breath for an instant. The air around him cooled, touched by the memory of endings, but not cruelty. It was the comfort of rest, the hush of twilight, the quiet understanding that all things must sleep before they rise again.

The scent of damp soil, of a storm long past, drifted in. Then came the whisper. It was not one voice, but many, a chorus of near-silent murmurs, the flutter of unseen wings in a darkened forest. It resonated not in the ears but in the chest, felt more than heard. Death had awoken, and it had not come for vengeance, but to remind them that balance had been restored.

The center of the mosaic responded to the awakening of the two sections. Where Life's green and Death's blue met, the nexus awakened. Color spun in radiant spirals, Life's emerald coils entwining with Death's midnight strands. The center pulsed with power. It shimmered like a living thing, hues merging and separating in an eternal dance. The floor beneath Xavier's feet seemed to breathe, the tiles warm one moment and cool the next, alive with something sacred.

The chamber thrummed. A symphony of harmony, contradiction, and unity filled the air. The energy did not tear or clash. It flowed, cyclical, whole. The mosaic had not merely awakened. It had accepted him.

The air cracked with magic, raw and unfiltered. A blend of creation and cessation flowed through the walls and pillars, through the very bones of the Syr'Vailen. The weight of it pressed against everyone in the room, yet instead of crushing, it lifted. They stood in the aftermath of something holy. Something reborn.

In Xavier's arms, Ella stirred. Her eyelids fluttered, her head shifting slightly to rest more firmly against his shoulder. Her breath deepened, and a flicker of color returned to her cheeks. The renewal had touched her. It had not healed her, but it had steadied her soul.

He stood at the center of it all, feeling the breath of the chamber, the pulse beneath his feet. The scent of life still lingered in the air, twined with the quiet chill of death. Serenity reigned and then, with the final flicker of light and the last swirl of mist, it faded.

The brilliance dulled. The breeze calmed. Yet what remained was not silence, but peace. The Life and Death sections of the mosaic had changed. No longer faded and cracked, their tiles now gleamed with permanence and power. The images etched within them had become frescos of color and depth, no longer mere representations, but living embodiments of their essence.

All around him, the villagers stood motionless.

Then came the next wave of prompts.

> **Know this!**
> Those who stood witness to the revitalization of the
> ley lines may now feel their own powers subtly altered

by what they have witnessed. The energies of Life and Death, intertwined in ways both delicate and dangerous, have left their mark on the very souls of those present. Their effects will linger.

Effect:
• +2 Charisma and Wisdom to those with Neutral alignment
• -2 Healing received and Damage done for those outside Neutral alignment

Xavier blinked slowly, the sheer intensity of the event having momentarily overwhelmed his senses. The last pulses of energy still echoed faintly in his chest, like the ringing after a bell tolls. As the world settled back into clarity, he became aware of the villagers doing the same, many exhaling at once, hands pressed to their chests or faces pale with awe.

Then, the prompts continued filling his vision.

You have completed quests: Sleeping Lines I and Sleeping Lines II.
Having started exploring the first level of the Deeps below the mosaic, you found not only one but two of the dormant ley lines. The ley lines of Life and Death have been revitalized, bringing equilibrium back to the natural order. The mosaic within the Syr'Vailen has shifted and now stands as a testament to your achievement, its radiance reflecting the harmony you have rekindled.

Rewards:
• Increased Mana in settlement lands
• Increased wildlife and quest opportunities
• +1500 Experience

> **You have been offered a quest:** Sleeping Lines III.
> Most of the ley lines that make up the nexus beneath
> your settlement remain dormant. Continue your
> exploration of the Deeps beneath the mosaic to find
> and restore the remaining lines, further increasing
> ambient mana and unlocking additional capabilities
> for your settlement. As this is a settlement quest, it
> will automatically be accepted when the appropriate
> conditions are met.
>
> **Conditions:**
> • Personal Level 15
> • Retain Mastery of the Syr'Vailen
>
> **Potential Rewards:**
> • Increased Mana in settlement lands
> • Increased wildlife and quest opportunities
> • +1500 Experience

Xavier dismissed the prompts with a weary mental push, exhaling through his nose as the last of them faded. He made a mental note to adjust his settings, forcing the system to withhold future prompts until manually requested. These bursts of information might have been tolerable in calm moments, but if something like this occurred during a battle, or worse, he wouldn't survive the distraction.

He turned his gaze toward Ella, still sleeping peacefully in his arms, and took one last look at the mosaic glowing beneath his feet, something had shifted in the world, something permanent.

#

Words etched themselves in brilliant letters, their elegant

script unfurling across Xavier's vision like a divine decree. A radiant symphony of chimes rang out in his ears, clear and

commanding, followed by a voice that echoed through his

soul:

"Hark and Hear! You have ascended in power. You are now Level 6!"

You have crossed the pivotal threshold beyond Level 5, stepping into a realm few ever reach. Where common individuals plateau, you rise, proving yourself as a true contender among the exceptional. This is no longer the path of the ordinary, your growth now marks the beginning of a legacy.
The touch of the divine lingers upon you, granting **6 attribute points** to shape your destiny, an exceptional gift elevated from the ordinary **4 points** granted to humans by the **Blessings of the Gods (Danu)**. Choose wisely, for these points will define your path. You have 3 days to assign them, or they will fall to the whims of fate.

A New Threshold Unlocked:
The horizon of your potential broadens. At this pivotal level, you are granted the power to choose a **Gathering Archetype** and a **Crafting Archetype**. These choices are more than roles—they are an extension of your soul's purpose, connecting you to the lifeblood of the world and the creations of your hands. Will you be the Harvester of nature's bounty or the Artisan of legendary wonders? The choice is yours.

Mastery Takes Root:
Your growing prowess earns you a unique boon: **20% skill allocation** to distribute among your known skills. This is your chance to sharpen the blade of a favored talent, forge new strength in an untapped domain, or balance your growth across disciplines. Let this moment

---

be a cornerstone of your greatness.

Rise, Seeker of Glory.
The world awaits your will. Seek adventure, seek
wisdom, seek love, and let your legend be forged in your
choices.
LIVE!

Xavier's legs gave out. He dropped to his backside with a
grunt, landing hard on the unforgiving stone of the mosaic.
The pain radiated through his spine and reminded him all
too clearly that he was, despite all appearances, still human.

He hissed between his teeth and reflexively clutched Ella
tighter to keep from jostling her. She stirred faintly in his
arms, her eyelids fluttering, then settling once more. Her
pulse remained steady, her breathing calm.

It had been a day of revelations, of awakening and
restoration, of miracles bound in ancient power. And now,
another truth began to surface.

Ella's eyes opened. They were heavy with exhaustion, but
clear. She blinked once, then twice, and finally lifted them to
his face. "I owe you an explanation," she whispered. "Seems I
have a chance to give it after all. I thought my choice would
take that away... but Vaeltheris chose otherwise."

Xavier frowned. "Vaeltheris? I know it's your blade, but...
how could it make a decision? Isn't it just a weapon?"

Her smile was faint but sincere. "Yes, and no. Take me to
my bed. I will tell you what I can."

He nodded, rising carefully to his feet once again.
The chamber had begun to return to its usual stillness,
though something subtle lingered in the air, a promise of
change. Around the edges of the room, the villagers were
beginning to stir and murmur among themselves, shaken
but unharmed.

Sylvie had released Emily at some point, but now walked away with one hand clasped tightly around the girl's, the other around her own son Pip. They departed without fanfare, leading the way toward the warrens. The crowd gradually dispersed behind them.

In the end, only four remained in the mosaic chamber: Xavier, Ella, Valkra, and Aelriva.

He turned and carried Ella away, stepping into the leylit tunnels that led toward the private chambers carved into the restored stone.

#

The room that now belonged to Ella had changed since Xavier had last seen it. Though still simple in its furnishings, it bore signs of care, touches of village life quietly seeping into the ancient stone.

A rough-hewn wooden chair stood beside the bed, its frame sturdy and new. A small table had been set nearby, holding a ceramic basin with a folded cloth, as if someone had prepared it for wounds they feared might come. The villagers had not been idle while he delved below. Even in fear, they had chosen hope.

Xavier laid Ella gently upon the mattress. She let out a soft breath as the blanket was drawn over her, her features peaceful now, almost fragile. He sank into the chair beside her, placing his hand over hers and holding it in silence.

For a time, neither of them spoke. Then, slowly, Ella took a deeper breath. She turned her head toward him, the movement stiff but deliberate. Her eyes found his, and when she finally spoke, her voice had changed. It was steadier now, clear, measured, touched with an almost ceremonial weight.

"I told you in the Deeps," she began, "of ancient civilizations lost to the ages. Empires broken by pride, forgotten through the ravages of time, or shattered by invasion and betrayal. To understand Vaeltheris, you must know of two such empires... the Sylmyrian Dominion and the Phoenix Empire."

Xavier remained silent, listening as her tone shifted further. She was not merely recounting facts. She was delivering a memory older than most could comprehend.

"Most of this knowledge has faded into myth. Few truly believe the Sylmyrians existed at all. But they did. They were scholars, crafters without equal, and masters of the ley lines. Their knowledge stretched beyond the arcane. They understood the very breath of the world. Their wonders were sought after by lord and commoner alike, forged not just with magic, but with meaning." She paused, gaze distant. "The Syr'Vailen is thought to be one of their creations. So is the great forge above it. Remnants of their glory... echoes of what was once a shining civilization."

Her voice softened slightly as she continued.

"The Phoenix Empire was no less mighty. But where the Sylmyrians were guided by councils of scholars and spellwrights, the Phoenix followed a divine hierarchy. A theocracy ruled by the Divine Emperor and enforced by zealous priests. Their cities, ziggurats, radiant gardens, sacred monuments, stood as symbols of divine purpose and order."

She turned her head fully now, meeting Xavier's eyes again.

"But power breeds envy. The Phoenix leaders saw their works overshadowed by Sylmyrian craft. The world sought Sylmyrian creations, and envy, once born, festers."

She did not need to say more. He understood.

"As often happens between great powers, their rivalry soured. Trade turned to suspicion. Suspicion into distrust.

Finally, then came war. The Sylmyrians wielded unmatched magical artistry, but the Phoenix Empire had divine backing, vast numbers, and fervor that bordered on madness."

Ella's fingers twitched beneath his hand.

"Rumors claim that one, or several, of the gods saw opportunity in this war. They whispered into the ear of the Phoenix Emperor. Promised him dominion, not only over the Sylmyrians, but over the future. The priests were told of rituals, blessings, divine fire. They listened. They obeyed."

Her voice darkened.

"For days, perhaps weeks, the Phoenix Empire bled itself in ritual. Sacrifices of slaves, beasts, harvests, gold. They poured everything into prayer and divine communion. And the gods answered."

She closed her eyes for a moment.

"A comet formed in the sky. Not a natural thing, but a burning sphere of stone and celestial flame, summoned by their rites. Its course was set, straight for the heart of Sylmyrian lands. Straight for this very city we are rebuilding."

Xavier leaned forward, his breath caught in his throat.

"But the Sylmyrians had not been idle," Ella said, eyes opening once more. "They knew what was coming. They were not just scholars. They were survivors. Their Ard'Maelor, the Forge Master, gathered the greatest minds and the strongest mages. Together, they wove a spell not to destroy the comet, but to divert it. To protect their people, even if it meant the end of their era."

She paused again. "And they succeeded. Just... not in the way they expected."

Her voice fell to a whisper.

"The comet veered off course. It struck the lands of the

Phoenix Empire instead, obliterating their temples, their monuments, their legacy. The devastation was near-total. Many believe the Blasted Expanse in the north is what remains of that scorched earth."

Xavier's voice came quietly. "And the Sylmyrians?"

Ella turned her head toward the bed's edge and fixed her gaze on Vaeltheris, which now rested on a linen wrap nearby.

"They survived. Not as mortals. But in spirit."

She drew in a breath, steadying herself.

"They created one final masterpiece. A soul-forged weapon, an Ethyr'Vael. Vaeltheris. More than a blade. It is the collective soul of their people. Their knowledge, their history, their skills... their very identities. Bound together. Preserved in that single artifact."

Her gaze fell to Xavier's.

"You asked how the blade could choose. That is how. It remembers. It decides. When I collapsed near the core, it sensed my end. And it gave of itself to protect me."

Her voice cracked slightly. "I do not know how many souls it spent to keep mine. But I feel the weight of it. The strain. It is diminished now. Its song... quieter." Tears welled in her eyes, but she blinked them away. "The strain has further weakened what it can do, and I don't know how or if it can be restored. I do know, however, that I trust you implicitly. I want you to become the bearer of the blade and lift its burden from my shoulders. Carry it forward. For them. For all of us."

She raised her hand. Resting in her palm was a small crystalline orb, faintly glowing with inner light. "Take this, it will bind the blade to your soul."

Hesitantly, Xavier reached out and took it from her. He turned it in his fingers, then looked up. "How do I do it?"

She gave him a faint smile. "It is magic. You must impose

your will upon it. It will respond."

He nodded once and turned his focus inward.

> **It appears you wish to bind the item "Vaeltheris, Eternal Song of the Blade" to your soul.**
> Binding is permanent. The weapon cannot be lost or stolen. If you die, it will return to you upon rebirth. It cannot be transferred to another without the purest intentions of your being.
>
> **Do you wish to proceed? Yes/No**

He focused on the word. "Yes."

The orb dissolved into his palm, warmth flaring along his skin. His head shot up as he heard Ella's speak as the action took place.

Ella's voice came softly, quiet, but filled with meaning. "By binding my blade, you have bound me. I am eternally tied to your side. Your trials are my trials. Your will is my will. Thus it shall be, until the gods fade and the stars fall."

Their eyes met once more the look in her eyes as she met Xavier's was hopeful, and in that look, Xavier understood. Ella had never simply been a guide. She had always been the bearer of a legacy, and now, that legacy lived on in him.

CHAPTER NINETEEN

Classes, and Skills, and Treasure Oh My!

Xavier sat quietly, Vaeltheris unsheathed across his lap. His thoughts churned. The truth about the blade, about Ella, about everything, it weighed heavily. He glanced to the side, to where Ella now lay curled beneath the blanket. Sleep had taken her at last, exhaustion settling over her like a veil after all she had endured.

The third time his eyes drifted to her, he noticed something new. A faint mark, high on her neck just behind her ear, barely visible unless one knew to look. He leaned in slightly. He wasn't sure if it was because her hair always covered it or if it was actually new. What had really caught his attention about it was the fact it matched his own mark, the one hidden on his inner wrist, that of the Ard'Maelor. It marked him as the master of the lands around the Syr'Vailen and as the Lord of the settlement.

"I guess that marks you as bonded to me," he murmured, voice hushed so as not to wake her.

Turning back to Vaeltheris, he exhaled through his nose. The blade's prompt had changed. It no longer held the deep red of a legendary item but instead shimmered with the rich gold border denoting mythic rarity.

You have discovered:	**Item Class:** Weapon

Vaeltheris "Eternal Song of the Blade"
Unique Ethyr'Vael "Soul Forged Blade"
Long ago, the ancient race of crafters known as the Sylmyrians were unrivaled in their art. Masters of enchanting weapons, armor, and mystical tools, they infused their creations with both beauty and lethal precision. But as the centuries passed, they foresaw the inevitable decline of their civilization. To preserve their knowledge and spirit, they gathered in a final, powerful ritual—a soul-forging rite that would allow them to live on within a single weapon.

Thus, Vaeltheris was born: a sword unlike any other, forged with the combined essence, skill, and memories of an entire civilization. With its creation, the Sylmyrians themselves faded from existence, their bodies turning

Item Rarity: Mythic
Item Quality: Masterwork
Weight: 1kg
Durability: Unknown
Damage: 30 – 45 Piercing/ Slashing
Traits: Though it appears sturdy, Vaeltheris is surprisingly light and perfectly balanced, almost as if it moves with the wielder's intentions rather than their strength. Its weight adjusts slightly to provide the ideal amount of heft for any strike, making it feel like an extension of the wielder's body.
Material: Vaeltheris is forged from a silvery, semi-translucent metal that gleams faintly with an internal light as if housing the embers of a forge within its core. This magical alloy is unbreakable, resistant to the ravages of time, and eternally sharp.

Form: The blade is slender yet slightly curved, designed for both grace and lethality. Faint, swirling patterns of to dust as their souls merged within the blade. Now, Vaeltheris is both a sword and a repository of ancient wisdom, holding the strength, spirit, and artistry of an entire race within its metal.

runes and filigree adorn its surface, glowing softly when attuned to the wielder's emotions or magic. These designs are etched so finely they appear to shift and ripple like liquid under certain light.

Special Traits:

1. **Living Steel:** The blade repairs itself if damaged (though breaking it is almost impossible). If chipped, the missing piece regrows with a faint shimmer.

2. **Ethereal Edge:** The sword's edge can phase slightly into an incorporeal state, allowing it to bypass certain magical defenses.

3. **Aetherforged:** The blade has the ability to shift its form to match the welders' needs. At the current level, it can change in size up to medium or down to tiny, the weapon's sheath will change to match.

4. Additional traits

may be discovered.

"Given what she told me about you," he spoke to the blade now, "I should not be surprised that you are mythic. A whole empire of people locked up inside you. How many thousands of souls does that mean I am responsible for now?"

Other than a slight brightening of its usual glow the blade didn't respond. Xavier hadn't really expected a response, though he found it interesting that prompts would change as he learned more information about something. That actually made him stop to think about how little he really knew of this world, its people, or even his own skills and abilities.

Leaning back in the chair once again he lay Vaeltheris across his knees and let his mind shift focus. It was becoming easier every time he tried to do it to pull up various interfaces. The fact they seemed to appear in his vision without any sort of device or headset still amazed him but it seemed to be a fact of life in this world. Soon his own character sheet appeared before his eyes.

Name: Xavier	**Level:** 6, 74% to Next Level	**Age:** 18
Race: Human	**Alignment:** Neutral	**Languages:** Basic, Sylmarian
Reputation: 600 – Who Are You Again? - Your name might be whispered in the winds, but most can't recall it. If you were a knight, you'd be the one who gets left out of the battle plan. People might nod at you in the market, but they're mostly confused.		
Stats		
Health: 140/140	**Stamina:** 120/120	**Mana:** 160/160
Attributes		

Strength: 12	Agility: 10	Dexterity: 12
Constitution: 12	Endurance: 10	Charisma: 14
Intelligence: 12	Wisdom: 14	Luck: 14
Resistances	Skills	Marks
None	See Skills Tab	Ard'Maelor - The Grand Forgemaster
Abilities & Traits		

Unbound Possibilities – While the inhabitants of Arath are constrained by rules limiting how they can grow and what they can learn you have been blessed by Danu to be unbound. These limits guide you but do not constrain you.

Linguist – You have the capacity to know, understand, and speak any mortal language

Unyielding Liberator - Having witnessed the devastating aftermath of a tyrannical assault, your resolve is as unshakable as your blade is sharp.

- **Strengthened Resolve:** Xavier gains a bonus to morale-based rolls and abilities when fighting against slavers, tyrants, or oppressors.
- **Justice Over Mercy:** In situations involving the abuse or enslavement of others, Xavier will prioritize swift and decisive action, often at the expense of diplomatic solutions.
- **Fearsome Reputation:** Enemies who learn of his deeds are more likely to falter in battle, intimidated by his uncompromising sense of justice.
- **Unbreakable Loyalty:** Those he rescues see him as a savior, and his reputation among the oppressed makes him a natural leader and ally to rebel causes.

His eyes widened as he noticed other changes to his stats that he had been unaware of. He searched through his options of tabs, a remarkably large number of options that he was going to have to figure out what each did, he soon found one simply called "Log." It held a running log, big surprise there, of everything that had happened to him from status changes to damage, to condition changes. Scrolling back through it slowly he finally found a notation after completing one of the puzzles in the crypt.

Congratulations: Your clever puzzle-solving has increased your Intelligence and Wisdom. (+2 INT, +2 WIS)

"So stats can grow outside of leveling. Good to know." He noticed that all of his attributes had a small plus sign next to them, reminding him that he had a couple of days to assign his new points before they would be assigned for him. He opted to put that off for now as he was unsure where he would be needing them most.

Another line in the log had stood out to him while he was searching for the change in his attributes. It read:

New Feature Unlocked: You may now choose an Archetype for Crafting and Gathering. These archetypes will help mold your role in the world around you. What path will you take to glory?

Exploring the tabs, he found the Classes screen. Three categories appeared: Combat (greyed out), Crafting, and Gathering. A prompt blinked when he focused on Combat:

You do not meet the criteria for selecting a Combat Archetype at this level.

He muttered to himself. "Not even a hint about when I will. Rude. Maybe someone else can help me with that. I'll have to ask Aelriva or Ella when she wakes up."

Turning his attention to the Gathering column he received a list of options, happily each option also provided a short list of subclasses, though that only made him curious about when he would be able to select one or more of those.

- The Forager – When nature hides its secrets, a forager finds them, whether they're buried in leaves, dirt, or dangerously close to poison ivy. "If it grows, glows, or bites back, I'll find a use for it."

- The Miner – Where others see stone and darkness, a miner sees potential, a glint of ore, the shimmer of gems, and maybe a little back pain. "Dig deep enough, and you'll find gold, or your third cousin who got lost down here."

- The Fisher – Patience, precision, and luck, qualities of a fisher who knows that sometimes the big one isn't just a story. "I catch fish the size of legends. And you just catch colds."

- The Woodsman – The forest offers much to those who respect it, timber for tools, sap for secrets, and birds to squawk when you're getting too close. "I don't hug trees, I chop them. Unless they hug back."

- The Scavenger – One man's trash is a scavenger's jackpot, especially when that trash still has teeth. "I don't find junk; I find pre-owned treasure."

- The Trapper – They set the traps, track the game, and collect the prize, whether it's fur, fangs, or something that should really stay in the ground. "I don't hunt. I let the beast come to me. Lazy? No. Efficient."

- The Botanist – A botanist speaks to plants, nurtures them, and occasionally tells them how much better they'd look in a potion. "Sure, I could eat this flower, but I'd rather sell it to someone who'll think it's magic."

- The Salvager – Ruins, wreckage, and rubble, it's not what's left behind; it's what a salvager can pry loose before someone notices. "Finders keepers, losers should've hidden it better."

- The Elemental Gatherer – When others shy away from the raw power of the elements, an elementalist sees opportunity in fire, wind, and stone. "Who needs a pickaxe when the lava does the heavy lifting?"

- The Survivalist – From tundra to desert, a survivalist thrives where others falter, finding resources no sane person would look for. "Oh, you packed rations? That's cute, I'll eat a cactus."

Each archetype seemed extremely useful in its own way. However, many of them seemed to involve hours if not days of backbreaking menial labor. As much as he had enjoyed gathering back on Earth when he was playing games, he didn't really think it would be his most preferred thing now that it was his life.

"Eww," he thought about mining, woodsman or even botany, "cubicle life but without the cubicle and more swinging a hammer or axe."

However much the subclasses of those archetypes seemed powerful and amazing he couldn't commit himself to those. A few of them stood out, however, forager, scavenger, salvager, and elemental gatherer. "What was a soul collector?" Focusing on the subskills didn't offer any further information and he mentally sighed once more. This place seemed dedicated to making difficult choices more difficult and he didn't have wiki or even a rule book he could use to research what precise path he would take.

"Maybe I am going about this the wrong way. Picking what crafts, I want to do may better help me to decide what gathering I focus on. It's not like I can't learn how to gather everything, I do have the ability to learn all skills thanks to Danu. These just seem to help specialize and probably help increase either the harvest or ability to find unique things."

He shifted over to study the crafting column.

- Blacksmith – Steel bends, blades sharpen, and fire obeys in the hands of a blacksmith—the ones who make heroes look the part. "You call that a sword? I've made better kitchen knives."

- Alchemist – Brews of brilliance, poisons of peril, an alchemist masters the art of turning 'maybe' into miracles. "Drink this, if it works, you'll thank me. If not...well, I'll learn something."
- Enchanter – The power of magic isn't in spells, it's in objects that hum with enchantments only an expert can weave. "Your sword's sharp? Cute. Mine sets people on fire."
- Carpenter – From bows that pierce hearts to ships that rule seas, carpenters are masters of wood and wisdom. "Measure twice, cut once. Ignore that advice, and you'll need new fingers."
- Tailor – Fashion, form, and function, a tailor stitches threads into stories, and cloaks heroes in destiny. "Oh, it fits poorly? Don't worry, the monsters won't notice."
- Jeweler – Every cut, every facet, a jeweler turns gems into treasures, and treasures into symbols of power. "A diamond's forever, but your money is mine."
- Leatherworker – From humble hides to legendary armor, a leatherworker ensures heroes stay nimble, protected, and fashionable. "Yes, it's dragon leather, no, you can't afford it."
- Rune Engraver – Symbols of power carved into steel, stone, or soul, rune engravers ensure that words do hurt. "I don't just write on swords. I argue with them until they glow."
- Artificer – Wheels spin, gears turn, and magic flows, an artificer's workshop is where machines come alive and marvels are born, "If it breaks, I'll fix it. If it explodes, that's your fault
- Cook – From rations to royal feasts, a cook turns ingredients into inspiration, and occasionally explosive dinners. "Don't ask what's in it, just eat. Trust me."
- Glassblower – Delicate as starlight, strong as magic, a glassblower's work is as fragile as it is powerful. "Handle with care, or handle a healer bill."

- Stoneworker – From statues to fortresses, stoneworkers carve mountains into monuments of ambition. "It's not just a rock. It's a really expensive rock."
- Relic Maker – From forgotten legends to new creations, relic makers forge objects that reshape history. "This relic belonged to a hero. Now it's yours, try not to die."

Again, there were so many choices, how could one ever make a decision especially since they didn't know what their skills could be or even if they could learn certain skills. The options overwhelmed him. They all sounded useful, and appealing in their own way.

Switching over to his skills tab gave him a new surprise. Each skill he had acquired was listed there along with their current rank but even this tab had evolved. He was now able to see how much progression he had per skill. He was also able to see something new. Alongside the skill level and progression value was a new column. His skills tab showed something new:

Natural Aptitude Level: 5 – Legendary Potential (Grandmaster Cap)

His brow rose. "Blessing of Danu really is no joke I can learn all of these skills to Grandmaster. I really should ask about skill ranks as well. Just another thing on my list of things I don't know enough about."

Resolving to reduce at least a little bit of that he reached over and laid a hand on Ella's giving it a reassuring squeeze before he rose from the chair and walked out of the room. It was time to learn and make choices.

#

The entrance chamber greeted him with its soft glow. He made mental notes about possible improvements before Aelriva appeared, shimmering into being just ahead of him.

He flinched. "Gods! I didn't call for you. How are you here?"

A twinkle lit the sprite's eyes, her form shifting through the various elements, though it seemed to linger on life and death aspects a little longer than the others now. "Yer will is known t' me, Ard'Maelor. Within the bounds o' Rynthavael, I shall always know where ye be and what aid ye seek."

"Alright," he said warily, unsure he really wanted something that could track him and knew his thoughts. Though she had been beyond helpful in the past so he eventually just accepted it and said. "I was hoping to find Braegor. I want to ask him about skill ranks and classes."

"Aye, I ken where the Gan Ceann is. He's over in the smithy, workin' away. Yer stonemason and carpenter team hae finished the repairs to the buildin' today, and the smiths were eager to get back to their craft. It doesnae hae the glory of the Great Forge yet, but I'd still counsel ye, nae to awaken it fully just now. It would draw too much attention, that it would."

She kept telling him not to awaken the forge. That council really started to make him question why. "So you have said, though you never explained. How could upgrading a building cause such an issue?"

She perched on his shoulder. ""The Great Forge is a Masterworks Sanctum, aye. There be many types o' Masterworks Sanctums, like the Eternal Hearth for cooks, the Prismarium for glassblowers, an' yer Great Forge, but there be only a handful o' each in all the world. When one is awakened or created, it brings great fame t' the one who played a part in its creation. An announcement rings out, tellin' the world of th' feat. Yer revitalization of th' ley lines was a momentous event in itself, but it pales beside the spectacle o' a new Masterwork Sanctum. Trust me, ye are nae ready t' defend it from those who would seek to take it from ye. Not yet, at least."

Xavier couldn't argue with her logic. Not if it was that

much of an event. He was still new to Arath and Rynthavael could barely be called a village. If something of that much importance was announced to the world, he had little doubt that some power would want to take it for themselves. "I understand now. Thank you Aelriva for explaining to me. I will keep the heart safe and hidden for now."

" Ye could store it in the vault. When the ley lines awoke, it opened up new passageways in th' warrens, and the vault an' armory are now at yer disposal, Ard'Maelor." She proposed.

warrens, and the vault an' armory are now at yer disposal, Ard'Maelor." She proposed.

That caught his attention. A vault and an armory, both from the ancient city that had been here. Xavier didn't think of himself as greedy but he knew eventually that his people would want to be paid for their work and the handful of coins he had managed to collect in his time on Arath were not going to pay for jack squat and he was pretty sure Jack had left town well before he got here.

"Braegor can wait," He said excitedly. "Show me to where these new rooms are. I need to see what we are working with."

The sprite lifted from his shoulder in a flutter of wings, and she was off back into the warrens with Xavier close on her trail. They wound down several passages and went past the pantry and the mosaic room before she paused in front of a new side tunnel. At the end of the short passage was a set of double doors.

"This be yer vault. The armory lies further."

"Awesome. Open it up and lets see what we are working with." Xavier moved towards the door but stopped when she spoke.

"I cannae. Only ye can."

He glanced at her and then placed a hand on either door

and pushed firmly. Nothing happened. The doors refused to budge no matter how hard he pushed. "I thought you said I could open these doors." He all but yelled at the diminutive flying woman. "They're not moving at all. Is there a key or a secret latch or something I am missing."

She sighed, he still hadn't learned much about his position. "They will nae open for anyone but the Ard'Maelor. Ye can change that if ye wish, but for now, only ye can open them. It is a vault, my lord. Did ye truly think the doors would just open? Additionally, it be the vault o' Cael'Anthir, the capital. Mere locks or secret latches would nae be enough to guard such valuables. Place yer hand upon the sigil." She fluttered over to a small plate in the door, where an intricate symbol was etched into the metal. "It will allow ye to open the lock an' the doors."

Xavier moved closer and peered at the small plate embedded in the large metallic doors. The symbol seemed to almost glow with an inner light. Reading the symbol aloud Xavier muttered. "Vaeska" pausing a moment to think he finished. "That which binds or secures. Well, if that couldn't be more obvious."

Placing his hand over the sigil he felt a surge of energy as his mark flared with energy. A resonant voice sounded in his head.

"Do you wish to access the Vault of Cael'Anthir, Ard'Maelor?"

"Yes." He answered with a grin.

Xavier grinned and simply said "Yes."

He could hear metal moving against metal and stone, the sounds of great bars sliding from their place with snicks and final booms before the twin doors parted in the middle, folding back away from him to leave the next room open. Xavier stepped through the doors and almost fell to his knees in disappointment. The room was empty.

Well not completely empty. There were shelves upon shelves lining the large hexagonal space and lined up neatly across the center of the rooms in several rows but that was it. No mounds of treasure, bags of coins, great stacks of metal or anything else of value. Sighing Xavier turned to leave the vault when Aelriva spoke up.

"Are ye goin' to leave what's left o' the treasure behind?" She flew through the door and towards the darkened back of the room where the light from the torches in the passageway didn't illuminate the shadows.

Xavier retrieved one of the torches from the sconce it was held in and followed her into the vault. On the back shelf he found three small chests and a single small bag.

Moving to the first chest, it stood about a foot and a half long, by a foot wide and only about 10 inches deep. The chest was made of sturdy iron reinforced oak the lid held a simple iron lockplate, worn but still functional, while the corners were capped with tarnished brass for added durability. He tested the lid and it slid open with ease.

When the light of the torch hit the leather lined inside of the chest his smile grew. The thing held easily hundreds of coins, a blend of copper, silver, gold and even the occasional silvery-white shimmer of what Xavier guessed to be platinum. He had no idea the conversion rate but this was a small fortune, he was positive. He dug into his pouch and pulled out the small handful of copper and silver coins he had found, adding them to the chest before closing it and turning the key in the lock. He placed the key into his pouch in place of the coins.

He turned to the second chest. It was smaller but more ornate. Polished mahogany was cornered with elegant brass pieces to complement the ornate brass inlay. Everything came together in a beautiful silver lock. Pushing the top open on the chest he found it was lined with velvet and separated into small sections. Each section had a collection of jewels.

Whereas the first chest was a wonderful find of money to help his village this was even more so as the gems were potentially worth far more than the coins themselves. Once again, he closed the chest and twisted the key sealing it shut. The silver key joined the first in his pouch and he turned his attention to the final chest.

It was the most unique one of the lot. Made of an ethereally pale wood with faint, swirling grain patterns that resemble frozen mist. The casket was small, almost delicate, yet unyieldingly strong. A softly glowing opaline gem was set in the top of the wood and Xavier gently laid his hand atop it. A faintly feminine voice sounded in his ears.

"Do you desire the casket open Ard'Maelor?"

Xavier's grin couldn't get any wider. He knew this had to be the best find in the vault just due to the construction and the magical lock. Me mentally chose yes and the casket opened to reveal shimmering white silk embroidered with faint Sylmyrian glyphs of protection and preservation. The silk was divided up into cushioned slots and tiny hooks to hold delicate items securely. The air inside carried a faint, timeless fragrance of juniper and ancient magic. Nestled in the ornate casket were five pieces of beautifully wrought jewelry.

You have discovered:	Item Class: Unknown
Magical Pendant	Item Quality: Unknown
	Weight: 0.09 kg
	Durability: Unknown
	Description: A silver pendant holding a Vaelshard crystal that shimmers with faint Sylmyrian runes. It

	hums softly near magical energy. **Traits:** Unknown
You have discovered: Magical Circlet	**Item Class:** Unknown **Item Quality:** Unknown **Weight:** 0.23 kg **Durability:** Unknown **Description:** A silverwood circlet lined with glowing Emberheart gems, carved with fiery runic designs. **Traits:** Unknown
You have discovered: Magical Ring	**Item Class:** Unknown **Item Quality:** Unknown **Weight:** 0.05 kg **Durability:** Unknown **Description:** A mithral ring with a Frostquartz centerpiece that radiates an icy blue glow. **Traits:** Unknown
You have discovered: Magical Bracelet	**Item Class:** Unknown **Item Quality:** Unknown **Weight:** 0.14 kg **Durability:** Unknown **Description:** A silverwood bracelet inlaid with Springstone fragments shifting between green and blue hues. **Traits:** Unknown
You have discovered: Magical Brooch	**Item Class:** Unknown **Item Quality:** Unknown **Weight:** 0.18 kg

	Durability: Unknown **Description:** A dark silver brooch with a Voidcrystal centerpiece that absorbs surrounding light. **Traits:** Unknown
You have discovered: Magical Amulet	**Item Class:** Unknown **Item Quality:** Unknown **Weight:** 0.12 kg **Durability:** Unknown **Description:** A mysterious amulet crafted from an unknown dark metal, its surface smooth yet oddly reflective, as if it holds a void within. Faint, shifting runes appear and disappear when gazed upon too long. **Traits:** Unknown
You have discovered: The Starleaf Earrings	**Item Class:** Common **Item Quality:** Well Crafted **Weight:** 0.05 kg **Durability:** 75/100 **Description:** Silver earrings shaped like delicate leaves, adorned with small sapphire inlays. **Traits:** Elegant design with subtle sapphire highlights.
You have discovered: The Moonlit Choker	**Item Class:** Common **Item Quality:** Well Crafted **Weight:** 0.09 kg **Durability:** 70/100

	Description: A black velvet choker holding a polished moonstone that reflects soft light. Traits: Simple yet elegant, enhances the wearer's graceful appearance.
You have discovered: The Golden Laurel Band	Item Class: Common Item Quality: Superb Weight: 0.14 kg Durability: 80/100 Description: A thin golden circlet designed to resemble a laurel wreath, with fine leaf engravings. Traits: A symbol of refinement and status, reflecting light beautifully.
You have discovered: The Amber Spiral Bracelet	Item Class: Common Item Quality: Well Crafted Weight: 0.18 kg Durability: 68/100 Description: A bronze bracelet spiraling elegantly, inlaid with large polished amber stones. Traits: Warm, earthy design with natural amber accents.
You have discovered: The Rosegold Ring	Item Class: Common Item Quality: Well Crafted Weight: 0.05 kg Durability: 78/100 Description: A slender rosegold band adorned

	with a brilliant-cut garnet reflecting deep red hues. **Traits:** Simple elegance with a bold, fiery centerpiece.
You have discovered: The Pearl Lattice Necklace	**Item Class:** Common **Item Quality:** Exquisite **Weight:** 0.23 kg **Durability:** 85/100 **Description:** A delicate silver necklace arranged in a lattice pattern, holding smooth, perfectly round white pearls. **Traits:** Timeless beauty showcasing unparalleled craftsmanship.
You have discovered: The Sunstone Brooch	**Item Class:** Common **Item Quality:** Superb **Weight:** 0.18 kg **Durability:** 82/100 **Description:** A polished brass brooch featuring a radiant sunstone centerpiece, glowing golden-orange. **Traits:** A bright, eye-catching piece symbolizing warmth and energy.

"Gods I need to find a way to identify magical items." Xavier bemoaned. Behind him a gentle bluewhite light flashed and more prompts filled his head.

You have discovered: The	**Item Class:** Rare

Veilshard Pendant	**Item Quality:** Well Crafted **Weight:** 0.09 kg **Durability:** 85/100 **Description:** A silver pendant holding a Vaelshard crystal that shimmers with faint Sylmyrian runes. It hums softly near magical energy. **Traits:** Enhances the wearer's ability to sense nearby magic and ley lines.
You have discovered: The Wyrmheart Circle	Item Class: Rare Item Quality: Superb Weight: 0.23 kg Durability: 90/100 Description: A silverwood circlet lined with glowing Emberheart gems, carved with fiery runic designs. Traits: Grants resistance to fire and amplifies fire-based spells.
You have discovered: The Frostbloom Ring	Item Class: Rare Item Quality: Well Crafted Weight: 0.05 kg Durability: 80/100 Description: A mithral ring with a Frostquartz centerpiece that radiates an icy blue glow. Traits: Grants cold

	resistance and minor frost magic abilities.
You have discovered: The Sylvanbrace	Item Class: Rare Item Quality: Exquisite Weight: 0.14 kg Durability: 95/100 Description: A silverwood bracelet inlaid with Springstone fragments shifting between green and blue hues. Traits: Enhances natural healing and connection to nature-based spells
You have discovered: The Nightveil Brooch	Item Class: Rare Item Quality: Masterwork Weight: 0.18 kg Durability: 88/100 Description: A dark silver brooch with a Voidcrystal centerpiece that absorbs surrounding light. Traits: Improves stealth and allows blending into dim environments.
You have discovered: The Amulet of the Unknown	Item Class: Legendary Item Quality: Exquisite Weight: 0.12 kg Durability: 100/100 Description: A mysterious amulet crafted from an unknown dark metal, its surface smooth yet oddly reflective, as if it holds a void within. Faint,

	shifting runes appear and disappear when gazed upon too long. Traits: Untrackable: Prevents detection by magical or mundane means, rendering the wearer immune to location spells, scrying, or divination. Unscryable: Conceals the wearer's presence and actions, shielding them from any form of magical observation or surveillance.

Xavier spun, the only other being in the room was Aelriva. "Did you do that?" He questioned the sprite. "You can identify magical items? Can you teach me to do it?"

"The power o' the Syr'Vailen allows me to ken the nature o' things. I dinnae ken how to teach this ability to another. It's nae based on skills or knowledge. It is simply the ley lines revealin' what is." Came her simple reply. There was almost a regretful tone in her statement as if she would teach him if it was within her ability.

"Of course, it wouldn't be that easy. Oh well, I guess I need to find a spell or something." Xavier said.

"Aye, there be many spells an' items that can help ye ken the traits o' magical items. Though findin' someone to teach ye magic might prove a bit difficult."

Xavier studied the newly identified magical items for a few minutes before he chose one. The Amulet of the Unknown was a definite necessity. Especially given the warnings Aelriva kept giving him about not being ready for the outside world to find his village. He may not have a way to hide it from the world yet, but he could hide himself and the attention that he would bring. He slipped the fine chain of the necklace over his head and tucked the amulet into his shirt. Then he closed the chest once again.

He finally turned to the small bag. It was a beautifully crafted item. Looking like a small satchel, its leather was rich dark blue with intricate silver threads laced through its surface giving the impression of starlight. Xavier raised an eyebrow as he looked at it. When he picked it up he received the prompt he was expecting.

You have discovered: Magical Bag	Item Class: Unknown Item Quality: Unknown Weight: 0.12 kg Durability: Unknown Description: A finely crafted satchel made from enchanted voidleather, its surface a deep midnight blue with swirling, faint silver threads resembling starlight. Traits: Unknown

Shaking his head slightly he held the bag out to the side and waited. After only a few moments the light shone behind him once again and the information about the bag changed.

You have discovered: The Voidtide Satchel	Item Class: Epic Item Quality: Superb Weight: 1.5 kg (Base) Durability: 90/100 Description: A finely crafted satchel made from enchanted voidleather, its surface a deep midnight

blue with swirling, faint silver threads resembling starlight. Despite its small exterior, it carries far more than it appears. A subtle hum can be felt when held, as if space itself bends within.

Traits:

- Dimensional Storage: Contains up to 20 slots, each capable of holding a standard item (weapons, tools, or small chests).

- Weight Reduction: Reduces the weight of stored items by 60%, significantly lightening the load for the user.

- Void-Sealed: Contents are immune to external damage and do not degrade while stored

Xavier could barely resist doing a little celebratory dance. This was every gamer's dream item. Bags of holding could make schlepping all the treasure and loot from a dungeon so much easier to accomplish, and now he had one.

Better yet this one would preserve anything put within it while reducing its weight. He quickly opened the bag and a visualization of a 4x5 grid appeared in his mind. It was all but empty currently, the exception being a small clear crystalline orb showing in the bottom right square. Xavier grinned and moved to unlock the chest of coins before tipping it and pouring all the clinking metal disks into the bag. As expected, the first row of the grid filled, one square with each type of coin and a number was superimposed over the image of each coin.

Copper Coins	276
Silver Coins	150
Gold Coins	70
Platinum Coins	4

He was thrilled with the effect. Reaching into the satchel he imagined grabbing a copper coin and he pulled his hand out holding one of the small disks as the number count in the bag decreased by one.

Now he couldn't resist dancing and chanting softly as he did. "I got a bag of holding, I got a bag of holding, I got a bag of holding." He dropped the coin back in and took Aelriva's hands dancing with her. The small sprite gasped in surprise as she was spun about and then released.

Xavier picked up the other two chests and carefully tucked them into the bag as well. Each one took up a space of their own and the weight of the bag increased slightly but Xavier now had the whole of his wealth on him. He then stuck his hand back in the bag and withdrew the little orb. It closely resembled the orb Ella had given him to bind Vaeltheris to himself earlier.

Focusing on the gem he got the prompt.

It appears you wish to bind the item "Voidtide Satchel" to your soul.
Binding is permanent. The weapon cannot be lost or stolen. If you die, it will return to you upon rebirth. It cannot be transferred to another without the purest intentions of your being.

Do you wish to proceed? Yes/No

Xavier's grin was spread from ear to ear now. The vault was a major discovery. Much more than he expected when he first saw the empty shelves. He was excited to see what was in the armory now. He focused on the word yes and the small orb sunk into his hand binding the satchel to his soul the same way had happened with the blade, and from what Ella had said herself, earlier.

"Alright Aelriva. Its time to see the armory. Then you can lead me to where Braegor is." Xavier considered for a moment then amended his statement. "Actually, lead me to the armory then go find Braegor and ask him to join me there."

He walked to the passageway, as soon as the two of them cleared the vault doors they swung ponderously closed with a resounding boom. Xavier jumped at the unexpected noise but quickly settled himself and followed the sprite towards their next destination, and Xavier smiled.

The past may have been buried, but its gifts were beginning to surface.

CHAPTER TWENTY

Weapons, Classes, and Spells

The corridor curved just as Aelriva had promised, two passages down from the main vault. The air here was still and faintly metallic, like iron left too long in shadow. Xavier paused before the iron-bound oak door at the end of the corridor, half-expecting resistance or another trial, but it opened without protest at the touch of his hand.

The mechanism responded exactly like the vault had, humming faintly as his palm pressed against the sigil plate. A subtle warmth bled from the ancient glyph before fading into silence. The heavy door creaked inward, revealing the room beyond.

He stepped inside, torchlight flickering across stone walls that were oddly bare of the decorative reliefs he had grown accustomed to in other parts of the ruins. The room was small, utilitarian. A pair of low benches lined the walls, their cushions long since rotted away to brittle husks. But it wasn't the benches that held his attention.

A grated window of iron mesh dominated the far side, flanked by twin sconces. Just beside it, an equally imposing iron door sat embedded in the wall, without handle or latch.

It reminded him more of a police station armory than a treasure hoard. He could almost imagine a clerk sitting behind that grate, handing out weapons to patrolmen. Curious, he stepped forward and lit the two sconces bracketing the window, casting the space in steadier light.

Beyond the bars, shelves and weapon racks stretched into the shadows. The outlines of swords, axes, and armor glinted dully beneath the dust. Despite the grime, he felt a surge of satisfaction rise in his chest. This was no empty tomb. This was a cache of forgotten strength.

He turned to share the moment with Aelriva, but the sprite was gone. For a moment, confusion tugged at his brow, then he remembered. He had asked her to retrieve Braegor.

Scrubbing a hand through his hair, Xavier chuckled under his breath. The request had slipped his mind entirely. Shaking his head, he turned back to the iron door beside the window, searching for the familiar sigil plate. It didn't take long to find, half-hidden behind a rusted torch bracket.

The same prompt greeted him when he pressed his hand to it.

> **Would you like to access this storage chamber?**
> Yes / No

He chose yes.

A soft chime answered, followed by the groan of ancient gears. The iron door unlatched and opened inward with surprising ease. Xavier stepped through... and stopped short.

The chamber beyond was larger than he'd expected. Deeper too, the walls vanishing into shadow beyond the torch's reach. It might have been magnificent once, but time had not been kind. Shelves sagged, crates were crumbling, and most of the metal bore the cancer of corrosion. Yet the structure itself held firm.

He raised the torch higher, catching the glint of a halberd's blade on the wall. Beneath it, a row of curved swords rested like sleeping serpents on a rack thick with dust. Some might be salvageable. Others, he feared, had already surrendered to rust.

Still, there was promise here. Not treasure, but foundation. Enough, perhaps, to begin arming those who would protect the village. He took another step forward, the sound of his boots echoing faintly in the hollow space. Behind him, the door remained open, the others would come and he would not be alone for long.

#

The stillness of the armory stirred as footsteps echoed faintly from the corridor. Dust danced in the lamplight as three figures entered the chamber. Aelriva floated ahead, her wings casting soft glimmers across the old stone. Behind her came Braegor, his head held aloft in one hand, and the young dwarven apprentice Rilsa, wide-eyed with wonder.

The Gan Ceann paused just inside the threshold, raising his head a bit higher to gain a better vantage. From his lifted perspective, Braegor's eyes swept across the racks, walls, and cluttered weaponry, cataloging what time had left behind. His expression didn't shift. For his kind, it was simply a change in perspective.

Rilsa stepped in slowly, turning on the balls of her feet as she took in the room. "I didnae think ye meant a proper armory," she breathed. "Figured we'd find a few old tools, maybe a half-rack o' rusted pikes. But this... this be somethin' else."

"It's not in good shape," Xavier said, brushing a hand along a dusty spear haft. "But it's more than I expected. It's a start."

They fanned out into the chamber. Aelriva hovered silently near the ceiling, her presence subtle, her gaze drifting like smoke toward the deeper shadows. Rilsa crouched near a buckled crate, her fingers already testing the toughness of rotted leather. Xavier moved through the rows, lifting blades and shifting armor pieces with careful deliberation.

Braegor's body, moving independently of his head now perched atop a high rack, sorted through the remnants with mechanical ease. One hand worked methodically, examining hilts and steel, while his head remained aloft, granting him a sweeping view of the room. It was an eerie but efficient rhythm.

Time passed and hope dimmed. A finely forged sword cracked near the tang when lifted. A breastplate had caved inward from corrosion. One shield had fused to the stone wall behind it. For every passable item, four more had succumbed to rot or rust.

Braegor's body paused. Then, with deliberate motion, he retrieved his head from the rack and set it back upon his shoulders. "Most of it's gone," he said quietly. "The steel's soft, the iron's warped. Time's taken its toll."

"But it's nae all ruined," Rilsa countered, holdin' up a torn jerkin. "The leather'll boil well enough. A bit o' stretchin', an' it'll patch up easy. Could make decent sets for a few o' the guard."

Xavier nodded, setting aside a shield with a cracked rim. "And the rest we melt down. Reforge. Not treasure... but a foundation maybe."

They returned to their work. Rilsa focused on anything salvageable for armor—straps, padding, buckles. Braegor collected blade cores, hilt materials, and any viable steel. Xavier did the lifting and hauling, shifting debris and sorting crates. In the quiet, the armory seemed to breathe again. Not as a tomb, but as something stirring back to life.

Then Rilsa's voice rang out from the far corner. "Back here, there's a cabinet. Looks untouched, it does."

Xavier crossed the room quickly. The iron-bound cabinet stood partially obscured behind a slumped rack. Its latch gave way with a reluctant creak, revealing shelves lined in faded velvet. Resting inside were three swords, two short, one long, and a pair of daggers. Though dulled by dust, their dark metallic gleam shimmered with unmistakable density.

Braegor stepped forward, his eyes widening. "Adamantine," he murmured. "By the gods…"

He didn't reach for them immediately. He just stared, reverent. "I've seen one piece of it in all my years. A ceremonial blade, locked away behind glass. But five? In one place?"

Rilsa leaned in slowly, her voice barely above a whisper. "These be real," she said. "Not replicas. Not rusted junk. These be blades that sing in th' forge hymns. Metal forged from th' bones o' th' world itself."

As Xavier stepped closer, a few prompts flickered across his vision.

You have discovered:	Item Class: Rare
Adamantine Short Sword x 2	Item Quality: Well Crafted
	Weight: 1.2 kg
	Durability: 50/100
	Damage: 42-68 (21-34)
	Damage Type: Piercing or Slashing
	Description: A sleek short sword forged from adamantine, its blade gleaming with a dark, polished luster. Despite its inherent resilience,

	centuries of neglect have dulled its edges and loosened the hilt slightly, but its craftsmanship ensures devastating strikes. **Traits:** - **Unyielding:** The blade is nearly indestructible, capable of parrying the strongest strikes. - **Armor-Piercing:** Bypasses conventional armor with ease, delivering devastating blows.
You have discovered: Adamantine Long Sword	**Item Class:** Epic **Item Quality:** Superb **Weight:** 2.0 kg **Durability:** 45/100 **Damage:** 51-102 (56–110 when wielded with two hands) (26-51) **Damage Type:** Slashing **Description:** A masterfully crafted long sword forged from adamantine. Time and exposure to the elements have slightly dulled its edge and caused minor corrosion on the hilt, but its exceptional material and design make it capable of tremendous

damage.
Traits:
- **Unyielding:** Nearly indestructible, ensuring it remains reliable in any battle.
- **Enhanced Reach:** Allows precise strikes at a longer distance.
- **Armor-Piercing:** Effortlessly penetrates heavily armored foes.

You have discovered: Adamantine Dagger x 2	**Item Class:** Rare **Item Quality:** Well Crafted **Weight:** 0.7 kg **Durability:** 40/100 **Damage:** 22-51 (11-25) **Damage Type:** Piercing **Description:** A compact and deadly dagger forged from adamantine. Years of abandonment have left its edge nicked and its grip slightly worn, but its adamantine construction ensures it delivers precise and powerful attacks. **Traits:** - **Unyielding:** Resistant to breaking, ensuring reliability in any scenario. - **Piercing Precision:** Ideal for slipping through small gaps in armor.

| - **Lightweight:** Allows for swift and silent attacks. |

Even dulled and worn, the damage potential was incredible. Xavier stared at the stats, then looked back at the weapons in his hands.

"These would be priceless back home," he muttered. Then, louder, "I'm assuming they're not common here either?"

Braegor let out a low laugh. "Common? Even King Ironthorn of Arenvalis has never held one. These are beyond rare. Artifacts in fact. A single blade could ransom a fortress."

"Arenvalis?" Xavier asked, eyes flicking up.

The smith nodded. "North of the Silverwood. The Wildlands stretch through it. Ironthorn rules from Thandor's Reach. Bramblegate sat on the southern fringe of his domain. We answered to no one, but we were close."

Xavier glanced back at the blades. "I may need to visit. If people are living like that, under chains or poverty, maybe they'd come here instead. Help us build something better."

Braegor finally lifted one of the daggers, turning it in his hand. The torchlight caught the metal, dancing across its flawless geometry. "Aye," he said, voice quiet. "Some would come for freedom. Others for hope. And a few? For blades like this. Give 'em all three, and they'll follow."

\#

"These blades are beautiful," Xavier said, slowly turning one of the short swords in his hands. "Surprisingly light. I thought adamantine was supposed to be heavier."

Rilsa gave a knowing grin, her fingers trailing along the edge of the long sword. "Aye, it is, till ye coax it into listenin'. A master smith shapes it t' balance like a duellist's dagger.

Takes more than hammerin' though. Takes skill, patience... an' a touch o' th' divine."

Xavier gave a few short test swings, marveling at the smooth, deadly flow of the blade. "Could either of you repair them? Fully?"

Braegor shook his head. "No. Not yet. I'm a journeyman, not a master. I can shape steel, maybe star-metal with care, but adamantine? That takes a different level of craftsmanship. And more than that... it takes the right forge."

Rilsa's tone lowered, reverent. "Aye. Ye'd need a place o' power, where th' flame runs deeper than stone an' th' bellows breathe the world's memory. A legendary forge."

Xavier's brow furrowed. "There are places like that?"

Braegor nodded, crossing his arms. "There are only three great forges that I know of. Khazrak's Crucible, in the dwarven kingdoms beneath the Ironspire Mountains. Ashenforge of Sal'tarak, to the far southwest, deep in the desert heart of the Saltwind Citadel. And the third, they say, lies across the sea—the Skyforge of Eryndral, in the Isles of Aelinthar. Myths speak of a fourth... lost millennia ago. Its name's been forgotten."

Aelriva floated silently nearer. Her voice, when it came, was quiet and certain. "The Celestium Forge. It was lost when th' empires fell, at th' end o' th' Age o' Empires. Some say it was th' greatest o' them all. 'Tis said th' forge was a gift from a goddess herself. It crafted more than blades. It crafted legacy."

Xavier's eyes remained on the weapons, his expression growing distant. The forge they had uncovered flickered in his mind, those ancient channels in stone, the hearth cold but intact. His gaze shifted to Aelriva. She caught his look, said nothing, but gave the faintest nod.

He returned his attention to the blade. "I need to learn

more," he murmured. "About this world. Its history. I'm stumbling in the dark here."

Rilsa snorted. "Then light a torch, my lord. Ye've got th' bones o' greatness in yer hands, but bones ain't enough. Ye need to ken how they walked before they fell."

"As to how one is made, my lord..." Braegor began, drawing a slow breath. "That's the stuff of legend. Supposedly, it requires powerful artifacts, relics from the elder days. Not just ore or skill, but catalysts bound to the world's primal roots."

Rilsa stepped closer, eyes alight with memory. Her voice took on the cadence of old forge-tales. "Gather close, an' hear th' tale o' Khazrak's Crucible," she said, her brogue thick with reverence. "Born in th' deep halls o' the Ironspire, when th' world was yet young an' th' mountains still whispered the secrets o' th' gods. For its heart, th' darin' King Khazrak wrenched the Molten Core from the fiery grasp o' Ignavyr, th' dread Titan o' Flame—his beard singed but his resolve unbroken."

Her hands moved as if sketching fire in the air. "Its flames hungered for purpose, an' so he fed 'em Eversteel Ore, th' unyieldin' metal sung into existence by the Stonefather's breath. But even fire an' ore couldnae birth legends without a steady hand upon the Anvil o' the Stonefather, carved from th' world's heart an' imbued with th' wisdom o' the mountain's soul."

Her voice dropped to a hush. "Thus, in th' roarin' depths, Khazrak's Crucible was born. A forge that shaped nae just metal, but the destiny o' all who dared wield its creations."

The final words hung in the air like the last reverberation of a hammer strike. Xavier exhaled slowly and looked again at the blades. They would wait, and for now, so would the forge.

#

The glow of the torchlight flickered across the adamantine blades, casting ripples of light through the dust-choked air. Silence had settled again, thick with thoughts and the weight of stories now remembered.

Xavier finally spoke, his voice quiet. "I've reached the point where I can choose my archetypes. One gathering. One crafting. I've been holding off, trying to figure out what fits... but nothing's stood out until now."

Braegor looked over at him, curious. "What's made ye bring it up now?"

Xavier set the short sword gently back into the cabinet. "This, all of this, it's made something clear. I'm not just swinging swords and scavenging ruins. I'm building something. I need to be part of that."

Rilsa leaned back against one of the stone pillars, arms crossed. "Most folk know their path from their kin. Me mother's side were smiths back t' th' foundin' o' Clan Thorgrimm. Her father taught her, an' she passed it to me. Me hands knew th' hammer before I could spell me own name."

Braegor gave a small nod. "Same here. My mother's father was a smith. I learned under him until his hands failed. My grandmother mined iron along the edge veins of the lower spires. That left its mark, too. Core skills tend to follow the bloodline. It's more natural than people think."

Xavier frowned slightly. "That's the thing. I don't know what my mother did, or my father. There's no line to follow for me." He didn't elaborate, and neither of them pressed.

He thought back to the books he used to read on Earth. One series had a main character who became an enchanter, crafting powerful weapons to defend his village. Another followed a blacksmith whose forge became the heart of a growing settlement. There was one about an alchemist who turned battlefield salvage into wonders, and another, his favorite, about a shaper who could mold any material into whatever he imagined. That one ended with the protagonist ascending to godhood, though, so it didn't exactly feel applicable, and he didn't have access to a skill like that anyway.

He turned toward Aelriva. "Why have I not seen any enchanted weapons or armor? I've found jewelry, and my satchel, but nothing else."

Aelriva fluttered near one of the overhead sconces, casting a faint light. "Enchantin' is a complicated craft, aye. Not only do ye require th' item t' be enchanted, ye need t' ken th' enchantment ye mean t' place upon it. Then ye'll need essence stones, filled with th' right level o' essence for what ye're enchantin'. More complex enchantments require more essence, mind ye. Finally, essence crystal must be ground, an' th' powder used. With essence crystal bein' what's needed t' make essence stones, it's nae easy t' come by for th' average crafter. Powdered essence crystal is needed for higher versions o' other crafts as well, so it be a rare an' precious commodity." She ticked off each point on her fingers as she spoke.

Xavier scowled slightly. He hadn't heard of essence stones or essence crystal until now. It sounded like one more layer of complexity to overcome if he wanted to improve the village. It also helped him narrow his path. Enchanting wasn't for him.

Smithing, while appealing, would tie him to a forge. He didn't have the time to spend hours hammering metal. Cooking, another interest, seemed similarly impractical. Too rooted. Too stationary. That left two options that stirred something deeper in him: Artificer and Rune Engraver.

He returned his gaze to Aelriva. "Can you tell me anything about Artificers or Rune Engravers?"

The sprite drifted closer. "I am sorry, Ard'Maelor. Much has been lost t' me over th' centuries as th' Syr'Vailen fell into dormancy. I do nae remember much beyond th' fact they be craftin' archetypes. They were both respected by th' Sylmyrians, aye. All craft was, however. As ye wake more o' th' ley lines an' level th' village, more should return t' me." She replied, once again there was a tone of sadness to her voice and Xavier wasn't sure if it was due to the lost memories or the fact she couldn't assist him.

Xavier nodded and brought up his interface. The two archetypes had been singled out and he focused on them in turn hoping to learn more.

Artificer: Masters of Arcane Craftsmanship
Artificers are inventors who blend magic and mechanics to create devices, constructs, and tools. They are engineers of the arcane world, always pushing the boundaries of what is possible by fusing innovation with magical theory.
"Why choose between magic and machines when you can just use both and call it brilliance?"
Sub-classes include – Gadgeteer, Machinist, Magitech Engineer, Tinkerer, and Rune-Tech Smith.

Rune Engraver: Masters of Magical Inscription
Rune Engravers are arcane artists who channel ancient power through symbols and glyphs, inscribing runes onto weapons, armor, scrolls, and even the land itself. Their craft shapes the very fabric of magic, bringing spells to life through precise etching and mystical design.
"Yes, it's just a squiggle, until it blows up your face."
Sub-classes include – Weapon Sigilist, Ward Crafter, Rune Artificer, and Scripter of Scrolls.

He was amazed at how much the two overlapped. Artificers pushed boundaries. Rune Engravers etched the very rules. Both felt... right. A part of him dared to believe he might take both someday. After all, his trait Unbound Possibilities said nothing was truly off-limits.

With a village to support him, perhaps he could become something more. His mind raced with the possibilities, golems, constructs, etched walls of warding, mobile tools, defensive sigils, even weapons of layered function. Forest guardians were impressive. But what if he could craft something that never faded? Something permanent.

"I've narrowed it down to two," Xavier said at last. "Rune Engraver... and Artificer."

Braegor blinked. "Rare paths."

"Aye," Rilsa said, pushing off the pillar. "Nae many go those routes. Enchantin's already tricky enough. But runes an' mechanisms? That's th' kind o' work that either makes legends—or corpses."

"They speak to me," Xavier said simply. "I haven't met anyone here who uses either path. But maybe that's the point."

He opened his interface and made his choice.

You have selected a Crafting Archetype: Rune Engraver
New Skills Acquired:
Rune Channeling (Level 1, 0%)
Infuse and activate etched runes with magical energy.
Enhances the power and stability of inscriptions.
+2% chance to successfully activate a rune
+2% rune efficacy
Rune Deciphering (Level 1, 0%)
Interpret or disable runes on items, structures, traps, or
ancient relics.
+2% chance to learn a rune
-2% chance to trigger traps or hostile glyphs

He felt the shift immediately... an intuitive grasp of

curves, angles, etched sequences that hadn't made sense before. Symbols pulsed at the edges of his thoughts, not words but blueprints of potential.

He smiled faintly. "And for gathering... I think I'll choose Scavenger. Makes the most sense with where I've ended up."

> **You have selected a Gathering Archetype: Scavenger**
> **New Skills Acquired:**
> **Keen Eye (Level 1, 0%)**
> *Spot hidden, overlooked, or valuable materials in ruins, battlefields, and forgotten places.*
> +2% chance to detect rare or useful objects
> **Trap Awareness (Level 1, 0%)**
> *Detect, assess, and disarm traps while scavenging.*
> +2% chance to disarm a trap
> -2% chance to trigger a trap

Xavier felt both new skills settle into place like missing tools suddenly found in a belt pouch. Subtle, but ready. They were quiet talents, but he knew instinctively they would save his life and maybe change others'.

He looked to Braegor and Rilsa. "Thanks for your help, even if you didn't mean to give it."

Rilsa grinned. "We'll take credit anyway, my lord. Just make sure ye don't blow yerself up scribblin' strange lines on things ye shouldn't."

"I'll do my best," Xavier said, smirking. "No promises though."

He gestured back toward the cabinet. "Please see to the weapons and armor as we discussed. We'll need them ready. I have a feeling that when more guards arrive, outfitting them properly will become a priority."

He hesitated, then added, "I'm granting both of you access to the armory. You can begin moving stock and organizing salvage as you see fit. I'll be giving access to Coren as well, he'll need it, now that he's Captain of the Guard."

#

Xavier stepped from the armory, the door easing shut behind him with a deep, echoing thud. Aelriva flitted silently at his shoulder, her sylvan glow casting soft ripples of amber and silver along the carved stone walls. The corridor ahead stretched in gentle curves, lined with moss-veined archways and ancient runes dulled by time. The air was still, save for the occasional flutter of her wings and the quiet press of his boots against smoothed stone.

They moved without words, following the faint breath of ley-touched air that still lingered in the hallways of the Syr'Vailen. It wasn't just a walk back to Ella. It felt like a return, to purpose, to responsibility, to something anchoring.

Xavier slowed his pace, then halted, turning inward. A subtle pulse echoed in his thoughts as his interface unfolded like an unseen scroll across his awareness.

You have 6 Attribute Points to assign.

His gaze traced the familiar spread of attributes, each line holding meaning now more than ever. Strength and Dexterity had their place but today was about growth. About crafting and comprehension... and survival.

He tapped Intelligence twice, each press like a key turning in a hidden door. Already, the runes from earlier seemed crisper, their patterns more fluid in his mind.

Then Wisdom, also twice, grounding intuition, bolstering the quiet sense that guided him in unfamiliar paths.

Finally, Luck. He chuckled to himself as he tapped it twice. "Still riding that dice roll, huh?" he muttered.

Attributes Updated.

> **Keen Eye** skill progression boosted by 20% from your skill growth allocation.

The change settled into him like a breath drawn after silence. The world around him hadn't shifted, but his sense of it had.

Aelriva gave a small, approving hum. "Not poor choices, Ard'Maelor. Not at all."

Xavier let the moment hang, then spoke. "Aelriva… when I first awakened the Syr'Vailen, I gained the skills for Life and Death magic. But no spells. How am I supposed to level those without casting?"

"I was wonderin' when ye'd ask about that," she replied, drifting ahead to face him mid-air. Her wings beat softly, stirring a faint breeze. "It's nae difficult, truly. I can teach ye a basic spell for each. It'll set ye down th' path toward mastery, sure enough."

Her form changed, an elegant shift that blurred light and shape. First, she radiated vibrant green as vines and curling leaves shimmered around her, blooming and unfurling like petals in fast-forward. She glowed with a warmth that resonated from the very stone.

> **You have learned a new Life Magic spell – Blooming Touch.**
> **Casting Time** – 6 seconds
> **Range** – Touch
> **Duration** – Instantaneous
> **Cost** – 15 Mana
> **Description**: Channel the vitality of the ley lines into a single touch.
> Healing Surge: Restore 18–24 HP.
> Revitalize Flora: Restore life to plants, soil, or nature-bound items.

Then, as though a wind passed through her, her glow

dimmed and cooled. Vines withered. Color drained into muted grays and blues, her wings trailing mist. The air grew heavier, touched by unseen murmurs and the soft scent of cold earth.

You have learned a new Death Magic spell – Wraith's Whisper.
Casting Time – 6 seconds
Range – 30 feet
Duration – Up to 1 minute (Concentration)
Cost – 15 Mana per 10 seconds
Description: Whisper dread into a foe's mind.
Target takes 15 necrotic damage every 5 seconds.
Target has disadvantage on attacks against you while affected.

The knowledge poured into his mind in a sudden surge like the first notes of a forgotten song returning mid-melody. His thoughts filled with motion and rhythm: the exacting gestures, the vocal tones and resonance shifts, the feel of ley energy as it coiled and flowed toward each spell's unique form. His body tensed for a heartbeat under the weight of it, and then... it passed, leaving clarity in its wake.

He blinked, steady once more. They reached the threshold of the chamber. Xavier pushed open the door. Warm firelight bathed the stone floor in amber glow, dancing against the walls in slow, flickering waves. The air here was softer. Quieter. As if the room itself respected the presence of the one who lay within.

Ella rested in her bed beside the hearth. Her hair fanned loosely over the linen beneath her head, catching the light with warm brown and gold streaks. Her chest rose and fell in an even rhythm now, her color no longer pale with shock.

Xavier crossed the room slowly. He lowered himself into the chair beside the bed and took her hand gently in his. Her skin was cool, but no longer cold.

He watched her for a long moment. Just breathing. Today had been filled with choices, and with revelations. With the stirrings of something greater than he could yet name, but here, at Ella's side, he found stillness.

His body ached, and his thoughts had begun to fray at the edges. But for now, they could wait. He leaned back, head resting against the smooth curve of the chair behind him. The warmth of the fire kissed his face. Aelriva dimmed her glow and settled near the hearth without a word. Xavier, Lord Vael and Ard'Maelor of Rynthavael, closed his eyes, and finally let sleep take him.

#

CHAPTER TWENTY-ONE

On the Road Again

"Hey Alex, good morning! You want your usual today?"

The voice pulled him from his thoughts like sunlight through fog. Bright, familiar, warm. His eyes drifted upward to find a smiling brunette leaning out the window of a little café. Samantha. Her cheerful tone and the scent of fresh coffee wrapped around him like a memory come alive.

"Oh, hey Sam. Yeah, that'd be great. Gonna need it to get through another day of work. I swear they come up with the most monotonous tasks just to keep us busy." He placed a hand on the counter, a soft grin tugging at his lips. "Do you have any of those fresh croissants too? I didn't eat, and my stomach's staging a rebellion."

She laughed, setting a steaming cup on the ledge beside a warm paper bag. "Lucky for you I stashed one."

Xavier reached for them… And blinked.

Samantha was gone. The smell vanished. The café faded like mist in sunlight.

He was still in the warrens, standing beside Ella's bed. His hand hovered inches above the blanket instead of a counter.

Confused and unsettled, he stepped back and sat heavily in the nearby chair. His heart raced. He pressed his palms against his face, then reached out and clutched Ella's hand, grounding himself.

What in the world was that?

He hadn't eaten anything questionable. He hadn't drunk anything but water. Had he fallen asleep standing up? Dreamed with his eyes open? Or was something toying with his mind?

The thought sent a cold ripple through his chest. He inhaled slowly, steadying himself, but the hairs on the back of his neck rose as another presence stirred in the room.

Across the bed, a figure now sat where no one had been a moment before. Danu.

The goddess of balance watched him with serene amusement, her vermillion hair cascading in waves over her shoulders, her smile calm as morning light. Her hand rested lightly on Ella's, fingertips brushing the unconscious woman's skin.

"My, how you have grown already, Alex," she said. "Only a handful of weeks, and you've a fledgling settlement, a soul-bound companion, and the power of two ley lines stirring within you. You've exceeded even my highest hopes."

Xavier stared, uncertain whether to speak or simply stare. She always looked so... vivid. Almost too much for the world around her, like color painted atop grey canvas.

He swallowed. "Why did I just see Samantha? Is she here too? Are others brought from Earth? You told me the world had problems, but not much else."

Danu's smile widened. "You've walked the ruins. Heard the stories. Met the races of Arath. Don't you find it strange how much they resemble the myths of your world?"

She gestured toward the spot where Samantha had stood moments earlier. "There is crossover, Alex. Through dreams. Through imagination. Since the first stories were told on Earth, they have drawn inspiration from here. Arath influences your world far more than most realize. Its echoes shape your legends."

He blinked, thoughts tumbling over themselves. "How is that even possible?"

"Faith and magic are sparse on Earth. Gods cannot dwell there. But influence? That is different. A whisper in a dream. A flash of inspiration. A story half-remembered. Your world develops rapidly. That pace makes it a mirror, a lens through which we glimpse what might be. We did not create your people's choices, Alex. But we nudged ideas. Inspiration does not equal manipulation."

Her voice gentled. "Be at peace. You aren't losing your mind. Being of another world, you see things that others here cannot. Most mortals look past such visions. Their minds are not made to accept them."

She laughed softly. The sound was delicate and strange, like bells beneath water. "A curious thing, is it not? That in a world of magic and monsters, some truths are still too strange to see."

Xavier leaned back, silent. His thoughts churned. How many things in Arath matched stories from Earth? After a while it was easy to see how many of the things he had seen or experienced in Arath could be found in the stories, games and myths of his home. He even saw some correlations between technology and some of the magics he had experienced so far. Had all of that stemmed from dreams?

He looked up slowly. "So you came to calm me down? Am I that important to you?"

"Yes and no," she answered. "You are a turning point, a fulcrum. I cannot tell you everything, nor should I. The more I shape your fate, the more it might twist into something worse. My domain is balance. And balance cannot be forced."

She stood, brushing imaginary dust from her gown. "This world is slipping further from what it should be. You have the potential to stop that. But only if you choose to. I cannot compel you. You must seek it yourself. Learn more. Wander beyond these woods. Or even within them. There is far more here than you know."

Her gaze lingered on him, warm and wistful. "I think you will choose rightly. You are a pinion of fate, after all."

Then she vanished. Not with a flash, not with a sound, but with absence. The chair beside the bed was empty. Her scent lingered for only a heartbeat.

Xavier exhaled through his nose and dragged both hands down his face. Was she even real? Was any of that? He didn't know, and that bothered him.

He couldn't trust her blindly anymore. She was too convenient. Too polished. Too manipulative in her kindness. She had brought him here, yes. But it was her fault he had been hit by the car in the first place.

He looked at Ella, still sleeping. Her breathing was faint but stronger than it had been. Her color was slowly returning. He reached out and stroked her hand, the faint calluses along his palm brushing her skin.

"I'm glad you're still with me," he whispered. "I don't know if I'd have made it without you."

She didn't stir, but Valkra, curled up at the end of the bed, lifted her head and blinked slowly at him.

Xavier smiled and stood. There was work to do. The village waited, the future waited, and somewhere beyond the treetops, answers waited too.

"No pressure," he muttered, turning toward the exit.

#

The echo of his footsteps followed him through the dim stone passages as he made his way upward from the depths. The air lightened gradually, growing warmer with each level, until the faint scent of earth and moss reminded him just how far below the surface they had come.

Before he reached the upper halls, a shimmer of blue drifted into view beside him, Aelriva.

The sprite hovered at his shoulder, wings faintly humming as she matched his pace. Her eyes glimmered with an almost expectant light.

"I've been going over the city interface," Xavier said, keeping his voice low so it would not carry. "Most of it still makes no sense. Half the tabs are greyed out, and the few that are open give almost nothing. But a couple of things caught my eye."

"Ask yer questions, Ard'Maelor," she replied. Her tone was calm, melodic, and lightly amused. "I'll offer what help I can. Though keep in mind, much o' what once was lies still beyond ye. Even I see only fragments at times."

He nodded. "It's the buildings and villagers tabs. I've seen what's being built outside, I've walked through them. But the interface says nothing's there. It's blank. The same with the villagers. I can see their names, but that's all. No details, no roles, not even how many we actually have. How am I supposed to manage anything if I can't see it?"

"Ah, well now, that be simple enough," Aelriva said,

fluttering ahead of him briefly before circling back. "Ye've no heart to yer village yet, Ard'Maelor. No steward named. No place t' center yer people. Homes and huts be a start, aye, but ye'll need a town hall if ye wish t' manage proper. With such a place, ye'll be able to assign duties, track yer people's needs, and see what troubles brew afore they grow too large."

Xavier frowned, processing that. It made sense. Back on Earth, he'd played plenty of settlement-building games. You never got access to certain features without upgrading your core structures. A hall, a steward, maybe a council later. It wasn't just gameplay logic anymore. It was how Arath itself operated.

"Alright," he said slowly. "So that's the bottleneck. No wonder everything feels stalled."

"Aye. Ye've built well, but without a seat o' guidance, even th' best stone will crumble. Ye'll need space carved out, not just for yerself but for th' ones who'll help ye shape this place. Only then will th' deeper paths o' yer interface open t' ye."

They stepped into the large entrance chamber that bridged the warrens and surface-level buildings. Light filtered through from the far corridor, casting golden patterns across the stone floor. Here and there, villagers sat sharing morning meals and quiet conversation. The ones who lacked homes still slept in the warrens, and this chamber had become a common gathering place.

Xavier paused as his eyes swept the room, then spotted who he was looking for.

"Thanks, Aelriva. I'll handle the next part."

The sprite gave a slight bow mid-air, her wings flickering silver as she turned and vanished through the upper arches.

Xavier crossed the room toward a rough stone table where

two men sat reviewing a half-unrolled parchment over their breakfast. Rhett, the carpenter, was a sturdy man with callused hands and a worn smile. Across from him, Orrik, the dwarven stonemason, was already chewing a thick strip of salted meat between comments.

"Morning, M'lord," they said in unison as Xavier approached and took a seat beside them.

Rhett pushed his empty plate back. "We were just going over the plans for the day. Few more homes nearly done, and we were talking about starting the livestock pens next."

Xavier raised a hand. "Hold that thought. The homes take priority, yes. People need places of their own. But before we build anything else, I need a town hall."

Both men blinked, pausing mid-motion.

"This chamber has worked so far, but it lacks any real functionality. I can't manage anything from here. What I need is a space that gives structure. A central place where I or Braegor can speak with others and oversee the needs of the settlement."

He pointed toward one wall, where open windows let in light but little else. "I don't want to block the warrens, so can we build outward from there? It'd put it closer to the center of the village, too."

The two craftsmen followed his gesture. A moment later, Orrik pulled a wide tube from his satchel, uncapped it, and began sliding out rolls of parchment. He flipped one over, cleared a space, and together they began sketching.

Xavier chuckled softly. Once they got going, the pair forgot he was even sitting there.

The design was simple, functional. Neither man was a true architect, and they had told him before they could only build what they understood. But that limitation didn't slow them down. The result was clean. A main hall set back behind the current chamber, with antechambers flanking each side. Double doors framed one end, and a raised platform was etched into the opposite wall. Offices lined the interior, giving it the feel of a small keep or court.

They slid the parchment over to him.

Xavier studied it, nodded, then looked up with a grin. "That's perfect. How soon can you start?"

Orrik scratched his beard. "Well, m'lord. We'll need more stone and lumber. Th' homes've used most o' what we salvaged from the ruins, and th' trees within the village proper be thinnin'. With more golems t' gather, we can keep pace. Might be able t' start on the foundation by Windspire morning."

Xavier blinked. "Windspire?"

The dwarf held up thick fingers, ticking off names. "Sunwake, Moonshade, Starcrest, Hearthfire, Dewfall, Windspire, Arathbond, and Nightveil. Then back t' Sunwake. Today be Starcrest."

"Three days," Xavier murmured. "Alright."

He pulled up the interface and opened the settlement magic tab. Sure enough, the village's mana pool remained full, and no golems had been summoned for the day.

He selected the only available spell and activated it.

Outside, stone shifted. Roots twisted. Earthen forms rose from the ground, shaped by magic and pulled from the very forest floor. Within moments, ten forest golems stood still and silent, awaiting commands.

"Done. I'll make sure Aelriva summons them each

morning. You'll have your workforce."

The men rose with satisfied nods, offered him respectful salutes, right fists over hearts, then gathered up their designs and marched off toward the golems.

Xavier remained seated, fingers steepled beneath his chin. The sprite had answered his questions. Now he needed to answer the ones the interface still left open.

#

Xavier remained seated long after Rhett and Orrik left, letting the sounds of the hall wash over him. Low conversation drifted from the gathered villagers nearby, punctuated by the scrape of tin plates and the soft clatter of wooden utensils. Light flickered gently from the sconces set into the stone walls, mingling with early sunlight that trickled in through the open entry corridor.

He pulled open the interface again. Tabs flickered to life, semi-translucent and layered across his vision like ethereal parchment. He focused on the Quests tab and began scrolling through the entries.

You have been offered a quest: Reforge the Past II
Having gained mastery of Cael'Anthir, it is up to you to restore it to its former glory and rebuild its people.
Objective: Raise the settlement to Level 2
Failure Penalty: Stagnation of growth. This is a bound settlement quest and cannot be refused.
Reward: +5000 Experience. Increased powers and capabilities for the settlement.

You have been offered a quest: Sleeping Lines III
Most of the ley lines that make up the nexus beneath your settlement remain dormant. Continue your exploration of the Deeps and restore the remaining lines to further increase ambient mana and unlock additional

capabilities.
Condition: Reach Personal Level 15. Maintain mastery of the Syr'Vailen.
Reward: +1500 Experience. Increased ambient mana, wildlife presence, and quest opportunities.

You have been offered a quest: Whose House I
While the lands surrounding your settlement fall under your purview, not all who dwell within them call you lord. Explore at least four unique locations and uncover their significance.
Reward: +500 Experience. Reduced danger from monster nests. Additional unknown benefits.

You have been offered a quest: Drums in the Deeps I
The unknown deeps lie beyond the reach of your current domain. Reclaim the first level beneath the warded nexus mosaic and uncover what lurks there.
Reward: +500 Experience. Increased resource access and other settlement benefits.

Xavier closed the quests tab and moved to the Settlement Level requirements.

Rynthavael (Cael'Anthir) – Level 2 Requirements:
Population: 49 / 100
Buildings: 6 / 15
Settlement Quests Completed: 3 / 5

"Not too far off," he murmured, narrowing his eyes at the population number.

He navigated to the Villagers tab. Names scrolled by, but something immediately caught his attention.

Ella was missing, so was Aelriva, and so was he.

He frowned, crossing his arms. That confirmed a theory. The interface didn't recognize Aelriva as a villager due to her bond with the Syr'Vailen. He could understand that.

But his own absence? Perhaps because he was the lord of the settlement and thus not counted among the general populace.

But what was different about Ella? Was it because she was still recovering? Or was it something deeper, something tied to her unusual nature?

He leaned back, lost in thought for several long moments. In the end, he sighed and closed the interface. He wouldn't solve that mystery today.

There was still progress to be made. Mentally, he reached out to Aelriva through their bond. Within moments, a faint shimmer coalesced over the center table. The sprite emerged in a ripple of soft light, her wings trailing faint azure sparks.

"Ye summoned me, Ard'Maelor?" she asked, tilting her head slightly.

He motioned her closer. "Before Emily's disappearance, you mentioned several nearby locations that might be worth investigating. One of my quests requires me to explore four unique places within our territory. With Ella still recovering, staying close makes sense. Which one is closest?"

Aelriva did not hesitate. "T' the north lies a place hidden from view. Hidden t' most, but not t' ye. These lands be yers now, an' they will answer. Head toward the mountains that loom o'er the trees. Ye'll find what ye seek afore the sun has passed twice."

Xavier narrowed his eyes. "Really? A riddle? You couldn't just say what it is?"

"I could guide ye," she said with a smirk, "but ye pledged my aid t' the crafters. I cannot be in two places at once. A riddle is more proper for a quest. Or do ye expect everythin' t' be handed t' ye on a silver platter?"

He gave her a flat look. "It's no wonder stories about sprites always say you lot are tricksters."

Aelriva's grin widened. Mischief twinkled in her eyes. She spun once in the air, her wings catching the light. "Tricksters we may be, but that be our charm. If ye need nothin' else, I'll return t' overseeing th' golems. Do not worry, Ard'Maelor. I'll keep watch over Ella while ye're away."

He nodded, already rising to his feet. She was right. He would not wait. Ella would want him to keep moving, and the village could not afford stagnation.

#

The corridors of the warrens were quiet as Xavier descended once more. Most of the village was awake now, focused on construction, food preparation, and tending the growing settlement. He passed through the winding stone paths, down past the sleeping quarters, and into the deeper chambers.

Ella's room was dimly lit, the glow-crystals along the wall casting gentle amber light across the curved stone. The air here felt still, almost sacred.

Valkra stirred slightly on the bed, stretching one paw outward before settling again beside the unconscious woman. The shadowmane cub blinked up at Xavier as he entered.

He knelt beside the bed and reached out to gently stroke the panther's head. "I'm heading out for a bit, Valkra. I need you to stay and watch over her, alright?"

The cub yawned, her small tongue curling as she blinked sleepily at him. She shifted slightly, making more room at Ella's side but clearly not planning to leave. It was all the answer he needed.

Xavier smiled faintly, then turned his gaze to Ella. Her breathing was slow but steady. Color had returned to her cheeks. There was still no sign of consciousness, but something about her presence felt stronger, less faded than before.

"I'll be back soon," he said softly, resting a hand briefly over hers.

He stood and gathered his gear from the adjoining chamber. Light leather armor, simple but reinforced. His satchel already organized. Vaeltheris, resting in its sheath. He felt the weight of the blade settle against his back as he slung it into place.

From there, he moved through the warrens toward the kitchen, drawn by the smell of baked bread and simmering broth.

Inside, he found Frieda and Greta moving in perfect rhythm, Frieda stirring a thick stew in a cast iron pot, Greta kneading dough beside a tray of hard biscuits cooling near the hearth. A few young helpers, including Emily, darted back and forth between tasks, taking instructions and carrying platters of food to the surface.

"Good morning, m'lord!" Frieda called cheerfully without even turning.

"Good timing," Greta added, dusting her hands off and gesturing toward the corner. "Pack's ready. Dried meat, cheese, biscuits, and some trail cakes."

Xavier offered a grateful nod. "You two are the true power behind this place."

Greta laughed. "Flatterin' words don't get ye seconds, but they do make the work lighter."

He gathered the food into his satchel, checked the straps, and thanked them both again before heading back toward the surface.

The light outside had strengthened. The soft warmth of mid-morning bathed the settlement in golden hues. He stood for a moment at the base of the new town hall foundation, surveying the land.

To the south and east, workers moved over rising homes, hammering beams into place and shaping stone for chimneys. Past them, small fields stretched toward the Silverflow River, where crops had begun to take root. Further east, a handful of Animari cleared land for gardens and penned animals. Golems labored silently in the woods, gathering timber and stone.

The village breathed. It was becoming real.

Xavier walked slowly around the outer wall of the central hall until he reached the north side. The woods pressed close here, and beyond them, the land sloped upward toward distant mountains. He remembered his first journey out with Ella, how they had followed the trail toward the Heart of the Forge. That felt like a lifetime ago, though only weeks had passed.

He already missed her beside him. Resolved, he adjusted the straps on his satchel and took a single step forward. A flicker of light appeared at his shoulder.

Aelriva drifted into view, her wings catching sunlight in a soft shimmer. Her voice was gentler than usual.

"Before ye go, I have one more gift t' offer, Ard'Maelor. A skill born o' perception. It'll help ye see the dangers that lie ahead."

She reached out and placed a small hand against his brow. Her form shifted slightly as she called upon the element of water, the blues in her wings and gown deepening to aquamarine. Cool energy flowed through his skin, and a rush of awareness settled behind his eyes.

A prompt opened before him.

Congratulations! You have learned a new skill: Insight (Level 1)

> The Insight skill enables you to perceive the physical, magical, and emotional states of creatures and people around you.
> Even at novice levels, you can identify their name, level, and vital resources such as health, mana, and stamina as percentages.
> As the skill improves, you will uncover deeper truths... vulnerabilities, strengths, and the nature of their essence itself. Observation becomes knowledge. Knowledge becomes power.

"Name, level, health bars," Xavier murmured. "You've turned me into a walking status screen."

"Aye," Aelriva replied with a small grin. "But one who sees clearly is harder t' fool, and harder t' break."

He turned to face her and took her hand for a moment. "Thank you. Truly. I didn't mean to imply you were holding back. This... this is a gift."

"I know. An' ye've earned it. Ye've grown fast, Ard'Maelor. Faster than I thought ye might. But Arath needs such growth."

He nodded solemnly. "Take care of them while I'm gone. I'll return as soon as I can."

"Aye. May the path open true for ye."

She vanished once more, her light dispersing into the morning breeze.

Xavier turned north, toward the trees. The woods rose up to meet him like an old friend, and with each step he left the sounds of the village behind.

Birdsong filled the canopy. Leaves danced on the wind. He walked steadily, keeping the mountains ahead of him in view, resting only when fatigue forced him to stop.

By nightfall, he had reached a grove at the base of a low

rise. The moons had begun to climb, emerald, crimson, and the pale silver disk that reminded him of Earth.

He climbed a broad-limbed tree and settled on a sturdy branch, fifteen feet from the ground. It swayed gently in the night air as he wrapped himself in his cloak.

Then he reached into his satchel and pulled free a worn leather-bound volume. One of the books from the ruins of Bramblegate.

Its title was faded. Its spine cracked. But the stories within had waited long enough. He opened it carefully and began to read beneath the light of three moons.

CHAPTER TWENTY-TWO

I am a Dwarf and I'm Digging a Hole

The night passed uneventfully. Xavier stirred to the soft rustle of leaves and the warbling rise of birdsong overhead. He shifted on the narrow tree limb where he had wedged himself, wincing as stiffness pulled at his muscles. Sleep had come in fits, and now his shoulders and hips protested the awkward position with every small motion.

Bracing a hand against the trunk, he stood and stretched. Morning sunlight filtered through the canopy, painting the forest floor below in dappled gold and shadow. He reached into his pouch, chewing slowly on a bitter leaf of forest sage to ease the ache that lingered in his back and neck. It helped. A little.

Once grounded again, boots pressing into damp earth, he set his course northward. Aelriva had said he would find the place today, some remnant of the past lost to the woods. He didn't want to waste daylight.

Still, as he moved, he kept to his habit. Eyes sharp, steps measured. Herbalism had changed the way the forest looked to him. Leaves shimmered faintly when they held properties of interest. Vines grew in patterns his eye now parsed with meaning, not just aesthetics. Here, a stalk heavy with potential poultices. There, bark used to mend torn flesh or staunch blood. He knelt often, harvesting carefully, always noting the growing weight of his satchel.

It reminded him of hiking the Cascade Range back home. Washington's peaks had offered solitude, but not like this. Not the full-throated wildness of Arath. There was no comparison, no contest. The Silverwood lived in a way Earth's forests never had. Every chirp, rustle, and snap echoed with a deeper resonance as if the forest watched him with curious eyes just beyond the trees.

His pace alternated between jogging and resting. When the sun climbed high and heat pressed against his shoulders, he slowed to a walk. There was no point in rushing blindly. He needed to find something specific, and the forest stretched endlessly in all directions. Eight hundred square miles of claimed territory, and he had no idea what sign he was supposed to look for.

Aelriva's guidance had been vague. Infuriatingly so.

Xavier muttered to himself. "So much for game mechanics."

No mini-map. No glowing quest markers. Even the maps scavenged from Bramblegate were useless here. Most were painted murals or stitched cloth panels meant for tavern walls, not for backpacks. He needed something he could use in the field, something living, something that—

He stopped, narrowing his eyes at the underbrush ahead. A worn trail curved through the ferns like the ghost of a path. Game trail, maybe, it was nothing special but still, he followed it.

For the next hour, he wound along that narrow trail. When nothing emerged, he veered away, zigzagging outward in wide arcs to check the terrain beyond. Every now and then, he paused, squinting into the green, frustrated. He should have asked Aelriva for more clues. Relying on luck wasn't enough anymore. Not with others counting on him.

A low, moss-covered boulder offered a place to sit. He slumped onto it, pulled out a strip of dried meat, and tore into it absently. His mind drifted to his skills tab. Maybe something there could help.

He opened the interface, eyes scanning the long list. The number surprised him. In just a few weeks, he had learned more than he thought possible, fighting, crafting, foraging, deciphering runes. It was a strange, surreal record of his time in Arath.

He skipped past the weapon proficiencies. He might need them later, but not now. Same with the crafting skills.

His eyes stopped at a line near the bottom: Keen Eye. Level 1. Newly added when he chose the Scavenger archetype.

The ability to identify hidden or valuable items, resources, or opportunities in an environment that others might overlook.

It sounded perfect. But there was no activation option. Just a passive effect. He sighed, closing the interface. That figured. He bit off another chunk of meat and let his gaze wander. Then he paused as his chewing slowed. The trees were different. He turned his head and looked back the way he had come.

He was right, they were distinctly different. Shorter, younger, thinner trunks and tighter spacing. If he hadn't been still, he never would have noticed. The contrast was too subtle while moving. But here, seated and still, the pattern revealed itself.

He stood and backtracked a few paces. Then he paused and compared again.

No doubt about it. This part of the forest had regrown

more recently. He began walking its edge, tracing the shift in growth pattern. After circling for half an hour, he realized the entire section spanned nearly two miles in radius and then it happened.

A faint chime echoed in his mind. His vision blurred for half a heartbeat.

> **Congratulations! You have learned a new skill:** Woodlore (Level 1).
> Woodlore represents an intimate connection to forests and woodlands. It encompasses knowledge of the ecosystem, the ability to interact harmoniously with the environment, and skills specific to wooded areas. Synergistic with Survival and Tracking. In forested regions, both gain increased effectiveness.
> The forest is alive. The wise learn its language. The foolish become its prey.

Xavier blinked, dismissing the message. When his gaze settled again, the trees looked different. Their age was clearer and their health more obvious. Even their arrangement seemed to hum with meaning. Whatever lay hidden here, he was close now.

#

The shift in the forest's tone followed him as he walked. What had once been wild and tangled now held a quiet deliberateness, as if someone had shaped this part of the woods long ago and the memory of it still lingered in the roots.

He retraced his steps toward the southeastern edge of the younger grove, letting his senses remain open. His pace slowed. His gaze swept the ground. There, half-hidden beneath a mat of leaves and moss, something angular caught his eye.

Xavier crouched, brushing aside the debris. A row of stones, laid with clear intent, revealed themselves. The moss clung to their edges, but the deliberate placement was unmistakable. A path, old and long-forgotten.

He straightened slowly, following the line of stone to the north. Then turned and looked south, back toward Rynthavael. "This runs both ways," he murmured.

The trail wasn't wide, barely more than three feet across, but it had once been carved with purpose. Roots had cracked the stone in places, and ferns poked up through the seams. Still, the layout persisted.

Why hadn't Aelriva mentioned this? If it ran south, it could very well lead directly back to the village. That made it important. A road for trade routes? It was especially important if more of the forest was hiding these kinds of ruins.

His fingers traced the edges of the nearest stone, feeling the weathered grooves. It wasn't just a road. This had been built to last. His newly acquired scavenger instincts buzzed.

He moved north along the old trail. Every so often, he paused to kneel and clear away another patch of moss or debris. Each time, the road continued. Each time, it reassured him that he was not just walking in circles.

It wasn't long before the path began to change. Not in direction, but in what surrounded it. The forest floor rose in uneven mounds. Some were too regular to be natural. He stopped at one, pressed a hand into it, and pushed aside the soft cover. Metal glinted beneath the dirt.

With effort, he pulled the object free. Rusted through and heavy in the hand, but still recognizable. A pickaxe head. The wooden haft had long since rotted away. He turned it over slowly and smiled as he realized this wasn't just a trail. It was a route to something that had once been worked. Something that had value.

Xavier set the pickaxe down, more intrigued than ever, and pressed forward. Curiosity quickened his steps. The way the path curved, how the trees leaned slightly back from it— it reminded him of places with stories. Of Bramblegate, of the caverns beneath Rynthavael, of the way Arath whispered its truths to those willing to listen.

Twenty minutes later, the forest answered his interest with a snarl. The ground gave way beneath his foot.

"Shit!" He cried out as he flung himself backward, just barely catching the lip of the collapsing earth. Loose soil crumbled around his boots, and a deep, hollow echo rose from below. He lay on his back for a moment, heart hammering.

A prompt flickered into view.

> **Quest Updated:** Whose House I
> You have discovered a significant place. Continue to explore this location to uncover its importance or details of its past. Doing so will meet the requirements of one of the four places required for this quest.

Xavier sat up and blinked the notification away. He took several deep breaths before crawling closer to the edge of the pit. The sinkhole had swallowed part of the stone path. Below, fifty feet down, he could see broken wood, rusted metal, and fragments of stone.

He strained to listen for sounds from the hole. Water dripped somewhere in the darkness, and beneath that... silence.

He studied the shaft's edges. Chunks of worked stone clung to the walls in uneven places, suggesting this had once been reinforced, perhaps even climbed. Sadly, the ladders and support structures had long since rotted through.

It was clear that it was no natural cave. This was a mine. His lips parted slightly. Aelriva had sent him here not for the road, but for what it once led to. Something hidden deep beneath the trees, and now, he had a way in.

#

Xavier circled the rim of the sinkhole, wary of triggering another collapse. The soil was unstable in several places, but after testing with his boot, he found a firmer patch of ground about a dozen feet back from the edge. A sturdy tree grew there, its roots wrapped deep into the earth.

He reached into his pack, pulled out a coiled rope, and exhaled as the weight lessened. He had not wanted to fill his satchel with its weight reducing properties before leaving, he remembered far too many gaming sessions where he had to continuously drop items, he had found to make room for more. Thus, he had debated leaving the rope behind before setting out but was glad now that he hadn't.

Looping the rope around the base of the tree, he cinched a tight knot and tested it with his full weight. The tree groaned slightly but held fast. Confident, he stepped to the edge, tossed the rope down into the dark, and began his descent.

The wall was uneven, pitted from age and collapse. His boots found purchase more often than not, but even so, chunks of crumbling stone broke loose beneath his steps, clattering down into the hollow with loud echoes that bounced unnervingly.

Halfway down, the walls began to glow. Patches of soft, greenish light clung to the stone, moss, faintly bioluminescent, like what he had seen in the Life Ley Line's cavern. He paused to brush his fingers across it, and for a moment, felt a pang of longing for Ella. Her steadiness. Her quiet guidance. Even her teasing smirks when he did something dumb.

He shook the thought away. Focus man you are going into a dungeon. Twenty minutes later, boots touched stone.

The shaft opened into a wide chamber littered with the remnants of broken ladders, snapped ropes, and long-decayed mining tools. Several rusted pickaxes lay among splintered wood and coils of rotted hemp. He nudged them aside with the toe of his boot.

There was no question now. This had once been active, and maybe... it could be again.

The village's smiths had been scraping together what ore they could find, but it wouldn't last. If this mine still held usable material, it could supply Rynthavael for months. Years, even.

A tight passage gaped at the far side of the chamber. At first glance, it looked natural, but as he moved closer, he could see where stone had been cut away, though once wide enough for carts, it was now narrowed by time and collapse.

He made a mental note: repairs would be needed before this place could be considered safe for work again. But that was a problem for later. For now, he had a passage to explore.

Xavier pulled a torch from his pack and lit the oil-soaked cloth. The flame sputtered, then flared to life, casting long shadows against the stone walls. Holding it high, he stepped into the narrow corridor, the tunnel swallowing him in its slow, spiraling descent.

The air grew damp, then wet. Walls dripped with condensation, and the stone underfoot turned slick. The tunnel twisted left, then right, a long curve that dipped deeper beneath the forest floor. Then it opened and the passage led into a vast cavern.

His torchlight flickered across damp stone and the clustered glow of mushrooms. Some were the size of his

WELCOME TO YOUR NEXT LIFE

head. Others blanketed the walls like a breathing carpet. Moss glowed faintly along the ceiling, mirroring starlight through a canopy of dripping stone.

The air was thick with spores. Xavier's throat caught immediately.

Coughing, he backed into the tunnel and fumbled through his pack. After a moment of rooting around, he pulled free one of his spare shirts, slipped it over his head halfway, and tied the collar tight around his mouth and nose. The makeshift mask helped, even if it made him look ridiculous.

He chuckled to himself, his voice muffled. At least no one was around to see it.

Torch raised again, he stepped into the cavern, careful with each footfall. Stalactites loomed above like jagged teeth. Pools of water caught the shifting light, refracting it into gentle prisms of green, blue, and gold.

It was beautiful in a haunting way. He moved further in.

A wide, flat mushroom caught his eye. Waist-high and thick as a stump, it looked solid enough to sit on. He moved toward it, needing a rest. As soon as he touched it, the cap burst.

A dense cloud of yellow spores exploded into the air. He reeled backward, eyes squeezed shut, breath held. His skin prickled as the cloud enveloped him. The cloth mask blunted most of the inhalation, but it wasn't enough to keep the sting from reaching his eyes.

They burned, and watered while he staggered. His vision blurred, he slammed into a wall, then bounced off a thick mushroom stalk. His foot caught on a ridge of stone, and he crashed to the ground. The torch skittered from his hand, tumbled across moss and stone, and landed with a hiss in a pool of water.

Darkness swallowed the room. For a few heartbeats, he lay there, blinking rapidly, eyes stinging, chest heaving. Only the soft glow of moss and mushrooms offered any light.

He sat up, cursing under his breath, and wiped his eyes with the edge of his sleeve. Still blurry but improving. He reached for the soaked torch, but it was useless now. The cloth had been soaked and was now limp and cold. He tossed it aside with a sigh and rummaged through his satchel for a replacement.

As his fingers closed around another torch, something caught his eye. A brighter light, faint and orange, like a firefly glow... but steadier.

He turned toward it. Nestled amid a patch of morels sat a squat, rounded mushroom, no bigger than his palm. It glowed like warm embers, casting soft light in a small halo. Grinning, Xavier stepped toward it.

#

Xavier crouched beside the glowing fungus, careful not to disturb the surrounding morels. The mushroom's light pulsed gently, like a slow heartbeat, suffusing the cavern floor with warm, orange hues. It reminded him faintly of a dying ember or a watchful eye.

He reached out and let his fingers brush the cap. As he did, something shifted in his vision. A soft pulse, a shimmer of recognition through the lens of his skill interface.

You have discovered:	Ingredient Class:
Glowcap Mushroom	Common
	Item Quality: Raw
	Weight: 0.01 kg
	Durability: 5/5
	Traits: A small, orange mushroom that glows with an

> inner light, providing dim illumination for approximately one hour. Shows signs of potential use as a minor antidote to certain natural poisons.

His Herbalism skill reacted instantly. Instinct guided his hands. He grasped the mushroom gently near the base and twisted clockwise. It came free without resistance, the glow undiminished in his palm. The moment he placed it in his satchel, another prompt followed.

Congratulations! You have gained a new rank in a skill: Herbalism (Level 10)
Herbalism is the art of gathering, identifying, and utilizing plants for their various properties—from healing wounds to crafting poisons.
You have advanced from **Novice** to **Apprentice**.
+20% to herb effect. +20% to harvest quantity.
Additional Effect: You can now identify more rare and exquisite plants and additional properties within familiar herbs.

+1000 Experience Earned

A rush of satisfaction washed through him. It wasn't just the level gain; it was the implication. Progress didn't require battle. Villagers could grow through harvesting, crafting, learning. If he wanted Rynthavael to thrive, this was how.

He smiled and tucked the glowcap securely in his satchel. Its light still glimmered through the leather seams. Then he looked back to the cluster where he'd found the first. Carefully, he gathered more.

One after another, the glowcaps came free, six in total. He left one out to use as a light source and stored the others, noting how the magical satchel still required individual inventory slots for each, but preserved their illumination within.

Cradling the last glowcap in his hand, he lifted it high. Its glow wasn't as strong as a torch, but it was steady and warm. Enough to see.

He wound through the cavern again, stepping carefully this time, avoiding the spore-heavy stalks. Moss underfoot muffled his footsteps, and the glowcap's light danced over stone and shadow as he approached the far side of the chamber.

Another tunnel waited there. This one sloped downward at a steeper angle, but not dangerously so. Xavier adjusted his grip on the glowcap and moved forward.

The deeper he went, the more the passage twisted. Smaller corridors branched off from the main path, some blocked with rubble, others narrowing into collapsed veins of dirt and stone. More than once, he had to backtrack from a dead end. Still, the tunnels hinted at a once-functional mine.

At the back of one narrow side-passage, something caught his attention. A faint shimmer, like light brushing across metal. He dropped to one knee, holding the glowcap low. The stone wall glinted faintly. Veins of ore.

He didn't recognize the metal. His mining skill was nonexistent, but the luster suggested something valuable. He touched the vein, marveling at how the stone still bore the signs of past tools, hammer marks and shallow cuts worn smooth by time.

Excitement stirred. He had been correct; this wasn't just a tunnel system. It was a full mine.

Real, functioning infrastructure. If he could clear the passages and stabilize the structure, this place could supply his village for generations.

He rose and moved quickly now, retracing his steps

to recheck every branch tunnel he'd dismissed. One after another, veins emerged from the gloom, some faint, some rich. The deeper he went, the clearer the picture became.

His happiness was effusive. This wasn't a prospecting site. It was a legacy.

Then, rounding another corner, he stopped cold. The rubble at the end of the passage was unmistakable, collapsed stone, cracked timber supports. Another dead end.

But this one was not empty.

Half-pinned beneath a heavy slab, a skeleton lay in crumpled repose.

Rotted fabric hung from its limbs. What might have once been a tunic or shirt was now little more than threads. A cracked lantern rested just beyond the reach of one arm, and the stone beneath it bore soot-stained scorch marks.

The hand had clawed faint grooves into the nearby rock, as if the owner had tried, desperately, to escape.

Xavier knelt, laying the glowcap on a nearby ledge. He bowed his head in solemn respect to the dead. Then, gently, he began to search.

#

Xavier moved with care, brushing away the loose dust and flakes of stone from what little remained of the figure's belongings. Time had taken nearly everything, clothing, pack, gear, but not all was lost.

A rusted tinderbox rested near the body's side, the metal warped but intact. Beside it, he uncovered several pitons, their steel dulled by years underground but still serviceable. He collected each carefully, tucking them into his satchel. Flint and steel, a potion labeled with Fire Resistance, two small silver ingots, and a purse of dwarven-marked gold coins were found within a rotted pouch beneath the remains.

He reached for the skeleton's exposed arm. Around its wrist, miraculously preserved, was a single leather bracer. The leather was dark with age, but supple, and the bindings still held firm.

He hesitated before removing it. "Thank you," he said softly, fingers working the straps free. "You won't be forgotten."

The bracer came loose easily. He placed it into his pack, then glanced toward the slab that pinned the other half of the body. No way to retrieve the second. It lay crushed beneath what could be several tons of stone.

He was about to rise when something half-buried beneath the debris caught his eye. A glint of metal, dim but unmistakable. Shifting a few loose stones, he revealed the object fully, a shortsword, perfectly preserved.

His breath caught.

The weapon seemed to drink in the glowcap's light. Its blade shimmered faintly with an orange hue, as if fire slept beneath the steel. The hilt was wrapped in heat-resistant leather, and the air around it radiated a subtle warmth that lingered against his skin.

You have discovered: Emberstone Shortsword **Description:** A short sword forged from Pyrestone, its blade emanating a faint orange glow with an almost molten sheen. Heat radiates gently from the weapon, making it warm to the touch even in the	**Item Class:** Rare **Item Quality:** Masterwork **Weight:** 1.5 kg **Durability:** 85/100 **Damage:** 18–24 **Damage Type:** Slashing or Piercing **Traits:** • **Radiant Heat:** Inflicts minor fire damage on every strike.

WELCOME TO YOUR NEXT LIFE

| coldest environments. The hilt is wrapped in heat-resistant leather, ensuring comfort for the wielder during prolonged combat. | • **Ignition Strike:** 20% chance to set flammable enemies or objects ablaze.
 • **Unyielding Flames:** Resistant to cold and frost-based effects. |

While the other items were great finds, considering how long the body must have been here the sword was amazing. Xavier turned it in his hand, testing its weight. Slightly heavier than Vaeltheris, but well-balanced. The blade gleamed in the dimness with a subdued, volcanic beauty.

He unsheathed Vaeltheris in his other hand and tested a few light swings, short blade in his right, dagger in his left. The pairing felt good. Not perfect, but solid.

A thought struck him, and he shifted Vaeltheris' form. With a silent pulse, the dagger lengthened into a shortsword to match the Emberstone blade.

It was still awkward, but workable. He let out a low chuckle. "We're getting there."

He sheathed both weapons and returned to the remains. There, half-buried beneath the rubble, he spotted the edge of a worn scabbard. With patience, he eased it free from the collapsed belt. As he did, a small pouch detached and fell into his palm.

He opened it with care. Inside, he found a delicate locket, its gold filigree dulled with age. The initials T.H. were engraved on its surface. Inside the locket, beneath a layer of dust, was a faded image, a young dwarven man with a thick beard and a shy smile.

Xavier held it gently for a moment, thumb brushing across the tarnished frame.

He set the locket aside and turned his attention to a second object in the pouch. A small journal, leather-bound, its edges frayed but the cover still mostly intact.

He flipped it open. The script was unlike anything he had seen. Angular, geometric strokes, inked in a faded copper-brown. The letters shimmered faintly, resisting understanding.

Then the world answered him again as a new prompt appeared.

> **Congratulations! You have learned a new language —**
> **Khazridan (Old Dwarvish).**
> This language is used in ancient dwarven texts,
> inscriptions, and records. It allows comprehension
> of archaic knowledge, including crafting methods,
> settlement histories, and personal journals.

The symbols realigned before his eyes. The words came into focus.

The journal belonged to a dwarven woman, never named, but clearly of the Hurnthar, more commonly known as the Stonedelver, clan of the Ironpeak Mountains. Her entries detailed the exploration of this mine, references to a place called Dun Karak, and the desire to make her name known among her people. He flipped to the final page.

"The crystals here hum with power, more than I've seen before. If I can bring back even one shard, it will all be worth it. I'll return to Dun Karak a legend."

Another chime and another prompt appeared.

> **You have been offered a quest:** Memories of the Fallen I
> For time unknown, this dwarven explorer has lain
> crushed in these tunnels. Who was she, and who did she
> leave behind when she crossed the threshold of death?
> Your only clues are a journal and a locket bearing the

initials T.H., and a city named Dun Karak.
Will you restore her memory to her kin?
Potential Rewards: Unknown.
Accept? Yes/No

Xavier didn't hesitate. "Yes," he whispered.

His quest log updated. The glowcap flickered gently beside him.

As he moved to close the journal, a folded piece of parchment slipped from its back cover and fell softly to the ground. He picked it up, unfolding it with great care.

It was no ordinary parchment. Enchanted vellum shimmered beneath his fingertips. Silver filigree edged its border, and the faint image of an incomplete map danced along its surface.

You have discovered:
Explorer's Map

Description: A finely crafted map made from enchanted vellum, its edges trimmed with silver filigree. The surface shimmers faintly, displaying an incomplete depiction of the world, with blank spaces waiting to be filled. Upon being soul bound to its owner, the map comes to life, updating with every new location the bearer has seen firsthand. The ink appears as if drawn by an unseen hand, flowing

Item Class: Epic
Item Quality: Exquisite
Weight: 0.3 kg
Durability: 90/100
Traits:
• **Soulbound Cartography:** Binds to its owner, updating automatically with every location seen firsthand.
• **Real-Time Awareness:** Reveals terrain, landmarks, and changes in environment.
• **Mark of Discovery:** Allows magical notations visible only to

to reflect real-time changes.	the owner. • **Localized Illumination:** Can highlight the owner's current location on command.

A small gemstone, much like the one Ella had given him when he bound to Vaeltheris, rose from the center of the vellum. He touched it without hesitation.

The gem dissolved into light, and the map shimmered. Color spilled across the parchment, shifting like ripples over water. Rynthavael. Bramblegate. The Silverflow. His entire journey drawn before him in delicate lines and soft washes of ink.

A prompt appeared.

> **Would you like to integrate the Explorer's Map with**
>
> **your interface?**

"Yes."

The upper-right corner of his vision flickered.

A semi-translucent minimap appeared. His position marked by a glowing dot. Nearby tunnels displayed in faint grayscale, but only the ones he had walked. Yet ahead, the faint image of a bridge began to resolve.

He bowed his head, the glowcap's light casting soft shadows over the page still open on the stone beside him.

"Thank you," he murmured again, voice quiet with reverence. Then he stood, packed the map, the journal, and the locket, and turned toward the bridge.

#

CHAPTER TWENTY-THREE

What We Find Behind a Mine

Before he moved off, he left a marker near the corpse of the fallen dwarf, a simple signpost in the system so the villagers could retrieve her and grant her a proper burial. She had left behind so much; he couldn't bring himself to leave her completely alone. Finished he moved deeper into the tunnels.

The soft pulse of the glowcap in Xavier's hand cast warm light across the tunnel walls as he moved deeper into the mine. The air had cooled further, damp and heavy, with the scent of stone, iron, and something older, something buried.

Every step traced lines on the new minimap integrated into his interface. He watched it occasionally shift as the grayscale filled in with the corridors he explored, tracing his steps like ink spreading across parchment. Dead ends resolved, loops closed, and branching paths blinked softly as he passed them by. This mine was far larger than it had first seemed.

Grooves in the stone marked the remnants of cart tracks, worn smooth by time. Rusted brackets jutted from the walls where lanterns might once have hung, and faded tool hooks showed where miners had once rested their equipment. Xavier ran his hand along the stone, noting places where ore still glinted faintly, waiting to be harvested.

He rounded a bend, where the air grew warmer. The temperature shift was subtle, but distinct, and the earth beneath his boots held a rising tension, pressure, faint vibration, something beneath the stone that pulsed with dormant heat.

Tapping the minimap in his vision, he zoomed out slightly. A faint reddish hue bled into the edges of the northern tunnels, a gradient that intensified the deeper he went.

Geothermal activity. Lava vents, perhaps, maybe ley-adjacent fire essence. Whatever it was, it explained the Emberstone ore... and hinted at danger.

As he advanced, a new shape appeared on the minimap ahead: a thick wall, squared on both sides. It was not a natural formation, not a tunnel. A door.

He slowed his pace as the corridor widened again, and sure enough, there it was, set into the stone with time-worn symmetry. A pair of massive stone double doors, carved with the faded remnants of dwarven script and inlaid with thin bands of tarnished metal. The symbols were mostly worn smooth, and several pieces of the stonework had cracked and fallen, but the doors still stood.

One was tilted slightly, its hinges damaged and sunken, but it remained closed. The other hung ajar, its edge splintered inward where something, whether blast or claw or time, had forced entry.

Xavier stepped closer, tracing the dwarven markings with his free hand. They stirred something in him. Not meaning, but memory. Echoes of craftsmanship. The bracer he had taken from the fallen explorer did not match the style. It was newer, foreign. That explorer must have found these tunnels long after they were abandoned and perished here, alone.

He realized that this was no mere mine. It was ancient, built with purpose and protected. Something about it felt familiar... eerily so. This place belonged to the same forgotten age as the ruins above back at his village. The same civilization. He was now certain this had once been part of the Sylmyrian city Xavier was rebuilding, and now it belonged to Rynthavael.

The glowcap's light filtered through the cracked opening, and beyond the doors he could see a short tunnel extending forward. Roughly hewn, less refined than the earlier sections, and sloping slightly downward.

He slipped through the gap and entered. Here, the air grew sharper. Not colder, but thinner. The stone underfoot was worn smooth in the narrow, the rest left jagged and uneven. He followed it, boots crunching faintly on gravel as the tunnel opened up to a ledge.

Then he stopped. Before him stretched a bridge, ancient and fractured, arching over a chasm so deep that even the mosslight from the cavern walls failed to touch the bottom. A low mist clung to the edges, curling like breath from the abyss.

The bridge itself was stone, wide enough for two to cross shoulder-to-shoulder in its prime, though time and collapse had rendered it uneven and cracked. On this side, a narrow ledge gave him just enough footing to approach it. The wall to his right offered a handhold. The drop to his left promised death.

He let out a slow breath, lifting the glowcap higher. "Of course," he muttered.

He checked the map again. The bridge was the only way forward. Whatever lay beyond it, deep in the earth, past heat and stone and ruin, it had been sealed, forgotten, and defended. Until now.

Returning to the precipice, he studied the ravine. A faint shimmer on the water below reflected dimly, strangely visible even in the dark. It made him uneasy. If his small mushroom light could be seen from that distance, so could others. The thought settled uneasily in his chest.

The ledge extended about forty feet in either direction from the door. On the left side, roughly fifteen feet away, was the foot of the bridge. Both ends of the ledge curved into the rough stone wall, and across the chasm, about thirty feet away, he could make out the shape of another ledge and hallway.

He sat on the edge, feet dangling, eyes fixed on the ancient structure. It was about six feet wide and spanned the thirty-foot gap. Its sides were eroded away. He had no training in stonework, so he couldn't judge the stability. Still, bridges had lasted centuries back on Earth. He just hoped this one would too.

He turned to the minimap. It displayed the same layout he observed: the deep ravine, the bridge, the far hallway. Beyond that was another chamber, crystalline and expansive. That had to be what the dwarf had written about in her journal. The map lit up with vibrant color where he had explored, but the surrounding world remained in grayscale, a memory of where the dwarf had gone. Landmarks appeared as outlines beyond her reach. It was powerful, but not omniscient.

Xavier returned to the bridge and peered at it again. A nagging sense of unease tugged at him. He almost stepped forward but froze. Several stones glowed faintly red to his eye. Pressure plates. His trap awareness skill had triggered.

He dropped prone, inching toward the nearest glowing tile, careful to keep his weight on the safe stone. It looked identical to the others, but something about it set his instincts on edge.

> **You have discovered a trap:** Pressure Stone Trap
> Your trap awareness skill has identified a new trap. This pressure stone trap seems to be designed to drop sections of the stone bridge into the chasm below if stepped upon.

Heart thudding, Xavier backed off and began mapping each trap in turn. Thirteen glowing tiles. He crawled the length of the bridge, marking each one with an upright arrow wedged in the cracks just beside them. If he had rushed forward, he would have triggered them all.

Chuckling under his breath, he whispered a silent thanks to one of his favorite authors. They always marked their traps. It saved lives. As he stepped off the bridge and onto the far ledge, a familiar prompt flickered before his eyes.

> **Keen Eye: Rank 2 achieved**
> **Trap Awareness: Rank 2 achieved**

Safely upon the far ledge once more Xavier began to examine it before going to the dark hallway. A cursory glance inside confirmed it was, in fact, a hallway and not rough stone walls. Now that he knew one of his skills would trigger a change in color to what he was seeing to indicate hidden traps he was curious what else it would trigger for other hidden items. Its description described it as "the ability to identify hidden or valuable items, resources, or opportunities in an environment that others might overlook." Sadly, nothing else on this side of the chasm revealed itself with a different color glow either.

#

Before moving deeper, Xavier paused beside the hallway's entrance. A narrow alcove had caught his eye, partially obscured by a broken slab of wall. He knelt and carefully cleared the space, slipping a small cloth-wrapped bundle into the recess. Inside, he placed the Potion of Fire Resistance, the silver ingots, and the purse of dwarven-marked gold that he had found with the skeleton, just in case. A fallback cache. He covered the stash with the flat stone panel and made a mental note of its exact location. If things ever went wrong, he'd have at least one ace hidden in the dark.

The hallway ahead was narrow, its arched stone ceiling just high enough for Xavier to pass without ducking. The glowcap's light shimmered faintly across the walls, catching on etchings carved directly into the stone. This was not raw tunnel but worked passage, and ancient. Even here, the craftsmanship held.

He stepped forward, and the stone responded. Not with movement, but memory. The air grew still. The faint scent of dust and age pressed close, and his footsteps echoed louder than before.

Intricate murals lined either side of the corridor, carved in bas-relief with masterful precision. At first, they told a tale of discovery: dwarven miners breaking through the surface rock, uncovering rich veins of ore, and descending deeper into the stone. In one panel, clusters of uncut gems sparkled with faint enchantment, and behind them loomed distant crystalline spires.

Xavier lingered at that mural. He could almost hear the tapping of picks against stone, the rhythmic crack of hammer to vein. Briefly, he touched the carving, and the crystals seemed to shimmer faintly in response.

As he continued down the hall, the tone of the story shifted. The next set of carvings showed calamity. A great collapse. Miners fleeing in terror, others buried beneath jagged slabs of stone. Shadowy figures, spindly and wrong, crept through the cracks. In the flickering light, their spider-like limbs seemed to twitch.

Xavier's hand moved unconsciously to Vaeltheris. The hallway grew colder.

The next murals depicted towering stone guardians, dwarven statues etched with weapons raised and gemstone eyes alight. Dwarven runes below them glowed faintly in the glowcap's light. He leaned in and read the ancient inscription.

By stone we toil. By stone we are protected. Let no shadow disrupt the harmony of the depths.

The words carried weight. Magic lingered in them still. He continued, each step drawing him deeper into history and into something else, something watching.

At the far end, the last mural filled the wall from floor to ceiling. A massive spider loomed at the center, its limbs stretching across a vast web that held entire mining parties trapped in its strands. The eyes of the creature gleamed, inset with tiny chips of some reflective stone. Xavier hesitated.

He stepped closer. The air here felt wrong. When he reached out to touch the web-carved stone, a jolt of static bit at his fingers. Then the hallway exploded with sound.

A piercing crystalline chime split the silence, followed by a pulsing, discordant hum. The tones were jagged, jarring. Runes lit along the walls, pulses of red and white racing in time with the rising soundscape. The air itself seemed to buzz and press in, charged with static energy.

Xavier stumbled back, heart hammering. Then he heard it... skittering. First faint. Then louder. Not just from ahead but from behind as well.

He threw his pack to the ground and drew both blades. A shadow flickered at the edge of his vision. Then another. The first spider lunged from the dark.

#

The huge spider hit him like a battering ram. Xavier barely managed to deflect its fangs with the crossed hilts of his blades, the force of the impact driving him back against the stone wall. Its eyes gleamed, black and wet, reflecting the crimson light pulsing along the runes.

Vaeltheris snapped upward in a quick slash, slicing along one of the bristled legs. The creature shrieked and reared back, only for a second spider to seize the opening. It darted in low, hooking claws along Xavier's ribs and tearing into leather and flesh alike.

Pain flashed through him. Xavier gritted his teeth and spun, driving his short sword into the spider's abdomen. The Pyrestone blade flared bright with inner heat, scorching the wound. The spider screamed, its legs flailing as it withdrew, but the first one was already on the move again.

It crashed into Xavier with the weight of a falling boulder. He twisted, barely evading the twin fangs that snapped where his throat had been moments before. Vaeltheris drove into its side, scoring a deep line, but not deep enough. Not fatal.

More movement. The third spider skittered across the ceiling, limbs whispering against the stone like dry leaves. The fourth crawled forward on the floor, head lowered, ready to strike.

"Always spiders," Xavier muttered. "Of course it had to be spiders. Giant, venom-dripping, horse-sized nightmares."

He feinted left and dodged right as the fourth spider lunged, claws tearing across the floor. Xavier leapt backward, but the ceiling-dweller took its chance, dropping from above. It slammed into him, driving him to the ground beneath its weight.

The wind left his lungs. Fangs scraped against his shoulder armor, and he barely got his short sword up in time to jam it between them. He twisted, shoved, and the blade flared again, burning into the creature's underside. It screeched and spasmed, legs curling inward as it collapsed atop him.

With a grunt of effort, Xavier rolled the dead spider off and scrambled to his feet, but the third one was already there.

It struck low, sinking venomous fangs into the meat of his calf. Agony roared through his body. Xavier dropped to one knee, breath ragged, vision swimming. The poison seared its way through his system, a sickly heat curling through his limbs.

He swung Vaeltheris in a wide arc, striking the spider across the legs and forcing it to retreat. Blood dripped down his side. His health bar flickered in his vision, and with it a grim icon: a pair of fangs with green droplets.

You are poisoned -2 damage per second for 30 seconds unless treated.

Xavier fumbled at his belt, but there were no potions. He cursed under his breath. No supplies. No backup. Just him… And two spiders.

Xavier roared and lunged forward, catching one mid-step. His short sword drove into its head, the Pyrestone flaring red-hot. The creature spasmed and collapsed.

The last one screamed and rushed him in a blur of claws. Xavier sidestepped, pain lancing up his leg as he pivoted. Vaeltheris caught the spider's thorax as it passed, and this time the blade cut true. The shimmer of enchanted steel sliced deep. It fell still.

Silence returned, broken only by Xavier's ragged breaths. Blood pooled around his boots. His limbs trembled. He dropped both blades and slumped against the wall.

The poison finally ran its course.

#

Xavier leaned against the stone wall, letting the last echoes of pain dull to a throb.

He took another look at his health bar and did some quick math. He had enough hit points to survive until the venom ran its course. A good thing, since he had no herbs or potions to treat it. That would have to change. He made a mental note to speak with the village alchemist. He needed to improve his herbalism and potion brewing skills if he planned to keep venturing alone. Or he could seek more life-based spells.

His eyes widened as a thought struck him. He slapped his forehead. "Spells. Idiot."

He quickly cast Blooming Touch. The gestures and incantation took only a few seconds, and as the life magic surged through his body, the worst of the wounds began to mend. The venom still burned, but the pain faded, and his health started to recover faster than it ticked away. He repeated the spell several times, buying precious seconds until the poison's effect finally ended and his wounds closed fully.

He exhaled in relief.

Returning to his prompts, he scanned the combat log and found something unexpected.

Congratulations! You have learned a new skill: Two-Weapon Fighting (Level 1)

The Two-Weapon Fighting skill allows a character to wield two weapons simultaneously, granting increased attack versatility and damage potential. While difficult to master, this skill rewards dedication with fluid combat techniques, improved accuracy, and devastating combos. Starting with small weapons and basic strikes, practitioners refine their ability to strike with both hands in perfect harmony.

"If one sword is good, two must be twice as good. Math checks out, right?"

-25% to main-hand hit/damage.
-50% to off-hand hit/damage.
At the Novice level, you are limited to small weapons in both hands (Daggers, Short swords, etc.)

He looked to his next prompt and smiled broadly. The fight had brought him closer to his next level.

For killing 4 giant wolf spiders, levels 5, 6, 7, and 8, you have been awarded 3,750 experience points.

Only 700 experience away from leveling. He stood and gave one of the corpses a half-hearted kick.

"Yeah. Who's dead now? Damn spiders."

Something about the body caught his attention. A soft glow, faint, familiar. Like the ones that marked plants under his herbalism skill. Frowning, he set his pack down again and drew Vaeltheris. Willing it to shrink into dagger form, he set to work.

About thirty minutes later, covered in ichor and exhausted anew, Xavier sat back on his heels. He'd gained more than just experience.

You have discovered:	**Item Class:** Uncommon
Wolf Spider Venom Sac * 7	**Item Quality:** Average
Description: A dark,	**Weight:** 0.2 kg
flexible sac harvested	**Durability:** 70/100
from a giant spider, filled	**Traits:**
with a viscous, pale-green	- **Toxic Essence:** Contains
liquid. The sac is slightly	enough venom for 3
translucent, revealing the	applications, each capable
venom swirling within. It	of delivering a potent
emits a faint, acrid odor	toxin when applied to

that tingles the senses and warns of its potency.	weapons or traps. - **Corrosive Nature:** The venom can weaken certain materials, such as wood or low-grade metals, upon prolonged exposure. - **Paralyzing Effect:** Victims hit by venom-coated weapons have a 30% chance of being paralyzed for up to 10 seconds.
You have discovered: Spider Silk Threads * 5 **Description:** A spool of shimmering, incredibly strong thread spun from the silk of giant spiders. It has a faint, iridescent sheen that reflects light in subtle hues of silver and gold. The thread is astonishingly lightweight yet tougher than steel, making it ideal for crafting and intricate repairs.	**Item Class:** Rare **Item Quality:** Well Crafted **Weight:** 0.1 kg (per spool) **Durability:** 95/100 **Traits:** - **Tensile Strength:** Can support up to 500 kg of weight without breaking. - **Flexible and Lightweight:** Ideal for creating fine, unbreakable fabric or reinforcing armor and tools. - **Enchantable:** Highly receptive to enchantments, making it a valuable material for magical items.
You have discovered: Spider Chitin Fragments * 16	**Item Class:** Uncommon **Item Quality:** Average **Weight:** 0.5 kg (per

Description: Jagged fragments of dark, glossy chitin harvested from the exoskeleton of a giant spider. The fragments are rigid, lightweight, and naturally resistant to damage, making them useful for crafting and reinforcement. Their surface is textured with natural ridges and patterns, offering both functional and decorative potential.

fragment)
Durability: 80/100
Traits:
- **Durable Material:** Extremely tough and resilient, ideal for crafting lightweight armor or tools.
- **Natural Camouflage:** The chitin's coloration blends well in dark or forested environments, making it ideal for stealth-based equipment.
- **Poison-Resistant Properties:** Provides moderate resistance to toxins when used in armor or gear.

Looking at the pile of materials, he briefly considered hunting more.

Then he reread the venom sac's description. The paralysis effect alone could have killed him. He would not go hunting for more then, not until he had antivenom. Maybe some resistance potions too.

He packed everything away. The satchel's enchantment handled the weight admirably, but even so, it now held a serious haul. Two more ranks in his survival skill had popped up during the harvesting, he hadn't even noticed.

That glow around the parts? A feature of survival, good to know. This solo trip had reminded him how far he still had to go.

He stood, cleaned Vaeltheris and his hands, and moved on. Toward whatever came next. He took a long breath, then another. The venom had passed, but its toll remained. His limbs ached. His tunic clung to him, soaked in sweat and blood. He then retrieved the Pyrestone short sword, it still radiated a soft, residual warmth. He sheathed both, then reached for his pack.

From within his satchel, he pulled a fresh glowcap and shook it gently. The fungus shimmered to life with a soft orange light, illuminating the far end of the hallway. He followed it, boots crunching across stone dust and spider remains.

The carved stone gave way to natural rock. The worked hallway ended, replaced by twisting caverns that wound downward, the walls slick with mineral sheen. He moved carefully, following the path marked on his minimap. It bent and narrowed, widened again, then opened into a vast chamber.

He stopped. The sight that met him stole his breath. Crystals, hundreds, thousands, jutted from the walls, ceiling, and floor. They ranged in size from needle-thin to the girth of a man's chest. Each one pulsed with faint inner light, glowing in soft hues. At first glance, they seemed to shine in a rainbow, but as his eyes adjusted, he realized there were only eight true colors.

Life. Death. Fire. Water. Earth. Air. Light. Dark.

These had to be the essence crystals he had heard about. He stepped forward, reverent.

With slow care, he tapped the pommel of his short sword against a nearby cluster. A section broke cleanly away. He caught the piece as it fell.

You have discovered:	**Item Class:** Rare
Life Essence Crystal	**Item Quality:** Superb
	Weight: 0.5 kg
Description: A golden-	**Durability:** 15/15

green crystal glowing with a soft, warm light. It symbolizes vitality, growth, and renewal, with delicate vein-like patterns running through its core.	**Traits:** - **Crafting Component:** Essential for creating healing potions, vitality-based enchantments, and restoration spells. - **Essence Stone Creation:** Refined into a Life Essence Stone, amplifying life magic or trapping the essence of natural creatures.

Xavier turned the crystal over in his hand, feeling the warmth of it pulse in sync with his own heartbeat.

He moved from node to node, testing and gathering a fragment of each kind. Each crystal triggered a new prompt, one for Light, then Fire, Earth, Death, Dark, Water, and Air. The traits varied, but they were unified in purpose: magical crafting, essence trapping, power refinement.

He soon had a large collection of each type of crystal in his satchel, which sagged slightly under the growing weight. Even with its weight-reduction enchantment, the cache he now carried was a small fortune in raw essence.

The chamber pulsed quietly around him, a cathedral of light and magic left forgotten under stone. And now, found again.

He crouched to lift one more crystal...and froze. Movement. A soft sound. Not footfalls, not skittering. A wet slither. Followed by the brittle tinkling of crystal shifting.

He backed away slowly, rising to his feet. Something was here.

From between two thick clusters of crystal, it emerged. A mass of translucent goo, shot through with razor-edged shards that shimmered as it moved. It pulsed like a living prism, its surface rippling with oily light. As it rolled forward, it scraped the cavern floor with a faint grinding chime.

Xavier's eyes widened. Unconsciously e reached inward, focusing and triggered Insight.

Name: Crystaline Ooze	**Race**: Crystaline Ooze	Disposition: Hungry
Level: Unknown	Class: Unknown	Active Effects: Unknown
Description		
The Crystalline Ooze is a mesmerizing, translucent creature, its gelatinous body filled with jagged shards of crystal that refract light in brilliant, shimmering hues. Its surface appears smooth and liquid, but it conceals razor-sharp edges that can slice through flesh and armor. The ooze moves slowly and deliberately, its crystalline structure grinding softly with a faint chiming sound. When it senses prey, it ripples and pulses, using its sharp shards and magical properties to attack and absorb its victims. Despite its beauty, it is a deadly predator, often camouflaging itself in crystal-rich caverns.		
Stats		
Health: 130/130	**Stamina:** 200/200	**Mana:** 100/100

It pulsed again... then lunged.

\#

Xavier hurled himself sideways, narrowly avoiding the lunging mass of the crystalline ooze. It struck the cavern floor with a resonant chime, sharp and eerie. Shards splintered outward from its form as it rebounded, cutting the air with gleaming edges. One sliced across his upper arm, shallow but burning.

He rolled to his feet and drew both blades in a single motion. Vaeltheris pulsed with cold light. The Pyrestone short sword glowed faintly with stored heat. The ooze rippled again and slid forward, unnaturally fast.

Xavier struck first, driving Vaeltheris deep into the creature's side. The blade entered smoothly but offered no resistance, like stabbing into thick fluid... or that odd green Jello grandma always served at Thanksgiving. The ooze shimmered and quaked but showed no sign of real pain.

A pseudopod lashed out. He ducked beneath it, slashing with the Pyrestone blade. The metal hissed as it met the ooze's surface, slicing through with a burst of heat. That drew a reaction. Steam billowed, and the creature recoiled slightly, crystals within its body vibrating erratically.

Then it exploded. Not with fire or sound, but with shards. The air filled with a sudden blast of crystal splinters, whirling in every direction. Xavier screamed and threw himself behind a stone outcropping. Several sharp slivers punched through his leather armor leaving him pin cushioned with the crystal pieces. The worst was one embedding in his thigh and a second that drew a furrow across his cheek. Blood splattered across the glowing ground.

He clutched his leg and cast Blooming Touch. The magic surged, slowing the bleeding and dulling the pain. He gasped, blinking through the haze of agony and lifted his head.

The ooze reformed, drawing its broken mass inward. A quick use of Insight told him it had taken real damage, but so had he.

Name: Crystaline Ooze	**Disposition:** Hungry
The Crystalline Ooze is a mesmerizing....	

Health: 63/130   Stamina: 200/200   Mana: 40/100

Not enough. He needed something stronger.

He reached deep, invoking the second spell he had learned, his only offensive one tied to death magic. Arcane syllables tumbled from his lips, strange and hollow. Shadows coalesced around his hand and formed into a writhing spear of dark energy.

He launched it. The necrotic blast struck the ooze dead center. Where it landed, the crystalline body turned murky. Dark veins spiderwebbed through its surface. The ooze screeched—no sound, just vibration, an oscillating whine that rattled his teeth.

It fled, inching back toward the far end of the cavern. But Xavier advanced, relentless. He cast again, despite the pain forming behind his eyes and the burning drain of mana.

The second spell struck with force, and the creature spasmed. The shards within its body darkened to black. Xavier's limbs trembled, his fingers shaking from exhaustion. Still, he did not stop.

He pressed forward, cast once more. The magic answered, barely. His vision blurred. The ooze shriveled inward, its fluid form collapsing around the blackened crystals. Its motion slowed. Then stopped.

The notification icon in the corner of his vision pulsed. He held the spell a second longer, just in case. Then released it and collapsed to his knees.

A radiant chime rang in his ears. Familiar now. Triumphant.

"Hark and Hear! You have ascended in power. You are now Level 7!

The touch of the divine lingers upon you, granting **6**

attribute points to shape your destiny, an exceptional gift, elevated from the ordinary **4 points** by the **Blessings of the Gods (Danu).** Choose wisely, for these points will define your path. You have **3 days** to assign them, or they will fall to the whims of fate. Your growing prowess earns you a boon: **20% skill allocation** to distribute among your known skills. This is your chance to sharpen the blade of a favored talent, forge new strength in an untapped domain, or balance your growth across disciplines. Let this moment be a cornerstone of your greatness.

Rise, Seeker of Glory. The world awaits your will. Seek adventure, seek wisdom, seek love and let your legend be forged in your choices. LIVE!"

#

CHAPTER TWENTY-FOUR

Taken

Xavier closed the level-up prompt with a faint smile, then turned his attention to the notification for defeating the ooze. His eyes widened. Two thousand, three hundred experience.

That single creature had nearly matched the reward for clearing entire dungeons. It was a harsh remind, the creatures inhabiting his lands were growing more dangerous. He would have to be more careful and focus on strengthening himself. He had only been in Arath a few weeks, but he was already level seven. That wasn't enough. Not with people relying on him.

Cautiously, he searched the crystalline cavern. After the ambush, he wasn't eager to be surprised again. The search took nearly an hour, but nothing stirred in the shimmering silence. It seemed the ooze had been the sole inhabitant.

Returning to the creature's remains, he grimaced. Whatever held its body together had dissolved with its death. The corpse had collapsed into a foul-smelling pool, its mass thick and viscous, the crystal shards that once floated in it now scattered throughout the muck.

He crouched nearby, eyeing the pool. If only he had a vial or proper tools, he might have taken samples. He extended a hand to retrieve one of the shards. That was a mistake.

The instant his fingers touched the goo, a sharp hiss erupted, and pain flared across his fingertips. His health bar ticked down several points. Xavier jerked back with a curse. The liquid was acidic. He wasn't sure how the crystals had survived inside it, but perhaps it was like the way glass held acid back on Earth. Maybe the shards were simply resistant.

After another moment of contemplation, he sighed and stood. With limited water and no idea how deep the caverns went, lingering wasn't an option. Still, before he turned to go, something near the edge of the chamber caught his eye, a faint shimmer half-buried in a narrow fissure near the far wall, just behind where the ooze had spawned.

He approached slowly, crouching beside the cracked stone. Nestled amid mineral dust, almost overlooked, was a small object that pulsed with subtle inner light. Reaching in carefully, he pried it free.

It was unlike the others. Dull on one edge, sharply tapered on the other, the shard seemed to glow faintly from within, not with external essence like most crystals, but something deeper, something resonant.

You have acquired: Shard of Resonance **Description:** A slender, translucent fragment pulsing with inner light that shifts through subtle hues depending on its environment. It hums faintly when held, vibrating in harmony	**Item Class:** Rare Component **Item Quality:** Exquisite **Type:** Essence-Bound Crafting Material **Weight:** 0.08 kg **Durability:** 20/20 **Traits:** - **Elemental Synchrony:** Naturally

with nearby magical fields. This Shard of Resonance is a rare crystalline essence-bound sliver, formed only under deep elemental convergence—typically at the heart of ley-touched ruins, ancient forges, or after significant magical events. Its inner lattice is attuned to both soul-signature and elemental resonance, making it essential for soulforging, high-tier rune architecture, and binding enchantments.

attunes to the strongest elemental field present during crafting (Fire, Water, Earth, etc.), enhancing alignment with that school of magic.

- Rune Stabilizer: When used during advanced rune crafting, prevents rune degradation and enhances spell imprinting success by +15%.
- Soulforge Catalyst: Can serve as a key medium when binding essence crystals, soul fragments, or sentient relics, ensuring stable fusion and extended durability.

Special Usage:
- Ley-Aligned Structures amplify the shard's responsiveness, allowing it to:
  o Lock onto ley signatures
  o Trace resonance pathways
  o Stabilize volatile soulbound enchantments

- May be consumed during legendary item reforging to grant a permanent trait such as:
  o **Harmonized Casting:** reduced essence cost when using spells tied to the item
  o **Echo Imprint:** allows item to remember the last spell cast through it and replicate it once

Xavier turned the shard over in his fingers. There was power in it. Raw, waiting, attuned to something he couldn't yet name. He tucked it carefully into his pouch, wrapping it in cloth to keep it safe.

#

He had a limited amount of water and didn't know how much deeper the caverns went. During his search, he had noticed another passageway leading even further into the depths, and it had not escaped his notice that the quest for "Whose House 1" had yet to update. The system still considered the location incomplete.

He had come to a crossroads. He could press on, knowing full well that the dangers would only escalate the deeper he ventured. Or he could return to the village and check if Ella had recovered enough to travel again. If she had, he could bring her and Valkra with him, and together, they might face whatever waited in the dark with greater confidence.

Ultimately, it was the thought of those who relied on him that guided his choice.

He had discovered the location. He had a map now, etched into his interface, giving him an easy route back. From what he could tell, it had been decades, perhaps even longer, since anyone had set foot in these tunnels. Whatever secrets they held would wait a few more days.

His mind made up, he rose and started toward the corridor that led back to the long hall and, eventually, the surface. He moved carefully. His ears strained for any signs of danger, the wet drag of another ooze, the chittering of hidden spiders. But the tunnels were still, the silence broken only by the echo of his own footsteps and the occasional drip of water from the ceiling.

Still it took hours. He hadn't realized how long he'd been below until he reached the narrow shaft that likely connected the Deeps to the forest above. When he looked up, he saw stars twinkling against a black velvet sky. Night had fallen. Deep night. It had been just after midday when he began his descent.

His rope still hung where he had anchored it earlier, a lifeline dangling through the darkness. He placed a hand on it and began the climb. It was more taxing than the descent had been. The damp stone walls offered little help, and the climb demanded every ounce of focus and strength he had, but his body responded with calm assurance. He was stronger now.

Back on Earth, he'd never been unfit, just average, dulled by years behind a desk and only occasional workouts. The gym had been maintenance, nothing more. Slowly, without noticing, he had softened. Here in Arath, that softness had burned away. His limbs moved with lean power. His muscles responded like coiled springs.

He climbed steadily, his breath deep, his thoughts distant. When he finally reached the top and pulled himself over the rim of the shaft, he lay there for a long moment on the forest floor. The air was cool and rich with the scent of pine and loam, a grounding contrast to the stifling weight of the tunnels below.

Then something moved. A flicker of white at the edge of his vision. Fast and silent.

He turned his head instinctively, eyes scanning the underbrush. Pain exploded at the back of his skull. The world tipped sideways, and darkness swallowed him whole.

#

Xavier drifted awake slowly, as if clawing his way through thick tar. His head pulsed with a dull, rhythmic ache that pounded behind his eyes and echoed through his skull. Darkness pressed in from all sides, not the gentle dark of sleep, but a dense, suffocating void.

He tried to move, but his limbs wouldn't respond. Panic surged, then was checked by instinct and logic.

His interface still shimmered faintly in the back of his mind. No blindness. No paralysis. His health was full. He was bound... and blindfolded.

His wrists were cinched tight, arms pinned to his sides. His legs felt similarly restrained. Something beneath him creaked with each jolt. He was being dragged.

A rough platform, a sledge maybe, scraped across the forest floor, jostling with every root and stone. His body shifted slightly with each pull, the vibrations humming along the wooden frame beneath his spine.

The cool touch of air hinted at forest night, not the cloying damp of the caverns. The scent of pine sap, crushed leaves, and fresh earth confirmed it. Somewhere above, branches creaked in the night wind. He was no longer underground.

Then came a voice. "Yes. He's awake."

It was feminine, calm and measured. There was a subtle, rasping sibilance to the words, almost a purr behind her consonants, like breath curling through a predator's throat. Controlled and cool, but not unkind.

He quickly realized she wasn't speaking to him. "No. That won't be necessary yet. The elders will decide."

A pause followed, long enough for Xavier to pick out the faint creak of leather, the soft thud of boots shifting in place. When she spoke again, her voice dipped lower, less formal now, but no less composed.

"I know the only humans this deep are raiders. But the elders will want to question him. Just like the others."

The final word lingered. Not in threat, but in certainty. There had been others. Captured? Interrogated? Executed?

Xavier tensed against the ropes, trying not to let the panic rise. The sledge rocked slightly beneath him with each pull forward, the forest floor groaning beneath its passage. He couldn't see, couldn't move, but he could listen, and think.

They had no idea who he was. No idea what he carried. No idea what killing him might do.

"Fine," the woman said at last, voice clipped and cool. "Give it to him."

Footsteps shifted in the brush, closer this time.

Then hands, large, practiced, grabbed his face. Fingers dug into the joint of his jaw, prying his mouth open. He tried to twist away, but a hard backhand caught him clean across the cheek. Pain lanced through his skull. The blindfold dimmed the blow, but not the sharp crack of it.

The same hand returned, more forceful now, wrenching his jaw wide.

A thick liquid spilled in. Bitter, metallic, clinging like cold sap. He gagged and jerked his head back, but another hand clamped over his mouth. A second pinched his nose.

No air. He kicked weakly, uselessly against his bindings. Swallow or suffocate. His body chose to survive.

The fluid slid down his throat like syrup laced with ice. Within seconds, his limbs began to tingle. A weight settled on his chest. The edges of thought grew soft, dimming beneath the slow tide of unconsciousness.

Dreamveil sap. He remembered reading about it. An Animari sedative used to subdue wild beasts or dangerous prey. Especially favored by pantherkin tribes in the high forests. Rare, clean, and lethal in high doses.

His mind began to spiral. They thought he was a raider. Thought he was like the slavers at Bramblegate. His breath slowed, and then the world slipped sideways again.

As the last threads of thought unraveled, one final conviction held fast.

They don't know who I am.

Then, nothingness surrounded him.

#

The haze of unconsciousness lifted like fog burned off by dawn.

Xavier stirred, limbs sluggish, body aching. He was upright now, still lashed to something solid, and propped against the base of a tree. His arms and legs remained tightly bound, but the blindfold had been removed.

He blinked, squinting against the filtered morning light. Shafts of golden sun pierced the mist above, glinting through dew-laced leaves. The air was clean and sharp, pine sap, fresh earth, and the smell of a fire.

A small, smokeless fire crackled nearby. A blackened pot hung over the coals, the scent of cooked meat and herbs drifting into the clearing. His stomach twisted painfully at the smell.

Then came the new sound, low, steady, primal. A growl.

Xavier lowered his gaze.

A massive feline lay stretched across the ground between him and the fire. Its fur was thick and white, patterned with charcoal rosettes that glimmered faintly in the dawnlight. A long, heavy tail curled beside its body. Its head was raised slightly, eyes fixed on him — a pale, unblinking blue, like shards of glacial ice.

It didn't move. It didn't need to. Every line of its body radiated coiled patience. Power. The kind of power that waited, measured, and then killed without hesitation.

Not a normal animal.

Xavier's pulse quickened. Not making the same mistake as he had with the spiders, he triggered *Insight*.

Name: Frostclaw		Disposition: Wary
Level: Unknown	Class: Unknown	Active Effects: Unknown
Description		
The snow leopard is a large, elusive feline native to cold, mountainous regions. Its thick, snow-white fur, patterned with dark rosettes, provides excellent camouflage in snowy landscapes. With piercing ice-blue eyes and a long, bushy tail for balance, the Snow Panther moves silently, making it a masterful predator. Renowned for its agility and strength, it can leap great distances and traverse treacherous terrain with ease. Snow Panthers are fiercely territorial and highly intelligent, often regarded as symbols of resilience and grace in the wild. Their natural stealth and survival instincts make them both feared and revered by those who encounter them.		
Stats		

| Health: 320/320 | Stamina: 500/500 | Mana: 100/00 |

Frostclaw, Xavier thought. Of course it has a name.

Movement beside the panther drew his gaze. A woman stepped into view, placing one hand lightly on the feline's broad head.

"I didn't think the dreamveil would keep you down that long," she said.

The voice was unmistakable, the same one he'd heard before blacking out. Low. Precise. With that subtle feline rasp in her consonants, a predator's breath curled into words.

She stood tall, athletic and sure-footed, wrapped in practical leather armor shaped for mobility and survival. Over her shoulders hung a pale fur-lined cloak clasped with carved bone. Her build spoke of quiet strength honed through cold terrain and harder battles.

Her body was covered in short, dense fur patterned like a snow leopard's, pale gray-white with soft black rosettes. The fur thickened subtly around her shoulders and neck, vanishing beneath her armor but visible at the wrists and along her jaw.

Her face was mostly human, but not entirely. A gentle feline curve shaped her cheeks and snout. Her nose was dark and feline, nestled between high cheekbones marked with rosettes. Her ears were pointed, furred, and alert. She didn't blink often.

A long tail, thick and tufted at the end, flicked once behind her.

Her eyes, gray-blue, slitted and unflinching, locked on him.

Xavier triggered *Insight*.

| Name: Lianna | Race: Iskari | Disposition: |

Froststride	(Snow Panther Animari)	Untrusting
Level: Unknown	**Class:** Unknown	**Active Effects:** Unknown
	Description	

The Iskari are a race of Animari descended from snow leopards, renowned for their stealth, resilience, and connection to cold, mountainous regions. With pale skin marked by faint rosette patterns and thick, snow-like hair streaked with silver or black, they move with feline grace and precision. Their piercing blue or gray eyes reflect sharp intelligence and a predatory nature. The Iskari thrive in harsh environments, leveraging their exceptional agility and survival instincts. Fiercely loyal and protective of their kin, they are skilled hunters, trackers, and warriors, embodying the quiet strength and adaptability of their snow leopard heritage.

	Stats	
Health: 200/200	**Stamina:** 210/210	**Mana:** 170/170

She watched him in silence, her hand resting on Frostclaw's head, the other near the curved blade at her hip. A well-crafted recurve bow was strapped across her back alongside a quiver of black-fletched arrows.

"You were unconscious for half the night," she said flatly. "I had half a mind to leave you here and let the woods decide your worth." Her tail gave a slight twitch.

Xavier didn't answer. Every part of her posture warned him that silence was safer... for now.

Lianna didn't move, but her voice carried across the camp with the same controlled sharpness. "Next time use less. We don't want to kill him yet."

Xavier turned toward the sound of movement overhead.

A second figure dangled upside down from a thick tree limb near the fire. He hung by his knees, arms loosely folded across his chest, pale fur ruffling in the wind. His snow-leopard coat was darker than Lianna's, streaked with silver and black. A long, sinuous tail swayed behind him in gentle rhythm.

His face bore the same hybrid grace, a soft feline snout, a catlike nose, rosette markings across his brow and cheekbones. His ears flicked subtly, tracking sound and scent with casual efficiency. His ice-blue eyes locked onto Xavier, narrowed with veiled scrutiny.

He grinned faintly, not cruelly, but with no warmth either.

Xavier triggered *Insight* once more.

Name: Liosan Froststride	**Race:** Iskari (Snow Panther Animari)	**Disposition:** Untrusting
Level: Unknown	**Class:** Unknown	**Active Effects:** Unknown
Description		
The Iskari are a race of Animari descended from snow leopards, renowned for their stealth, resilience, and connection to cold, mountainous regions. With pale skin marked by faint rosette patterns and thick, snow-like hair streaked with silver or black, they move with feline grace and precision. Their piercing blue or gray eyes reflect sharp intelligence and a predatory nature. The Iskari thrive in harsh environments, leveraging their exceptional agility and survival instincts. Fiercely loyal and protective of their kin, they are skilled hunters, trackers, and warriors, embodying the quiet strength and		

Stats		
adaptability of their snow leopard heritage.		
Health: 170/170	**Stamina:** 150/150	**Mana:** 200/200

They were siblings. And neither looked particularly interested in negotiation.

Liosan tilted his head slightly, tail curling and uncurling in silent tempo. His gaze moved from Xavier to Lianna and back again.

Xavier returned his attention to her. Lianna's expression hadn't changed. Her eyes were still sharp. still wary.

He was breathing, that was something, but trust had not been extended, and from the silent twitch of Frostclaw's ears and the still tension of the camp, he knew one wrong move could change that quickly.

#

Lianna's gaze didn't waver. Her posture shifted slightly, a quiet readjustment of weight, one furred ear flicking back toward the woods behind her, then forward again. Her tail moved with more tension now, curling once, then falling still as she stepped closer.

Frostclaw remained exactly where he was, his massive head tracking her steps with idle confidence. Xavier could still feel those ice-blue eyes on him, passive but not relaxed, just waiting.

Lianna stopped just out of reach. Her hand rested lightly on the hilt of her blade, but she made no threatening motion. Her stance spoke clearly enough. "Who are you," she asked, "and why are you in the Silverwood?"

The question landed like a stone in a still pool. Her voice was even, precise, each word measured like it was being weighed for truth the moment it left her mouth. Her ears were angled toward him, alert to more than just his words, listening for the pace of his breath, the tremor in his tone, the lies behind his eyes.

Xavier hesitated. He considered the bindings around his limbs, the panther at his feet, the two Iskari who watched him like scouts assessing a wounded animal. He couldn't afford the truth. Not all of it.

"My name is Xavier," he said slowly. "I live deeper in the forest. I was exploring a location I hadn't seen before and was just trying to make my way back home when I was... ambushed."

He kept his voice steady. Not too fast. Not too defensive.

"I mean you no harm. I didn't even know anyone else was nearby."

Lianna narrowed her eyes. Her tail flicked once behind her, quick and sharp.

Liosan dropped from the tree branch without a sound. He landed in a low crouch, his movements effortless, the fur along his limbs shifting with the impact. He straightened, arms crossed, tail curling slowly behind him. His eyes never left Xavier.

"Troll shit," Lianna snapped suddenly, the growl in her voice rising. Her ears flattened for a heartbeat before resuming their upright posture. She stepped closer, boots sinking slightly into the soft loam.

"We know what you are. You're with the raiders. You got separated from your pack while scouting one of our villages, didn't you?" Her voice sharpened. "Liosan found only one set of human footprints down there. Yours."

She gestured vaguely behind her, toward the path Xavier had taken from the ruins below.

"You are a long way from the Wildlands, little human,"

she said, voice bitter. "No one is coming to rescue you."

She turned her back on him, signaling, without fear or doubt, that she didn't see him as a threat. Not now, not tied as he was, and definitely not with Frostclaw at his feet.

The great cat let out a soft chuff, its ears swiveling in tandem with its mistress's movements.

Liosan moved to the fire and crouched beside it. He picked up the cooking pot and stirred it with a carved wooden ladle. Xavier could smell the savory broth thick in the air. It made his stomach growl, loud and involuntary.

Lianna heard it and shot him a glance over her shoulder. Her face was unreadable, sharp and undeniably beautiful in its feral way, but cold.

"We'll reach the foothills before nightfall," she said aloud, speaking to her brother. "The elders will decide what to do with him. If he talks, they might grant him a quick death. If not…"

She didn't finish the sentence. She didn't need to, it had the intended effect.

Xavier's heart pounded. He tested his bindings again, but the knots were expertly done. There was no play in the rope. No weakness to exploit.

He looked up again. Liosan's eyes met his.

There was no malice in them, only watchfulness. Like a predator that had seen men bleed before and didn't care for their excuses.

Xavier felt the despair beginning to rise.

Then he clenched his jaw. No. Not like this.

He wouldn't die a prisoner, bound and nameless. If they took him to these elders, he would have to make them listen. To believe. He didn't know how, not yet, but there had to be a way.

He forced his breathing to slow. He measured it, grounded it. For now, he was alive, and he still had a chance.

#

Time passed in slow, grinding silence. The forest around them had begun to stir, birds rustling in high branches, insects humming at the edges of the clearing, the faint creak of trees shifting with morning light. But at the campfire, all was still.

Xavier sat with his back braced against the hard wood of the sledge, his arms bound to his sides, legs wrapped tightly in rope. Every muscle ached. His spine throbbed. His shoulders burned. His wrists, rubbed raw by the coarse fiber, throbbed in time with his heartbeat.

And his stomach... It twisted with a dull, angry ache, growing sharper with each breath. The scent of the stew boiling above the fire was maddening, thick with spice and marrow and game meat. It coated the inside of his nose, clung to the back of his throat, and taunted his empty belly with every curl that reached his nostrils. His mouth was dry. He swallowed hard on nothing.

Across the fire, Liosan crouched in near perfect stillness. His snow-leopard-patterned fur caught the light as he stirred the pot with a carved wooden ladle, the rhythm slow and unhurried. His expression remained unreadable, watchful, and guarded.

Xavier's mouth parted slightly. He hesitated... then pushed the word out. "Please."

Lianna's ears twitched where she leaned against a tree nearby, her posture relaxed in theory but never in truth. Her tail stilled for a moment, then curled once behind her.

Xavier licked his lips. "I haven't eaten since yesterday morning," he said, voice cracked with dryness. "Could I... just have a little? I'm not trying to buy favor. I just..."

He trailed off. His pride fought with his need. His eyes closed for a moment. "I'm starving."

A long pause followed. The fire popped once. Liosan looked up but did not speak. His pale blue eyes drifted toward his sister in a silent question, his tail moving in a lazy figure-eight behind him.

Lianna pushed off from the tree with a subtle shift of her hips. Her boots crunched faintly over pine needles as she approached, every step smooth, deliberate, feline. Her short fur shimmered in the light. Her eyes were cold and steady.

"You think we owe you something," she said at last, not a question. Her voice was quiet but edged in steel. "That we should reward trespass and lies with kindness."

Her tail twitched again, sharper this time. The faint breeze carried her scent, pine oil, cold stone, worn leather.

"No," Xavier said. "I don't." He lifted his head, barely. "I just... I thought maybe you weren't monsters."

Lianna halted just in front of him. Frostclaw stirred slightly at her side, lifting his head a few inches, ears angled forward.

"We aren't," she said, voice cooler now. "That's what separates us from your kind."

Her gaze bore into him, gray-blue and glinting like steel beneath ice.

"We don't starve captives. We don't break bones for sport. We don't drag children in chains through mud to prove dominance. We remember who we are."

She crouched smoothly, her knees folding beneath her in a fluid motion. One hand reached toward the pot, scooping stew into a wooden bowl. Her other hand hovered near her blade the whole time, even if she didn't draw it.

"We remember," she repeated, quieter this time. "Even

when you forget."

She lifted a spoon, tested its heat, then brought it to his lips.

"Open." Came the soft command.

Xavier did. He let her feed him.

The stew was thick, flavorful, peppered with chunks of tender meat, sliced roots, and some leafy green that had a bitter, grounding taste. The warmth spread through his stomach like a blanket, dulling the ache, though it did nothing for the tight knots of anxiety coiled in his chest.

Lianna didn't speak again as she fed him, five spoonfuls, no more. When the bowl was empty, she stood, wiped the spoon clean, and returned to the fire.

Frostclaw's gaze followed her for only a heartbeat before resettling on Xavier. The massive snow panther had not so much as twitched his muscles in all that time, save for a single quiet breath.

Liosan remained kneeling beside the pot, but his posture had changed, no longer loose and casual, but alert. His ears shifted toward every sound, every twitch of Xavier's limbs. His tail no longer moved.

Then, without a word, he vanished into the woods. One moment he was there. The next, the forest had claimed him.

Xavier blinked at the space where the Iskari scout had been. The stillness that followed was not comforting.

Lianna resumed her position near the edge of the clearing, leaning against the base of a wide-barked tree. Her arms folded across her chest. Her tail curled loosely at her side, but her eyes never closed. She wasn't resting.

Frostclaw adjusted his position near the fire, but did not lie down. Instead, the beast shifted forward slightly, placing a single heavy paw in front of Xavier, just shy of touching his boot.

The paw opened. Claws, curved and glinting, extended in slow precision... then retracted again. A soft rumble vibrated in the snow panther's throat. Not a threat. Not quite. Just a reminder.

Xavier's breath hitched. He didn't move again.

The ropes still held. His hands were numb. His legs half asleep. But for the first time in hours, his stomach wasn't empty. It gave him a thin thread of strength and hope, enough to hold on.

He leaned his head back against the wood behind him and exhaled slowly through his nose. They thought he was a raider. They were taking him to their elders, and time... was running short.

#

A few hours later, Xavier stirred as movement rocked the frame he was bound to. The sledge beneath him shifted, its wooden runners scraping softly over packed earth and dry pine needles. He felt his position shift slightly as the weight at his back tilted forward.

Lianna and Liosan were moving him. He remained still as they lifted the front end of the sledge. The wooden handles, carved with notches for rope, were eased into a harness of leather and fur. Frostclaw grunted low in his throat as the final buckles were secured along his shoulders. The snow panther bore the burden without resistance, muscles rippling beneath dense rosette-patterned fur.

Once everything was fastened, Lianna stepped back to Xavier's side. She crouched beside him, gloved fingers tugging on the knots around his wrists and ankles. She tested each one with quick, efficient jerks. Satisfied, she reached behind his head and secured the blindfold once again, cinching it tight.

"I swear I mean neither you nor your people harm," Xavier said, voice strained. "I just want to return to my home."

"Quiet," she snapped. "Your fate is in the hands of the elders now. I recommend you hold nothing back from them. If they are satisfied with your answers, you will get a swift death. If you vex them, then they have ways of making you spill the truth."

She stood, her footsteps receding. A moment later, the sledge began to move again. The harness creaked slightly as Frostclaw began to walk, dragging Xavier over the uneven forest floor. The sledge jolted with every root and slope, rattling his bones and pressing the bindings tighter around his limbs.

Xavier fell silent. With his eyes covered, he focused inward, toward the strange sense that had never quite faded since his arrival in Arath. That subtle awareness pulsed faintly within his mind, like an instinct rooted in something deeper than memory. A map without a surface. He could feel his direction, even blind.

They were moving north. The incline beneath the sled had changed. The earth was climbing. He was being taken toward the foothills, toward the Ironspire Mountains, the small map in his head confirmed this to him.

CHAPTER TWENTY-FIVE

Bound By Three, Proven By Deeds

The map in Xavier's interface updated in real time as he was dragged through the forest. Even without his sight, he could track their rapid movement. Judging by the shifting position of the confluence at Syr'Vailen, they were covering nearly three times the distance he could travel on foot in a day. Fifteen miles had already passed beneath him, all while bound and blindfolded.

He gritted his teeth and tried not to dwell on the humiliation of it. At least the map still worked. That, and the chance to finally review his interface, offered some small comfort. He pulled open the character tab with a thought and immediately triggered the familiar prompt.

> **You have reached Level 7.**
> **You have 6 attribute points to assign.**

Xavier quickly allocated his points. +2 Constitution, raising it to 14. A little more health could mean the difference between surviving or dying if this meeting with the elders went sideways. +2 Charisma, just in case talking might actually get him somewhere. +2 Luck, for the same small voice that always nudged him to invest in it.

He sat in silence, pondering the strange intuition. Was it fate? Divine whispers from Danu? Or just his subconscious pushing him toward the right path? He shook the thoughts away. No sense dwelling on something he'd likely never understand.

Time passed, long, dragging hours filled with jostling movement. When the forest trail grew smoother and the pace quickened, Xavier knew they were climbing toward a more established path, perhaps leading to a hidden settlement. With nothing else to do, he began reviewing his skills tab again. The list had grown impressively long in the short time he'd been in Arath.

Something caught his eye as he scrolled. His Daggers skill was still gaining experience, despite his recent shift toward short swords. Curious, he selected it and received a helpful tooltip:

Daggers (9 – Novice)
Progression: 83%
This skill will evolve into *Small Blades* upon reaching Level 10.

He grinned internally. So that's how it worked. Weapon skills could merge and evolve. If Daggers became Small Blades at Level 10, then it might encompass short swords, stilettos, and other similar weapons.

That raised another question. What else evolved? He tapped through his other skills and began to notice a more complex pattern. The ranks didn't shift every five levels as he'd first assumed. Instead, they followed a structured tier system. Novice at level 1, Initiate at 5, and Apprentice at 10. But Apprentice extended all the way to level 24. After that came Journeyman, spanning levels 25 to 49. Then Adept from 50 to 74. Craftsman picked up at 75 and held until level 99. Master dominated the hundreds, from level 100 through

149. And at the very end, Grand Master stood alone at level 150.

He frowned. Only when he reached level 10 had he received a notification about bonus experience. Did that happen at every new rank, or only at specific milestones like the start of Apprentice or Master? The system seemed deliberate, but maddeningly opaque. Gods, how he wished someone could just explain the rules.

He sighed. Gods, what he wouldn't give to have someone who understood this world's mechanics. Ella might know. But she was likely worried sick right now, assuming she hadn't tried to gut someone to find him. Aelriva might know too, but he doubted she'd appreciate being bombarded with questions. And Lianna? The cold Iskari tracker clearly thought he was barely worth the effort to drag north. She'd probably stab him for asking about skill progression.

He shook his head and tried something else to distract himself. With a thought, he opened the City Interface... or tried to.

> **You have attempted to access the Rynthavael Settlement Interface from outside your area of influence.**
> **Access denied until you return to your domain.**

"Well," he muttered aloud, voice muffled behind the blindfold, "guess that answers that." At least now he knew. He was officially outside his land's borders.

A familiar weight settled on him, that gnawing, restless need to understand. He cycled through the rest of his interface tabs, gear, stats, logs, until he stopped on a stray thought that had been bugging him for days. Time. How many days had it been since he arrived? Were weeks the same length here? Were the months?

He focused on the idea and received an unexpected

prompt.

> **Would you like to display time and date in your interface?**
> Yes/No

Xavier would have facepalmed if his hands hadn't been bound. Mentally, he selected yes. A new icon appeared in the bottom right corner of his vision, gleaming softly.

18:58 – 22 Bloomrest 13097 (200 AoOD)

He blinked. Bloomrest? That was a new one. He tapped the icon again, pulling open more details.

> Bloomrest – Third month of the calendar
> 40 days in the month
> 16 months in a year
> Current Era: 13097, Year 200 of the Age of Order's Dominion

Sixteen months? The realization hit him like a slap. Earth's twelve-month calendar seemed quaint in comparison, and this world had been tracking years for over thirteen millennia. A calendar system that old, still in active use? Earth was practically an infant in comparison.

He recalled Danu's words, how Arath had touched Earth's myths and dreams. Maybe she hadn't been exaggerating.

#

Before he could reflect further, the dragging stopped. Silence pressed in around him. Xavier stiffened, straining his ears. Boots shifted in loam. A breath caught nearby.

Xavier's breath caught. The air felt different... less wild, more measured. The ever-present rustle of trees faded into structured silence. He strained his ears, listening.

The blindfold came off without warning.

Torchlight stabbed into his eyes, and he winced, blinking furiously against the sudden flare. His captors had brought him indoors, or perhaps into a sheltered glade. He couldn't yet see the surroundings, just flickering shapes caught in silhouette, dancing behind the firelight.

From his left came a voice, sharp and familiar.

"Elders, we found this human emerging from a collapsed tunnel deep to the south within the Silverwood."

It was Lianna. The steel in her voice was unmistakable, cold and unyielding.

"He was too far east to be seeking elven lands," she continued. "And nowhere near any of the human settlements that engage in trade. The only thing that fits is that he was part of a raiding party. Maybe a new recruit, or one of their noble-born sympathizers. His weapons are better than the usual scum carry. Could be a bored lordling slumming with murderers."

She had clearly spent the journey crafting that speech. It was thorough, damning, and delivered without hesitation.

Xavier barely had time to process her words before a massive shadow stepped into the torchlight, blotting it out with sheer size.

The figure towered over him, broad-shouldered and bristling with dark fur. Eyes like molten amber regarded him with measured contempt. The creature's scent—earth, iron, and old stone—hit Xavier like a wall. A hand rested on a massive axe strapped to its back, but it did not yet draw it.

Insight Triggered.

Name: Thror Ironpaw	Race: Ursari (Bearkin Animari)	Disposition: Wary
Level: Unknown	Class: Unknown	Active Effects:

		Unknown
Description		
The bearkin Animari, or Ursari, is a race of humanoids embodying the traits of bears. Known for their immense strength, resilience, and protective instincts, they are the steadfast guardians of their people and lands. With broad, powerful frames, thick fur-like hair in shades of brown, black, or silver, and deep-set amber or dark brown eyes, they project an aura of unyielding determination. Ursari are natural warriors and defenders, deeply tied to earth's strength and endurance, and their stoic demeanor hides a deep well of wisdom and patience.		
Stats		
Health: Unknown	**Stamina:** Unknown	**Mana:** Unknown

Thror grunted, unimpressed. "He does not look like much. Any one of our Wardens could bring him down before he raised a blade."

A soft, feminine voice answered from the shadows, still from Xavier's left. "Calm, Thror. I do not believe he is one of the raiders. I say we hear his words."

That voice, measured, serene, cut through the tension like a cool breeze.

Xavier seized the moment. "My name is Xavier," he called out, projecting his voice past the torchlight. "I come from Rynthavael. It's a village deep in the woods. We built it on the ruins of a lost place, right now it's refuge for survivors of raider attacks. If you've been targeted, then we have a common enemy."

He twisted his head, trying to see who else stood beyond the firelight. The torchbearers shifted. Light fell in new angles.

Six stood together behind Lianna, each robed in natural hues of greens, browns, silvers. Their clothing seemed grown, not sewn, adorned with antlers, feathers, stones, and bark. Each wore a unique torc at the throat and a circlet across the brow. No two shared the same sigils or ornamentation. They radiated presence. It was not power flaunted, but simply there, undeniable.

Xavier triggered Insight on each in turn, the results filtering into his mind in a controlled rush.

Name: Kaelith Moonstride	**Race:** Lynari (Lynxkin Animari)	**Disposition:** Neutral
Level: Unknown	**Class:** Unknown	**Active Effects:** Unknown
Description		
The lynxkin Animari, or Lynari, is a race of humanoids embodying the traits of lynxes. Known for their sharp vision, independence, and agility, they thrive in roles requiring clarity, adaptability, and precision. Lynari possess lithe and graceful frames, often with tawny, silvery, or gray fur-like hair streaked with black. Their piercing golden, amber, or green eyes reflect intelligence and an uncanny ability to detect hidden threats. Distinctive tufted ears and subtle whisker-like facial markings highlight their feline lineage, further enhancing their air of mystery. Deeply connected to air's vigilance, the Lynari are natural strategists, scouts, and mediators, blending sharp instincts with careful deliberation to guide their kin through the challenges of both wilderness and society.		
Stats		
Health: Unknown	**Stamina:** Unknown	**Mana:** Unknown

Name: Sylara Dawnshade	**Race:** Cervari (Deerkin Animari)	**Disposition:** Curious
Level: Unknown	**Class:** Unknown	**Active Effects:** Unknown

Description		
The deerkin animari, or Cervari, is a race of humanoids embodying the traits of deer. Renowned for their wisdom, grace, and nurturing spirits, they are deeply connected to the natural flow of life and harmony. Their slender frames are complemented by soft, earthy-toned hair, often adorned with subtle antler-like growths or decorative markings. Their serene green or hazel eyes reflect a profound empathy and calm strength. Cervari are skilled healers, spiritual guides, and mediators, embodying life's gentle yet persistent growth and fostering balance within their communities and the natural world.		

Stats		
Health: Unknown	**Stamina:** Unknown	**Mana:** Unknown

Name: Veyara Frostwhisper	**Race:** Iskari (Snow Leopardkin Animari)	**Disposition:** Untrusting
Level: Unknown	**Class:** Unknown	**Active Effects:** Unknown

Description		
The snow leopard Animari, or Iskari, is a race of humanoids embodying the traits of snow leopards. Known for their stealth, agility, and resilience, they thrive in harsh, cold environments, such as mountainous		

regions. With pale skin marked by faint rosette patterns and thick, snow-like hair often streaked with silver or black, they exude an air of quiet strength. Their piercing blue or gray eyes and fluid movements reflect their feline grace and predatory instincts. Fiercely loyal to their kin, Iskari are natural hunters, trackers, and warriors, blending primal intuition with sharp intelligence to navigate both wilderness and social challenges.

Stats		
Health: Unknown	**Stamina:** Unknown	**Mana:** Unknown

Name: Arvyn Flamefeather	**Race:** Falconi (Hawkkin Animari)	**Disposition:** Wary
Level: Unknown	**Class:** Unknown	**Active Effects:** Unknown

Description

The hawkkin animari, or Falconi, is a race of humanoids embodying the traits of hawks. Renowned for their sharp eyes, precision, and discipline, they are the vigilant protectors of the skies and masters of aerial tactics. Their lithe frames are accented by feathers that blend seamlessly with their hair, often in shades of gold, brown, or gray. Their sharp, piercing eyes, usually golden or bright brown, miss no detail. Falconi are natural scouts, hunters, and tacticians, embodying air's freedom and vigilance while protecting their kin from above with unmatched dedication.

Stats		
Health: Unknown	**Stamina:** Unknown	**Mana:** Unknown

Name: Lyselle Silvermist	**Race:** Vulpiri (Foxkin Animari)	**Disposition:** Intrigued
Level: Unknown	**Class:** Unknown	**Active Effects:** Unknown

Description		
The foxkin Animari, or Vulpiri, is a race of humanoids embodying the traits of foxes. Known for their cunning, charisma, and agility, they excel in diplomacy, negotiation, and intrigue. With sleek, fiery red or coppery hair, sometimes streaked with black or white, and sharp, playful eyes in hues of amber, green, or gold, they radiate a sly charm. Their slender frames and quick movements reflect their natural adaptability. Vulpiri are master negotiators, spies, and strategists, embodying life's clever resourcefulness and thriving in both social and wilderness challenges.		

Stats		
Health: Unknown	**Stamina:** Unknown	**Mana:** Unknown

Name: Khoran Dusksworn	**Race:** Duskhari (Pantherkin Animari)	**Disposition:** Wary
Level: Unknown	**Class:** Unknown	**Active Effects:** Unknown

Description		
The pantherkin Animari, or Duskhari, is a race of humanoids embodying the traits of panthers. Enigmatic and precise, they are masters of stealth and shadow, thriving in dark forests and shadowed terrains. Their smooth, dark-toned skin is complemented by sleek black or deep midnight blue hair, and their golden or green eyes shine with piercing intensity. Duskhari move with silent		

precision, blending seamlessly into their surroundings. Known for their patience and strength, they are natural shadow warriors and tacticians, channeling earth's unseen power and embodying the stillness before the strike.

Stats		
Health: Unknown	**Stamina:** Unknown	**Mana:** Unknown

Xavier's mouth went dry. Every Insight check came back with the same glaring absence, no stats, no class, no level. Only race and disposition. In games that usually meant one thing: they were significantly higher level than him. Possibly much higher.

For non-combatants to have that kind of power... it was staggering. Either these were warriors of extraordinary caliber, or their influence and skill ran deeper than blade and spell. Likely both.

He bowed his head, carefully, to each in turn. Respect offered freely, not demanded.

Kaelith's voice cut through the air at last. Barely above a whisper, but it carried the weight of command. "Untie him, Lianna. We will speak to him as an individual, not a prisoner."

Lianna stiffened. Her tail flicked behind her, jaw clenched as she looked ready to argue.

"You were wise to bring him bound and blindfolded," Kaelith added. "Your vigilance has kept this haven hidden. The raiders have not found our enclave yet due to you and the Wardens. Do not mistake our words for reproach."

Lianna blinked, then nodded sharply. She stepped toward Xavier, her knife flashing in smooth arcs as she severed his bindings.

Xavier slumped forward, catching himself as sensation rushed back into his legs. The cold had seeped into his muscles. His knees buckled, and he dropped to a sitting position with a wince. Lianna loomed just behind him, blade still in hand, watching like a hawk.

He didn't blame her. He was a stranger in front of their leaders. Soon, Xavier was able to look up to the surrounding individuals. Other than Lianna there was no outright hostility from any of them. Instead, their features displayed emotions ranging from mistrust to disinterest to curiosity. He was an unknown element. His words had the semblance of truth if lacking details.

After a moment and at a nod from the Lynari, who seemed to be the head of the group, Sylara stepped forward. The Cervari elder wove her fingers through an intricate pattern, golden light spilling from her palms. The warmth flowed over him like sunlight through water. Every ache, every cramp, every lingering sting faded in an instant.

Xavier's status log flashed with a vague notification: Healed by unknown spell.

He stood slowly, eyes on the elders.

"I want to help," he said clearly, voice steady. "Tell me what I need to do to prove I mean you no harm."

The silence lingered after Xavier's question, stretching like a taut bowstring.

He kept his gaze fixed on the Lynxkin who had spoken, Kaelith, though she had not yet given her name. Her golden eyes met his, unreadable. Around her, the other elders shifted slightly, considering.

It was Lyselle, the Vulpiri, who broke the quiet. "Send him with the Wardens," she said brightly. Her voice had a light, playful edge, but there was no mistaking the weight behind it. "They leave soon to hunt the raiding party that struck

Tilsen. If he helps recover the captives and brings them home safely, I will say he's earned some trust."

Xavier turned back to Kaelith, awaiting her response. The Lynari studied him in silence for a long moment, then stepped forward until she stood directly in front of him. Though she was smaller than the others, her presence loomed larger than any.

"Do you swear," she asked softly, "that you mean my people no harm?"

"Yes," Xavier replied at once. "I swear on everything I have that I didn't even know you were here, let alone mean you harm."

Kaelith tilted her head. One ear twitched. "What was that?" she asked, voice lilting. "I did not quite hear you."

He frowned, puzzled but obliging. "I swear on everything I have that I didn't even know you were here, let alone mean you harm."

Her eyes narrowed slightly, and she leaned in. "Once more, if you would. Just to be clear."

Xavier hesitated. Some instinct prickled at the base of his neck. But retreating now would only make him look guilty. "I swear on everything I have," he repeated slowly and firmly, "that I didn't even know you were here, let alone mean you harm."

The moment the last word left his mouth, a sudden pressure dropped over him, like unseen chains wrapping tight around his chest and limbs. It wasn't physical. It was something deeper. Weight without form. A judgment without voice.

Kaelith smiled faintly. "It is done."

Xavier's eyes widened. "What is?"

"You swore three times before the Circle of Elders," she

said gently. "That invokes the Ritual of Three. Your words are now bound by witness and tradition. If you had lied, the gods themselves would have struck you down where you stood."

His throat went dry.

Kaelith's smile faded. "That does not mean we trust you. Not yet. Will you go with our Wardens, then, and help us reclaim those who were taken?"

You have been offered a Quest: Break the Bonds I
Quest Type: Mandatory
Trigger: The Ritual of Three has bound your words. Your trait *Unyielding Liberator* enflames your resolve. You cannot refuse this quest.

Quest Objectives
•   Assist the Verdantspire Wardens in tracking and eliminating the raider party responsible for the destruction of Tilsen.
•   Rescue any surviving Animari captives.

Failure Penalty
•   Due to your trait, refusal is impossible.
•   Failure will result in the death or enslavement of captives and the complete loss of trust from the Animari of Verdantspire Haven.

Potential Rewards
•   +5000 Experience
•   Increased trust with Verdantspire Haven
•   Improved diplomatic relations between Verdantspire Haven and Rynthavael

---

Xavier exhaled slowly as the prompt faded. He had been tricked, and it had been done cleverly, subtly. Kaelith had drawn him into the oath without ever declaring her intent. And yet... he couldn't be angry. This was a chance to prove himself, not just to them, but to Arath itself.

He straightened his posture and met Kaelith's gaze. "I will do everything in my power to assist in freeing your people Kaelith."

She blinked once. Her ears twitched. "You know my name," she said softly. "Yet I have not spoken it, nor have any of the others."

"I know," Xavier replied, unflinching. "Your presence told me."

Her eyes narrowed slightly, but she nodded. "Then allow me to return the courtesy. I am Kaelith Moonstride, High Speaker of Verdantspire Haven. With me are my fellow elders—Thror Ironpaw, Sylara Dawnshade, Veyara Frostwhisper, Arvyn Flamefeather, Lyselle Silvermist, and Khoran Dusksworn."

Each nodded in turn as she named them. Xavier bowed his head respectfully to each.

"Lianna will return your belongings and brief you further," Kaelith continued. "She will escort you to food and rest. The Wardens move swiftly. You will join them."

She turned and strode away, the other elders following without a word. The torchbearers vanished with them, taking the brilliance of their light as they left.

Xavier was left in the dim glow of the firepit, alone except for Lianna.

She stepped forward, arms full of his gear. Her face was carved from stone. If she disagreed with the elders' decision, she did not say so. She simply held out his things and waited.

Xavier reclaimed his belongings in silence. He re-buckled his swords, slung his pack, and adjusted the satchel across his chest. Lianna said nothing. She turned and stalked away into the forest paths of the settlement; he followed.

#

The path Lianna took curved gently through towering trees, the forest canopy thick with woven walkways and elevated dwellings. Verdantspire Haven revealed itself in layers. Homes carved into trunks or suspended between branches glowed with bioluminescent moss and lanterns of shimmering stone. Wooden bridges arched over hollow glades where Animari moved with practiced ease. Everything breathed with harmony, alive, cultivated, hidden.

Xavier followed; eyes wide reminding himself of a tourist back on Earth. He had no idea how such a place had remained secret. Hundreds moved through the forest paths around him. Thousands, perhaps. A living stronghold disguised as wilderness.

Lianna offered no commentary, simply walking at a clipped pace.

When she came to a stop, it was in front of a small shop that looked like a blend between a streetside food cart and a sit-down restaurant. A half-sphere canopy of woven root and hide shaded a smooth counter of polished wood. Steam drifted up from copper cauldrons set into the cooking stones behind it, and the scent of spiced broth and grilled meat filled the air.

The sight struck Xavier with unexpected force. It reminded him of home, of Samantha, the barista with bright eyes and a crooked smile who worked the sidewalk café on his way to work. She always had his order ready before he spoke, teased him when he came in late, and never let a morning pass without a clever quip.

A pang of sadness clutched at his chest before he could push it down. He blinked, and the image faded. He was still in Arath, far from coffee and city sidewalks.

"Xavier," Lianna growled, snapping his name.

He blinked again and turned toward her. "I'm sorry, what did you ask? I was thinking."

"I asked if you wanted stew or roast," she said, expression unreadable.

Behind the counter, a young Animari woman with sleek fur and dark whisker markings waited patiently. Her features were smooth and aquatic, her fingers webbed, her eyes round and dark. Otterkin, Xavier realized. She wore an apron wrapped tight around her middle and a carved bone hairpin that held back her slick, dark hair.

"I... uh..." he glanced at the steaming pots. "What are you having?"

Lianna exhaled in mild irritation and turned to the otterkin. "Two bowls of selkhar stew, Kianna."

She placed a silver coin on the counter.

The woman, Kianna, smiled and turned to her cauldrons, moving with swift grace. She ladled out two steaming bowls of rich, dark stew, each served with a thick slice of crusted bread and a few roasted tubers with blackened edges. She passed the trays across the counter without a word.

Xavier took one with a nod of thanks. As his hands touched the warm wood of the tray, a soft notification blinked in the corner of his vision.

Language Unlocked: Avara
You have acquired foundational knowledge of a regional Animari dialect.
New Word Learned: *Selkhar* – "From the Sea" (seafood-based)

He followed Lianna to a nearby bench carved from petrified root. It wound in a spiral around a low stone table, polished smooth by use. She sat without ceremony. He joined her more slowly, inhaling the scent of the food.

The first bite confirmed his suspicion. The stew was incredible, deep, briny flavor layered with spice and smoke, punctuated by the occasional burst of root sweetness. Fish, shellfish meat, and herbs he couldn't name melded into something that tasted like hearth and ocean all at once.

He closed his eyes for a moment, savoring it. They ate in silence until Lianna broke it.

"Tilsen was a new settlement," she said. "Barely one cycle old. Thirty-three families. Craftsmen, scouts, gardeners. The raiders struck between our patrol rotations. They were precise, quiet."

Xavier set his spoon down, wiping at his mouth with a rough linen square tucked under the bowl.

"That matches what we found at Bramblegate," he said. "Ella and I discovered the ruins. Survivors taken. The rest... gone."

Lianna's hand tensed around her spoon. A small crack echoed from the wood as she clenched it tighter than needed. "You saw Bramblegate?"

He nodded once. "We searched the town. It was full of burned homes. Tracks leading east. We think they've got a central base somewhere, but we haven't found it yet."

Lianna's jaw flexed. Her tail lashed once behind her before settling. "You speak of these things with ease," she said quietly. "As if they were facts to catalog, not people, not lives."

"I speak of them the only way I can," Xavier replied. "But they're not numbers to me. I buried some of the bodies with my own hands."

The silence that followed felt heavier than before.

Finally, Lianna's shoulders relaxed by a fraction. "Stories say humans don't care," she murmured. "That they look the other way while we're hunted and sold."

"I'm not one of those humans," he said, voice steady.

She didn't reply, but she didn't argue either.

The rest of the meal passed quietly. When they finished, she rose without preamble, brushing crumbs from her fingers. "It is time. We will meet Liosan in the forest. He has the last known trail."

Xavier stood, gathering his pack and gear. He followed the dangerous woman, he still had a feeling she would rather shoot him than help him but fate, well the devious little Lynari elder, had decreed they work together, and he was in no way going to try and cross her will.

CHAPTER TWENTY-SIX

The Howl of Freedom

Xavier followed Lianna eastward, slipping through the gates of Verdantspire Haven and into the moon-dappled forest beyond. Shadows stretched long beneath the towering trees, and the hush of night wrapped around them like a living thing. They had barely gone a few hundred paces when a blur of white muscle and fur thundered past him.

He stumbled back in alarm as Frostclaw streaked between them, the snow leopard's powerful frame cutting through the underbrush like mist through stone. Xavier instinctively angled his stride away from the massive beast, giving it space even as he tried to match Lianna's effortless pace.

Before he could catch his breath, a new prompt flashed across his interface.

> **Lianna wishes to add you to her party. Do you accept?**
>
> **Yes / No.**

A grin tugged at his lips. She might still distrust him, but she was honoring the High Speaker's request. That alone felt like a win. He mentally selected Yes.

The interface shimmered. New panes unfolded beside his own health and stamina bars, displaying small portraits of Lianna, Liosan, and Frostclaw. Bars for Health, Stamina, and Mana appeared beneath each, and then, another icon blinked into view. It resembled a winged foot overlaid atop a tree canopy.

The moment it appeared, his speed surged. Wind whistled past his ears. Branches seemed to bend aside, and his boots barely touched the forest floor. He laughed aloud, giddy with the rush.

> **Status Effect Applied:** Forest Runner. Granted by party leader Lianna Froststride.

He tapped on the icon, curiosity piqued. The details confirmed the boost in speed and agility, especially in wooded terrain. His attention shifted to Lianna's portrait, and when he focused on it, a short summary appeared, more detailed than he'd seen before.

Name: Lianna Froststride	Race: Iskari (Snow Panther Animari)	Disposition: Wary - Neutral
Level: 27	Class: Ranger (Beastmaster)	Active Effects: Forest Runner, Beast Bonding
Description		

The Iskari are a race of Animari descended from snow leopards, renowned for their stealth, resilience, and connection to cold, mountainous regions. With pale skin marked by faint rosette patterns and thick, snow-like hair streaked with silver or black, they move with feline grace and precision. Their piercing blue or gray eyes reflect sharp intelligence and a predatory nature. The Iskari thrive in harsh environments, leveraging their exceptional agility and survival instincts. Fiercely loyal and protective of their kin, they are skilled hunters, trackers, and warriors, embodying the quiet strength and adaptability of their snow leopard heritage.

Stats		
Health: 200/200	**Stamina:** 210/210	**Mana:** 170/170

Xavier's eyes widened. *More than four times my level...* He thought.

No wonder his Insight skill had struggled to detect much earlier. If Lianna was this powerful, he could only imagine how high the Elders ranked. It stirred something inside him, a drive he hadn't yet voiced.

He had a new goal. Catch up to the twins. At the very least, reach a level where he could stand beside them with confidence. A glance at Liosan's icon revealed he matched his sister's level, though his class read Rogue (Assassin). That explained a lot.

He lengthened his stride, gradually closing the gap between himself and Lianna. Frostclaw loped somewhere ahead, a silver shadow in the dark.

"Lianna," he called softly, his voice steady despite their speed. "Once I've proven myself, and if you're willing, would you teach me more about beast bonding? I... I've befriended a shadowmane panther."

She didn't reply at once, and her pace never slowed. Then, sharply, she turned her head toward him.

"You befriended a shadowmane?" Her voice was incredulous. Her piercing eyes narrowed, studying him anew. "They are rare beyond measure. Most never leave the Shattered Expanse. Even the Duskhari struggle to bond with them, and they are born to the task. When, exactly, did you travel to those forsaken lands?"

The suspicion in her tone cut like a blade. Xavier didn't

flinch. Instead, he told her everything.

Lianna didn't interrupt often, but when she did, her questions were pointed, precise, and demanding the sort of detail that only truth could provide.

Xavier recounted the moment he and Ella had stumbled upon the mother shadowmane locked in brutal combat with the shardfang wolves. He described the heavy silence after the fight, the way Valkra had pressed her small, trembling body against him once the dust had settled. He spoke of burying the fallen mother, of how the cub had refused to leave their side, and how Valkra had since followed him of her own will.

When he finished, the forest filled the space between them with wind and rhythm. The sound of their feet striking loam, the hush of leaves brushing past their shoulders, the far-off cry of some nocturnal predator, it all passed in silence.

Lianna didn't speak, but she did glance at him, sidelong. Not once, but twice. The tight line of her jaw loosened, and the hard edge in her eyes dimmed, not fully, but enough to notice. She was beginning to wonder who, exactly, this human was.

"You told the elders your village was made up of survivors," she said finally. "Bramblegate, was it not? I have seen it on maps. It was no hamlet. You expect me to believe it was destroyed?"

Her tone was skeptical, but it lacked the earlier bite.

"Sadly, yes," Xavier replied, his voice low. "Ella and I were headed there, hoping to find people willing to join us in rebuilding. We had only just found Valkra when we saw the smoke rising. We ran, but we weren't fast enough. By the time we arrived, it was all but gone."

His hands curled into fists at his sides.

"We managed to save a few," he continued. "Some were

still in cages. Others were being... tormented. We struck down the last of the guards with their help and brought them back with us to Rynthavael. Among them were several Animari. One of them has helped train me in archery. She's on the town guard now."

Lianna slowed. Her hand dropped to Frostclaw's head as the great cat emerged from the brush and padded alongside her. The two moved as one, a single force of focus and instinct. She didn't look at Xavier at first, but when she did, her expression was thoughtful.

"I want to see this village," she said. "I once heard rumors that Bramblegate welcomed Animari, but I dismissed them. It seems I missed my chance to see if the stories were true." Her voice darkened. "In most lands, it is not so. My people are hunted in the Wildlands. Enslaved."

The words were simple, but heavy.

Xavier's breath caught. His pace faltered.

"I knew... I knew slavery existed here," he said slowly, "but hearing it like that... knowing entire peoples are targeted..." He shook his head. "It's wrong. All of it."

Lianna glanced at him again. She said nothing, but her silence, this time, did not feel like dismissal.

They ran on in quiet, the trees thinning slightly as the Ironspire Mountains crept closer on the horizon. The wind shifted, bringing with it the scent of snow and stone. The world grew colder.

The silence between them deepened. It no longer felt as if a distance were between them in that depth, instead it felt like understanding.

#

The trees grew shorter as they climbed. The undergrowth thinned, giving way to moss-slick stone and patches of coarse mountain grass. Peaks loomed ahead, jagged silhouettes against the twin moons. The forest floor sloped upward, drawing them closer to the Ironspire foothills.

Without warning, Lianna halted. Xavier followed her gaze upward.

A pale shape hung upside down from a thick branch high overhead, knees hooked casually around the wood, a glinting blade in one hand and an apple in the other. Liosan's white hair swayed gently in the breeze as he carved off a slice of fruit and popped it into his mouth.

He waved cheerfully at Lianna, then turned his ice-blue gaze toward Xavier. The grin he offered was sharp around the edges… playful, but not warm. Instead, his eyes were judging and measuring.

Xavier stared, unable to decide whether he was more amazed by the assassin's perch or by how effortlessly the twins accepted it.

In a hushed voice, Lianna called up to her brother. "He is here at the High Speaker's request. She charged him to aid us against the raiders. He swore three times he means us no harm." She folded her arms, her body language indicated that she was done with that topic. "Have you found the camp?"

Liosan unhooked his legs and dropped. He twisted midair, landing silently on his feet in a crouch, blade still in hand, apple slice resting atop it. He took another bite, then nodded toward the mountains.

Xavier blinked. That should not have been possible.

Lianna let out an audible sigh and rolled her eyes. "You know full well you need to tell us more than just wave vaguely."

From a belt pouch, she drew a small, folded map and laid it across Frostclaw's back. The snow leopard didn't flinch. This, it seemed, was routine. Liosan stepped around to the opposite side and studied the map. After a moment, he tapped a point on the northern slope.

Xavier's interface pinged, and a new icon flared to life on his map.

Raider Encampment Identified.

He smiled faintly. Efficient, even if dramatic.

Without another word, the four of them set off. Xavier did his best to keep pace, though Lianna and Liosan moved with uncanny ease, and Frostclaw flowed like a ghost between them. The moonlight filtered through the high trees, casting silver nets across the path.

The foothills rose steadily beneath their feet until, at last, they crested a narrow ridge and peered down into a shallow valley. The raider camp lay below.

Dozens of tents dotted the basin, their canvas flapping gently in the night breeze. A cluster of wagons formed a crude wall at the valley's mouth, their broad backs turned outward in a crescent. In the center, a large fire burned bright, casting flickering shadows across the clearing. Near it, several larger wagons were arranged in a loose circle, cage wagons, Xavier realized. Slavers' wagons.

His stomach twisted.

Overhead, the two moons hung low, one bleeding violet light, the other casting a red sheen across the camp. The mixture lent the scene an ominous, otherworldly glow.

As he watched, something shifted in his vision. Small glowing symbols began to appear above the heads of figures below, faint but unmistakable. Xavier leaned forward, blinking in disbelief as more and more icons manifested.

He counted quickly. Fifteen. Eleven human-sized, four massive wolves.

The symbols moved slowly, some patrolling the camp's edge, others loitering near the fire. There were no markers on civilians, no children, no innocents. Only targets.

Xavier exhaled slowly. Even with four of them, this would be no easy fight.

Beside him, Lianna studied the camp in silence. Then, without looking away, she began to speak.

"Those three near the far treeline. Sentries. Lio, take care of them. When I see their marks vanish, I'll eliminate the two closest to us. Frostclaw will handle the wolf."

Liosan gave a quick nod and vanished into the underbrush. One moment he was crouched beside them, the next he was gone without sound or ripple.

Lianna turned her head toward Xavier. "Stay with me. We'll move into the camp once the sentries are down. I can silence at least two more on the way. But once my arrows fly near the fire, the alarm will sound. I hope those blades of yours are more than ornament."

Xavier met her gaze and gave a solemn nod. "They are, and your people will breathe free air tonight, or I'll die trying."

The words left his mouth before he could stop them.

Gods, did I really just say that? He thought to himself.

Lianna raised an eyebrow, a smirk tugging at the corner of her mouth. She shook her head slightly. "I will hold you to that, human."

Then she was moving, and Xavier followed, slipping down the ridge toward the wolves and men below.

The wind shifted again, colder now. Death was coming for those below and they hadn't realized it yet.

#

The forest swallowed them once more. Crouched low, bow already in hand, Lianna moved with fluid precision. Xavier mirrored her as best he could, but every step felt like a gamble. Each crunch of leaves beneath his boots, each accidental nudge of brush, rang far too loud in his ears. Compared to the others, he felt like a clumsy ox.

They moved steadily downward, circling the camp. Frostclaw split away halfway down the ridge, vanishing into the trees without a sound. Xavier assumed the great cat was headed for the wolf Lianna had marked. There was no sign, no signal, just trust between beast and ranger.

He wondered if he and Valkra could ever reach such synchronicity. He hoped so.

Suddenly, one of the sentry marks on the far side of the camp vanished. Then another. A moment later, the third blinked out, followed by a faint, distant scuffle. No raised voices. No alarm.

Xavier felt his pulse steady. They had a chance.

Lianna moved like a shadow between the trees. She reached a low rise, unslung her bow, and drew an arrow in a single motion. Xavier, crouching just behind her, watched her target—a lone raider standing near the edge of the camp.

There was no warning. Just a soft whistle of wind. A hsst of arrow whispering through the air. The arrow struck the raider clean through the eye. He crumpled without sound.

Lianna had already drawn a second arrow. Her next shot hit the throat of her second guard target before he could cry out. He fell beside the first, gurgling softly.

The perimeter was broken. They pressed on, edging closer to the firelight.

That was when Xavier noticed it.

A faint shimmer in the dirt, barely perceptible, like a

reflection that didn't belong. He reached out to signal Lianna and crept forward on hands and knees.

The shimmer resolved into a spiral of tiny symbols, etched in the soil with impossible precision. They pulsed faintly with inner light, responding to his presence.

His breath caught. It was an actual rune. Not decorative. Not mundane. This one was real.

He extended his hands, careful not to cross the spiral's threshold. A strange tension filled the air near it, like static before a storm. Instinct told him to keep his distance, and he listened.

The sigils hummed faintly in his mind, aligning with something inside him.

> **You have discovered a new rune:** Warding Rune of Alarm.
> This rune will generate a loud alarm sound when triggered.

Excitement bloomed in his chest. His class, its whole purpose, was awakening.

He focused on the shape of the rune, visualizing its pattern, its logic. Then, one by one, he imagined the key sigils inverting. They responded. With a silent pulse, the spiral unraveled, the glow extinguishing like a dying ember. The rune was gone.

His interface pinged.

> **Rune Learned:** Warding Rune of Alarm
> **Rune Deciphering Skill Increased**

Grinning, he glanced at his rune list. One entry now glowed beneath the heading. His first.

Lianna moved beside him. She crouched low, her eyes scanning the earth. She said nothing until the faint residual flash of the deconstructed rune faded from view. Then she nodded once, curt and approving. "Nicely done."

They moved on.

#

They reached the edge of the camp.

Lianna pressed against the side of a heavy wagon, Xavier crouched beside her. Beyond the rim, the fire still blazed bright, casting dancing shadows across the gathered raiders. Four men sat in a loose circle, sharing dried meat and passing a skin of what looked like strong liquor. They laughed quietly among themselves, weapons nearby but forgotten.

Closer to the fire, three massive wolves lounged near a fifth man. He was lean and scarred, his left shoulder wrapped in overlapping layers of scale armor. He sat on a low stool, sharpening a short dagger and slicing chunks from a slab of roasted meat. Each time he tested the blade, he tossed the meat to one of the wolves and resumed his work.

Just beyond them, the tent flaps stirred. There was still no sign of how many were within.

Lianna didn't hesitate. She rose just high enough to line up a shot and loosed a single arrow toward the handler. It struck, but not cleanly. The man had twisted at the last second and took the shaft in the shoulder rather than the throat.

He roared in pain and staggered to his feet.

Lianna cursed under her breath and fired again, but the moment of surprise was lost.

The wolves snapped to alertness, eyes glowing in the firelight. Then they charged. Two of the beasts were nearly on them when Frostclaw exploded from the darkness.

The snow leopard struck like a falling boulder. He

slammed into the charging wolves, sending them sprawling in a tangle of limbs and snarls. Blood sprayed as his claws raked deep, and his jaws locked around the neck of the closest one. Bone cracked. The third wolf veered wide and lunged for Frostclaw's exposed flank.

Xavier sprang into action. He drew Vaeltheris in one hand and the Emberstone shortsword in the other, blades gleaming in the flickering firelight. One of the raiders had grabbed a halberd and rushed toward him. He met her head-on.

The Emberstone blade arced upward, striking her forearms before she could bring her weapon to bear. The elemental metal hissed against flesh, leaving smoking wounds. She shrieked and fell back, clutching her arms.

Another raider came at him from the left, sword raised.

Xavier twisted, bringing Vaeltheris across in a defensive sweep. Their blades met in a jarring clash, sparks flying. Xavier pushed forward, trying not to lose his footing.

Lianna moved like a storm. She had drawn a long dagger, wielding it in her off hand while her bow spun in the other like a blunt staff. She knocked aside weapons with the curved limbs of her bow, stepping into the openings to carve deep, bleeding gashes into exposed flesh.

Every motion was lethal. Every step precise.

Xavier could barely keep track of her as more raiders poured from the tents. One held a weighted net in one hand and a cudgel in the other. Xavier cursed and began circling, doing his best to keep other enemies between himself and the trapper. If that net caught him, he was finished.

Then a voice rang out from the largest tent.

A pulse of black energy burst from within, sweeping across the battlefield like a shockwave.

Xavier staggered.

His health bar dropped dangerously. A glance showed the others had taken hits as well, less than him, but still notable. Pain lanced through his chest, cold and heavy.

The tent flap parted.

A man stepped into the firelight, robed in black with silver thread glinting along his sleeves. A collar of etched obsidian clung tightly to his throat, and in his right hand he held a bone-white staff. He raised his arms and began to chant.

The collar flared once, then dimmed as his incantation rose. Before he could finish, a blur of motion surged from the shadows behind him. Liosan. The assassin appeared with a wicked grin, eyes gleaming.

He plunged his dagger deep beneath the caster's raised arm, sliding it between the ribs. The robed man shrieked and dropped the staff, clutching his side. Liosan drove the dagger down again. And again. The screams were soon cut short.

Around them, the captives in the wagons stirred. The necrotic wave had struck them too. They cried out, voices filled with fear and pain, their cages rattling. Xavier's heart twisted. He dared not look away from the fight, but the sound of their suffering clung to his ears.

On the far side, Frostclaw continued his vicious assault. One wolf lay still. The second tried to rise, only for the great cat to slam it back down and rip into its neck. The third, the one that had flanked, darted in to bite at Frostclaw's legs, searching for an opening.

And then the handler rose. The arrow still jutted from his shoulder, blood trailing down his armor. He held a long polearm with a bladed ring at one end, a man-catcher, and in his other hand, a vicious, barbed whip. His eyes burned with rage.

Lianna turned to meet him.

The whip cracked through the night, and she cried out as it tore across her shoulder. She ducked the next swing of the man-catcher and rolled, coming up just in time to deflect another lash with her bow.

She fought with gritted teeth, pain etched into every motion.

Xavier didn't see how long she could last. But he had his own problems.

A fresh wave of raiders poured from the far tents, drawn by the noise. They were sloppier than the others, half-dressed, weapons poorly gripped. Still dangerous.

Xavier grunted as he blocked another clumsy swing, then drove Vaeltheris into the raider's gut. Blood sprayed. The man dropped.

Another came. Xavier met him with the Emberstone blade, searing through leather and muscle. His breath came in ragged bursts, arms shaking with fatigue. Xavier's blades left blood and agony in their wakes, though he was not as skilled as the other two of his party, his opponents seemed to be the lesser armed and armored raiders. Part of him felt cheated at being left with the seeming dregs of their enemies, another much louder part of him shouted that first part into submission and was just thankful to be alive and only minimally injured.

Xavier stumbled back, breathing hard, blades dripping. The last raider in front of him dropped to his knees, clutching at the gaping wound Vaeltheris had carved across his stomach. Blood pooled quickly. The man collapsed face-first with a final, rattling breath.

Xavier turned, scanning the battlefield.

Lianna still held her ground, blood running down her side

from a dozen whip cuts. Her bow struck out in tight arcs, knocking the man-catcher aside each time the handler tried to close the distance. Her dagger flashed whenever she found an opening, drawing fresh blood across the slaver's legs and arms.

Frostclaw mauled the final wolf in the background, his fur streaked with red but his movements just as fluid and vicious. The caged prisoners were crying now in fear, pain, and confusion. Some reached through the bars, others cowered in the corners.

Xavier took a step toward Lianna, intending to help... and that was when he saw the flap of the central tent shift.

Another figure emerged.

This one was tall, armored in dark half-plate that shimmered with oil-slick polish. A brutal-looking man, his face half-shadowed beneath a narrow steel helm, held twin scimitars. One glowed faintly with a crackle of electric blue.

Xavier barely had time to react before the first blade lashed out low, slicing cleanly across his calf.

Lightning exploded up his leg.

His body seized. He tried to scream, but the sound caught in his throat. Every nerve screamed at once. His grip faltered. His knees buckled.

And then the second blade came down.

The tip of the scimitar punched through his leather cuirass just below his collarbone, sliding deep into his chest. He felt it pierce the flesh, then something vital. Air escaped his lungs in a wet gasp.

The world tilted.

The armored man yanked the blade free and turned, already moving toward Lianna.

Xavier fell to the ground, breath caught in his throat,

vision swimming.

Somewhere, far away, impossibly distant, a horrified and pained scream echoed in a suddenly empty room, the bed disheveled by the abrupt vanishing of its occupant. Ella had vanished.

The sound pulled at something in his soul., but he couldn't reach it.

His heartbeat slowed. The chaos of battle dimmed, its edges softening. Laughter. Screams. The crack of a whip. The thrum of magic. All of it drifted away as if heard underwater. He felt the warmth leave his limbs. Then the cold came.

His vision narrowed, the stars overhead shrinking to pinpricks in a sky that was suddenly far too vast. The moons above blurred together, purple and red fading into a single smear.

And then... Nothing.

The saga continues in Book 2 – Shadows Over the Wildlands.

CHAPTER TWENTY-SEVEN

Appendix 1 - Lovo's Abridged Guide to the Races of Arath

Greetings, fellow seeker of wonders. I am Lovo, a humble traveler who has roamed the untamed reaches and hidden corners of Arath, where legends breathe life and magic weaves through every stone and shadow. From the sunlit spires of Velanor's trade cities to the shadowy depths of the Underdark where the Del'shĕ whisper secrets, I have ventured with an unyielding thirst for discovery. The vibrant cultures, unique beings, and perilous landscapes of this world have been my teachers and companions. In these pages, you will find not just knowledge of the races and peoples that call Arath home but a reflection of their stories, their struggles, and their triumphs. May this guide inspire you to tread paths unwalked and to see the beauty in the vast tapestry of life that stretches beyond the horizon.

Aetherborn

The Aetherborn are beings of raw magical energy, their forms shimmering with a faint, otherworldly glow. They are semi-translucent, their skin radiating hues of silver, blue, or violet, as though lit from within. Aetherborn often appear androgynous, their features smooth and ethereal, with glowing, pupil-less eyes that seem to pierce through the veil of reality. Their presence feels both calming and unsettling, as they hover or glide with an unnatural grace, leaving faint trails of light in their wake. Despite their mysterious origins, they exude a sense of timeless wisdom, as though connected to the very fabric of the universe.

- **Abilities**:

  ○ **Ethereal Step**: Aetherborn can phase momentarily out of the material plane, allowing them to avoid attacks or pass through obstacles.

  ○ **Arcane Attunement**: Their deep connection to magic grants them innate talent in spellcasting, particularly in illusion and divination.

  Magical Resilience: They possess resistance to magical effects, shielding them from harmful arcane forces.

- **Culture**: Aetherborn do not form traditional societies, as their origins are often isolated and unpredictable. Instead, they gravitate toward areas of strong magical energy, such as ley lines or ancient ruins, where they study the arcane or meditate on the mysteries of existence. Aetherborn see their lives as fleeting and seek to leave a meaningful mark on the world, whether through profound magical discoveries or as mentors to aspiring mages. Their enigmatic nature often leads others to revere or fear them, and their presence is sometimes seen as an omen of great change.

Animari

The Animari are humanoid-animal hybrids, embodying the traits, instincts, and spiritual essence of their animal archetypes. Each subrace displays unique physical features and abilities tied to their lineage, blending primal power with human intelligence. Animari are deeply connected to nature, often drawing strength and guidance from their ancestral spirits. They are diverse and adaptable, thriving in various environments from dense forests and windswept plains to icy tundras and shadowy jungles. Their settlements, shaped by their animal instincts, prioritize harmony with the natural world, reflecting a deep respect for life's interconnectedness.

Aelori (Lionkin)

The Aelori are majestic and commanding, their golden or tawny fur and flowing manes (in males) exuding power and authority. Their piercing amber or green eyes seem to shine with a mix of wisdom and intensity, while their muscular builds speak to their unmatched strength. Aelori are natural leaders, their very presence inspiring those around them to act with courage and unity. Their movements are deliberate and graceful, like a lion stalking its prey, blending calculated strength with innate elegance. Known for their honor and bravery, Aelori often take on roles as warriors, diplomats, or tribal chieftains.

- **Abilities**:
  - **Lion's Roar**: A deafening roar that terrifies foes and emboldens allies, turning the tide of battle.
  - **Ferocious Strikes**: Their sharp claws and raw power make them fearsome in close combat.
  - **Leadership Prowess**: Aelori inspire confidence and coordination among their allies, enhancing group effectiveness.

- **Culture**: Aelori society is structured around hierarchical prides, with leaders chosen through trials of strength, wisdom, and loyalty. They hold deep respect for their ancestors, often seeking guidance through rituals and meditations. Aelori believe in the importance of balance between power and compassion, often serving as protectors of weaker Animari tribes. Their settlements are fortified and elevated, designed to reflect their vigilance and dominance. Seasonal hunts and grand feasts are central to their culture, celebrating the unity and prosperity of the pride.

Cervari (Deerkin)

The Cervari are graceful and serene, their antlers often branching like living works of art, adorned with moss or flowers. Their fur ranges from soft browns and russets to snowy whites, perfectly camouflaged within their forested homes. Large, expressive eyes radiate a calm wisdom, and their slender frames are built for agility and speed rather than brute strength. Cervari move with an almost otherworldly elegance, appearing to glide through their environments without disturbing them. Known for their deep connection to nature, they embody the balance and harmony of the natural world.

- **Abilities**:
  - **Empathic Connection**: Cervari can communicate with animals and sense disturbances in the natural order.
  - **Healing Touch**: They possess a gentle, innate magic that allows them to soothe wounds and ailments.
  - **Antler Defense**: In times of danger, their antlers serve as powerful tools for self-defense, delivering precise and impactful strikes.
- **Culture**: Cervari are the spiritual guides and healers of the Animari, often serving as druids or shamans who

safeguard the balance of nature. Their settlements are hidden within sacred groves or dense forests, blending seamlessly with their surroundings to avoid detection by outsiders. Rituals celebrating the seasons and life cycles are central to their culture, often involving music, dance, and offerings to the spirits of the land. While peaceful by nature, Cervari are formidable when protecting their homes and allies, using their wisdom and agility to outmaneuver their enemies.

Duskhari (Pantherkin)

The Duskhari are sleek and shadowy, their fur often black or deep blue, shimmering faintly under the light of the moon. Their piercing eyes, in hues of gold or icy blue, seem to glow in darkness, giving them an unnervingly predatory gaze. They move with a quiet confidence, their muscles taut and ready to strike at a moment's notice. Duskhari are masters of stealth, able to vanish into the shadows as if they were never there. While they are often solitary, their presence commands respect and caution, as they are known for their precision and cunning.

- **Abilities**:
  - **Shadowmeld**: The ability to become nearly invisible in low-light environments, making them masters of ambush tactics.
  - **Silent Predator**: Duskhari move without a sound,

making it nearly impossible for enemies to detect their approach.

- ◦ **Razor Claws**: Their sharp claws deliver swift and lethal attacks, ensuring they can dispatch foes quickly.

- **Culture**: Duskhari value independence and personal strength, often living solitary lives or forming small groups where each member contributes unique skills. They are highly disciplined, spending years perfecting their craft, whether it be combat, espionage, or another art. Duskhari culture revolves around adaptability and survival, and their young are trained in the ways of stealth and cunning from an early age. While they prefer to avoid large conflicts, they will not hesitate to protect their territory or allies with calculated ferocity.

Equaris (Horsekin)

The Equaris are tall and imposing, their equine features blending power and grace. With elongated faces, hooved feet, and flowing manes, they resemble majestic steeds, their frames built for strength and endurance. Their fur varies from earthy browns and blacks to dappled grays or whites, often with streaks of silver in their manes and tails. Equaris carry themselves with pride, their steady gait and upright posture reflecting their unyielding resolve. They are swift and tireless, often revered for their ability to traverse great distances and weather even the harshest environments.

- **Abilities:**

  o **Unyielding Endurance**: Equaris can sustain prolonged physical exertion, making them invaluable in battle or during long migrations.

  o **Stampeding Charge**: Using their immense strength, they can deliver devastating charges, trampling foes with their hooves.

  o **Enhanced Stamina**: Their robust constitution allows them to resist fatigue, environmental hazards, and physical strain.

- **Culture**: Equaris are nomadic, thriving in open plains and vast grasslands where they form tightly bonded herds. Their culture revolves around movement and freedom, with each member contributing to the collective survival of the group. They revere the wind and open skies, often holding rituals to honor the spirits of the plains. Equaris tribes are led by chieftains chosen for their wisdom and strength, and disputes are resolved through ceremonial races or trials of endurance. They are known for their hospitality, often sharing stories, songs, and sustenance with travelers who respect their ways.

Falconi (Hawkkin)

The Falconi are humanoids with avian features, their sleek, feathered forms reflecting the majesty and precision of raptors. Their sharp golden eyes can spot the slightest movement from great distances, and their talon-like feet are formidable weapons. Falconi feathers vary in shades of bronze, gray, or white, often with patterns resembling hawks or falcons. They are built for speed and agility, their compact, muscular frames giving them unparalleled control in both ground and aerial maneuvers. With an air of quiet discipline, Falconi are vigilant protectors of their kin and territory.

- **Abilities**:

    ◦ **Keen Eyesight**: Falconi can see with incredible clarity over long distances, making them expert scouts and hunters.

    ◦ **Glide**: While not capable of full flight, Falconi can use their feathered arms to glide gracefully through the air.

    ◦ **Talon Strike**: Their sharp talons allow them to deliver precise and powerful melee attacks.

- **Culture**: Falconi are highly disciplined, with their society emphasizing loyalty, vigilance, and duty. They often live in high-altitude settlements, building homes into cliffsides or atop tall trees where they can watch over the surrounding lands. Leadership within Falconi tribes is earned through merit, with elders and warriors alike proving their worth through acts of bravery and service. They revere the skies and hold elaborate aerial ceremonies to mark significant life events or celestial alignments. While they are wary of outsiders, Falconi value alliances built on mutual respect and shared goals.

Felvari (Catkin)

The Felvari are lithe and agile, their feline features lending them an air of charm and mystery. With pointed ears, whisker-like facial markings, and long tails, they embody the cunning and grace of their feline counterparts. Their fur varies widely, from solid blacks and whites to intricate tabby or spotted patterns, often shimmering in the light. Their eyes, typically bright green, amber, or blue, are striking and ever-watchful. Felvari are natural explorers and opportunists, known for their playful yet resourceful nature.

- **Abilities**:

  - **Feline Agility**: Felvari are capable of rapid, acrobatic movements, easily scaling walls or navigating tight spaces.

  - **Night Vision**: Their slit-pupil eyes grant them superior vision in darkness, making them exceptional nocturnal hunters.

  - **Sharp Claws**: Their retractable claws are not only

effective in combat but also useful for climbing and gripping.

- **Culture**: Felvari society is loosely organized, with individuals often prioritizing personal freedom and exploration. They thrive in both urban environments and dense forests, adapting effortlessly to their surroundings. Despite their independence, Felvari maintain strong family bonds and often return to their communities after extended periods of travel. They are known for their love of storytelling, treasure hunting, and clever tricks, and their homes are often adorned with trinkets and trophies collected from their adventures. Felvari festivals are vibrant, featuring music, dance, and feats of agility.

Leporini (Rabbitkin)

The Leporini are small and nimble, their long ears and fluffy tails giving them an unmistakably rabbit-like appearance. Their fur, soft and often in neutral tones like white, gray, or brown, provides excellent camouflage in their natural habitats. With their compact, wiry builds and spring-like legs, Leporini are swift and agile, capable of bounding over obstacles with ease. Their bright, inquisitive eyes and perpetually cheerful expressions reflect their optimistic outlook on life.

- **Abilities**:
  - **Bounding Leap**: Leporini can jump incredible distances, making them difficult to corner or capture.
  - **Quick Reflexes**: Their heightened awareness allows them to evade danger and react swiftly to threats.
  - **Acrobatic Grace**: Leporini excel in physical maneuvers, often using their agility to outwit opponents.

- **Culture**: Leporini are communal and cheerful, their villages often bustling with activity and laughter. They value craftsmanship and are known for their skill in farming, cooking, and weaving intricate textiles. Leporini hold grand seasonal festivals that celebrate life and community, featuring games, music, and feasts. Though peaceful by nature, they are fiercely protective of their homes and will band together to defend against threats. Their quick thinking and resourcefulness make them adept at resolving conflicts without resorting to violence.

Lupari (Wolfkin)

The Lupari, or Wolfkin, are humanoids embodying the loyalty, agility, and tactical prowess of wolves. Their angular, wolf-like features include pointed ears, sharp canine teeth, and bushy tails, while their fur-like hair ranges from ash-gray to earthy brown or jet-black, often streaked with silver or white. Their piercing eyes—amber, icy blue, or deep green —seem to glimmer with intelligence and determination. Lupari carry themselves with a quiet confidence, their movements swift and purposeful, evoking the coordination and vigilance of a wolf pack. Known for their deep sense of camaraderie, they are natural leaders and protectors.

- **Abilities**:
    - **Pack Tactics**: Lupari excel when working with allies, gaining tactical advantages in group combat.
    - **Keen Senses**: Their heightened hearing and sense of smell make them exceptional trackers and hunters.
    - **Howl of Rally**: A Lupari's howl inspires their allies, increasing morale and coordination during battles or challenges.
- **Culture**: Lupari society revolves around the concept of the pack, with strong emphasis on loyalty, unity, and mutual care. Pack leaders, or "Alpha Guardians," are chosen based on their ability to protect and inspire

their kin. Lupari villages are often hidden within forests or mountainous regions, designed to protect their communities while allowing room for hunting and roaming. Rituals such as ceremonial howls and communal feasts celebrate milestones and strengthen bonds. Though they value peace, Lupari are fierce and unrelenting when defending their pack or territory, often leading other Animari tribes in coordinated efforts during times of conflict.

Lynari (Lynxkin)

The Lynari, or Lynxkin, are enigmatic and perceptive Animari, their sharp features reflecting the independence and mystique of their lynx ancestors. They are lithe and agile, their fur-like hair often a mix of tawny, silvery, or gray tones, streaked with black patterns. Their distinctive tufted ears and keen, golden or green eyes grant them an air of mystery, while their subtle whisker-like facial markings highlight their feline lineage. Lynari are known for their unparalleled vision, able to spot details others might miss, making them natural scouts, strategists, and mediators.

- **Abilities**:
  - **Heightened Vision**: Lynari can see exceptionally well, even in low-light conditions, making them adept at spotting hidden threats.
  - **Silent Step**: Their natural agility allows them to

move silently, making them difficult to detect.

- ◦ **Strategic Insight**: Lynari have a natural talent for reading situations, allowing them to anticipate enemy movements or resolve conflicts diplomatically.

- • **Culture**: Lynari thrive in roles requiring clarity, adaptability, and precision. Their communities are small and decentralized, often located in forests or mountainous terrain where they can live in harmony with nature. Lynari elders, known as "Moonstriders," are revered for their wisdom and often mediate disputes among Animari tribes. They value independence and self-reflection, with young Lynari encouraged to embark on solitary journeys to discover their purpose. Despite their preference for solitude, they are fiercely loyal to their kin and will defend their communities with calculated ferocity when threatened.

Selkiri (Sealkin)

The Selkiri, or Sealkin, are aquatic Animari, their smooth, water-resistant skin and streamlined forms perfectly adapted for life in coastal and underwater environments. Their appearances are marked by gray or mottled patterns reminiscent of seals, with webbed hands and feet aiding in their unparalleled swimming abilities. Their dark, glossy eyes and sleek builds allow them to move effortlessly through water, making them natural navigators of the seas. Selkiri radiate a calm and tranquil energy, their movements as fluid as the waves they call home.

- **Abilities**:
  - **Aquatic Adaptation**: Selkiri can hold their breath for extended periods and swim at remarkable speeds.
  - **Cold Resistance**: Their dense, water-resistant skin protects them from cold temperatures, allowing them to thrive in icy waters.
  - **Ocean's Call**: Selkiri have a natural ability to communicate with marine life and sense changes in ocean currents.
- **Culture**: Selkiri live in coastal villages or underwater settlements made from coral and stone, often near reefs or kelp forests. They act as guardians of the seas, protecting marine ecosystems from overfishing and pollution. Spirituality plays a significant role in their culture, with ceremonies and songs dedicated to the ocean's deities and spirits. Selkiri are skilled fishers, traders, and navigators, their maps and charts prized by sailors. Though generally peaceful, they are unyielding

when defending their waters, employing guerrilla tactics to outmaneuver larger naval forces.

#

Serpenti (Snakekin)

The Serpenti, or Snakekin, are sleek and cunning, their smooth-scaled skin and serpentine eyes giving them a mysterious and dangerous allure. Their scales range from deep greens and browns to striking black or gold patterns, while their slit-pupil eyes shimmer with intelligence and subtle menace. They often possess forked tongues and sharp, angular features, enhancing their snake-like appearance. The Serpenti move with a hypnotic grace, their every action deliberate and calculated, embodying the predatory precision of their serpent ancestors.

- **Abilities**:

  - **Venomous Defense**: Some Serpenti can produce venom to enhance their bites or weapons, incapacitating foes.

  - **Enhanced Perception**: Their acute senses allow them to detect vibrations and subtle changes in their surroundings.

  - **Silver Tongue**: Serpenti are naturally persuasive and adept at manipulation, making them skilled negotiators or spies.

- **Culture**: Serpenti are often secretive, their

communities hidden within swamps, deserts, or dense jungles. They value subtlety and adaptability, with social hierarchies often determined by cunning and intellect rather than physical strength. Many Serpenti are alchemists, crafting potent poisons and antidotes from their environments. Their rituals often involve the shedding of old skin, symbolizing renewal and personal growth. Though mistrusted by some for their secretive nature, Serpenti play crucial roles as diplomats, scouts, and even shadowy protectors of Animari society.

Ursari (Bearkin)

The Ursari, or Bearkin, are imposing and powerful, their broad frames and dense fur making them stand out among the Animari. Their fur comes in shades of brown, black, or white, and their bear-like features include rounded ears, sharp claws, and a thick, muscular build. Despite their intimidating appearance, Ursari are known for their calm and contemplative nature, their slow, deliberate movements hiding immense strength and endurance. When provoked, they are ferocious defenders, capable of overpowering most foes with ease.

- **Abilities**:
  - **Unstoppable Strength**: Ursari possess immense physical power, capable of lifting or breaking through heavy obstacles.

- ○ **Natural Resilience**: Their thick fur and sturdy frames provide resistance to cold and physical blows.

- ○ **Furious Wrath**: When enraged, Ursari can enter a berserk state, amplifying their strength and endurance.

- **Culture**: Ursari are solitary by nature, often living in remote mountain forests or cold tundras. Despite their isolation, they serve as spiritual guides and guardians for Animari tribes, offering wisdom and protection during times of crisis. Ursari traditions are deeply rooted in balance, with rituals honoring both their primal strength and their introspective, peaceful side. Their homes are simple yet sturdy, designed to endure harsh climates. While they prefer peaceful resolutions, Ursari will unleash their full fury when defending their kin or their lands.

Vulpiri (Foxkin)

The Vulpiri, or Foxkin, are cunning and charismatic Animari, their bushy tails, pointed ears, and sharp features embodying the slyness and agility of their fox ancestors. Their fur is vibrant, often in shades of fiery red, snowy white, or midnight black, with striking patterns that enhance their allure. Their quick, darting movements and ever-watchful eyes suggest a constant state of alertness, while their charming smiles often mask their shrewd minds. Vulpiri are natural problem-solvers and negotiators, adept at navigating both physical and social challenges with wit and ingenuity.

- **Abilities**:
  - **Keen Intuition**: Vulpiri have an uncanny ability to read people and situations, making them skilled negotiators and manipulators.
  - **Agile Reflexes**: Their dexterity allows them to evade attacks and navigate difficult terrain with ease.
  - **Sly Trickery**: They can use minor illusions or distractions to mislead enemies or escape danger.
- **Culture**: Vulpiri are social and resourceful, often thriving in villages near human settlements or secluded woodland communities. They are master traders, entertainers, and diplomats, known for their sharp wit and ability to diffuse tense situations. Their festivals are lively and colorful, featuring music, storytelling, and performances that showcase their playful nature. Vulpiri emphasize adaptability and cleverness, encouraging young members of their communities to travel and learn from the world. Though generally

peaceful, they are fiercely protective of their kin, using cunning and deception to outmaneuver more powerful foes.

Centaurs (Velstari)

The Centaurs, or Velstari, are nomadic beings with the upper body of a human and the lower body of a powerful horse. Their dual nature combines human intelligence and adaptability with the strength, speed, and stamina of their equine halves. Centaurs are striking figures, their human torsos tall and muscular, often adorned with braided hair, tribal markings, or ornaments made from natural materials. Their lower bodies, covered in sleek fur, display a range of colors from earthy browns to gleaming blacks and dappled grays. Known for their connection to nature and the stars, Centaurs often act as guides, traders, and protectors of sacred lands.

- **Abilities**:
  - **Unmatched Speed**: Centaurs can traverse great distances at high speeds, outpacing most land-bound creatures.
  - **Incredible Stamina**: Their powerful builds allow them to endure long journeys or grueling combat without tiring easily.
  - **Celestial Awareness**: Their innate connection to the stars grants them superior navigation skills and

the ability to predict weather or celestial events.

- **Culture**: Centaur society is deeply spiritual, guided by the cycles of nature and celestial patterns. They live in migratory tribes, often following seasonal paths that sustain their way of life. Leadership is shared among elders known as "Starguides," who interpret celestial signs and lead their people with wisdom. Ritual dances and storytelling under the stars are central to their culture, often used to pass down knowledge. While generally peaceful, Centaurs are fierce defenders of their territory and traditions, their sheer speed and strength making them formidable opponents.

Dwarves (Dorn'Vathrin)

The Dwarves, or Dorn'Vathrin, are one of the most enduring and industrious races in Arath, their deep connection to stone and metal shaping their culture and identity. Stocky and muscular, Dwarves are typically shorter than humans but broader in build, their strength and resilience unmatched. Their skin tones often reflect the hues of the mountains or mines they inhabit—ruddy, bronzed, or dusky—while their hair and beards, always meticulously groomed, range from fiery red to deep black and shimmering silver. Known for their craftsmanship and engineering prowess, Dwarves are master builders, miners, and artisans.

Dorn'Thrazik (Mountain Dwarves)

The Dorn'Thrazik, or Mountain Dwarves, are traditional and militaristic, dwelling in towering strongholds carved into the hearts of mountains. Their gray or ruddy skin and dark hair reflect the harsh, rugged environments they inhabit. They are fiercely protective of their homes and relics, their fortresses often resembling labyrinthine masterpieces of stonework.

- **Abilities**:

  - **Stoneborn Resilience**: Exceptional resistance to cold, high-altitude effects, and physical injuries.

  - **Master Smiths**: Renowned for their skill in forging weapons and armor, often imbued with runic enchantments.

  - **Mountain Adaptation**: Natural climbers and navigators in rocky terrain.

- **Culture**: Mountain Dwarves are deeply traditional, their society organized into clans that value honor, duty, and loyalty. They engage in regular martial training to defend their homes from trolls, goblins, and other threats. Sacred forges and ancestral relics are central to their identity, and they revere deities associated with the earth and fire. Festivals often involve grand feasts and contests of strength or craftsmanship.

Dorn'Haldrik (Hill Dwarves)

The Dorn'Haldrik, or Hill Dwarves, live in rolling hills and valleys, their homes often blending into the natural landscape. Slightly leaner than their mountain kin, they possess warm, earthy tones in their skin and hair. They are known for their hospitality and dedication to farming and craftsmanship, creating goods that are as practical as they are beautiful.

- **Abilities**:

  - **Agrarian Expertise**: Bonuses to crafting, farming, and woodworking.

  - **Sturdy Constitution**: Resilient against disease and environmental hardships.

  - **Community Builders**: Their cooperative nature enhances group efforts, from construction to combat.

- **Culture**: Hill Dwarves are pastoral and community-focused, their lives centered on family and tradition. Storytelling and music play an important role in their culture, with each generation passing down tales of heroism and wisdom. Their settlements often serve as trade hubs, connecting neighboring races through barter and diplomacy. They are skilled brewers, known for creating some of the finest ales in Arath.

Dorn'Durzath (Dark Dwarves)

The Dorn'Durzath, or Dark Dwarves, dwell in the lightless depths of the Underdark, their pale or ashen skin and coal-colored hair adapted to the subterranean world. Their glowing red or orange eyes allow them to see in near-total darkness, but they are sensitive to bright light. Known for their secretive nature, they are masterful crafters of enchanted weapons and armor, often using rare, magical materials found deep underground.

- **Abilities**:

    ◦ **Superior Darkvision**: Enhanced sight in low-light and pitch-dark environments.

    ◦ **Stealth and Deception**: Bonuses to stealth, enabling them to move unseen in the shadowy depths.

    ◦ **Runic Enchantment**: Expertise in imbuing items with powerful magical properties.

- **Culture**: Dark Dwarves are insular and fiercely protective of their secrets, their settlements heavily fortified and hidden from intruders. While some clans trade rare goods with surface dwellers, others remain hostile, guarding their realms with ferocity. Their society values innovation and precision, with an emphasis on creating artifacts that blend engineering and magic. Religious ceremonies often involve fire and glowing runes, symbolizing their connection to both the earth and the arcane.

Dorn'Nethrin (Deep Dwarves)

The Dorn'Nethrin, or Deep Dwarves, live in expansive mines and underground labyrinths, stretching beneath entire regions of Arath. Their rough, metallic-hued skin and milky or silver eyes reflect their deep connection to the earth's veins of precious minerals. Known for their perseverance and resourcefulness, they are the ultimate explorers and miners of the dwarven world.

- **Abilities**:

    ◦ **Tremor Sense**: Can detect vibrations in the ground, allowing them to sense movement or potential collapses.

    ◦ **Mining Expertise**: Bonuses to appraising and extracting precious gems and ores.

    ◦ **Seismic Resistance**: Naturally resistant to tremors and seismic activity.

- **Culture**: Deep Dwarves are deeply spiritual, seeing mining as a sacred act of uncovering the earth's hidden truths. Their records and maps of the underground are unparalleled, often detailing ancient tunnels and forgotten cities. Exploration and excavation are central to their culture, and their homes are adorned with gems and minerals they've unearthed. They maintain strong bonds with their clans, often uniting for grand expeditions.

Dorn'Valkari (Sea Dwarves)

The Dorn'Valkari, or Sea Dwarves, live along coasts or underwater, their bluish-green skin and hair resembling the ocean's hues. Their coral-encrusted armor and shimmering pearl accessories speak to their deep connection to the sea. Sea Dwarves are skilled shipwrights and pearl divers, their fortified underwater settlements marvels of engineering.

- **Abilities**:
  - **Aquatic Adaptation**: Natural swim speed and the ability to hold their breath for extended periods.
  - **Waveborn Resistance**: Resistance to pressure and cold in deep waters.
  - **Maritime Expertise**: Bonuses to shipbuilding and navigation.
- **Culture**: Sea Dwarves blend dwarven traditions with maritime lore, worshipping ocean deities and spirits. Their settlements, often built from coral and stone, are bustling centers of trade, with goods ranging from rare pearls to finely crafted tridents. Festivals involve songs and dances inspired by the rhythm of the waves, celebrating their connection to the ocean. While

peaceful, they are fierce defenders of their waters, often repelling threats with cunning naval tactics.

Elves (Shělan)

The Elves, or Shělan, are one of the oldest and most graceful races in Arath, their ageless beauty and deep connection to nature and magic setting them apart. Tall and slender, Elves possess angular features, pointed ears, and eyes that shimmer with hues reflecting their magical or elemental affinities. Their skin tones range from pale alabaster to sun-kissed bronze or obsidian black, depending on their subrace. Renowned for their longevity and wisdom, Elves are often seen as keepers of ancient knowledge, protectors of natural realms, and masters of arcane arts.

Del'shě (Dark Elves)

The Del'shě, or Dark Elves, are a mysterious and secretive subrace who dwell in the shadowy depths of the Underdark. Their ebony skin gleams with a faint sheen, while their silver or white hair contrasts starkly with their dark features. Their glowing eyes, in shades of red, violet, or pale blue, enable them to navigate their lightless homes. Known for their mastery of shadow magic and stealth, Del'shě are often both feared and misunderstood.

- **Abilities**:
  - **Superior Darkvision**: Del'shě can see clearly in complete darkness.
  - **Shadow Magic**: Innate abilities include creating

magical darkness or stepping between shadows.

- ○ **Subterranean Adaptation**: Resistance to poison and other hazards common in the Underdark.

- **Culture**: Del'shě societies are often matriarchal and highly structured, with a strong emphasis on hierarchy and loyalty. They worship deities of darkness and cunning, holding grand ceremonies in honor of the moon and stars they rarely see. While often portrayed as ruthless, many Del'shě are philosophers, inventors, or protectors of forgotten knowledge. Their cities are architectural marvels of bioluminescent fungi and crystalline structures, blending beauty and functionality.

Ge'shě (High Elves)

The Ge'shě, or High Elves, are the most sophisticated and politically influential of the Elven subraces. Their skin glows with a faint radiance, ranging from golden hues to pale ivory, while their hair often appears silver, gold, or platinum. Their eyes shimmer with colors as vibrant as gemstones, reflecting their affinity for magic. Known for their mastery of arcane arts and elegant diplomacy, they are often leaders among the Shělan.

- **Abilities**:

- ○ **Arcane Expertise**: Ge'shě have natural talent for

magic, excelling in enchantment and divination.

- ◦ **Fey Grace**: Enhanced agility and reflexes, making them difficult to hit in combat.

- ◦ **Innate Magic**: Can cast minor spells without preparation.

- • **Culture**: Ge'shě live in majestic cities of marble and crystal, often perched atop hills or surrounded by enchanted forests. Their society values art, knowledge, and diplomacy, with scholars and artisans holding high status. They govern through councils of elders, whose decisions are guided by divination and centuries of experience. Festivals celebrating celestial events, such as eclipses or comets, are lavish affairs filled with music, dance, and magical displays.

Gol'shě (Sun Elves)

The Gol'shě, or Sun Elves, are radiant and charismatic, their golden skin and fiery red or golden hair reflecting their connection to the sun. Their eyes often gleam like molten gold or amber, and their presence exudes warmth and vitality. Revered as spiritual leaders and bringers of light, they are often seen as symbols of hope and resilience.

- • **Abilities**:

- ◦ **Radiant Aura**: Their presence inspires allies,

granting bonuses to morale and resistance to fear.

- ○ **Sunlit Magic**: They excel in spells related to fire and light, as well as healing.
- ○ **Solar Resistance**: Naturally resistant to fire and radiant damage.
- **Culture**: Sun Elves live in open, sunlit regions such as deserts or plateaus, where they construct gleaming temples and golden spires. Their society revolves around worship of the sun and the cycles of day and night, with rituals performed at sunrise and sunset. Known for their diplomacy and generosity, they often act as mediators between other races. Festivals celebrating the summer solstice are grand events, featuring parades, fire-dances, and offerings to their solar deities.

Mak'shě (Moon Elves)

The Mak'shě, or Moon Elves, are nocturnal mystics and dreamers, their pale, almost luminescent skin and silvery-blue hair reflecting their connection to the moon and stars. Their eyes, often resembling the night sky, shimmer with shades of silver, lavender, or deep blue. Known for their calm demeanor and introspective nature, Moon Elves are spiritual guides and keepers of celestial knowledge.

- **Abilities**:

- ◦ **Lunar Magic**: Innate abilities to manipulate illusions and calm emotions.

- ◦ **Night Vision**: Superior vision in low-light and dark conditions.

- ◦ **Starry Guidance**: Enhanced ability to navigate by celestial bodies.

- **Culture**: Moon Elves live in secluded forest glades or atop high plateaus, where the night sky is clearest. Their society is deeply spiritual, revolving around the cycles of the moon and the passage of constellations. They are masterful stargazers and astrologers, often sought out for their wisdom and prophecies. Festivals coincide with phases of the moon, with the full moon being particularly sacred, celebrated through ceremonies of dance, song, and meditative reflection.

#

Mec'shẻ (Sea Elves)

The Mec'shẻ, or Sea Elves, are aquatic adventurers and guardians of the ocean, their sleek, streamlined forms adapted for life in water. Their skin is often tinged with blue or green, while their hair flows like seaweed in shades of aquamarine, silver, or black. Their eyes, large and reflective, resemble pearls or ocean depths, aiding their vision underwater.

- **Abilities**:
  - ◦ **Aquatic Adaptation**: Swim speed and the ability to breathe underwater.
  - ◦ **Waveborne Magic**: Proficiency in water-based spells, as well as minor control over tides.
  - ◦ **Oceanic Vision**: Enhanced perception in underwater environments.
- **Culture**: Sea Elves live in underwater cities constructed from coral, shells, and bioluminescent materials. Their culture revolves around the ocean's rhythms, with festivals held to honor storms, tides, and marine life. Skilled sailors and navigators, they often assist surface dwellers in crossing treacherous waters. Their settlements are tightly knit, emphasizing collective survival and harmony with marine ecosystems.

Tu'shě (Wood Elves)

The Tu'shě, or Wood Elves, are the protectors of forests and sacred groves, their earthy appearance blending seamlessly with their natural surroundings. Their skin is often tan or bark-like, and their hair comes in shades of green, brown, or auburn. Their eyes, resembling polished amber or mossy jade, are both watchful and wise. Agile and stealthy, they are experts in archery and guerilla tactics.

- **Abilities**:

- ◦ **Natural Camouflage**: Proficient in hiding and moving silently in wooded environments.

- ◦ **Archer's Precision**: Exceptional skill with bows and ranged combat.

- ◦ **Druidic Connection**: Minor abilities in druidic magic, such as summoning vines or sensing nearby wildlife.

- **Culture**: Wood Elves are deeply attuned to the natural world, living in tree-top villages or hidden forest enclaves. Their society emphasizes balance, with druids and rangers often taking on leadership roles. They hold seasonal festivals to honor the earth and its cycles, with rituals involving music, dance, and offerings to forest spirits. Though peaceful, they are fierce defenders of their homes, using their knowledge of the terrain to outwit and ambush invaders.

#

Gan Ceann (Dullahan)

The Gan Ceann, or Dullahan, is a mysterious race of humanoids defined by their ability to remove their heads. Unlike myths that depict glowing skulls or flaming eyes, their heads are as lifelike as any other humanoid's, requiring them to either hold their heads in hand or place them down nearby when separated. Their skin is much like that of

Humans, varying in tone from pale alabaster to deep bronze, with no outwardly unnatural markings. The only sign of their ethereal nature is the faint, ghostly glow emitted from the base of their necks when their heads are detached. Despite their unnerving appearance, the Gan Ceann are deeply intelligent and often serve as intermediaries between the mortal and spiritual worlds.

- **Abilities**:
  - **Detachable Head**: The Gan Ceann can separate their heads and control both their bodies and heads within a limited range. This allows for nique vantage points and strategic advantages in combat or exploration.
  - **Ethereal Glow**: The faint light emanating from their neck when headless provides dim illumination and wards off minor undead or hostile spirits.
  - **Mental Resilience**: When headless, they gain resistance to mental influences such as charm, fear, or telepathic intrusion.
  - **Disorienting Presence**: The unsettling ability to place their head in unexpected locations can confuse or unnerve opponents.

#

- **Culture**:

The Gan Ceann are a reclusive people, often forming tight-knit communities in secluded, mist-shrouded valleys, ancient ruins, or dense forests. Their society is deeply spiritual, revolving around rituals that honor their ancestors and maintain the balance between the living and the dead. They view their unique headless nature not as a curse but as a sacred connection to the spiritual realm, granting them insights into the ethereal plane. Leaders, called "Luminarchs," are chosen for their wisdom and ability to mediate between their kin and the spirits.

Gan Ceann festivals are hauntingly beautiful affairs, marked by processions of headless figures carrying lanterns and playing ethereal music on flutes and strings. These ceremonies often serve to honor the dead or celebrate pivotal moments of celestial alignment. Though largely peaceful, the Gan Ceann are formidable when provoked. In battle, they use their headless condition to confuse foes, leveraging their heightened resilience and the ability to manipulate both their bodies and heads in tandem.

#

- **Legends and Perceptions**:

Among other races, the Gan Ceann are regarded with a mix of awe and fear. In some lands, they are seen as protectors of sacred boundaries or guides for lost souls. In others, they are treated as harbingers of death or ill fortune, avoided and mistrusted. Despite this, the Gan Ceann remain focused on their role as mediators between realms, striving to maintain harmony and understanding in a world that often struggles to comprehend their nature.

Gnomes (Fennari)

The Gnomes, or Fennari, are a race of inventive, curious, and whimsical beings, known for their small stature and boundless energy. Standing shorter than most other humanoids, Gnomes possess a wiry build, with sharp, expressive features and hair that often seems untamable. Their skin tones range from earthy browns to pale cream, with bright eyes in shades of blue, green, or amber that sparkle with mischief and wonder. They are natural tinkerers, artisans, and scholars, driven by an insatiable curiosity about the world and a deep love of storytelling and creation.

Fennar'Silvari (Forest Gnomes)

Forest Gnomes, or Fennar'Silvari, are closely tied to nature, their lives entwined with the rhythms of the woods and the creatures that dwell within. Their hair often mirrors the colors of the forest—greens, browns, and even the occasional auburn—and their skin carries a slight bark-like texture. Small and nimble, they are masters of blending into their surroundings and forming bonds with woodland creatures.

- **Abilities**:
  - **Natural Camouflage**: Exceptional at hiding and moving silently in wooded environments.
  - **Beast Whisperer**: Innate ability to communicate with small animals and call for their aid.
  - **Druidic Magic**: Proficiency with minor nature-based spells, such as controlling plant growth or summoning light.
- **Culture**: Forest Gnomes live in treehouses or burrows that harmonize with their environment, often hidden from outsiders. Their society emphasizes community and environmental stewardship, with druids and herbalists often taking leadership roles. They celebrate the changing seasons with vibrant festivals, marked by music, dancing, and feasts made from foraged foods. Though peaceful, they are resourceful defenders of their homes, using illusions and guerrilla tactics to ward off

threats.

Fennar'Tinkeri (Tinker Gnomes)

Tinker Gnomes, or Fennar'Tinkeri, are industrious and inventive, constantly experimenting with new devices, alchemical formulas, or magical constructs. Their wiry frames are often smudged with soot or grease, and their wild, colorful hair reflects their chaotic energy. Known for their ingenuity, they are equally adept at creating brilliant inventions and catastrophic accidents.

- **Abilities**:
  - **Artificer's Insight**: Natural proficiency with crafting, repairing, and dismantling complex machinery.
  - **Quick Thinker**: Enhanced problem-solving skills and improvisation under pressure.
  - **Alchemical Aptitude**: Skilled at brewing potions and using explosive or defensive gadgets.
- **Culture**: Tinker Gnome societies are bustling workshops, filled with the constant clatter of tools and the hum of arcane energy. Their settlements often resemble labyrinthine collections of interconnected labs and homes. Collaboration and competition coexist in their culture, with inventors frequently holding exhibitions to showcase their creations. While their

inventions sometimes cause chaos, their contributions to engineering and magic are invaluable.

Fennar'Nethri (Deep Gnomes)

Deep Gnomes, or Fennar'Nethri, are a reclusive and pragmatic subrace that thrives in the shadowy depths of Arath's underground caverns. Their skin carries the hues of stone—gray, slate, or pale silver—while their eyes gleam with the soft glow of luminescent minerals. With their compact frames and quiet demeanor, they are perfectly adapted to life in the dark, where they mine precious gems and metals.

- **Abilities**:
  - **Superior Darkvision**: Exceptional ability to see in pitch-black conditions.
  - **Stone Sense**: Innate ability to detect weak points, seams, or traps in stone structures.
  - **Gemcraft Expertise**: Proficiency in appraising and refining gems into enchanted items.
- **Culture**: Deep Gnomes live in hidden subterranean cities carved from stone and illuminated by bioluminescent fungi and crystals. Their culture values precision and craftsmanship, with elders revered for their wisdom and skill in mining and gemcraft. Though they avoid conflicts with surface dwellers, they are fierce in defending their territories from

subterranean threats like drow and mind flayers. Festivals often involve elaborate carvings and light displays, showcasing their artistic mastery.

Halflings (Velethrin)

The Halflings, or Velethrin, are a cheerful and resilient race, known for their small stature and boundless optimism. Rarely standing taller than four feet, they have round faces, curly hair, and warm, earthy skin tones. Their eyes, often bright shades of green, hazel, or blue, shine with curiosity and kindness. Halflings prefer a simple life, valuing home, family, and community, though some are driven by wanderlust and the call of adventure.

Veleth'Bryn (Hearthfoot Halflings)

Hearthfoot Halflings are the quintessential Halflings, embodying their race's love of home, hearth, and community. Their hair is typically curly and ranges from sandy blonde to deep chestnut, while their skin is sun-kissed from tending their farms and gardens. They are hearty and cheerful, always ready to lend a hand or share a story.

- **Abilities**:
  - **Lucky Resilience**: An uncanny knack for avoiding danger or misfortune.
  - **Community Spirit**: Bonuses to group tasks and morale.
  - **Green Thumb**: Expertise in agriculture and

herbalism.

- **Culture**: Hearthfoot Halflings live in pastoral villages with cozy, earth-covered homes built into hillsides. Their lives revolve around family gatherings, communal feasts, and festivals celebrating the seasons. Hospitality is central to their values, and their doors are always open to weary travelers. While they prefer peace, they are surprisingly resourceful and tenacious when defending their homes.

Veleth'Darun (Wanderfoot Halflings)

Wanderfoot Halflings are adventurous and nomadic, their sun-kissed skin and weathered clothing reflecting their love of travel. Their hair is often wind-swept and untamed, and their bright eyes sparkle with curiosity. Wanderfoots are known for their storytelling, often weaving tales of distant lands and daring exploits.

- **Abilities**:
  - **Wayfarer's Instinct**: Enhanced navigation and tracking skills.
  - **Quick Reflexes**: Natural agility allows them to dodge danger.
  - **Charming Presence**: Bonuses to persuasion and storytelling.

- **Culture**: Wanderfoot Halflings travel in colorful caravans, forming tightly knit bands that serve as both family and community. They make a living through trade, performance, or craft, bringing joy and wonder to those they encounter. Their festivals, held at crossroads or oases, are spectacles of music, dance, and shared stories. Though they rarely stay in one place, they leave lasting impressions wherever they go.

Veleth'Umbran (Shadowstep Halflings)

Shadowstep Halflings are a secretive and enigmatic subrace, living in the shadows of dense forests or hidden urban districts. Their dusky skin and dark clothing allow them to blend seamlessly into their surroundings, and their quiet, deliberate movements make them excellent scouts and spies.

- **Abilities**:

  - **Shadowmeld**: Can become nearly invisible in dim light or darkness.

  - **Silent Step**: Exceptional stealth and evasion.

  - **Keen Intuition**: Bonuses to perception and detecting hidden dangers.

- **Culture**: Shadowstep Halflings live in small, secretive communities, protecting themselves through anonymity and careful planning. They value self-reliance and discretion, often taking on roles as spies, couriers, or protectors of ancient secrets. Their festivals are rare and private, involving symbolic rituals that honor the cycles of the moon and stars. Though wary of outsiders, they are fiercely loyal to those they trust.

Humans

Humans are one of the most widespread and diverse races in Arath, characterized by their ambition, adaptability, and innovation. Their physical appearance varies greatly, from pale-skinned northerners to sun-bronzed desert dwellers, with hair and eye colors spanning nearly every spectrum. Despite their relatively short lifespans, Humans are known for their resilience and capacity to shape their environment, often founding thriving cities and empires. Their cultures are incredibly varied, reflecting the unique challenges and resources of their homelands.

Kingdom of Arenvalis (Wildlands Humans)

The humans of the Kingdom of Arenvalis hail from the rugged Wildlands, where survival often depends on strength and cunning. With weathered skin and strong physiques, they are accustomed to harsh environments and a life of constant toil and conflict.

- **Capital: Thandor's Reach** – A sprawling, fortified city perched on a plateau overlooking the Wildlands, known for its massive iron gates and thriving marketplaces.

\#

- **Ruler: King Rorik Ironthorn** – A pragmatic and battle-hardened leader, famed for uniting the nomadic tribes into the Wildlands Confederacy under his reign. His rule is defined by a delicate balance of maintaining the Wildlands' independence while fostering trade and diplomacy with neighboring regions.

\#

- **Abilities**:
  - **Enduring Resilience**: Resistance to environmental challenges like extreme heat, cold, or hunger.
  - **Practical Prowess**: Bonuses to crafting, fortifications, and mercantile negotiations.
  - **Battle Hardened**: Increased stamina and strength in combat.

\#

- **Culture**: Kingdom of Arenvalis society is fiercely independent, with a focus on resourcefulness and self-reliance. Their settlements are heavily fortified trade hubs, often surrounded by harsh wilderness. They value pragmatism over tradition, and their leaders are often chosen through merit and survival skills. Festivals celebrate their resilience, featuring competitions in hunting, forging, and storytelling.

#

- **Ironhaven** – One of the widest-known settlements in the kingdom is the trade center of Ironhaven. This crossroads settlement is home to one of the largest slave markets and notorious for the number of mercenary and slaver companies that call it home.

Velanor (Eastern Coast Humans)

The humans of Velanor are cosmopolitan and competitive, excelling in diplomacy, commerce, and artistic innovation. Their appearance varies due to the diverse population of their bustling trade cities, which are melting pots of different cultures and races.

- **Abilities**:
  - **Master Traders**: Bonuses to negotiation, appraisal, and bartering.
  - **Cultural Adaptability**: Gain advantages when interacting with other races or learning new skills.
  - **Artisan's Touch**: Proficiency in crafting intricate and high-quality goods.
- **Culture**: Velanor is a hub of innovation and cultural

exchange, its cities filled with grand markets, art galleries, and academies. Their society values ambition and creativity, with success often celebrated through public ceremonies. Velanor festivals feature parades, performances, and showcases of new inventions or artistic creations. They thrive on diplomacy and trade, maintaining alliances with various kingdoms and enclaves.

Tidewatch (Southern Coast Humans)

Tidewatch humans live along the coasts of Arath, their lives deeply intertwined with the sea. They are expert sailors and shipbuilders, with tanned skin, salt-kissed hair, and a rugged, adventurous demeanor.

- **Abilities**:
  - **Maritime Expertise**: Bonuses to navigation, shipbuilding, and fishing.
  - **Weathered Resilience**: Resistance to water-related hazards like drowning or hypothermia.
  - **Ocean's Call**: Enhanced perception near or on water.
- **Culture**: Tidewatch society revolves around the sea, with fishing, trade, and exploration forming the

backbone of their economy. Their rituals often involve honoring ocean deities through offerings and songs, and their festivals feature boat races, seafood feasts, and displays of maritime prowess. Tidewatchers are known for their adventurous spirit, often venturing into uncharted waters in search of new lands and treasures.

Minotaurs (Kharosians)

The Minotaurs, or Kharosians, are a proud and powerful race of bull-headed humanoids, standing taller than most other races. Their muscular builds and horned heads make them imposing figures, while their fur-covered bodies and hooves reflect their connection to their beastly ancestry. Despite their fearsome appearance, Minotaurs are deeply honorable, adhering to strict codes of conduct and loyalty. Their horns, which vary in size and shape, are symbols of their personal strength and status.

- **Abilities**:
  - **Gore Attack**: Minotaurs can use their horns to deliver devastating charges.
  - **Labyrinthine Mind**: They have an innate ability to navigate mazes and complex pathways.
  - **Unstoppable Strength**: Their immense power allows them to break through barriers and overpower foes.

- **Culture**: Minotaur society is centered around honor, tradition, and personal strength. They live in labyrinthine cities or fortified enclaves, their architecture reflecting their cultural focus on mazes and structured order. Leadership is earned through trials of combat, wisdom, and strategy, with chieftains serving as both rulers and spiritual leaders. Their festivals are grand displays of physical prowess, including wrestling, horn-decorating contests, and ceremonial dances that tell stories of their ancestors. Minotaurs are fierce in battle but deeply loyal to their allies, often serving as guardians or champions of justice.

Zar'kaan (Marked Ones)

The Zar'kaan, or Marked Ones, are individuals with infernal, demonic, or abyssal ancestry, their fiendish traits marking them as outcasts or powerful beings depending on the culture they inhabit. Their skin often carries unnatural tones—deep reds, shadowy grays, or ashen whites—while their horns, tails, or glowing eyes betray their otherworldly heritage. Some Zar'kaan bear intricate markings or brands on their skin, believed to reflect their infernal lineage or magical prowess.

Infernal Zar'kaan

Infernal Zar'kaan are descendants of devils tied to the Hells. They are calculating, charismatic, and ambitious, their features smooth and polished, with horns that curve like a crown. Their glowing eyes, often gold or crimson, hint at their infernal cunning.

- **Abilities:**

    o **Hellfire Magic**: Proficiency with fire-based spells and resistance to fire damage.

    o **Silver Tongue**: Bonuses to persuasion and deception.

    o **Infernal Resilience**: Increased durability against magical and physical attacks.

- **Culture**: Infernal Zar'kaan often act as rulers, advisors, or manipulators, their natural charisma and intellect making them skilled leaders. Their societies value order and hierarchy, with power earned through strategy and cunning.

Abyssal Zar'kaan

Abyssal Zar'kaan are tied to the chaotic demons of the Abyss. Their jagged horns, feral eyes, and wild demeanor reflect their volatile nature.

- **Abilities:**

    o **Chaotic Fury**: Bonuses to strength and damage

when enraged.

- ◦ **Abyssal Endurance**: Resistance to poison and necrotic damage.

- ◦ **Unleashed Power**: Can temporarily enhance physical abilities at the cost of control.

- **Culture**: Abyssal Zar'kaan are often shunned for their unpredictable nature, but their strength and passion make them formidable allies. They thrive in loosely organized groups where individual power is celebrated.

Shadow Zar'kaan

Shadow Zar'kaan bear the marks of fiends tied to darkness and shadows. Their features are subtle but unsettling, with faintly glowing markings and eyes that pierce through the gloom.

- **Abilities**:

- ◦ **Shadowmeld**: Can blend seamlessly into shadows, becoming nearly invisible.

- ◦ **Dark Magic**: Proficiency in illusion and necrotic spells.

- ◦ **Ethereal Step**: Can momentarily phase into a shadowy plane to evade attacks.

- **Culture**: Shadow Zar'kaan live in secretive enclaves

or among societies where their skills in espionage and subterfuge are valued. They are often misunderstood but revered for their mastery of darkness and illusion.

#

* * *

ABOUT THE AUTHOR

Xander Rose

Xander is a fledgling author who is expanding from writing short stories to full novels. His areas of focus are LitRPG, GameLit, and Fantasy. He hails from the Pacific Northwest.

THE ARATH SAGA

Life was ordinary—mundane, even—until a fleeting moment changed everything. Distracted by a stranger on the street, Alex never saw the car coming. In an instant, the world he knew disappeared, and he awoke in a realm unlike anything he'd ever imagined. Transported to a land of danger, magic, and untamed beauty, Alex must navigate a new reality where survival is a daily battle. Everything he once took for granted—comfort, safety, even the rules of nature—has been stripped away. But armed with the lessons from his favorite books and games, Alex is determined to forge his path and discover if he has what it takes to thrive in this second chance at life.

Welcome To Your Next Life

"When the heavens burn and the earth does sigh, a mark long forgotten shall pierce the sky..."

Xavier never asked to be reborn. Yet when a dying world calls out for balance, he finds himself pulled through the veil of reality into Arath, a land bound by ley lines, fractured by ancient betrayal, and suffocating under divine watch. Armed with only instinct and a soul-bound blade, Xavier must forge new alliances, challenge cruel slavers, and awaken forgotten magics buried beneath the forest of Silverwood. But with every step, the gods take notice.

Shadows Over The Wildlands

"Bound by chains yet fated to free…"

The deeper Xavier digs into Arath's corruption, the more sinister the truth becomes. Infiltrating the slaver stronghold of Ironhaven, he uncovers a conspiracy centuries in the making, one that marks the Animari for eternal bondage. But not all chains are visible. When he meets Lythara, a succubus bound by an infernal pact, Xavier faces an impossible choice: defy a devil-backed kingdom, or become its next pawn. As the earth stirs beneath Rynthavael, rebellion ignites, but every act of freedom comes with a price.

The Iron Oath

TBD

Ashes Of The Blasted Dawn

TBD

The Ivory Citadel

TBD

Sands Of The Forsaken Flame

TBD

The Tides Of War

TBD

The War Of The Gods

TBD

The End Of An Era

TBD

The Last Kael'sharyn

TBD